The

CW01559053

Suni Samara

ISBN: 9798264416200

Independently published

© Suni Samara

The Invisible Cage

By

Suni Samara

About the Author

Suni Samara is a carer, writer and artist from Scotland. Her parents moved from India to settle into Scotland, in the 1960s. Her debut novel 'The Invisible Cage' is a fictionalised account of her life, both own voices and diverse fiction. It is an adult novel with coming-of-age aspects that may also appeal to YA readers. Suni is a Science graduate and taught mainstream Science and special needs education. She enjoys drawing and has submitted pieces of her work to the Big Art Show She currently lives with her 2 daughters in Glasgow.

About the Book

"You can't see the bars or the lock, but they are there. I am a prisoner."

Meet Anoushka:
Edinburgh biology student, dutiful Indian daughter, great marriage material. She's everything to everybody and yet – she's nothing. She's invisible in an invisible cage. This is the year that changes her life.

Dedication

To my two wonderful children, Maya and Shanti,
whose love, strength and resilience continues to inspire
me every day.

Part 1
The Match

Chapter 1

We're all sitting around the table in silence: Mum, Dad, my brothers, Aditya and Akash, and my younger sister Lalita. I'm shaking at this point, more scared than I thought I'd be, now that it's come to this. I trust my parents and they trust me – sometimes I think I should get an award for being the most meek and dutiful daughter in Scotland – but this is a gigantic step and my head and my heart are battling over whether it's the right one. I guess you can take the family out of India, but you can't take India out of the family. 'And why would you want to?' I can see their astonished, no, horrified, faces now, if I said that aloud.

Dad's picking up the phone now, very carefully, like it's a ritual, and he starts dialling the number. He smiles to show that it's ringing, but we all tense up when he licks his lips, ready to start.

'Hello, Mr Tilak? This is Mr Malhotra.' There's a fraction of a pause, which makes me wonder how many times my dad has rehearsed this – first impressions, and all – then he gets straight down to business. 'I'm phoning regarding a marriage proposal.' Lalita gives an involuntary squeak at that and claps her hand over her mouth; my strict mum just smiles and puts a finger to her lips.

Dad's in full swing. 'You recall meeting my sister-in-law, Sonu, in India? And telling her that you have a son who is now at the age of marriage...' Then there's a lot of yes, yes and yess-ing, until, glancing over at me, as if to remind himself, he manages to get some more all-important facts in. 'Anoushka is twenty-two years old. She was born on the 21st of April 1971 at 5.30pm...yes, that is the 21st, in the evening. She is in her final year of studies at one of the local universities here in Edinburgh. She is approximately five feet two inches tall, with tanned brown skin–' He listens for a second, then qualifies that. 'Yes, lightly tanned brown skin.'

That must pass muster, even if it makes me a feel a bit like a prize cow at the Royal Highland Show – not that I should complain because I'm dying to know what the boy looks like – because Dad stops talking, except for a chorus of 'Hmms' and scribbles a few notes on the pad in front of him. Once he lays his pen down, he says, 'Thank you. Mr Tilak. I, too, will consult my guru and we can talk again later in the week. Goodbye.'

He's barely put down the phone before he's giving us the lowdown. 'Ravi Tilak is five feet ten with fair skin. He has finished his degree in Law, has a good position in a prestigious firm and is ready to get married imminently.' Dad beams at my mum; job done.

Is that it? I want to ask, but, of course, I don't. Instead, I remind myself that this is only the first step.

'How does his father sound?' Mum asks.

'He sounded very pleasant.' Dad nods. 'But we'll have to wait and see what the guru says.' He taps the notepad, on which he's jotted Ravi Tilak's birth details to pass on, a sign that any marriage plans will stop right here if our astrology charts aren't compatible.

Ravi Tilak. I mouth the name, acutely aware that this might be the name of my husband. I'm still scared, but excited too, now that the boy has a name. I wonder if he feels the same, hearing Anoushka Malhotra for the first time. Sometimes I wish I already knew what Mata Rani (Hindu Mother Goddess) has planned for me: the blessings of a good husband and kind in-laws should be guaranteed for a good daughter, surely? But what if I have some karmic debts to pay off to the mother goddess? Something that makes me the Cinderella of an arranged marriage.

It's something that's bothered me since I was barely a teenager.

When I was fourteen, my parents took me to see the guru at the Mandir, our temple, already keen to enquire about my future prospects of a match with another respected family. It's a vetting process all Indian girls go through, and I wasn't complaining. After all, even at that age, I'd decided that it was going to be my ticket out of here. Away from the narrow life in a city I never saw. Away from the stifling family expectations of being the eldest daughter. Away from the divide of being Indian and Scottish, which actually meant being neither. They'd give me a good education, my mum and dad, I knew that – and they have – but for them, it's never been about me having a career, just another way to up my stakes in the marriage lottery.

That day at the Mandir, I was outwardly neat and calm, but inside, I was all over the place; hormones, I realise now, all muddled in with anxiety and hope. I remember untying my laces and placing my shoes in the great entrance. My eyes were drawn to the centre of the hall, where beautiful murtis of devis and devas entwined with golden jewellery. They dripped with diamonds and pearls, dressed in the finest kurtas and saris. I wanted to get lost in the intricacy of the abstract colours and patterns. If they swallowed me up, the thoughts firing off at my brain would be gone too: How am I supposed to find a husband so soon? Surely, I'm too young for this? What will he be like? What if I'm stuck with someone horrible to me? What if I don't find a husband? What if nobody wants me? What if I have to stay at home forever…

Then I saw Achariya ji (the priest) walking towards me.

'Aaja, beta. Come here, little one.' He spoke with a gentle, reassuring voice, and I was convinced he could read my thoughts.

'Namaste, Achariya ji,' I whispered back.

He beckoned us towards a corner of the huge hall, and sat across from us, me flanked by my parents, before taking out a roll of paper held together by coir twine. I knew it was my astrological chart, and I had to hold my legs down to stop them from twitching. It turned out that my intended husband was the least of my worries.

'Child, you will not find happiness until the age of forty,' was what the guru said.

Looking back, I can see how cruel it was to write off half of my life like that, something that not even a circus psychic would do for kicks. At the time I didn't really process it because his next bombshell, the one my parents took to heart, was how I, Anoushka Malhotra, was on a scale of ten out of eighteen in terms of spirituality. This, he told us, impressively, was guru-level – and, 'To mould and strengthen your faith, Anoushka,' was precisely why I was destined to endure a quarter of a century of pain and suffering. I watched as my parents, amazed and teary-eyed, thanked God for not encouraging them to follow my grandad's advice – given when I was a disappointing, sickly baby girl, turning blue from my first asthma attack – to take away the burden and, 'Let her die.'

All in all, quite a day that was.

And now, here I am, sitting at the table, tempting fate again, by listening to a marriage proposal before I've even finished college, let alone reached middle-age or spiritual enlightenment. It's not even my doing; my Auntie Sonu from Mumbai is the one who took it upon herself to stalk a textile millionaire visiting from Bradford, discover her (yes, her! I like that; the aunties are on the fence) handsome and brilliant little brother and decide that I was the way to inveigle our family into the Tilaks' distinguished circle. Too good to be true? Maybe, but apparently formidable Auntie Sonu has done her homework via grilling mutual friends: the Tilaks are well-known throughout West Yorkshire and the East Midlands, and their son and heir does exist and is eligible. Suddenly, our fractured family has come alive, and everyone is planning the first wedding in years.

Lucky me. No really, I do mean it. Lucky me

Chapter 2

It's only a week later, and Dad has already been to see the guru. He arrives home, Saturday lunchtime, more excited than I've ever seen him. My mum's in the kitchen, cooking – Mum is always in the kitchen, cooking, or else she's in one of the Aunties' kitchens cooking – and he calls her as soon as his key's in the lock. I'm upstairs in my bedroom, studying, and I creep out on to the landing, holding my breath.

'Madhu? The guru said everything is fine,' he shouts. 'At least half their stars meet. It's a possible match! He instructed us to see the family and to take relevant steps.' Dad beams at her, while I stand frozen at the top of the stairs – my legs won't work. 'I've already called Mr. Tilak from work to tell him and I'm going down to see them at the weekend.'

'So soon?' My mum is wiping her perfectly clean hands on a tea towel and frowning.

'Soon is good. This is our daughter's future.'

'Yes, Dev. And our introductions must be carefully planned. Anoushka? Anoushka, come down,' Mum orders, looking up at me. 'You heard the news. We have to get ready for the Tilaks.'

My frozen legs suddenly thaw to jelly, and I grab hold of the banister as I make my way down. 'Are we all going, then? To Bradford?' I ask. 'I thought–'

'Of course we're not,' Mum snaps; I can see she's making a mental list. 'That wouldn't be right at all. But we have to present you properly.' She glances down at her watch and then at me, looking me up and down; I'm still in my college clothes, which are black and white and plain, modest but not traditional – I can see it in my mum's eyes. 'Go and get changed, Anoushka.

Something suitable.'

'Suitable?'

'For photographs. We need professional photographs. Dev.' She turns to my dad, but he's way ahead of her, striding to the house phone that they still keep in the hall – they're like a machine – and tapping in numbers. Three minutes later, we have an appointment in a photographic studio.

'But what about my hair? My make-up?' I wail as Mum bundles me in to a green and silver salwar kameez.

'We'll stop at Auntie Deepti on our way over. Sharmila will see to you.'

Sharmila's my cousin, and she'll never be at home on a Saturday. I start to say this, but Mum cuts me off. 'What is the point of having a beautician in the family if she doesn't work for the family? Now, jewellery. Very important…' She bustles away to her own bedroom, where I can hear her opening drawers and picking through what she calls her heirlooms.

What's the rush? I think, it's all moving so fast. But I can't deny the little bubble of excitement that's deep in my insides. It makes a change from Saturday afternoon studying and reading and helping out with the housework. Maybe soon I'll have my own house to look after. Well, at least I'll balance cleaning and studying better than I can here. My fingers start shaking, so when Mum comes back with an array of bangles and chokers and earrings, she has to fix the clasps.

'A little flush on your cheeks is good,' she tells me. 'You look nervous, innocent. But no worry lines, Anoushka. You don't want to look old. This is just the start.'

Those words keep coming back to me during this whirlwind of a weekend. This is just the start. I keep wondering if Ravi Tilak is going through the male equivalent, primped and preened to make a good impression. My dad will meet him, alongside Mr and Mrs Tilak, but he'll also be given photographs to bring home to us; our family will pore over Ravi's portrait in the same way that they will go over my face and skin and clothes with a magnifying glass. That gives me the creeps, just a bit. Marks out of ten, like I'm auditioning for the Big Brother TV show, or something, except the contract is life, not a few weeks. Mum and Dad think that's a good thing, reassuring – that I'll be taken care of forever. Forever. This is just the start of forever. Stop it, Anoushka, I tell myself. That's me all over, revelling in the angst, because it's not really angst at all; my parents know what they're doing. They've planned for it since I was a baby, so they're not going to pick the wrong boy and so they're not going to make me marry the wrong person. They mean that when they say it, I know they do. No pressure, then, folks. I'm still day-dreaming when we get to the studio.

'Anoushka? Anoushka!'

My mum's glaring at me, and the photographer – a hobbity little man with wonky eyes and a look-at-me camera lens – snaps his fingers.

'Stop dreaming, Anoushka, and put your shoulders back,' Mum orders. 'We haven't got all day! Good husbands don't hang around, you know.' She gets a vigorous affirmative nod from Auntie Brindi, the hobbit's dumpy wife, and they start nattering in staccato Hindi. I mean, Hindi is always staccato, but two middle-aged women talking husbands, is next level.

'Does she not want to marry?' Auntie Brindi stares at me, and repeats herself in English, as if I'm too Scottish to understand her – our – first language.

'Of course she wants to marry. Anoushka, tell

Auntie that you want to marry.'

What she means is, Anoushka, keep the side up, tow the family line. I nod in agreement.

'I just expected it to be a bit well...more romantic,' I add. You know, more Love Actually than a conveyor belt.

The two women click their tongues and wiggle their heads, like it's a choreographed prelude to shimmying across the stage in their saris.

'Romantic? You want dancing and an audience?'

'Life is not Bollywood, Anoushka–'

'Why are you laughing? Why is she laughing, Madhu? This is no laughing matter.' Auntie Brindi turns her back and mutters about children.

'Dev?' Mum shouts. 'Dev, where are you? We need the family shots now.'

Well, if ever I'd had designs on being a supermodel instead of a biologist, they're long gone after today. I cross my fingers that the hobbit knows what he's doing because I'm not doing this again; he was quite keen to airbrush in the Taj Mahal as backdrop – vetoed by Auntie Brindi, which raised her up in my estimation – so he can surely photoshop a grimace into a smile and add in a demure-but-not-too-demure background effect.

Ravi Tilak, please be worth it.

'Make him The One,' I beg Mata Rani, staring into the darkness before I go to sleep that night. 'Let me do something to make Mama and Papa proud of me.'

It's a long week. My parents are preparing for the introduction to the Tilaks as if they're sitting final exams followed by tea with the Queen at Holyrood Palace. I can hear them through the thin walls of our house, muttering late into the night. Mum is angling to go down to Bradford with him, I know she is, but it's not the done-thing and Dad's having none of it; he's a by-the-book (and that's the Indian book) man, heedless of the consequences.

When I get home from college on Friday afternoon, Mum is making pakora as if gram flour is going out of fashion. Every surface is covered in deep-fried snacks.

'Eat. Eat.' She urges me when I'm barely through the kitchen door. 'I need to keep busy, or I will worry about your father's journey. He should be there within the hour.'

We both glance over at the wall clock. The second hand has been snapped in half as long as I remember, but the main ones tick stolidly round. It's almost four.

'You're early. I hope you didn't miss your class. Did you come straight home on the bus? I should have asked Arjun to collect you.'

I grab a pakora and stuff it whole into my mouth, anything to stop me blurting out the truth: one, that it's bad enough my dad insists on meeting me from college every day; I don't need my little brother to fill in for him, and two, I haven't had classes on a Friday afternoon since my first year. It's three precious hours all to myself, three hours where I can do anything, go anywhere, be anyone. So, what if all I do is sit in the library behind a pile of books? Sometimes I buy a bland white sandwich and a weak hot chocolate from the second-floor vending machine. They're not nice but it's what ordinary students do; their lives too busy to think about real food and family meals. Once or twice I've even taken the sandwich into the library and eaten it under the table…How shameful is that? Not the breaking of the rule itself, but that it's probably the worst rule this twenty-two-year-old woman has ever broken. Uh…No, it isn't, though. That would be Donald. Nobody knows about Donald, not that there's anything to know, we're just misfit ships that pass in the hallway, but my family wouldn't see it that way.

I take a plate, filling it with more pakora, and root in the cupboard for the tamarind sauce. My mum's face relaxes, there's nothing she likes more than feeding people – I can see her pleasure in my eating struggling with her need, now we're in the marriage business, to remind me that a fat bride isn't as appealing as a thin one.

'This is a late lunch.' I gesture at the plate. 'Forgot to take mine, so I worked in the library.'

'Then take more,' she urges. 'Rice? Do you want rice? No? Then I must clear up and get these into the freezer. I want to be ready for your father's phone call.'

'He's not meeting the Tilaks today, though, is he?' I mumble through the snack. I picture him in his best suit (straining a little at the stomach, the proud demonstration of a good wife, good cook, good income), hugging his briefcase full of happy family photos of the Malhotras, with me as the money shot – fingers crossed. My dad is no salesman, other people usually do his bidding.

Mum shakes her head. 'I just want to remind him how important this is, Anoushka.'

And she does precisely that when the phone rings half an hour later. She holds the phone out and I hear Dad say, 'I've arrived safely in Bradford. It's small. Not very clean.' (I can hear him puffing up that he's come from the more classy Edinburgh). 'Don't worry about a thing and I'll give you a call after I've been to the Tilaks' house.'

Mum replies, 'Be careful now, Dev. Remember to look out for everything and watch carefully how Ravi Tilak and his parents respond to your questions. This is our daughter's future on the line.' She moves the phone closer to her ear until I can no longer hear his actual response but he's consoling her; her shoulders sag a little and she's murmuring, 'Ha…ha,' which means 'Yes'.

As soon as she places the phone down, I jump in with, 'Is Dad okay?'

'Dad's fine and he'll be seeing the Tilaks later on this evening.' She's tapping her teeth with her forefinger through the words.

'Why are you worrying then?' I ask her. I know it's a serious situation, the whole marriage thing. I know how sheltered I've been – still am – but my parents are always supremely organised. If Mum is hesitating… 'Mum?'

'I just hope everything is alright, Anoushka. Happiness is in a girl's kismet, her destiny is laid out when she is born. Whatever we do, we can't ignore that.'

She looks deflated somehow, a muscle in her face, just near her mouth, twitching. For the first time ever, I feel like the grown-up, as if I need to protect her. It's weird. I try to put her mind at ease.

'Mum, whatever Mata Rani decides to do will be for the best. That's what you always tell me, isn't it? If it's right, we'll know. If it isn't, we'll know. It's just the first match, isn't it. Some people have three or four.'

Mum opens her mouth, but before she can say anything, an upstairs door bangs, there's thunder on the stairs and Lalita barges through the door, yelling, 'I'm hungry. Feed me, Mama.' She looks between us. 'What are you talking about?'

Mum's in-control face switches back on and our moment, such as it was, is gone. 'Anoushka, make some tea,' she says. She turns a big smile on Lalita. 'Dad is meeting Ravi Tilak tonight. We're talking about weddings. Isn't that exciting?'

'Has he got a brother?' my little sister asks. 'I could marry the brother. We could have a double wedding.

What do you think, Anoushka? Oh – only if he's good looking, of course,' she adds.

Mum snorts. 'You're too young for marriage, Laly. One wedding at a time.'

'Yeah. You can practise on Anoushka's and then mine will be perfect.' Lalita grins at me.

Out of the corner of my eye, I see my mother's lips tighten slightly but she says nothing. What can she say? She'd deny it but there's an element of truth: they sent me to one school where I got bullied for being a little brown girl whose English wasn't great, so they sent my sister to a different school. They didn't let me have any friends outside our (Indian) social circle, so I stayed home studying and got my own way about university. Now they're a bit – just a bit – more lax with Laly so she won't be as quiet and geeky as me. I'm not complaining, that's what older sisters are for, isn't it? And I get to do everything first. Laly will never have that.

'Ravi Tilak,' she says. 'My brother-in-law, Ravi. I can't wait to see what he looks like, can you, Anoushka?'

'I'm bursting,' I admit, and we start giggling. I am dying to see what he looks like, which is hypocritical because the thought of him and his family ogling me and passing judgement is icky. Unless he falls in love with me at first sight, and his parents see me as the daughter-in-law they crave. Then it would be okay. Okay, Anoushka: faulty logic, double hypocrite.

We spend the whole evening chatting, saying things over and over again, like, 'I wonder what he's like? I wonder if he looks like those hunks on the Indian channel? I wonder how brainy he is?'

I get no studying done whatsoever.

We all stay up later than normal – even my brothers – pretending that we just happen to be really interested

15

in the David Attenborough on the telly. But Dad doesn't ring.

Chapter 3

He looks exhausted when he comes in. The traffic, he moans. He could have got to India faster.

'Dev!' The world might think my dad is head of our family, but even he bends to her will when my mother uses that tone – something she only ever does behind closed doors. 'We're waiting. Anoushka is waiting. You didn't phone us. Please tell us about the Tilaks.'

'Ah.' He eases his jacket off and hangs it over the banister; Mum is so distracted, she forgets to tell me to take it upstairs and put it away. 'Ah. The Tilaks. I didn't want to phone you, Madhu, I wanted to tell you myself…' a big fat slow smile spreads over his face '…about your prospective son-in-law.'

My mum claps her hands together and gives a half croak, half squeal. My own heart is thumping. 'I'll make some tea,' I say, pre-empting them both. 'If you promise not to start the story till I come back.' I've never before splashed milk and water into mugs with such abandon, but I take more care on the carrying of the tray to the dining table. For once I doubt Mum would have noticed. Absently, she pats the chair beside her. Laly's on her other side.

'Sit, Anoushka. Your father has much to tell us.'

It's an instruction to both of us, and Dad clears his throat as if he's making a speech. 'Ravi Tilak is twenty-five years old. He has an LLB Law degree and works as a top executive in a firm of solicitors in Bradford– What's that, Anou?'

'So, he is a lawyer? Or a solicitor? Or what?' I ask.

Dad shrugs, as if to say, a degree is a degree, don't be picky. And Mum shakes her head.

'A prestigious firm,' she reminds me.

'He doesn't drink or smoke,' Dad goes on. 'He has received outstanding awards for his achievements and, he has met Queen Elizabeth.'

Pause for applause. Dad couldn't be more thrilled if he'd created Ravi himself. He takes a gulp of his tea and looks over at Mum, who is gripping her mug but saying nothing. I expected questions to putt out of her like a power drill. I wonder if she's also thinking that the boy seems to be too good to be true. Dad must read that in our faces because he hurries on.

'This is exactly what I have been told by Mr and Mrs Tilak and their extended family,' he stresses. 'We will be very lucky and privileged to get into this family. I have a very good feeling, Madhu.'

'Did you meet him, the boy?' Mum asks.

Dad scratches his head. 'No. But for the very best of reasons. At this early stage, he is leaving his marriage in the hands of his parents. He trusts them implicitly. Out of respect for us, and for Anoushka, it is his wish that we, the adults, meet first. He told me so himself,' Dad adds importantly. 'Madhu, he phoned me from his office. He left a Board Meeting to do so. And he invited us both back next weekend, to meet him.'

Mum blinks rapidly. 'Do you hear that, Anoushka? Ravi Tilak sounds like a good man.' She's itching to plan the visit but she's doing her duty by her daughter. 'What did he think of Anoushka?' she asks suddenly. 'Did he like her photograph?'

'Mr and Mrs Tilak were pleased.' Dad pauses. Oh help. 'Ravi is waiting until he's got to know more about her–'

Mum gives up playing it cool; why shouldn't she? Every moment of her life as a mother has been a journey to this point. I want to be impressed, but call me cynical, there's a fine line between smarmy and perfect. I'm neither; I most definitely want to see the goods before I get carried away with the romance of it all. Still, I know better than to be as crass as saying that, and if I know my mum, she's not going to wait another five minutes, let alone five more days to see what Ravi Tilak looks like.

Dad knows her, too; she doesn't have to ask. He motions at me to bring his briefcase over, from where he always leaves it in the hall, at the side of the telephone table, and on the table he unclicks the locks and opens it up. For a second I feel as if I'm in a bank heist movie, checking the loot for counterfeit notes with a gun at my head, but inside, there's nothing but three discarded ties, all tangled up – my dad hates wearing ties and he always pulls them off as soon as he can then loses them – and a thin brown envelope bearing a photographer's stamp, just like the one that we sent the Tilaks. Dad hands the envelope to Mum.

'Have you looked already?' she asks him.

He shakes his head. 'No. But I know what the young man looks like. Mr and Mrs brought family pictures with them–'

'Wait,' Laly says. 'Didn't you go to their house? What if it's a scuzzy Council one on a dodgy estate?'

'Laly! Stop it now, or go to your room,' Mum scolds. But she turns to Dad for an explanation.

'They have the builders in. Renovations and remodelling, they say. Major stuff.' Dad waves the question away. 'They showed me a large, framed picture of Ravi's graduation, all of them grouped around the family piano.'

A piano, no less. I wonder if he plays. I wonder if he'll play for me? We're not a musical family by any means, but I'd like my children to learn something. I tell myself not to get carried away, it's probably his sisters who did the music while he, brainy and the boy, got extra maths lessons. I watch as my mother opens the envelope. If this really were a film, she'd do it elegantly, with ceremony, but this is 24 Granton Road, and her fingers are shaking as she yanks the pictures out. She yelps suddenly, not a good sign – how bad can he be? – but it's just a paper cut, to which she gives scant attention, before gobbling up the images in front of her. I have to sit on my hands to avoid snatching them from her. It's not like I'm shallow enough to demand ten-out-of-ten tall, dark and handsome, just a man who looks nice – kind, I mean – and I like the look of.

'Fine-looking chap,' she decides finally. 'A bit on the thin side, but that's why a good wife can cook.' She looks pointedly, with a certain satisfaction, at my dad's paunch. He pats it, and they smile at each other.

I could scream. 'Mum? Let me see?'

'Patience, Anoushka.' But smiling, she passes them across the table.

There are three photographs. The biggest one, the main one, shows him in his graduation outfit – smart suit under a black gown that's blowing out in the wind. He's got his degree parchment rolled up in one hand, and he's smiling at something beyond the camera. His eyes aren't very clear, as if he's squinting in the sun, and his hair is slicked down against his head, quite old-fashioned but probably for the occasion. He's definitely dashing rather than geeky. If I were a casting director, I'd give him the role of the boy next door who is safe to take your daughter out. The two smaller photos are more formal, in a studio, I'd say. They're of him and his family. If I'm honest, the first unconscious thought I have is 'firing squad' rather than Happy Families, though they deserve the benefit of the doubt – don't I know how awkward these shoots are. Mrs Tilak is not photogenic, her glasses are huge, and she has a big brown mole blending into her top lip.

She's a squat, sturdy woman, who looks strained, old. Then again, she's had one, two, three…I count six adult children but, of course, some of those could be in-laws…and it looks like Ravi is one of the youngest, so hers is unlikely to be a glamorous life. Mr Tilak, on the other hand, is smooth-skinned with sausage fingers resting on her shoulder. I feel a twinge of sympathy for her, a wife who has given her youth and energy to her family. The last picture is Ravi and his parents alone, and they all look happier, more relaxed – relief that the photography session is almost over, probably.

I could like Ravi Tilak, I think.

'Well, Anoushka?'

I look up to see Mum and Dad staring at me.

'Well?' Mum prompts again.

Slowly, I nod. 'I think you should go and visit them next weekend,' I say.

They're not known for being overly-demonstrative but at this moment, you'd be forgiven for thinking I'd just handed them a Maharaja's fortune.

Chapter 4

I'm constantly suffering deja vu all this next week. The anticipation. The stress. Mum runs around like a goddess possessed, getting her hair set, her best saris pressed and altered, and hinting confidentially to everyone she knows that a big family decision is on the horizon. I wish she wouldn't; the pressure of the knowing looks from the Aunties is crushing.

After they leave on the Friday morning, I do something I've never done before, I skip lectures. I just want some peace and quiet. I don't even want to think, just to put the telly on and watch repeats of The Bill. Their lives – the actors and the cops they're pretending to be – are amazing. Some of them are only my age and imagine waking up and knowing you're going to chase the bad guys or entertain thousands of people. Meanwhile, I get driven to college, do some experiments that have been done endless times before, eat a packed lunch, get driven home and do as I'm told. I wish I knew how to get my life started. At least getting married will be something different. I can start as I mean to go on, a different Anoushka; I know it's in me somewhere.

'Aye, right, hen,' I jeer myself. Easy to say, but what do I know? In Indian families like ours it's only proper, growing up, for girls to stay away from boys, keeping themselves pure for their future husbands. I've been asked out once or twice by boys at university but never accepted, so they've mostly given up. Twenty-two and never been kissed. I've no bloody idea what to expect. Donald is the only boy that I talk to every week, and that's because he's my lab partner, and when I say talk, I mean things like, 'Pass me that test tube,' and 'What results did you get from Sample A?' He's my height with reddish hair and freckles and he has these soft and plump baby hands, and he always looks so hungry. Literally hungry. One day I caught him kicking the vending machine in the lower corridor; it had stolen his money but kept the crisps he wanted. I offered him some of my lunch, and after he did that Scottish polite thing, saying, 'Och, no, no, I couldn't,' he wolfed it down. Now I pack more, on lab days, just in case. He'll miss me today. Maybe.

The house is quiet alright, but I'm too restless to enjoy it. I snack all morning and drink too much tea, until I'm too lethargic and fat-feeling to do anything. When the phone rings, I nearly fall off the settee. I remember in time that I'm not supposed to be home for another couple of hours, so the answer-machine records the message.

'We're in Bradford,' Mum announces. 'We're due at the Tilaks' at five. Anoushka, we'll phone you afterwards. Make sure you get the dinner ready for the boys coming in. Everything is in God's hands and for the best.'

'Thanks, Mum,' I mutter. It's only two o'clock now, and I'm beginning to wish I'd gone in to the library, after all. Normal girls my age, those who aren't chosen to be Indian and don't have to be protected from the evils of Edinburgh society, would have friends to talk to. Not me. I've never had a chance. I've got cousins by the truckload but they're idiots – the ones who aren't sniffy about me going to Edinburgh university. Even my mum says that's just envy and I should ignore it – which is actually hilarious coming from her because she doesn't really see my need for a degree except that it should attract the right sort on my marriage-o-meter. Dad thinks it 'gives me something to do' while I'm waiting, after all, my undergraduate studies are free and doing science is more respectable than getting a job in BHS or touching people in a beauty salon like Sharmila.

Growing up in Scotland was quite the challenge. It didn't help that for the first three years of my life we lived in Glasgow, then my mum and dad decided to take us all back to India. Maybe they expected a royal conquering hero's welcome home, but it didn't work out. Nobody has ever really explained why, but my dad couldn't get the office jobs he wanted and I was sick all the time – this was the time when my grandfather made the infamous statement that I should be left to die of my asthma – after a couple of years we came back, probably with our tails between our legs, as it was to Edinburgh.

The English language was never really my forte, and after all that time in Mumbai it was broken and singsong. Put me in an all-white British school in 1984 and people laughed, a constant sense of isolation and loneliness dangling over me. The bullies were more stupid than cruel – but that's easy to say in hindsight – and the worst thing was their relentlessness. They never gave up. I was chased down corridors, the mocking laughter and racist remarks a permanent soundtrack – and they couldn't even get that right; I was a filthy wee Paki my whole school life, no matter never having been to Pakistan in my life. Because we'd been away, I didn't really fit into our own cultural network either, so I fitted in nowhere. Every night without fail Mum scrubbed me hard in the bathtub so I would have the paler and prettier skin my Dad constantly told me I needed. There's another memory I have of my delightful grandfather and that's him telling me that if I couldn't be a boy I had to be a very good girl. His actual words were, 'From the day you're born into a traditional Indian family as a girl, it is a curse. If you're from a small village in India and don't have much income, it can be impossible to save money. This is why you're lucky if you don't get drowned at birth for simply being a girl or terminated early.'

How would I ever forget that? My self-esteem, never great, was at its all-time low in high school. I'm smart enough now to have worked out that this isn't all my fault, but it doesn't make it any easier to overcome, especially with a family that can't or won't see any of it. Not that I'd dare bring it up – what's the point, anyway? Perhaps all parents believe they love their children, but I don't think that mine like me very much.

If there's one thing I'm determined of, all of that stops here. Too many people don't learn from history, but I'm going to.

I drag myself far enough out of my pit of self-pity and self-righteousness to get my brothers and sister their evening meal, and then we all hang around bickering and biting our metaphorical nails waiting for the phone to ring – and it will, on the dot. My mother is nothing if not an on-the-dot type of person. The credits to Coronation Street are rolling when she calls, so I zap off the TV, and hold my breath.

'It's going well.' High praise, indeed, from Mum. 'The family is of a very high standard and Ravi Tilak has all the qualities that we would look for in a husband. What?' My dad says something in the background, and she continues with, 'They were very impressed with your photo, and they are overjoyed with the turn of events…'

That's a definite cue. 'Events, Mum?'

It's my dad who comes on the line. 'Anoushka, the Tilaks are travelling back up to Edinburgh in convoy with us tomorrow. Mr and Mrs Tilak will join us for dinner tomorrow evening, and all being well, Ravi will come for lunch on Sunday. Strike while the iron is hot, eh?'

In the background, Mum's shouting instruction about getting the house shipshape and ordering ingredients for a feast. I don't need to listen to the detail. I'm far too busy imagining the day after tomorrow being the day I will quite possibly meet my husband.

The second my parents walk through the door, I'm in trouble. Thank goodness the Tilaks didn't come straight home with them, though part of me wishes they had, to see how differently my mother would have reacted to what she immediately called my, 'Carelessness, you stupid girl.'

For once, Dad is peacemaker. 'It doesn't matter,' he soothes her. 'Don't blame Anoushka this time, Madhu, she was over-excited that it's all going so well. Let's keep calm, remember what's at stake.'

'Huh.' The shrug is her giving in, and she holds up her hands, as if in surrender.

What is it all in aid of? Me, ordering meat from the specialist butcher – the exact meat from the exact butcher that we always use when company is invited. Except that I wasn't listening last night when Mum was on the phone telling me not to do that because the Tilaks are vegetarian and so we'll need a whole new menu from Adil's Grocers at the top of Leith Walk.

I put the offending meat in the freezer, Dad goes out to collect the vegetables, and my mum is placated by being able to show off a spick and span house (which I got up at six to ensure) not burned down by the boys under my (assumed) lax supervision, nor filled with Lalita's rowdy, giggly friends. A cup of tea and a pile of cardamom biscuits the butcher always randomly throws in, seal the deal I'm out of the bad books again, and she's ready to spill all the Tilak gossip.

'Ravi's father, Kabir, is Manufacturing Director of West Riding Woollens and his mum, Dukkha, sits on the Board. As a girl she worked for the Indian Civil Service.' She emphasises their names; being on such familiar terms makes Mum very smug.

'They live with Kabir's brother, his wife and son, although they are currently on an extended visit in India, with a view to re-settle there. We met in the Victoria Hotel, in the city centre. They'd taken a suite for us. Apparently, they still have workmen in their home – a new conservatory and landscaping.' More smugness – of a different kind – as she takes in our own immaculate but small kitchen. 'Ravi himself was most kind to us. He served the tea, Anoushka!' Her eyes sparkle at that, and I can see that it's a string my brothers will be adding to their unsuspecting bows very soon.

'He even called your father 'Dad' and asked him how many sugars he wanted in his tea. Everyone found this very funny and that there were roars of laughter echoing around the room.' She laughs reliving it, before turning serious. 'Mr Tilak – Kabir – promised that the girl marrying his son will be treated like a princess. What she wants, she will get, irrespective of what it is. Do you hear that, Anoushka? He said he would love her more than his own daughter. He even went the great lengths to say,' she lowers her voice at this, as if marvelling, 'he will quit smoking if his daughter-in-law asks him to! Imagine that, Anoushka.'

'Wow.' I'm not sure how else to respond to such effusion. Maybe I should be marrying the dad. There is one thing I'm genuinely curious about. 'What did Mrs Tilak say to all this?'

'Ravi's mother agreed with everything her husband said, smiling constantly.'

I bet she did. But no, that's unfair of me. 'And the dowry?'

Mum's starry-eyes get just that bit more starry. 'Kabir stressed that all his family wants is a well-qualified daughter-in-law – absolutely nothing more. Ravi himself said the same thing about a wife.'

We look at each other, for once in solidarity; this is a huge thing. Unexpected. In many Indian families – I'd say most, the ones I know, anyway – it's tradition for the girl's family to give a dowry to the boy's family. It might be furniture, clothes, gold jewellery, cars, money… It's always struck me as ironic that the girl's family has to do this, I mean they're already handing over their precious daughter to complete strangers. In fairness, the boy's lot should be giving gifts.

'Nothing more?' I check. 'For real?'

'Genuinely,' Mum confirms. 'Kabir said that if we should want to offer a token, to respect tradition, he would leave that to us to decide, but it's unnecessary and should be for you and Ravi; icing on the cake, he said.'

Nice move; keeps our family's pride – my Dad's, as the man and head of the house, especially, intact; demonstrates their generosity; and doesn't leave us at a disadvantage if we're not as well off as them. Oh, I'm not being cynical, I hope with all my heart they are simply lovely people. I'm just keeping my feet on the ground because one of us has to, and my mother, the down-to-earth Madhu Malhotra has already fallen in love.

We've got this far when Dad arrives home, laden down with the makings of a week's worth of banquets.

'Anoushka, bring in the rest,' he puffs. 'Two bags in the boot. Chop chop.'

'What is this all about?' Doing as I'm told, I return, holding up the rest of the shopping, and then plonk it down; Mum gives me the nod to join her in unpacking. 'The vegetarian thing? You're saying the Tilaks are veggies?'

'Ye-es.' Mum and Dad share a look.

'Um...What does that mean?' Uh oh, is this the fly in the ointment?

'Vegan. They're vegan.' Mum concentrates on slicing onions. 'Ravi's wife will need to abstain from all animal products: eggs, fish, poultry, milk. As well as meat.'

Crap. Luckily, I bite that back. Is it such a big deal, though? I eat all those things because that's what I've been given – and you don't refuse food or waste it in our house. If I was given different things, or if I learned to cook them, I'd eat them instead. I think. Marriage is give and take, don't they say? Compromise...Hang on–

'What about my non-negotiable stuff?' I ask. 'The temple. They can't expect me to give that up.'

'No, no, no.' Dad holds his hand up. 'We explained how you are a devoted follower of Mata Rani, Goddess in Hinduism, and that you always go to the temple. We asked them to be very clear in their feelings about this–'

'The Tilaks respect your beliefs and will allow you to follow your own religion,' Mum takes over. 'You would be free to go to the temple whenever you wish.' She wiggles her knife in my direction. 'The only stipulation is this vegan, vegetarian nonsense.'

'Madhu!'

'You agree with me, Dev. You've eaten my food for twenty-five years. Anoushka has eaten my food for twenty-two.' Mum is complacent in her true colours. 'Nobody's perfect. The Tilaks included. Anoushka can eat proper food when she comes to visit us.'

My lips twitch, and the next minute all three of us are laughing out loud.

'Well, Anoushka, what do you think?' Dad asks, when we've calmed down. He says it casually, but I know everything is hanging on my answer. They might be hard on me, my mum and dad, stricter than I'd like, and it drives me mad that they always think they know best (though I hope they do in the marriage stakes) but if I say no to going any further with Ravi Tilak as a prospective husband, they won't force me. They'll never let me forget the one that got away, but they wouldn't ever force me.

A little bubble of excitement pops inside me. What do I have to lose? All I'm agreeing to today is meeting this boy. If we don't get on, then that's that.

'They sound like a wonderful family,' I say – totally honestly. 'I'd like to meet them. I'd like to meet Ravi. Thank you for finding him.'

Mum makes a choking sound and Dad bounds across the kitchen and wraps me in a big hug, something he's barely done since I was a little girl, poorly in India. When he releases me, tears are rolling down his cheeks. This starts me and Mum off.

'Don't, Dad. We're supposed to be happy,' I say.

He wipes his eyes with the back of his hand and turns away. I know he's already embarrassed, by the gruff voice he uses to say, 'It's a shock, realising my oldest daughter is ready to leave our family and begin a new life without us. What will we do without her, Madhu?'

'As my mother did without me. It's the circle of life.' Mum sniffs. 'My, these Adil's onions are strong today. My eyes are watering.' And she's back to her usual stoic self.

It's just as well. Emotion unsettles all of us, and besides that, Dad has unwittingly said something that will need a lot of thought. And planning. If – when – I marry, I shall be going to live with strangers. Not just one stranger, but a whole extended family. I might meet them half a dozen times, but they'll still be strangers. That excited bubble slowly grows a veneer of fear.

Chapter 5

4.45pm. They're going to be here any minute, Mr and Mrs Tilak. I've still got a stomach twirling like the Cirque du Soleil.

I keep tapping my nails on the wooden surface of the dining table, and Mum keeps flapping at my hand to stop me. Dad's pacing the hall and my brothers and sister, all spruced up and varying from excitement (Lalita) to veiled boredom (Arjun) are watching the clock with me.

Flurries of thoughts cloud my mind; the quieter everyone is, the more it creates fuel for the snowstorm raging in my head. All this, it's such a strange situation – being so intently inspected and judged to see if I'm good enough for someone's precious son. And not just me, but my whole family. It feels like a test. A test I can't study for, worse than my university exams, even the finals. What if I fail my family? What if I'm not keen on the Tilaks? Do I then still meet Ravi, or call it all off today? It's an added pressure to think of him sitting in the Travelodge waiting for their report.

When a car pulls up outside and two car doors slam, everyone instantly fixes their posture, my mum runs into the kitchen to check on the simmering chai, and Dad brushes down his grey suit before opening the front door. False alarm; we collectively sigh and slump. It's just Dad's lot from Mumbai via Glasgow, Auntie Sonu and Uncle Pavan. They're loud and a bit brash but confident enough to carry it off as being posh. Above all, they're on our side – mind you, the fact Auntie Sonu is bearing gifts in the guise of a golden woven basket of fresh pakoras, helps their cause. We can all hear her and my mum whispering nineteen to the dozen, stirring a lot more than the spices, I bet.

One of the curtain ties is twisted; Mum will frown at that, so I go over to fix it. I raise my arms to flick it out and settle it – and freeze. From the living room window, I saw a silver car approach the house and pull cautiously into the driveway, blocking Uncle Pavan's prized BMW. A sixth sense alerts my parents, who step out of the house to greet their prospective in-laws in the traditional Indian way – exchanging hugs, handshakes and pleasantries. Thankfully, my dad turned down Auntie Sonu's suggestion of garlands of flowers to put around their necks.

My brothers and sister and I make nervous faces at each other, waiting until the visitors are ushered in. The boys press themselves into the background, but Lalita nudges me forward, pointing to her mouth and performing a beaming smile. I try, but I'm sure it's more of a grimace. In the hall, Mrs Tilak is making a show of taking off her coat, slowly, so that she can politely give our house the once-over. I can't fault her for that; it's only what my mum and dad would have done yesterday in Bradford, and it gives me chance to look at her.

First impressions are how tightly her mud-brown sari is wrapped around her plump waist, trying (and I have to say it, sadly failing) to make her look a couple of stones lighter than she is. A lady who likes her curries and ladoos; I press my lips together to stop a giggle escaping. Her chunky gold earrings and long, thick gold neck-chain are a less than subtle sign that the family has money and her hair is in a very tight perm, like a bird's nest. I almost expect a wee birdie to pop up. What's the betting she talked her way into the hairdresser earlier this week and got a rush job done? Watching her, watching us, I'm taken by how like

Auntie Sonu Mrs Tilak is – which means they'll either love or hate each other. I'm so absorbed in that hair and the way she and my aunt are circling one another that I miss her first glance at me.

There's a little smile on her lips, but her eyes (behind the hideous over-sized glasses) are razor-sharp, drinking me in. I swallow. I think I look good – more than good-enough daughter-in-law material, especially given the Tilaks' effusively low expectations. I'm wearing a beautiful, deep-green chiffon Indian chemise with matching trousers, that neither overwhelms nor accentuates my skinny size 10 frame – elegant and modest, I'd thought, when I got dressed this morning. My dark brown hair is loose, shiny on my shoulders and there's no sign of the nerves-induced sweat trickling down my back. Out of nowhere my mind flashes with the final exams I should be studying for instead of participating in this charade of a suitability contest, and I lose balance slightly, concentration shot.

My prospective mother-in-law notices it all. There's a split second where I can see her deciding how to respond, before she comes forward and rests her hands lightly on my shoulders. My mum is hot on her heels and it's to her Mrs Tilak speaks, "Madhu ji, it's so nice to finally meet your daughter.'

Mum widens her eyes at me, and I manage a quiet and respectful, 'Namaste Auntie ji. Welcome to Scotland.' I'm careful not to sound overly Scottish, though.

'It's so nice to be here,' she says, and if it sounds wooden, well, it only matches my effort.

The boys and Lalita are introduced and although Mrs Tilak makes no move towards them, nor they to her, there's a round of amicable smiles. I know Laly well enough to sense her eyes home in on that

unfortunate mole – and the three stiff hairs that
protrude from it – and I will her not to blurt out a
home remedy. She doesn't. She doesn't say anything,
nobody does, but before the silence gets awkward, the
men barrel in and save the day. Oozing bonhomie, my
dad says, 'Come in, come in, Kabir. Meet my family.'

'Yes, yes, we have waited for this auspicious day.'
Mr Tilak clumsily pats my arm. 'As pretty as her
picture, Dev,' he approves, and I cringe inwardly. It's
like I'm six and about to dance for them. 'Don't you
think, Dukkha?'

Put on the spot, his wife gives the kind of lip-twitch
the Queen might offer when faced with a well-meaning
but inferior curtsey, and my heart meets my boots. I
smile to cover it, telling myself it's this parade she's
uncomfortable with, not me, but I can't help
remembering Mum's, 'Manners maketh man', that she
trots out on social occasions.

'Tea!' Auntie Sonu booms from the doorway,
carrying a loaded tray in such a way that her bangles
jangle. 'Mr Tilak? Mrs Tilak–'

'Kabir.' My possible father-in-law points at himself.
Auntie Sonu nods graciously and her eyes slide to his
wife. When she says nothing, he adds 'And Dukkha.
Please. No ceremony.'

'Dukkha, may I serve you tea?' My mum reaches for
the pot, deftly elbowing Auntie Sonu to one side. The
old but still beautiful teapot, kept specially to serve
chai on special occasions, is Mum's pride and joy. I will
the Tilaks to comment on it, but no god is listening.

'Very kind.' Mrs Tilak inclines her head. 'Can Kabir
and I have a little juice first?'

Ouch. It's a small request, perfectly reasonable, but
it wrong-foots the hostess.

'Er…yes. Yes, of course.' Mum is flustered, her eyes
raking over the groaning tray, from which juice is

patently absent. Accordingly, she shifts the blame to her sister-in-law. 'Sonu? Could you fetch the glasses and some orange?'

There's a little skirmish over the next few minutes, a flurry of brittle explanations and apologies, as we all realise that Scottish 'juice' is actually diluting squash whereas Mrs Tilak is expecting freshly squeezed fruits. Eventually served, she wrinkles her nose, laughs, and pronounces it, 'Delicious.' Then she proceeds to sip it throughout the rest of the afternoon. Mr Tilak gulps his down in one, hands back the glass and holds his hand out for tea and snacks.

Seated in the best armchair – which isn't any different to the others, other than it's by the window and has a side table next to it – with a rainbow platter of jewel-coloured sweet treats in reach, Dukkha Tilak seems to relax. And with that, the rest of us relax too. My brothers and sister are released to their rooms (bribed with a box of sweets to keep quiet and come down without a fuss when it's time to say goodbye) and the grown-ups – I've never felt more like a child – talk about traffic and house prices and mutual acquaintances in India. I don't say much; I'm not expected to – being seen and not heard is as pertinent for Indian daughters-in-law as it was for Victorian children – but I smile till my jaw aches and nod until my neck's stiff.

When there's a natural lull in the conversation, Mum motions to me to stand up. 'Come and help me with dinner, Anoushka,' she says, and I'm pleased to scoot out of the room and gulp down a tall glass of water. My mum does exactly the same.

'Most unladylike,' she whispers, and the two of us bite back our giggles.

Under cover of the noise of the fridge opening and closing and the kettle boiling, she asks me, 'Well? What do you think of your prospective mother-in-law?'

'She's starchy,' I mutter back. 'A bit scary.'

Mum doesn't argue, but she says, 'Let's give her the benefit of the doubt. Put it down to nerves – she was all silently sweetness and light in her own home. I expect there's a happy medium.'

'Yeah.' She's got a point. After all, I don't want to be judged on the grinning, nodding-dog impersonation I've been giving them all afternoon. 'Mr seems friendly,' I add.

'Mr knows his place under the thumb,' Mum says, surprising me. She puts her hands on her hips. 'Anoushka, the most important thing you can learn about marriage is that it's best when the wife is in charge, but she lets the husband believe he's in charge'.

A cough at the door makes my mother's head whip round and so interrupts my first real piece of marital advice. Mrs Tilak is standing there, looking uncomfortable. My first thought is that she needs the loo, and I'm wondering whether I should point out the bathroom to save her the embarrassment of asking, when Mr Tilak appears behind her, her coat is in his hand. Dad is bringing up the rear, as if they're forming a queue at a soup kitchen.

'Is everything alright, Dukkha?' Mum asks.

'Of course, Madhu.' She smiles and the mole on her lip winks at me. 'We're just saying goodbye.'

'But the food – you must be so hungry.' Mum sweeps a hand around the kitchen. 'Dinner is ready…Dev,' she catches Dad's eye over Mr Tilak's shoulder, 'tell them. There's no need to worry, it's all vegetarian.'

My dad couldn't get a word in if he tried, Mrs Tilak is shaking a vehement head (and yet, her birds-nest hair still doesn't move an inch). 'We wouldn't dream of troubling you. We're going to eat with Ravi this evening, and we'll return, with him, for lunch tomorrow. Is 1 o'clock alright?'

'Well, yes. If you're sure.' Mum's deflation is tangible and in that second, I could slap Mrs Tilak. She's Indian; she's marrying her child off; she knows how insulting it is as a visitor, not to stay and eat till you're over-stuffed and groaning at the stomach. And it's not me being over-sensitive, even Mr Tilak looks shame-faced, and as for Auntie Sonu – loitering where she has no business to be, behind the serving hatch on the living-room side – she hisses through her teeth, scandalised.

I don't know whether Dukkha Tilak is downright mean but doesn't want to burn her bridges yet, or whether she's genuinely, if crassly, not wanting to overstay her welcome, but the million degree temperature drop at least pierces her thick skin.

'Perhaps we might take Ravi some of your delicious snacks, though? To whet his appetite for tomorrow's feast?' she says. She turns to me and smiles. 'Anoushka, would you make us a basket?'

And with that she's apparently redeemed herself. Everyone scurries about making the Tilaks a hearty picnic for their hotel room. Am I the only one who thinks she'll ditch it in the industrial bin at the end of our road? All I know is, that food should be prepared and received with love and blessings – and if she can't take it in that spirit, she's equally getting none from me. I curse every poor innocent pakora I pack into her stupid basket.

Chapter 6

Even though it's really early, I take myself off to bed as soon as we've eaten. (Without saying a word, Mum put all the vegan stuff to one side and cooked us chicken, fish, even pork – something we rarely have out of respect for my dad's many Muslim friends – with a side of egg curry. I'd not much of an appetite but I made sure I licked my plate clean; we all did).

I've got so much to think about but most of me wishes I could shove my head under the pillow and forget it all. I've failed already, haven't I? Dukkha Tilak doesn't like me. I don't think she likes our family, full stop. I stifle a groan and try and take some deep breaths. I realise what else has been niggling at me: these arrangements have been made in a very peculiar way. The norm in Indian families is that the parents and son arrive together to see the prospective girl. So, the only explanation is that Dukkha wanted to check me out – check all of us out – before allowing her son to get involved. I lick my dry lips over and over, afraid that the worst will happen – that she'll go back to the hotel, have Ravi pack up all their belongings and drive straight back to Bradford. The shame of it. My mum and dad will be gutted.

The telephone rings once, twice, and I know it will be the family, wanting to know how the afternoon has gone. If I wasn't so down, I'd listen at the door to hear my mum's take on it all, but I'm too depressed. I give up trying to sleep, though. I wonder about going to find Lalita, but I don't want to talk about it all. The best thing I can do is meet Ravi tomorrow and see how that goes. Meantime, I'll get my books out and do some studying. A few pages of maths and statistics should calm me down, but the numbers just blur, and I read lines of Donald's cramped left-handed writing over and over. I wonder what he would think about all of this? We know nothing about each other's lives outside the Science Building. 'Oh, Mata Rani,' I say aloud, 'Please give me a sign.' And I swear the words have hardly left my mouth when there's a commotion downstairs.

My bedroom is at the back, so I don't know who the late night visitors are, or if they come in a car, but the front door opens and closes and there are muted voices of people being ushered in. I'm curious rather than worried – it's not the noise of an emergency or a drama – so I figure somebody will come and get me if I'm needed. I don't feel like facing anyone – but it seems like that's my hard luck. Seconds later, light feet run up the stairs – it's Laly; the boys are like monsters and my mum and dad tread more heavily and slowly, hauling themselves up the banisters – and she taps on the door and sticks her head round. Her eyes are bright.

'I knew you'd be awake,' she whispers, inserting her whole body into my room. 'But you don't have to be, if you don't want to. Wink wink.'

'What is it? What do you mean?'

'I mean, that your mother-in-law has come back to stay the night–'

'What?' I screech, far too loudly, and clap my hand over my mouth just as Lalita goes, 'Sshh. She'll hear you.'

'Apparently, the hotel doesn't live up to expectations so she's moved out. Noises outside her room or something. Er, like, it's Saturday night? What does she expect? Anyway, Mum's running round like the Queen just arrived and Madame Mother-in-law is hinting you should be here to wait on her.'

'I–' But I can't carry on because I have no idea what

to say.

'The husband and Ravi aren't here,' Laly adds helpfully. 'She got a taxi. They don't need respite 'cos they're not as sensitive as her.'

I haven't got any choice, have I? 'I'll get dressed,' I mutter. 'Go and tell them I was studying. I'll just throw some clothes on.'

'K.' Laly pulls a face and sticks her tongue out, but I'm not sure if it's at me or Dukkha. She wanders off and I scurry around to make myself look presentable. I'm squaring my shoulders – literally, I am – to go down the stairs when Mum's voice floats up.

'There you are, Anoushka. Here she is, Dukkha. She'll show you to the spare room, won't you Anou?'

'What? Yes, of course.' I shake my head to get the fog out. The unexpected guest is standing po-faced beside my mum, a big carpet-bag type thing at her feet. 'Hello, Aunti-ji,' I say politely, as I swoop down and pick it up – what is in it? Has she nicked the kettle and towels. 'Follow me up and I'll show you your bedroom. I'm sorry there was a problem with the hotel.'

I'm talking over my shoulder, but she's not answering. Mum does, instead. 'Unforgivable,' she announces. 'We won't give our business there in future. But it gives us a chance to spend some more time together, doesn't it, before Ravi arrives tomorrow. That's a silver lining.'

'Hmm,' says Dukkha.

It's such a non-committal non-reply that I suddenly wonder if this is a ruse to catch us on the hop. Maybe she's going to find fault and so Ravi won't be allowed over to introduce himself. Though why would she do that? Surely, they'd be better off doing a midnight flit and scuttling back down to Bradford without this pantomime. Stop over-analysing, Anoushka, I order

41

myself. I push open the spare room door and hoist the overweight overnight bag onto the end of the bed.

Dukkha Tilak glances round and does a tiny shiver. It is colder than the rest of the house, a bit more sparsely furnished too. I lean over and crank up the radiator, hoping it works. I have a random picture of fishing a handy Allen key out of my pyjama pocket and bleeding the radiator, a spit of boiling water hissing through her birds nest hair. I'm sure that wouldn't be the kind of practical daughter-in-law she'd appreciate though. A bit too workman-like.

'Maybe you can stop day-dreaming, girl, and run me a bath?'

'Eh? Yes. Sorry. Right.' Her words cut across my thoughts and I pull myself together. Wow. Nothing like being straight to the point, and making yourself at home, is there? I hope the immersion is on. As I cross the landing and grab two towels (the neat guest ones that are too small but look neat and new; Mum won't forgive me if I get out the bobbly family ones) I force myself not to apologise for the lack of an en suite bathroom.

'That's enough. I'm not expecting spa treatment,' she snaps over my shoulder and makes me jump as I'm squirting Radox into the swirling water. 'I'll test the water. I've a very specific tolerance that you'll only learn in time.'

'Of course, Auntie-ji. Can I do anything else? Would you like tea?' Say no, say no, say no...

'You can leave it beside my bed. I'll go straight there after my bath. I'm exhausted after all this trouble.'

'Yes, Auntie.'

'Good girl,' she says, totally unexpectedly and pats me on the back. Alright, it's the kind of praise you'd give a dog you're allergic to, but it's a breakthrough of a kind.

'Enjoy your bath,' I say. Enjoy your bath? What kind of idiot remark is that, I ask myself as I stomp down the stairs and put the kettle on. It's deadly quiet except for the gurgling water pipes; everyone else has vanished behind their own bedroom doors. Well, I hope none of them needs an urgent pee because Dukkha's in no rush to vacate the bath. It's at least half an hour and feels like half the night before I hear the plug being pulled and time it just right to get hot tea to her bedroom without another run-in. Well, Mata Rani, if this is a sign, it's a cryptic one at best.

It's a very long night. I can't settle, knowing that this Jekyll and Hyde woman is sleeping in the opposite room. I hear her stirring and going across to the bathroom, and I can't decide if she's not bothering to keep the noise down or if the darkness just amplifies everything. I wonder what I'd do if I hear her creeping downstairs and out the front door, Mum's best candlesticks and china cups hidden inside that big bag…maybe there's no husband-in-the-wings, after all. Maybe she and Mr Tilak are fraudsters, professional scammers. I stifle a giggle but it comes out like a hiccup and I hear her footstep freeze outside my door. Stranger-danger, that's what I'm feeling, and the giggle turns to a silent sob as I remember that this is my potential forever mother-in-law I'm thinking so badly of.

It's still early when I go downstairs, still in my jammies and un-rested, but determined to look on the bright side. Mr Tilak's nice enough and Mrs is just…odd. Nervy and suspicious. I try to imagine my mum scoping out the family and home of a wife for one of my brothers, and there's no question that they'd come across as a bit weird too. Most families probably do to outsiders – and especially outsiders that they're testing to see if they'll be joined in holy matrimony. I won't judge Ravi by his parents in the same way that I hope nobody – including him – judges me by mine. It's my role, in this courtship ritual to wait hand and foot on the groom's family, so like her or not, I've a position to keep up.

Full of Pollyanna resolutions, I nearly scream when I see Dukkha already sitting silent and poker-straight at the kitchen table. She's on the edge of the chair, with her handbag on the edge of the table, like someone about to leave a restaurant if she's not served within the next thirty seconds. In the stark light of day, her full face of make-up – red blusher and crimson lipstick – is clown-like, scary clown-like, and I swear her artificial curls haven't moved overnight. That's some hairdresser she has on retainer. I want to ask her age – mid-fifties? – because she's false-looking, like one of those dolls you get in a plastic can and stand on your dressing table.

'Good Morning, Anoushka,' she says.

'Morning, Auntie-ji,' I reply as nicely as I can. I'm about to ask if she had a good night, when she beats me to it.

'Did you sleep well?'

'Er, yes, thank you.' I white-lie because I'm surprised. It's probably a trap: she wants me to ask her exactly that so she can complain. So I don't.

'Good.' She nods that stiff head of hers. 'You made me comfortable at a late hour. I appreciate that.'

What? Would the real evil mother-in-law please step forward and remove this imposter. 'Right. Good,' I manage. 'Er, Auntie-ji…'

'Yes?'

I want to say, enough of the pleasantries, and just tell me if I get the seal of approval for your obedient son to leave his hotel room and come and meet me today, but of course I don't. Instead, I ask her if she'd like tea or coffee.

'Can you please make me a cup of chai tea?' she asks. 'Do you know how to make that?'

'Of course I know how to make chai!' The words are out before I can temper them. But it's a stupid question: don't all Indian girls have that basic level of training before they are listed on www.findmeahusband.in – even soon-to-be science graduates. 'I mean, I hope I can make it in the way you like,' I add.

She gives a brittle little laugh. 'It's not a test, dear,' she says, even though we both know it is.

She leaves me to it for a minute, and then says so quietly that I might have missed it, 'Anoushka, do you like me?'

Er, I mean, what? Did she really… She did. Who over the age of about six asks something like that? 'Of course,' I say brightly. 'Of course, Auntie-ji.' With difficulty, I bite back the, 'Why?' and the obvious retaliation, 'Do you like me?' hangs awkwardly between us. I don't want to know.

She doesn't expand on her question, or reply to me; she sits there humming a little tune I can't quite make out. For a second it does occur to me that she's not quite all there – Alzheimer's or something. But nah, she's sharp as a tack and plain weird. I concentrate on boiling the milk and measuring out sugar with all the concentration I give my lab work. I wonder what Donald would make of this, suddenly pops into my mind, and I try not to smirk. Mum comes to the rescue; I might have known she'd sleep with one ear open.

'Namaste, ji. How did you sleep?' she says to Dukkha, which feels like a step too far – the ji bit I mean; why should Mum be so respectful when it's not reciprocated? Especially since, an off-hand, 'Fine. Fine,' is the only reply. Still, my mum doesn't seem in the least bit bothered, so why should I be.

I place a cup of the steaming tea in front of each of them and then make myself an instant coffee, listening in to their chat as I do so. They're soon picking through their various acquaintances, seeking out mutual contacts and tip-toeing around titbits of delicious gossip; nothing too close to home. Dukkha's guard is down – or else she's a BAFTA-winning actress – and she seems more normal, less ogre-ish. Please.

With a few totally indecipherable words, I excuse myself to go and get dressed. There'll be no studying today, I know that. But at least the cooking's taken care of. We've all yesterday's food and then more, plus whatever the aunties drop over – they might sneer at it being veggie but they'll suffer making something meat-less, just to come over and get a look at Ravi. Who wouldn't? In other matches, Laly and me would be right up there, ogling the talent. I snigger to myself as I race into the bathroom and slam the door: if anyone deserves hot bath water today, it's me. It should be taken for granted that I'll get to hide away and pamper myself this morning, but having Dukkha here already, well, that confuses the plans. Will she be part of the primping? Crammed into my bedroom, straightening my best outfit and picking over the jewellery. Surely not. Nor will she be kitchen crew. Both are an overfamiliarity too far and I bet she's a stickler for etiquette. She certainly hasn't made this easy for any of us, herself included, I think. With any luck she'll 'rest' in her room, or Mr T will come and take her for a walk.

Mata Rani herself must be in my corner today, because when I emerge from the bath, it's to Laly banging on the door. I open it a crack and her mouth is close by. 'You can come out now,' she says. 'The mother-in-law from hell has gone back to the hotel to change her clothes and make a re-entrance with her beloved son – when all the work is done, of course.'

'Thank goodness.' I feel the tension seep out of me; a temporary reprieve that makes me feel about a hundred years younger, and with a whoosh, I'm excited about meeting Ravi all over again.

Laly chases me into my bedroom and we sit, giggling, on the unmade bed.

'What was all that about anyway?' I wonder out loud. 'She couldn't have suffered one night in a Travel Lodge? It's not as if it was somewhere on the Cowgate during the Festival."

Laly shrugs. 'Maybe she's like the Princess and Pea-'

'Yeah, right. Like our spare room is palatial.'

'True. In that case she's either doing it as a daughter-in-law-test, or she's just plain horrible.' Laly looks at me. 'Fingers crossed it's the first one, or she'll be a cow to live with.'

'Laly! Mum will hear you.' Then I spoil it by adding, 'Crap. You're right. But…'

'But?'

'She was nearly nice to me in the kitchen earlier.'

'Wowie. Well, as long as Ravi is a 12 out of 10 and not a mummy's boy, you're all set.' Laly crosses her eyes and pulls a face.

We both freeze when the doorbell rings downstairs, but the fact it's pushed open straightaway and voices echo down the hall, means it's just Auntie Sonu back with an entourage. Mum calls Laly and me, and we hang over the banister for a few minutes. She's got Auntie Deepti with her and all the little cousins between them, already dressed up in their brightest Indian suits. They shoo me back to my room, telling Laly to get me ready, 'In case they're early,' Auntie Sonu calls up the stairs.

'They won't be early.' I laugh; that would be the height of bad manners. 'Oh!' When Auntie Sonu glares at me, tapping a toe on the carpet, and widening her eyes, Mum looks down at her own feet, and I realise I'm being short-sighted. Dukkha Tilak's true colours suggest she might do anything, whether she's testing me or otherwise.

'And when they arrive stay upstairs,' Auntie Sonu orders. Then she mutters – I don't know if she realises I can hear her, 'Madhu, you'd do well to keep Laly out of the way all day. She's younger and lighter-skinned; if the mother's mentioned that to the son, who knows how it could all go.' There's a pause, and for good measure, she adds, 'Laly's figure is better, too. Or is it just because she's three inches taller?'

Way to go, Auntie. She really knows how to boost a would-be wife's self-confidence. Laly hears her too and snorts; she's no intention of getting married to anyone who isn't really rich and really good-looking and really, utterly, madly in love with her. And she'd never, like never, put up with Dukkha Tilak. But that's Laly, she's the youngest so she doesn't know the meaning of 'compromise'.

Anyway, it's not the done-thing for the little sister to marry first.

'Yeah, let's go and choose your lipstick.' Laly raises her voice and rolls her eyes at me. 'Gotta impress them. D'you think Orange Capucine or Beige d'Eau will go best with your degree certificate and graduation gown, Anou?'

'At least Anoushka doesn't have such a mouth on her,' Auntie Sonu shouts after us, but she doesn't mean it, she never does; she secretly admires Laly, she's always saying that Laly takes after her, and what an addition to her three strapping sons a daughter like Laly would have been.

My bright pink outfit with the fine gold threading has been hanging in the wardrobe just waiting for this day. The green and black with the silver is second-in-command, ready to change into for dinner; it's more fancy than the day-time pink, supposed to be more sophisticated, so that Ravi gets to see two sides of me. My lips twitch as I wonder what side of me he'd see if I waltzed down to greet him in my white lab-coat – or better still, saggy leggings and sloppy hoodie. It would almost be worth it to see Dukkha's face but I'd never have the nerve, nor could I bear to see the utter horror on my mum and dad's faces if I did. Auntie Sonu would disown me there and then and pack me off to some ancestors' village in Dhanushkodi or somewhere equally godforsaken.

'Earth to Anou. Er, come in, Anou…' Laly's standing looking at me, with her hands on her hips. 'There's no point in having stars in your eyes till you've actually seen him,' she says.

I don't bother telling her what I'm really thinking. Instead, I wriggle out of my jammies and get myself all dolled up. Auntie Deepti hauls herself up the stairs with a basket of beautician's goodies filched from Sharmila – who couldn't get the afternoon off; a rich client who pays for her to go to their house, apparently – and she paints my nails in a weird pearly pinkish-cream. 'It's good,' she praises herself when she's finished. 'Modest but fashionable. A statement colour.' She snaps a line of photos, from a little digital camera, to show to Sharmila later on – she says. I expect my hands and feet will be on show in the beautician's window, a before and after. Behind her, Laly holds up the box and points and laughs silently – Auntie Deepti is quoting the marketing bumf. She might have convinced herself but to me my fingers and toes just look anaemic.

49

'Why didn't you just say that to her?' Laly asks me, when the auntie has gone, and I'm gloomily holding up my hands to make sure they dry. 'You're such a bloody people-pleaser, Anou.' She shakes her head. 'What are you going to do if you don't like this Ravi guy? Put up with him and his smelly socks and grey jocks for fifty years so as not to offend anyone?'

The horror – despair? Fear? Naked hope? Which of them, all of them, must show on my face because she backtracks and softens (which she never does; she'd swear red was yellow and night was day rather than be challenged). 'I don't mean that exactly,' she says. 'But you do have to toughen up. You don't want to be running around after the Tilaks like you do around us, do you?'

'I never knew you noticed,' I murmur, and it might be the right moment for a bit of a heart to heart, if it wasn't exactly the wrong moment because there's a sort of Mexican wave of voices downstairs that indicates our company is here.

Laly grabs my hand, and putting her finger to her lips, we sneak out of my bedroom into Mum and Dad's, which overlooks the driveway at the front. We stand back, well behind the nets – I just know that Dukkha will look up to check, and gloat if she sees us – and watch a blue Toyota Carina pulling in. Mr Tilak is driving and Mrs is in the passenger seat; it's impossible to see anyone in the back. When he cuts the engine, none of them gets out straightaway. I'm too far away to know, but I bet Dukkha is giving them last minute instructions; when she twists around and apparently says something over her shoulder, I know I'm right.

'She's telling him to be a good boy and mind his manners.' Lalu nudges me and we giggle. 'Now, Ravi, love, has thee got a clean 'anky in ta pocket?' she mimics in a truly bad Yorkshire accent that Dukkha doesn't have. 'Don't show us up by drooling over your beautiful bride-to-be. Oh, and…' She lowers her voice, 'Don't mention the skeletons.'

'No, no – do mention them.' I nudge her back. 'As long as they're little ones. How else will I get to know what I'm – I mean, what I might be–' I correct myself, 'marrying in to?' I'm laughing along with her, but ouch, there's a bit of it too close to home. We've all got skeletons, haven't we? There's about a million innocuous things in our family history that Mum and Dad would be mortified if we blurted out: Uncle Zaki getting (wrongly, they insist) arrested; pretending to be out when the insurance man came round (I was about eight); Laly and me nicking a hair bobble from Patel's (we picked it up off the floor and didn't think about it being shoplifting) and Mr Patel came round later with another one, allegedly because he was sad we hadn't enough money to buy them. Oh, Mum was utterly humiliated that time.

We grab each other, and I'm more or less holding my breath, as the car doors open below us, and the three occupants get out. The boy emerging from the back is obscured by Dukkha, who's making a fuss of checking inside her handbag and smoothing her sari down, but I can see he's wearing a black shirt and dark grey trousers. He ducks his head down to reach back in to pick up something from the seat. It's a suit jacket that he slips into and settles the collar.

'Your knight in grey suited shining armour,' Laly says.

'He looks alright from here.'

'Yeah, so does Dukkha, but we've seen the fright she is close up.'

'Ssh!' I know it's coincidence (and my guilty conscience) but the birds-nest hair chooses that moment to turn in our direction. There's a funny –

that's not funny – little smile dancing on her lips, and I just know that she knows we're here, watching. Damn.

'He's thin,' Laly observes. 'But that's better than fat. You'll be expected to feed him up.'

'And he's got his own hair.' What I can see looks dark and silky.

'For the next few years anyway. And he mightn't take after his old man, anyway.' Laly grins wickedly. 'Though bald is better than Worzel Gummidge.'

'Laly!'

'What?' She looks sideways at me. 'You think it, I say it.'

Touché, as they say.

We creep back to my bedroom under cover of the fuss going on downstairs. There's a flurry of voices, of welcomes, of fake laughs and people talking over each other – why are British people obsessed with the routes they drive and how long they take? In my whole life, I've never had visitors who didn't create a whole conversation over the roadworks, services, and weather conditions on the A9. I suppose I should be grateful that the Tilaks are part of the in-crowd; it's one common denominator between our two families. I'm still straining to hear Ravi's voice amidst the shrillness of the aunties but they obviously troop into the sitting room and close the door. There appears to be a constant murmur of chatter, which raises my spirits. Half of me is wishing I was a million miles away, whilst the rest of me is desperate to hear what's being said. If my brothers were sisters, they'd be all tuned in and taking turns to rush up here and tell us what's going on, but as it is, there's just Laly and me looking at each other. I'm sitting on my hands so as not to bite my horrible but neatly painted nails.

The digital clock beside my bed clicks over agonisingly slowly. It's worse than setting up an experiment that you know you can't check on for x number of hours. Usually when that happens Donald and I go and raid the vending machine or try and get ahead with our write-ups – we're the only ones who don't go to the pub; the rest of the group has got used to that and begs or expects us to keep an eye of their specimens too. Well, it's something to do. I tense up a few times, then relax – as much as I can – when the door opens but it's someone going to and from the kitchen.

'Tea,' I say, redundantly. 'It's either all going well or the conversation needs a boost.'

'They'll be up to get you in a minute.' She looks at me and frowns. 'What would happen if there's like a colossal fall-out and the Tilaks leave…' One glare from me and she hurries on with, 'Rhetorical question, obviously. The mother-in-law granted permission for them to come so you've already got one foot in.'

She's right. I cheer up a bit. Dukkha could have escaped twice now, yesterday and this morning, yet she came back instead of hot-footing it back to Bradford, pleading a migraine or the universal 'family emergency'. All I've got to do now is win over Ravi – if I want to. But no, it's not what I want, it's what my mum and dad want. I know better than to say any of this to Laly, but she's flapping her hand at me.

'Someone's coming up. You're on, Anou. I'll be right behind you blending into the wallpaper in case the catch of the day sees me and throws you aside. G'luck.'

It's Auntie Deepti they've sent up; Sonu won't want to miss overseeing the refreshments. It's a bit of a blur even as it happens, but she holds my hand and leads me into a room full of people. They don't actually stop talking as I sidle in, and she nudges me to perch on the end of the sofa next to Dukkha. I say a very quiet

Namaste, but keep my eyes down, which is less good old Indian modesty than fear I'll blush or trip or say something stupid if I catch anyone's eye, but the upside is how I'll get Brownie points for it. I might have imagined it, but I'm sure that Dukkha looks in my direction and rests her hand on my shoulder. It's the most fleeting of nano-seconds but I'm sure she does and it throws me totally off course. Is she being nice or holding me back or is this my imagination?

I'm saved by Auntie Sonu – and I bite my lip because I've never before had grounds to say that – bustling in with a silver tray, my mum following meekly behind her like an in-between maid. Silence falls and the whole room watches as they go back and forth to the kitchen and then lay everything out on the dining room table. I have this sudden and crushing memory of a high school trip to the King's Theatre to see An Inspector Calls – the play where society crumbles and the stage set breaks up into a million pieces. It's like a momentary panic attack and my heart rate goes mental. Luckily, nobody is looking in my direction, and at the other end of the room, neither Mum nor Auntie Sonu spill the chai. It's now or never, I think, and I take advantage of the moment to pluck up courage and look (under my lashes) at Ravi, diagonally opposite me.

He's not looking at the groaning food table or at me – which I'm grateful for, although it could have been a very Richard Curtis stolen-and-shared glance scene. Instead, he's staring at the wall clock and twiddling with his fingers.

I hope to God he's nervous rather than bored.

I do see that he's nice-looking, at least. I mean, I want to sneak a few more looks, not run from the room. His suit is a nice one, probably not tailormade but definitely not one of those ill-fitting rumpled ones that go shiny. Men buy them from Burtons for job interviews, then forget to shine their shoes–

My eyes swivel down to Ravi's feet, and – another point in his favour – his black shoes are laced up and polished, and there's no mud on the heels. Oh, help, I think, I'm turning into my mum; that's exactly the kind of thing she'd check when my brothers go out. She's even been known to clean them herself. Double help. Does that mean Dukkha cleans my possible-future husband's shoes and if so, I'll end up doing it too…

I'm not sure if a tiny moan escapes me, or a little squeak. Probably it's only an intake of breath but Ravi turns his head and catches my eye. It's only for a fraction of a second before we both look away, but it's my instinct to smile and I'm glad that it's his, as well. A little warm feeling dares to creep towards my heart.

Chapter 7

'Anoushka? Will you pass round the tea and snacks?' my mum says in her best we've-got-company voice.

'Of course,' I all but whisper and go over and collect the two cups and saucers she's holding out. 'Mr and Mrs Tilak,' she instructs. Years of needing a steady hand for experiments and dissection have prepared me perfectly for this moment, and I hand over both without a tremor or the hint of a spill. Mr Tilak gives me a broad beam of a smile and I have the feeling he'd squeeze my knee if I was sitting beside him; I'm not sure if that's good or bad. Mrs gives me a less wholesome but seemingly benign upwards flick of her lips, which has to be good. Auntie Sonu is heavy breathing importantly right behind me, a plate in either hand. She's keen to list the pedigree of each of the snacks and sweets, so I turn obediently back to my mum.

'This cup,' she announces, reverently, 'is for Ravi.' She all but winks at me, and I deliberately don't look in the direction of Laly, who really is lurking in the corner; it's like I'm offering myself laid out on a saucer.

I put the drink carefully on the side-table tucked in next to his chair, and hear him say, politely, 'Thank you, Anoushka.'

I nod my head and risk a glance, to discover he's smiling up at me. Split-second impressions that he's neither got awful sticky-out teeth nor a horrible voice, mean I instinctively, positively grin at him, before realising and snapping back to demure. Mum gives me a cup of chai and a sort of sideways wide-eyed jerk of the head that says, 'Good girl, nobody's running away, it's going okay, now go and sit yourself back down, you can have cake later because there's nothing worse than food stuck in your teeth and remember not to slurp or gulp, we're not at a chimp's tea party.' I know this because she's been saying a variation of it all my life.

I slide neatly back in beside Dukkha, who's on her second round of snacks and hoovering up them up as quickly as Auntie Sonu, swollen up with joy, can tip them onto the plate. I remember that brilliant phrase all fur coat and no knickers and decide I'm seeing it in action with Mrs Dukkha Tilak. I take a very ladylike sip of my hot sweet tea and smile gently at the crumbs sticking to the mole on her mouth.

Once she's finished eating, she seems a bit twitchy, and I wonder if she's about to up-sticks again. Like, is this it? The first visit for a marriage match is always much more driven by the boy's family, so it's quite possible they'll call a halt – but she wouldn't be rude enough to walk out on two meals, surely? That's taking the upper hand too far…Even worse, she's giving these dainty little coughs, clearing her throat, and I'm all of a sudden terrified that she's choking. Hell, if she dies in front of me I'll never get married and even worse, I'll be resigned to a lifetime of Mum and the aunties passive-aggressively debating whose food did the terrible deed.

I want to laugh when I realise how wrong I've got it. She's just trying to get the attention of the away-with-the-fairies Mr Tilak. He finally clocks her and

puffs up as if he's about to make a speech. Please, no. I wait for him to tap his spoon on his cup.

He doesn't. When the clunking of crockery and the refusals of more refreshment are over, and there's a lull, he sort of half stands up – not unlike he's in the early throes of a heart attack (I saw it happen once in the cafeteria at college; it was undiagnosed angina but we only learned that later) – and that's enough to get everyone's attention.

'Hmm. I think it's about time these two young people, er, Ravi and Anoushka, formally meet each other,' Mr Tilak says, his eyes fixed on his wife's for approval; I can imagine the coaching that went into the timing.

Dad jumps in, on cue. 'Splendid idea.' (Splendid? My dad has never before said 'splendid' in my hearing). He rubs his hands together, shares a satisfied nod with Mr Tilak, and looks around. The two fathers have done their bit, the women will now take charge. And they, naturally, need no second bidding. A loud and animated debate ensues as to how best Ravi and I will best get to know each other: kitchen: no privacy; hall, stairs and landing: no dignity; garden: too cold. It'll have to be the spare bedroom, as approved by Dukkha whose night there clearly reassured her it was far from a passion-inducing boudoir. I have no input and neither does Ravi, we both sit there like spare parts ready to be choreographed into position. I'm a tale of two halves again: overwhelmed with gratitude that Act 2 of the show is going on so that I can finally talk to my co-lead, versus petrified that I'm about to be locked (metaphorically) in a bedroom with an utter stranger and forced to talk to him. No pleasing some folk.

Auntie Sonu races up the stairs like a devil possessed 'to prepare the room', Auntie Deepti vying for second position. I can hear them both giggling as they apparently rearrange the furniture; when they lean over the banister to call us up, I expect to see the double bed dragged out on to the landing and upended against the wall – it isn't. Mum beckons me and Ravi to follow her (I'm surprised Dukkha doesn't move), which we do, and the aunties usher us into the spare room, me to balance on the very side of the bed –

to get more comfortable feels too decadent, too risqué – and Ravi to sit on a kitchen chair they've placed diagonally opposite. I have to admire their last minute ingenuity: it's not a large room, yet even if we both prostrate ourselves and then stretch out our legs and arms, we still won't be able to touch each other. They back out of the room, leaving the door wide open, and shuffle across the landing and – reluctantly, I know it – down the stairs. Auntie Sonu, at least, would have loved to linger in earshot and be first with the, 'How's it going?' gossip.

When Ravi and I are as alone as it's possible to be in a house full of ear-wigging relatives, we carefully don't look at one another. It seems neither of us has a script for this bit. Silly, isn't it? I've spent a lot of time thinking about how meeting my husband-match might be, but it's been in a sort of fade-to-black fuzz, at the end of which we announce ourselves, dimpled and blushing. There's no nitty-gritty about how the conversation will go. What an oversight, Anoushka: you don't go in to a setting without a hypothesis– I realise, at this point that Ravi has taken the initiative:

'Well,' he's saying, like a contestant on a gameshow on telly, 'I expect you want to know about me. I'm Ravi, I'm twenty-five and I'm a lawyer at Kendricks, Patel and Leigh in Bradford…' There's a bit about him being on the fast track to promotion in the near future, and I know I should be hanging on his every word to fill in Mum and Dad later on, but I'm distracted by his posh voice. He sounds really English, like someone who lives in a manor house and has servants. It's a good thing, it's nice on the ear but I'm all the more conscious of my Scottish accent. It's not thick and incomprehensible, but it's nothing like his, nor is it the sing-song little Indian girl that people seem to expect after they've heard my parents, who are as Indian as the day they left there...He runs out of things to say and adds, 'What about you? You're studying?'

'Yes.' I sound a bit croaky, so I clear my throat, and say it again. 'Yes'. This time it rings out in the quiet bedroom. 'At Edinburgh Uni. I'm going to sit my Finals in May. An Honour's Degree in Applied Biology. I'm hoping to get a 2:1.' I'm not sure what else to add because what I do after graduating depends whether I get married or not. I want to do my PhD but my parents aren't having it. 'Where did you study?' I ask instead.

'Sheffield. I wanted to go to Oxford or London but I didn't like to leave the family. Like you, I expect.' He sounds quite earnest. 'I believe family to be the most important thing of all. I'm now independent and want to have my own children. I have enough money to look after a wife and after some years will be able to afford a house for us. Of course, there's always a place with my parents.'

Some years. Some years with Dukkha. Frying pan and fire come to mind. Hmm. But he clearly has plans for a home of his own. 'A home and children is a wish of mine, too,' I agree. It's true, but I wish I didn't sound so much like a Jane Austen heroine saying it. He flushes at that, and I do, too, and we smile at each other properly for the first time.

'Do you want to work first?' he asks. 'With your degree, I mean.'

I hesitate here, though, sure there's a right answer, and not sure what it is. 'Maybe,' I hedge. 'I could work in research or do a teaching diploma. But really,' I decide to go for broke, 'I'd like to do my PhD. If that's not a problem.'

'I'm sorry?' He looks at me, puzzled. There's a little cleft, not quite a frown, between his eyebrows that's very cute. 'Why is it a problem?'

'If...if...er...my husband didn't agree.' I try to be delicate; he doesn't know I'm hanging on his answer.

'Oh! Oh, I see.' His face clears. 'I'm sure a good husband would support your dreams. I myself studied Law and Business Management and thought investment banking was a good choice. Then I realised I liked law but not so much business. Luckily I had a lot of options.'

'That's good.' I nod far too enthusiastically, not sure why that's relevant, but who cares? Marriage to Ravi Tilak could be the way to my PhD. That's a very real pro. So as not to look too keen on studying, I add randomly, because I can't think of anything else. 'Er, my Dad said you'd be okay with me still going to the temple?'

'Of course.' His nod puts mine into perspective. 'Your beliefs are very important. You would be happy to be vegetarian in my mother's house?'

'Definitely.'

The conversation dries up a bit then. I'm wracking my brains, and he looks a bit like a deer in the headlights too. It's on the tip of my tongue to share how archaic this meeting is, putting us on the spot like this, but I decide I don't know him well enough – enough? I don't know him at all. I sneak a look at the bedside clock: fifteen minutes have ticked by. Ravi catches me looking – and, thank you, Mata Rani, it breaks the ice. We both laugh out loud.

'You're very beautiful, Anoushka,' he blurts out – literally making me jump. 'I am hoping to find a beautiful, clever wife, who wants to be a mother, and who is happy to join my family. It is my parents' dream, too. Would you–'

I freeze when he stops, afraid he's trying to find the words to ask me to marry him and fearing that the weight of expectation on me will make me say yes. I swallow, wondering if there'll be a decent cooling off period; he's a lawyer, after all. But the silence is screaming and the look in his eyes is agonising, so I can't help myself but to prompt him. 'Would I what, Ravi?' It's the first time I've used his name and a frisson creeps over me.

'You, er…Would you…' he repeats. 'Anoushka, would you agree to see me again? Can we tell our families our match is positive? Without obligation but positive?'

'Yes,' I say slowly. 'Yes, alright.'

He breaks into a big – relieved – smile, and stands up, and that seems to be that. It's the without obligation that's sticking with me. It's exactly what I want, isn't it; the get out clause, and it's sensible. So why does it make the request seem only lukewarm?

Downstairs, though, as we shyly stick out heads around the door, the news of our decision is taken so well, I do start to feel warm and fuzzy. Mr Tilak looks suffused – there really is no other word – with joy and even Dukkha unbends enough to kiss my cheek and invite me to visit the whole family in Bradford. Mum and Dad are smiling, as well, albeit briefly leaning into each other, in an exhausted our-job-is-done sort of way. I mustn't forget how very stressful all this is for my parents. It always is for the girl's family, who are treated as lower in rank than the boy's, and expected to give so much more. Frequently, the boy's family believe they can do and say whatever they want and the girl's lot will accept it, no questions asked. It's the way of Indian culture, though I don't really understand why – I know if I try to explain it to anyone non-Indian, it'll sound ludicrous that one family treats another as inferior because they have a son to wed and not a daughter. To be fair to the Tilaks, their opinions on the dowry and such are enlightened and I should be thankful, but…let's just say a sneaky little bit of me wonders if there's anything more to it than them being kind and generous people. I mean, Dukkha doesn't exude altruism.

I'm over-thinking again – Mum is baring her teeth through her smile and her eyes are boring into mine. Snap out of it, Anou, they're saying, be charming not difficult. Laly intercedes under cover of a 'quick freshen up', at which all the women present smile knowingly and let us go. The aunties take the opportunity to arrange a rota for toilet visits and getting the little cousins' hands washed; I can hear them as Laly corners me.

'Well?' she asks, hustling me into my bedroom and leaning on the door, closing behind her. 'Is he The One? You looked reasonably stars and roses when you came down but you're bloody hard to read.'

'I don't know about The One.' I do a quick check of my face and hair in the mirror and decide it's all fine. 'But he seems nice. Normal. We laughed.' I look up and catch Laly's eye. 'What? What more do you want? I met the guy for twenty minutes. I'd say that's a shining endorsement.'

'It's not that French thing where you swoon into a fit and can't bear to be separated ever again, though?' she accuses.

'A coup de foudre.' I grin. 'I'm not you, Laly. I'm the sensible oldest daughter, remember. You can have the fairy tale, I'm taking the safe option.'

'So when are you meeting again?'

'We're going to. 'Without obligation.' He asked me. But we didn't make an arrangement.'

'Well, do it,' she orders. 'Before they leave today. Take some control, Anou, or this whole thing will run away from you.'

'I will,' I promise her. 'Come on, I'm ravenous,

aren't you? Even for veggies.'

'Ooh, I'm wrong, it must be luurve,' she says. 'You want food and you've stopped looking scared stiff.'

She's right. Whatever happens, I've done the worst: met the Tilaks and Ravi head on. And it's alright. I know what I'm dealing with now. Anything is possible.

Auntie Sonu's foghorn voice calls us downstairs, sending Laly to the kitchen and manhandling me to sit beside Ravi at the dining table. It's been pulled out to accommodate all of us – the little ones banished very happily to the kitchen – but even so it's a squeeze. I don't know about Ravi but my thighs and shoulders are tense with not bumping into his; I'm more glad that Dukkha isn't on my other side as I really don't want to be literally rubbing shoulders with someone so rigid.

The resultant lunch is a jolly, celebratory affair, with dishes whirling around, compliments flowing, and a bonhomie I have only seen at weddings – this is just a foretaste! It's lovely to see everyone in such good spirits, so much so that even the baby cousins' cake-fight is laughed off by Auntie Sonu. If only every day could be like this. Ravi and I get to share a few more details too. We talk a bit about hobbies, and if he's a bit stay-at-home, well, so am I; we've both been studying or working hard. I'd rather he was a homebird than a cage fighter or a trainspotter; I'm not sure which of those would be worse to be dragged along to – or to be left at home in favour of. His best friend is his cousin, Anoop, and I'd have to say mine is my cousin, Sharmila – after Laly. We both like films, so we tentatively wonder if we could meet at a cinema sometime soon, as I can't imagine the stress of being plonked in our lounge with a video and some samosas, while the rest of the family crams into the kitchen. Cringe.

All in all, I decide I'm left feeling good about this match. Dukkha is a thorn, but seeing her more relaxed – by which I mean keeping her husband in mind of good manners by a series of surreptitious hand gestures, and bossing Auntie Deepti, who's taking it on the chin in support of the reason for the lunch – I accept she's probably a bit of a stinger rather than a total prickly cactus of a woman. She wouldn't do as Laly's mother-in-law (I mean, who will?) but I'm easy-going and easy-pleased; life's easier that way. You might say I'm cautiously optimistic, which sits well with Ravi's no obligation.

I don't think anything of it when Dukkha asks if she might use the telephone. Mum waves her into the hall as if she's one of the family and the desultory chat continues over the dregs of the sweets we're pushing on each other even though we're all stuffed. The visit is winding down, and I'm not sorry. I'm tired of being on show, and looking forward to deconstructing it all with Laly, and getting an onslaught of feedback from Mum and the aunties. Ravi and his dad are doing the 'let's make a move' shuffle, when Dukkha bursts back into the lounge, her whole face one big smile. It transforms her.

'Good news,' she cries, her eyes rolling beneath the eternally static birds-nest. 'Dev, Madhu, I have spoken to the priest. He has studied their charts; the stars are aligned; no doshas. He has chosen a date for the wedding of dear Ravi and Anoushka!'

I'm not sure that she even notices the speechlessness with which her words are greeted, she's elevated into her own little world. Ravi and I look at each other and I can see he's as shocked as I am, and despite the situation, it's nice that he and I are bound together in our response. Another sign, Mata Rani? The superstitious little niggle within me is glad there is no dosha evident; bad energy is frowned upon and if it were mine, I'd never be let forget it.

'When? When is the suggested date, Dukkha?' My Dad is first to pull himself together.

'The 22nd of September,' she announces confidently.

'Five months.' I can see my mum mentally counting it out.

'Isn't it perfect?' Dukkha claps her hands together.

I can't do this. I can't. It's all moving too fast. We've only known each other for twenty minutes and haven't even set a second date, let alone talked about the actual marriage. But it's like one of those domino games where they're delicately balanced till you give one a push and then they all start toppling. I'm not brave enough to object outright, but I look around the room, not caring if anyone picks up on desperation.

Beside me, Ravi gets to his feet. 'Thank you, Mum,' he says. 'It's an honour that the priest feels Anouskha and I are a match. Thank you, Mr and Mrs Malhotra, too, for agreeing to let us start on this long journey. Might we end today looking forward to the next steps? Five months might be too short or too long, but let's keep it as a goal. Anoushka?' He looks down at me and lays his hand very lightly on my shoulder. Do you agree?'

All I can manage is a nod – and a deep sigh of relief when I see the lawyer in Ravi has calculated his audience exactly. Everyone can interpret his words how they wish, and everyone is smiling again; even Dukkha retains her giddy edge. As for me, well, I asked for an ally and I'm not sure if Ravi is the most likely or unlikely source. It's certainly the most unlikely.

And it's told me one thing: in the split second he spoke up, I knew it. For better or for worse, Ravi Tilak is the man I'm going to marry

Chapter 8

'What's happening? Why aren't they going? Madhu?'

Auntie Sonu and Auntie Deepti are in unison, like the chorus in a Bollywood movie; their jostling to look out of the window while making sure anyone outside doesn't see them only add to the routine.

'I don't know,' Mum snaps. 'Maybe the car won't start. Maybe they pray before driving.'

'I will go and check–'

'You'll do no such thing, Dev. We'll look like idiots if they pull away as you go out.'

'And they'll know we were spying on them,' pipes up Laly.

Mum gives her a look. 'Make yourself useful and run upstairs and see what you can see from there,' she orders. 'Not you, Anou. You sit on the sofa and look calm, in case they come back in. Deepti, Sonu, let's clear quickly – just in case.'

The front door has closed behind the Tilaks, but before our combined Malhotra clan can drop their company faces and chew over the afternoon – with added relish – the trio needs to actually leave. The three of them are just sitting in the Toyota, like they're in a traffic jam. Laly's feet thunder above our heads. Then silence.

'Well?' Everyone looks at her as she comes back.

She shrugs. 'Dunno. But they're talking a hundred to the dozen. Could be an argument.'

I struggle to keep looking calm. What if they've changed their minds? What if something has put them off us, just at the point when I'm warming to the idea?

Another minute passes while we all look at each other. Then my dad says, reasonably, 'We can't ignore them any longer. I'll go out, Madhu.' He holds up a hand to stop her opening her mouth. 'I can offer them my AA card.'

Mum humphs, but under her breath, and we all watch Dad leave the lounge and open the front door as if he's going off to war. It's as if he's given the Tilaks a cue: Mr gets out of the car and they walk towards each other. Dukkha and Ravi sit tight.

'It's like a cowboy film,' Laly hisses – mindful, I'm sure, that the door is open. 'Pistols at dawn.'

'Ssh. Quiet,' Mum warns.

But we can't hear anything. I start to get up, but Mum pushes me down. 'Stay.'

'They look happy,' Laly translates for me. 'No punches, just lots of arm-waving and stuff. Oh – Ravi's getting out now. He's talking, too. Wait. He's going back to fetch Mrs T…' She squeaks. 'Watch out, they're all coming in.'

Like an ensemble cast warned that the curtain's going up, everyone finds a spot and starts doing something; innocent faces all round. Talk about obvious.

'We thought you'd gone. What a lovely surprise,' my mum trills, fooling nobody. Thank goodness it's Dad's head that appears in the doorway first. 'What?' she mimes.

He licks his lips. 'Good news. Good news,' he says, sounding like a doctor about to report his patient might be crippled but hey, they're alive. 'Er…Madhu, Anoushka, could we have… er… a quick word? Maybe in the kitchen–'

'Nonsense!' Dukkha's flushed face and rigid perm pop up, the rest of her body pushing past him into the room. 'This is a moment to share. We're all in agreement,' her eyes flick around the room, 'aren't we, Madhu?'

'I'm sure we are.' Mum has never sounded less sure of anything.

As for Dukkha, if I didn't know better, I'd swear she was drunk, or high on something. I've never been either but I've seen the fallout from the Students Union often enough.

'All is in alignment,' she announces. 'Our priest has given a date. Our families have bonded. Our children have agreed a match. Hmm?' She doesn't pause, she grabs a quick breath, while we all look at her in various speechless levels of tentative agreement. 'We have decided there is no reason to delay the Rokka ceremony*. Why wait? It will happen here and now!' She smiles – no, she doesn't, even in my state of shock, I read it as a leer, a triumphant leer – as if she's the victor in some kill or cure competition. She is preening.

For a second, my mum looks as if she might fall over, but she catches my dad's eye (I can't see what she does: encouragement? Despair?) and rallies supremely. 'Anoushka, Laly. Upstairs now, please. We can't embark on something so important without a change in outfit. You understand, Dukkha ji.'

We need no second bidding; we're out the door and up the stairs, even as Dukkha's voice floats after us. 'Of course, of course,' she's saying, 'Sonu and Deepti will assist me, I'm sure. The men can be free to do their male things…'

'What "male things" and where are they gonna do them – in the garage?' Laly snorts in my ear, but that's the least of my concerns.

'Mum, I can't do this now,' I say, as she shepherds us into my bedroom and closes the door. 'I'm not ready. I just met him.'

'But you do like him?' she puffs, collapsing onto the bed. I don't need to ask her if she and Dad were in on this; the one saving grace is that it's clearly a surprise to them too. I'd never trust them again if it were otherwise.

'Yes, I like him but I thought we'd have more time...'

'Give me a minute.' Mum's brain is clearly working at full speed, trying to sort this out. Finally, she says, 'Right. You like him. We like him. The Tilaks are a good family. There is a match here–' She raises her hand to stop me interrupting; is she convincing me or herself? 'Hear me out, Anou. In Hindu tradition, the Rokka is nothing more than public confirmation of that. It is the first step in the marriage journey, a bond of unity between two families. Yes? Anou, yes?'

'I suppose,' I agree, if unwillingly. She's literally right but everyone knows that it means the wedding's a done deal.

'Actually, Anou, think about it – this afternoon really was the Rokka already, in all but name. To refuse to, to seal it, is a rudeness I don't think we can face.' Her mouth sets firm as she's talking, and I know that look. In the space of five minutes, less, my mother has come full circle from shock to acceptance and is telling me what I have to do. She hits home with, 'If we, the Malhotras, don't go ahead now, it reflects badly on the Tilaks, and they will withdraw their offer – Dukkha will, I know it. So, as a good and dutiful daughter, if you like this boy...Of course, if you don't, if you were mistaken earlier,' her eyes challenge mine; the witch, 'say now, and that's the last we'll mention of this match.'

I look at Laly but she's oddly quiet. She gives me a sympathetic smile but the slight shrug of her shoulders means she's either decided I'm on a loser here and may as well give in or that she's with Mum – it has been known – and can see the Rokka is logical.

I sigh. 'Give me a minute.' Bottom lines: I didn't

argue when Dukkha announced the priest's date; I
agreed it was a potential match; nothing is irrevocable;
I don't want to disappoint my family; and the big one –
I do like Ravi. Not half an hour ago I said, and meant,
that he was the man I'm going to marry. I sigh again.
What's to lose except my self-respect and my family's
reputation if I refuse. And a tiny voice whispers
naughtily in my ear, you might gain a PhD. 'Let's do
it,' I say. 'I'd better put on another salwar suit, hadn't
I?'

Once Mum goes back downstairs to give Dad the
discreet nod – from the scurrying around and the
comings and goings (doing what, precisely?) everyone
else has taken the ceremony for granted. I can even
hear Auntie Sonu proclaiming to nobody in particular
what an excellent and totally obvious idea it is. 'Two-
faced old cow,' I mutter, and Laly snorts, so I turn on
her. 'As for you, you traitor, you're my sister. Why
didn't you back me up?'

'What? Back you up in what, exactly?' She sounds
affronted. 'It's not like you said, "No way, Jose, get me
outta here," and threatened to slit your wrists, is it? I'm
not a mind reader. You looked surprised, but not that
bothered.'

She's right, I know that. There's a million times in
my life where I wish I'd grown a backbone at the time,
but then again, only in a handful have things not
worked out in time.

'Anyway,' she goes on, 'you can still ditch him
before the engagement, can't you? I mean, he seems
cool but what if he's a perv underneath? And it'll be
much easier to call it all off on the phone instead of in
front of everyone down there now, especially old
witchy-head with the mole. Wait, and you could even
get Dad to do it.'

'How can two sisters be so different?' I look at her,

half in admiration, half in disbelief at the nonsensical sense she spouts.

'And I'm not done yet,' she assures me. She opens the wardrobe door and roots to the back, to an outfit protected by a paper cover. This she pulls out with a flourish. 'Ta da! They spring the Rokka on you, you need something to wear, Cinderella.'

A slow smile spreads over my face. 'Mum is going to rage.' Laly is making loose and free with the very expensive outfit I've been saving for the engagement.

'Let her. She hasn't a leg to stand on and she'll know it.'

It's not the leisurely getting-ready I envisaged, much more a hectic quick change as if I'm playing the lead in a community pantomime, with a soundtrack of stage: the aunties scurrying around at Dukkha's command, getting more sweets ready – no Indian celebration is complete without stuffing more and more sweet stuff down another's throat, and the Tilaks had obviously come prepared with a car boot-full – and Mum and Dad in the hallway, muttering over the money and whether they could cobble enough together by raiding the housekeeping and borrowing from Uncle Pavan.

'£201 into the envelope, Dev. Where is an envelope? A business one, long and white,' Mum is fussing.

'Madhu? Madhu!' That's Auntie Sonu, screeching up the stairs. 'The silver tray? You have a silver tray ready?'

'The sideboard,' Mum calls. 'Back left. It will need a little polish–'

'No need, no need.' Dukkha's school-girlish glee is seriously weird, her giggle more grating than her moaning. 'We have brought our family silver… Kabir, to the car again…'

There's a sharp intake of breath from the landing,

followed by, 'Such nonsense,' I hear Mum hiss at Dad. 'My daughter, my silver.'

'One-nil to Mum,' Laly says.

'More like an extra-time penalty point,' I add gloomily, and immediately tell myself to snap out of it. If this turns out to be a model perfect marriage, I don't want my memories of the Rokka soured by my temper. I put on a brilliant smile and leer at Laly, who jumps back in mock horror.

'Hounds-of-hell, Anou, you look like your mother-in-law already,' she announces, far too loudly.

'Sshh,' I hush her and we giggle behind our hands. It loosens something within me and I acknowledge the ludicrous nature of what we're doing – a pointless set of actions in this day and age: so pointless why wouldn't I go along with it? It's like Scottish people and Christmas; they all do Christmas but none of them believes in a baby Jesus being born.

'Will you kiss him today?' Laly whispers in my ear, and that starts us off again. I might actually be hysterical. It will be a long time, the wedding, until I kiss Ravi Tilak.

Downstairs, there is an ooh and an aah from the women – I don't know why; I look the same as before but with a fancier dress – as Laly pushes me into the lounge. Ravi has been moved to the sofa, and my dad is awkwardly offering him a long white and gold scarf to drape over his shoulders. Equally awkwardly, Ravi is trying to arrange it, and I have to resist a crazy urge to go over and do it for him. Dukkha, of course, is there to fuss expertly. He sits obediently still, lifting his chin towards her until I expect her to spit on a hanky and wipe a smudge off his face. As Dukkha turns away, I catch Ravi's eye and he gives me a teeny-tiny shame-faced smile, and I forgive him instantly. His mother is such a piece of work.

'Anoushka, sit here beside Ravi,' she orders. 'Put this on.' She has a matching scarf, which she hands to me nicely enough, but I'm left – thank the gods – to drape it becomingly over my own head. In the doorway, I see my mum itching to sort me out, but her hands are tightly gripping the prized silver tray, and she's just waiting for the nod. Mr Tilak snaps a couple of photos, and not to be outdone, my dad has set my brothers up to do the same. Ravi and I offer startled, rictus smiles as matching as our scarves, and then it's Mum's cue to present the tray.

As well as the sweets and the white envelope, there's a little pot of red vermillion powder mixed with rice and water to make a paste. Funnily enough, this – for the dot that will be placed on our foreheads – is actually called a tilak, and I only just bite my tongue to stop myself announcing that to the room and looking like a total idiot. Instead, I watch under my lashes as Dad smears the red dot above Ravi's nose – not without difficulty; I think Mum needed a bit more water to make the paste the right consistency, but I suppose better that than too runny - and pushes a too-big piece of Indian sweet into Ravi's mouth, and while his cheeks are bulging, drops the wad of cash onto his lap so that Ravi jerks his knees in defence. 'Here, you go, son,' Dad says. My youngest brother hands Dad a precarious pile of five boxes of the best quality Indian sweets, and he hesitates before placing them at Ravi's feet. It's all more Crackerjack, Cabbages and Kings, than Bollywood-polished… Stop it, Anoushka, I tell myself, a running commentary on the cack-handedness of my dad is not appropriate but – honestly? This would look so absurd to an outsider.

The thoughts are rushing me like a kaleidoscope, so that I barely notice my turn for the sticky itch of the vermillion paste, the cloying sugary cake passed from the edge of Dukkha's talons to my mouth. I'm still chewing as Mr Tilak and Dukkha loom over me to place a gold pendant and chain around my neck, while my mum and dad do the same to Ravi.

And–

That's it. More or less. As tradition dictates, Mum hands a beautiful and hideously expensive teal green embroidered silk sari to Dukkha, and if I'd still been chewing I'd have choked, because it's the one she's been saving for herself to wear at my wedding since I was eighteen. I hope Dukkha appreciates it; she just inclines her head regally and accepts the package. And Dad gives Mr Tilak £51 and another box of sweets. There's a little song and dance as Kabir Tilak refuses the cash, keeping only the one pound coin as a sign of goodwill.

Just like that, our families are bonded.

'Anoushka, beta. Welcome to our family,' Dukkha says, before turning to the rest of the room, smiling beatifically. 'Baadhiya, congratulations, everyone,' she trills.

'Baadhiya,' repeats Mum loudly, not to be outdone.

There's a sort of collective sigh, everyone loosens up – except me and Ravi – and some murmurs of more tea come from the aunties. Dukkha nips that in the bud. 'Thank you, ji, but we will be heading back home now. It will be late when we arrive.' She looks pointedly at her watch, as if everyone but her had delayed proceedings.

Dad looks at Mum and gets in first. 'Yes, we totally understand. Thank you for accepting our daughter into your family.'

Dukkha inclines her head graciously. 'Ravi, Kabir. Let us go,' she says.

'Have a safe journey back to Bradford,' Mum adds lamely.

There's a communal round of Namastes and they're gone. It's perfunctory to say the least and I'm left wondering, did that actually just happen?

* Rokka ceremony – engagement ceremony

Part 2
The Engagement

Chapter 9

A week after the match meeting, and the Rokka that still feels like an afterthought, life has changed in some ways but mostly it's the same. At least on a practical level: I'm spending the Easter holidays swotting for my Finals; the Tilaks are back in Bradford; Auntie Sonu has gone back to do some meddling in Mumbai for a few weeks; and my mum and dad are cautiously planning for an August wedding (eek, can't believe I'm saying that) while all the way consoling themselves that plans are plans and will be useful whatever date we actually go with (or maybe I'm projecting on to them, but I suppose it's reassuring that not everything is cut and dried). Laly is torn between thinking I'm mad to be considering a date so soon, and thrilled with the alleged spontaneity and therefore romance of it.

We haven't got round to making arrangements for mine and Ravi's 'date' to see a film together yet – we will, I hope, but logistics are against us; midway between Edinburgh and Bradford is still more than a hundred miles, and convention keeps us apart anyway – but we have started chatting on the phone. I'd like to write letters, too, but Ravi isn't keen, he says he dictates reports and would find composing a letter too like an exam. I can understand that – and at least there's no risk of Dukkha intercepting our sweet nothings (innocent as they are) and broadcasting them or sniggering. It's good to hear each other's voices, anyway. There's a dusty telephone extension point behind their wardrobe in Mum and Dad's bedroom that's never been used, so I talked them into letting me buy another phone handset. They're letting me go in there in the evenings, so at the grand age of twenty-two, I can have a private phone call. Yippee. Talking on the phone in our hall is a free for all, like one of the old-fashioned party lines we had when I was a kid; everyone's listening and thinks nothing of chipping in as they walk by. Ravi says he has a mobile phone and that he'll buy one for me so that we can talk any time we like – that's made Laly's eyes widen!

Well, mine, too, if I'm honest. I know that Auntie Sonu said the Tilaks were well-off but listening to Ravi, it's on a grander scale than I imagined. Or maybe it's that Ravi earns a lot of money and can help his parents out a lot. He talks about good investments he made at the American Bank, and this year he's going for partnership in the legal firm. When he gets it, he's buying himself a new car – an Audi 80 RS 2, which doesn't mean much to me but he clearly loves the idea. My little brothers are well-impressed and keep showing me pictures of them. I still think a car is a car, but the best thing is Ravi says when I pass my driving test, I can have his old one. Imagine me with a mobile phone and a car! I am clear, though, that these are perks of getting married (if we get married) not the reason to do it. Ravi is the reason, and the more I talk to him, the more I believe it's a good match. He seems to think so too. I've heard stories – mostly from Auntie Deepti and Sharmila – of girls who meet their prospective husband once or twice and that's it: they get engaged and then married without sharing more than a couple of conversations. Sometimes it's like a really strict protocol, others it's turned out to be indifference on the boy's part; he's been told it's time for a wife and expects she'll just fit in. I see how that was the case in the 1950s or even the seventies, but this is 1993! It happened to Sharmila's best friend, Mona, who got married last year, though. Sharmila says Mona knows the staff in the Co-op better than her husband because he hardly ever spends time with her, he's with his brothers and friends. But he's polite to Mona and she really likes her sisters-in-law so she's happy living with the family.

That sounds really sad to me now but Mum and Dad would say it's how marriage works: you trust the match, then you get to know each other after the wedding, and it takes time. It makes sense, but surely there should be a spark? My parents aren't the kind you can ask a question like that. I mean, my mum was literally imported to Scotland from India, to marry my dad, and she was only sixteen. Sixteen. She was a child. Ravi laughs, too, at the thought of asking Dukkha and Kabir Tilak. Already, he and I have established a rapport that I didn't expect. Nobody has ever paid me as much attention as Ravi does. He phones exactly when he says he will, talks for thirty minutes and tells me all about his life; I'm learning so much about him, and feeling better about Dukkha. She's still a bit of a spectre at the feast but day by day the idea of living with Ravi outweighs the fear of living with her. Fingers crossed.

'Anou? Anou – phone. It's Ravi.' That's my mum shouting. Even though I'm waiting for the call, she insists on answering it. She tries to draw Ravi in to some chitchat but so far he's managed to avoid everything beyond the how are you greeting.

'Hi, Ravi,' I say, snatching up the receiver in the bedroom. The phone stays live at my end until I call out, 'I've got it, Mum, you can hang up now.' I don't know how long she'd shamelessly listen in if I wasn't on to her. Maybe I should let her be; it would save the grilling I get every bloody night the second he's gone. 'Hi, Ravi,' I say again in a softer voice. 'How are you?'

'I'm tired,' he says. 'It's been a very busy day and my assistant is useless. I'm glad I have you waiting for my call, Anoushka.'

'Poor you.' I plonk down on the floor and wind the telephone cord around my fingers. 'He's the one you'll be able to get rid of when you're made a partner, yes?'

'Yes. I'll be able to interview for my own staff – an assistant and a secretary – who can really support me, and who want to learn.' He sighs. 'They don't listen at all. Everyone should take lessons from you, Anoushka. You're a great listener.'

'I hope so,' I say. 'I want to support you. I mean, when... if...'

He chuckles. 'Why can't you bring yourself to say it? And not if, but when... when we get married. Go on, say it.'

I'm not sure why it still feels so awkward. 'I don't want to take anything for granted,' I protest. 'Ravi, we didn't know each other a month ago. What if...' What if it all goes wrong?

'Say it, Anoushka,' he insists. 'Go on, "When we get married". Go on.'

'When we get married,' I agree, as quietly as I can. I wouldn't put it past my mother to be wiping down the doors or polishing the banister with her ears flapping like Dumbo's. The second I've settled down to study, she phones the aunties with a daily update, and what she doesn't know she makes up – I've heard her, but it's nothing new. I suppose when you're a housewife for thirty-odd years, you learn to make your own entertainment.

'That's better,' Ravi's saying and I smile at the approval in his voice.

'It's just such an alien thing – getting married. And so soon.' I explain. 'I didn't think it would be this easy.'

'What can I say? Our parents know how to make a good match. Unless–'

'Unless?' I quite like it when he falters, as

reassurance I can do, I've been brought up on that. And being able to placate. And console. Dutiful older daughter, remember? Supremely prepared for wife skills – well, some wife skills, anyway.

'Unless you aren't sure? Unless you might not want to.'

There's a touch of the lost little boy in him now and I wish he were here so I could give him a hug – I expect we might be on hugging terms now, in the real face-to-face, non-Indian-arranged marriage world. 'Of course I want to marry you, silly.' It's true. 'It's just overwhelming. You know, the most important day in a girl's life. Blah Blah.'

'I love you, Anou,' he blurts out so suddenly that I nearly drop the phone. He's not said that before, nor has he called me Anou, which is somehow more intimate than the declaration. 'I loved you the moment you handed me tea and I love you the more we talk. I need you to marry me, Anou. Please. Anou?'

'I...er, I love you, too,' I whisper, my mouth so close to the phone as I can taste the plastic. It feels so awkward, the words so contrived and I don't know why I'm blushing. I have to hold back a giggle – I've never told a boy I love him before. I don't think I've ever told anyone at all; we're not a terms of endearment type of family.

'Good. So it's good news my mother is finalising our formal engagement. Four weeks from today.'

He's bright as a button again, and I'm reminded of my dad when something doesn't go his way, or brothers when they were little and broke their LEGO: give them a snack or a sweet and there's smiles all round in a nano-second. Men are simple beasts – I don't know who said that, but it's clearly true (trust me, I'm a scientist talking). But wait – what? What did he say? I madly backtrack, not wanting to lose my

'Good Listener' badge so early in our relationship. Luckily, Ravi hasn't noticed that I'm having more of a conversation with myself than with him tonight; it's one of the things Mum complains about, me being 'in my head' too much. Well, durr, I used to think, where else? But as I've got older, I get it.

'Your mum is? Already? Do my parents know?' My confidence dips, just a little. When it's just me and Ravi talking, I'm fine, but mention the formalities and it all becomes a bit real again. In another life we could elope to Gretna Green or the Maldives or somewhere but there's no Indian or Hindu or culturally-respectable equivalent. We'd both be disowned.

'We have had the Rokka. We have a marriage date. Why wait?' It's a rhetorical question; I can hear the shrug in his voice, but I answer anyway.

'Four weeks. Is there really time?' I'm actually thinking of my revision and lab work; I've a wild image of telling Dr Moffat, my forthright Glaswegian tutor, I'm missing my mock practicals for a formal engagement ceremony that I've just been told is happening and I've no real say in. She only just held her tongue when Donald put his grandma's funeral above presenting a poster at RGU's international conference last year. She'd probably report me to Student Services who would home in on arranged versus forced marriages and hurriedly arrange a drop-in clinic at the Union.

'Anoushka? You seem distracted tonight.' Ravi, sounding disappointed, interrupts my over-active imagination.

'No. I mean, sorry. I'm just thinking of my exams and getting the family down to you. I–'

'Oh, we think it would be best if we do it in Scotland. All you need to do is dress up and look pretty.'

And cook, clean, arrange another party, put up half the family and – oh, my God, have Dukkha to stay again. None of which I say, obviously. 'That's kind,' is what comes out. 'I'd thought it would be at yours. You know, with you having a big house, and us having had the Rokka here...' Whoops – does that sound grudging? 'We're happy about all that, of course,' I hurry on. 'And it would save us time and travel.' I should be pleased that Ravi's family isn't a slave to tradition. Shame, though. I won't get to see the Tilak's lavish home so soon – and I bet that'll be Mum and Laly's first thought.

'That's settled then.' Ravi sounds supremely pleased. 'My mother will phone yours later. Now, I need to eat. Goodnight, Anoushka.'

'Goodnight,' I echo, head whirling. Have I just dreamed this? is a phrase that's constantly in my head just now. I wait for him to finish with 'I love you,' but he doesn't.

Chapter 10

There was a film out last year, Groundhog Day. Dad had been given a family ticket for the Cameo cinema – I've no idea why, he usually gets hampers from clients, full of whiskey or haggis, which none of us likes, and he gifts on, so we were all excited – and we all went. We even got popcorn, though Mum sniffed, and refused to share; she kept dipping into her bag for the proper food she'd brought from home. Anyway, that concept, where the same day happens over and over again, reminds me of the lead up to our engagement being exactly like the preparation for the first meeting – that turned into the Rokka – with the Tilaks. Thank God, they can't turn the engagement into the wedding… can they? Nothing more should surprise me with Dukkha being the one-woman committee and instigator of my future. If only I could do what Bill Murray did, and change the parts I don't like.

'Why here? Do they mean right here, or at a hall here? Or a hotel? Why not at their fancy mansion in Bradford?' This is my mum, three times a day to me and my Dad. 'Are we not good enough?' Then she gets on the phone to one or other of the aunties and changes her tune to, 'So kind of them to take the initiative and to heck with tradition, all to make life easier for us. Especially in our humble home. Of course, they have experience of our hospitality.' Honestly, the woman swithers from suspicion to pride like the weather – not to mention the ingratiating gratitude whenever she's on to Dukkha. I can't decide whether the two of them are going to end up best friends or arch rivals, and from her confusion, neither can Mum.

'I hope you know what you're doing,' she grumbles

at me, as I chop-chop-chop endless vegetables and she squints at yet another recipe for making them taste like meat for our side of the family, who will go home – shock, horror – 'hungry' because they've been denied their carnivore rights at the expense of the Hindu hippies from England and their vegan-y pretentions. 'If you get all anaemic and yellow, don't come crying to me.'

'I can get all the iron I need from beans and nuts…' It doesn't sound that appealing to me even as I say it, and I can see her lip curling, so I hurry on, 'And you're mixing anaemia and jaundice, you don't get jaundice from vegetables, Mum.'

'Huh. We'll see.' She shakes her head and glares at me. 'And how many more times, Anoushka! You don't use a bread knife to cut potatoes. You'll cut yourself to ribbons and bleed to death on my kitchen floor.'

'Well, if she's that weak and anaemic she won't spill much blood, will she?' Laly waltzes in and grins at me, giving Mum a two-finger salute behind her back. 'Can I have something to eat. Something proper to eat?'

'Of course you can, beta.' Mum wipes her hands on her apron and scurries around making my sister – who has two hands, two legs, a brain and could probably rule the country already – a plate of goodies, while she plonks herself down at the table and waits. She reaches over and grabs a couple of slices of carrot from my pile and starts rolling them in parallel lines. 'Whoops,' she says as one hits the floor, but she makes no attempt to pick it up.

'Oy.' I slap her hand. 'Why aren't you helping?'

'She has homework.' Mum speaks up. 'Not that you'd know it. And zero cooking skills. Whereas, you, Anoushka, need all the practice you can get if you insist on marrying vegans.'

'Yeah. And I'm a veggie-free zone. You better check

out the nearest Kentucky Fried Chicken to Maison Tilak for when I come to visit.' Laly grins at me. 'Make sure your love-nest bedroom has a decent drainpipe for you to shin down to the nearest kebab van when you go to bed starving.'

'Ha bloody ha.'

'Anoushka,' Mum shouts. 'Wash out your mouth – And will you be careful. What's got into you?'

That's in response to me chucking down the (wrong) knife, which bounces – miles away from Laly but she flinches and ducks extravagantly – and clatters off the edge of the table.

'Right. That's it,' I yell back. Well, it's a yell for me; dutiful little Anou never raises her voice in anger. 'If this marriage, the one that you all arranged for me, and told me not to mess up, is such a bad idea, then I give up. I'm not marrying Ravi Tilak. Alright? Is everyone happier now? Let's throw a steak on the pan and celebrate.' I lower myself onto the spare chair, breathing heavily. Laly and Mum are looking at me with their jaws hanging open. 'Sorry,' I mumble.

'Hey, hey. What is happening here?'

Shit. Even Dad's got up from watching the News. Why, now of all times, when freedom is months away, do I let them get to me? 'Nothing, Dad. Sorry,' I say but Mum's having none of it.

'She says she's not marrying him, Dev,' she tells him. 'Actually, she shouted at me that she's not marrying him. What are we going to do? What have I done to deserve daughters like these?'

'Excuse me? Leave me out of it.' Laly turns wide eyes on Mum. 'I'm just waiting for my dinner.'

'Tsk tsk.' Mum clucks, whirls around to ping the microwave, sticks a dish in front of Laly (who calmly starts eating) and continues her rant without a pause. 'The Tilaks – what do we tell them? The shame on our family.'

Dad looks bewildered. 'Madhu, calm yourself. Anou...Laly,' he looks between us, clearly torn, 'one of you, make your mama tea.'

'I don't need tea,' Mum says. 'I need an explanation. Is she marrying Ravi Tilak or not?' She won't look over at me.

Dad does though. 'Anou? Answer your mother, please. What is the problem–'

I can't speak, my mum is in full sway.

'One minute, it's all "I love you"– I knew she was listening in. Typical ' –the next, the match is off. My nerves won't stand this.'

Laly is smirking beneath her roti and I deflate. I can't win. 'Of course I'm getting married,' I say. 'I was just cross with all the teasing. I shouldn't have shouted. Sorry, Mum, Dad.'

Dad frowns but nods. 'Madhu?' he says.

Mum lets us hang for a minute, then shrugs. 'Jitters,' she announces. 'Wedding jitters. Though why, I don't know. Do you not trust your parents to make a good match, Anoushka?'

For fuck's fucking sake! It takes me everything I have not to speak out of turn – whatever Dukkha throws at me it won't be this bad, it won't. There's no pleasing either of them, but Dukkha can't even hang on the coat-tails of my mother's passive-aggression. 'Of course I trust you, mummy ji,' I say and you can't tell it's through gritted teeth. I incline my head to the mound of potatoes. 'What's next? Okra or aubergine?'

'Courgette,' she says. 'And use the paring knife this time. I need to phone Dukkha Tilak.' She's still muttering away as she wipes her hands on her apron, I close my ears but not before I catch the, 'Four weeks. Four! I don't know what she's supposed to wear. What was she thinking, to take the engagement salwar already…'

Laly and I grin at each other and do a quick High Five when Dad's wandering back to the telly, then she frowns. 'Anou? If Mum and Dad don't know where the engagement is going to be, why are you murdering all these vegetables? We're never going to eat them all.'

I pause, with my knife – the paring knife – ready to decapitate half a dozen slightly-shrivelled courgettes. 'One-up-man-ship.' I spell the syllables out as I slice. 'Mum doesn't want to be caught out. She's convinced Dukkha will arrive unannounced or send round all her extended family, and there'll be nothing to eat except roast animal.'

'Oh. Well, if they don't, you can take them as dowry, right?'

'You're soooo funny.'

'Amongst other talents.'

I'll miss having my little sister around, I think, as she wanders off to convince Dad to drive her over to Auntie Deepti's so that Sharmila can shape her eyebrows – Laly is self-conscious of her heavy beetling brows that aren't heavy or beetling to anyone but her – though she tells Dad it's for help with some graphic design homework. I was right about Ravi; he's the youngest child and all his brothers and sisters have left home. His sister, Heera, is a business woman in Mumbai, his brother Galu and family live somewhere in Yorkshire, and he's another brother, Rohit, they don't really talk about. 'His wife died in childbirth and he's never been the same man since,' is all that Ravi has said. It's less a secret than a tragedy; there's no mention of a baby, so I'm guessing he or she was lost too. 'You can see why my mother wants only the best for me,' Ravi also said. I think that's a compliment. Anyway, it means that I'm not going to a home filled with sisters-in-law and toddlers and a pecking order –

that could be the best of sorority houses or a nest of
vipers – just one filled with Dukkha. There are girl
cousins, though, Ravi says, and cousin's wives. I won't
be entirely alone. I don't like to tell him I'm quite
looking forward to being alone, just for a bit. That said,
though, I'll miss Laly.

By the time Mum comes back, I've chopped and
bagged and labelled a greengrocers' haul, and all she
has to do is run a beady eye over the piles before we
hurl them into the freezer. Her heart's not in it, though,
she doesn't seem to notice we're not filling the freezer
with due care and attention. The feistiness of earlier
has, worryingly, gone but I know better than to
confront her.

'Good girl, Anoushka,' she says absently and pats
me on the arm. 'When you've tidied away, bring some
tea through, yes?'

I take my time. Dad's not back yet, and I hear the
theme tune to Coronation Street start up, and then be
hurriedly silenced. Mum pretends she doesn't watch it
but there's nothing that puts her in a good mood like
muttering away at the likes of Reg Houldsworth and
Curly Watts.

'Nonsense,' she snorts, jerking her head at the TV
screen, when I go in and place a mug beside her. I curl
up at her feet, on the floor, and she strokes my head for
a second or two. The adverts play on in the
background and it's curiously peaceful. My mum and I
have these moments. Occasionally. It lasts till Dad
returns, and looks for his tea. It's all ready and waiting
in the pan, I just need to heat it, and add a bit more
sugar – Dad has a very sweet tooth – but again, I delay,
giving them time to have the hurried and muted
conversation they're going to have after Mum spoke to
Dukkha.

They both look up at me and smile as I hand Dad

his tea.

'I think I might go up and do an hour or two's study. Unless you want me?' The question is right there, screaming to be answered, but needless to say, it's ignored.

'Goodnight, beta,' Dad says.

'Goodnight,' mum echoes.

I spend the rest of the night wondering whether I'll be getting engaged here in the house (surely not?) or at Granton Village Hall (not posh enough for the Tilak clan?) or the Caledonian (far too posh for the Malhotras). It's all in Dukkha's hands, and my parents are downstairs coming to terms with her decision.

Chapter 11

'How does The Bonnington sound?' Mum asks brightly, as I drag my weary, jammied, body to breakfast. I did not sleep well.

'Huh?'

'Anouskha, keep up,' she scolds, setting a plate of kitchari down in front of me. 'Eat. We have much planning to do.'

I put my head down and eat, even though I'm not that hungry. That way Mum will talk and I won't ask the wrong questions.

'It's a nice hotel – not too fancy but with class, and very convenient, really. A good choice.' She chatters away, telling me everything I need to know about my engagement arrangements. I have no say; do I want any say? My mum and dad have always made all the decisions about my life so I wouldn't know where to start. 'A lovely big function room leading to the garden, Dukkha says. We'll get caterers, of course.' She sniffs. 'We can't trust a Scottish hotel to prepare proper food. Deepti-ji will know the best...'

When her monologue is drowned out by the kitchen taps on full blast, I put down my fork. 'So everything is good with the engagement? You made the arrangements with Dukkha?' Treading carefully here. 'In four weeks' time?'

'Yes. Yes. It will be a beautiful day. One to be proud of.' Mum turns from the sink. 'On Saturday we'll shop for a new dress for you.' Her face twitches and she tut-tuts at me. 'You can't wear the same one twice, but Anou – twenty minutes for the Rokka, the salwar suit you were saving? I suppose I understand your enthusiasm.'

Enthusiasm? It was an ultimatum, I think – being tired puts me in a bad temper – but this is a truce: the nearest Mum will get to forgiving me for wearing my engagement dress prematurely.

'I've got to get ready.' I get up, rinse my bowl out, and push in my chair as I pass it again. 'Tell Dad to wait for me, okay?'

'You could take a day off to help me with the arrangements?'

'Can't, Mum, sorry. Finals in a few weeks, remember? I don't want to fail now.'

'Hmm. Shame.'

She doesn't mean it and I'm not sorry but it's a dance we do. I could miss the day at college because it's still technically the holidays. This week's labs are voluntary, catch-up-and-revise sessions for those who are behind. Me, I'm way ahead, as always, but I'm still first with my lab coat on or seated at all the extra lectures. Partly it's that I've nothing else to do, but over the last year Dr Moffat's been using me more and more as a graduate teaching assistant. 'It will be all to the good if you apply to do your PhD here, Anoushka,' she tells me. 'You are going to apply?' It's taken for granted in the department, by me, too, because what else would I do? Teach? Even though I'm good at the GTA stuff, I'm not sure if I want to spend my life shepherding primary school kids around or coping with bored-to-sniggering teenagers learning about the reproductive system. Mata Rani, no. Donald is the only one who demurs. 'I'd tell you to get a life, Anoushka,' he says, 'if that wasn't the pot calling the kettle black.' Well, that's what I'm doing now, isn't it, getting a life. Except, I think, as I pull on my jacket and check I have my purse and keys, I'm not sure it's the life either Dr Moffat or Donald will be expecting.

There's no time like the present.

I stow my belongings in the locker room and go to tap on the frosted glass door that doubles as the staff office and general storeroom. It's far too small, but immaculately organised, courtesy of Dr Moffat and Donald – the official GTA. I'm not a naturally tidy person, but I've learned from them, and we all know exactly where everything is. It's soothing. You know precisely where you are with Bunsen Burners and petri dishes.

I poke my head round the door, and see the two of them, either side of her desk; it looks like a supervision session. 'Oh, sorry. I'll come back–'

'Anoushka, come in.' Dr Moffat beckons. 'We're just about finished here.'

'Talking PhDs,' Donald adds. 'Wondering if we, you and me, I mean, are in competition.' He stretches out a foot to push the third stool towards me – and to show he's just joking. He's into bio-technology and botany, which a lot of the field would still find incompatible and too out-there but not Dr M, so his PhD is all wrapped up as far as I can see. I've no idea, really, what I'd research. There are always lists of topics and supervisors advertised and I was expecting to pick one of those, for convenience more than interest. A bit like an arranged marriage – I'd fall in love after the event.

'About that… As you're both here…' They are both looking at me with interest as I hoist myself up onto the stool, and I can feel a flush creeping across my face and neck. I know they're expecting to hear I've decided on a subject, which makes me think I'm letting them down. 'It's my PhD,' I say in a rush. 'The thing is, well, I'm getting married.'

The words fall into a crushing silence.

'In August,' I hurry on, to fill it – I might as well get it all out there at once, anyway. 'I'll be moving to

Bradford, to live with my…my…' (brown-skinned or not, there is a full-on blush now flooding my cheeks) '…my husband's family. Our engagement is in four weeks. I hope you'll both come.' Really, Anoushka? As if. But I have to say something and it's enough for them both to recover.

'Well, congratulations. Congratulations.' Donald leans over and takes my hand, shaking it in a grand gesture, which makes us both laugh. 'I didn't know…'

Me neither, I think, as he peters out and Dr Moffat jumps in. 'Not what I was expecting to hear,' she says briskly. 'I thought you were going to tell me that you'd sold out to Glasgow Caledonian or were defecting to RGU.'

We all laugh again; an inside joke about the rivalry in the Scottish Uni system.

'No, never.' I hesitate again. 'Look, it is arranged and it is quick, but that's how it works in our culture. And it wouldn't be going ahead if I hadn't agreed, and weren't happy about it. My fiancé is a lovely man and his family seem… generous. There's a surprisingly good success rate for arranged marriages. Forced marriage is different, of course, and nobody is forcing me into anything…' Shut up, Anou. I can hear Laly's voice saying something along the lines of she protesteth too much, which is the extent of her knowledge of Shakespeare (do I mean Shakespeare?)

'God forbid,' Donald says lightly. 'There's a stubborn streak in you that gets results. I trust your judgement every time.'

'Thank you.'

'Seconded,' Dr Moffat adds briskly. 'It's a shame about the PhD though.'

'Oh, sorry, it's not that I can't do one. In fact, it's more likely I will…My parents didn't…I mean, Ravi does…' I stop, breathe and say, 'I hope I can do it in

Yorkshire. That's all,'

'Right-oh. Good. Great news. But that's me off.' Donald gets up. 'See you this afternoon, if you're around.'

I watch him leave the room, taking the seconds to let out a deep breath of air; this has all gone better than I expected. I mean, I didn't expect either of them to tell me I'm an idiot to my face but part of me expected to see it in their eyes. When I look back at Dr Moffat, she's looking me, speculatively.

'I did wonder, you know, about you and him.' She indicates Donald's retreating presence.

'He's my best friend.' As I say it I realise I mean it, even if he is also my only one.

'Good. I've enough corrosive liquids in my lab, without unrequited tears. And – forgive me – but you really are happy about your marriage?' Her eyes are searching but I can honestly meet the glance.

'Yes. Yes, I am,' I tell her.

'Then my sincere congratulations. I hope you'll be very happy. And I'm sure a Yorkshire University PhD is passable.' She smiles, before nodding across at the schedule taped to the wall. 'Better get going just in case anyone else actually turns up today. Set them up for molecular colonisation.' She shakes her head. 'First year stuff, but I despair...' Then as I open the door and exit,

'Oh, and Anoushka?' she calls after me.

'Yes?'

'Seriously, there are a lot of decent science departments in that area: Leeds, Bradford itself, Sheffield Hallam. Any one of them would be pleased to have a PhD student like yourself.' She's busy checking something on her desk and doesn't look up. 'Have a think about it carefully, that's all.'

'I will,' I say. 'Thanks, Dr Moffat.'

'Och. Call me Gillian, will you? Or I'll have to call you Mrs…at least until you get that doctorate.'

'Mrs What?' Donald says a few hours later, when we meet in the corridor outside the vending machine.

'Sorry?'

'Thy mysterious boyfriend's name? You'll be Mrs What?'

'Oh. Tilak. He's called Ravi Tilak.'

'Great. Well, Mrs Tilak-to-be, let me buy you a drink today in lieu of an engagement present.' He raises his palms to the machine. 'It's a special occasion so we could go to the canteen or the Union but the lines will be longer.'

'Hot chocolate from here is fine,' I say. 'Thank you – oh.' My lethargic departure from the house reminds me what didn't I do. 'I haven't brought any food today. My mum distracted me.'

'Mums and wedding talk.' Donald nods. 'Then, let me get you a sandwich too – cheese savoury? Ham salad?'

There's an alleged common room at the end of the corridor, really just half a dozen seats, a coffee table and a noticeboard. It's too much of a thoroughfare for anyone to pause at longer than rearranging their vending machine goodies into the right hands, so we always get a seat.

As we open our simple sandwiches and sip at the lukewarm sludge I secretly really like, I'm conscious that there's a slight awkwardness between us. Or maybe it's just me. Donald's chomping away stolidly, if not with the gusto he demonstrates when I've given him a Tupperware box or Thermos of something homemade. In three years – two and a half of being lab partners – we've not shared as much personal stuff as I have this morning. It's left us on an equal footing that for me has somehow slipped, just a little. I wonder if our friendship will survive past Finals? Unlikely. And that just adds to all the things that put me at sea; I've no idea any more what life will look like beyond August.

'Two older sisters, one divorced, one a single parent,' Donald says suddenly, so in tune with my thoughts I wonder if I have blurted something out loud. 'My parents never mention girlfriends to me because they secretly worry – wrongly – that I'm gay, but men don't have boyfriends in the Highlands and Islands and calling me a bachelor has connotations. So I'm a Scientist to the neighbours, Down There In Edinburgh and that about covers it.' He takes another big bite, and I wait to see if there's more. 'Relationships are weird. Now, how about we get back to what we know and talk about cell theory and homeostasis?'

'Sounds good to me.'

We even get seconds of hot chocolate to celebrate – and I've a distinct feeling that might be the most unconventional thing either of us has ever done. Still, what's weird behaviour when there's one of you, makes you a club if there's two.

Chapter 12

It does put the whole PhD up there as A Thing though, alongside the engagement, And wedding. I sit and stare out of the car window, mulling over it, as Dad negotiates the end of day traffic on the bypass. Getting married is, like, a day in my life, it's not a career choice. Or is it? I don't know what way to look at it. If I move to Bradford – I'm not sure when that thought will seem real, I might as well be thinking, 'If I go into Orbit' – then how much time will being married take up? Ravi is at work all day, the senior Tilaks have their mega-businesses to run, so they'll presumably be out too. Even if I am doing all the cooking and household chores, they won't fill all the days. Here, there are six of us, and I do more than my fair share and study full time – and that's only enough because I stretch the studying to the nth degree, even if I want to do it here and commute a bit–

But no. If I do that I'll be expected to come home all the time. Mum would never countenance me being in Edinburgh and not visiting for dinner, overnight, a weekend. I'll have a foot in both camps for the next three years, and I'll never escape.

'Are you alright, beta?' Dad's voice makes me jump. 'You're very quiet today.'

'What? Oh, yeah. I'm fine.' I pull at the seatbelt that's grazing my neck and shuffle in my seat. 'The traffic is awful and it's not even five o'clock.'

'Closures. Diversions. Always building works,' he complains. 'When I was a young man I enjoyed driving. Not now.'

'If I learned to drive I could be your chauffeur. Come and collect you from work and drive you home.'

Dad roars with laughter. 'Beta, in a few short months you will be a married lady. That's a suggestion for your husband. Ask him to teach you to drive.' He keeps chuckling as if it's the funniest thing he's ever heard.

'I have asked him and he said he'll buy me a car.' But the words aren't loud enough for him to hear. I'll just get a patronising, 'Yes, beta, of course he will.' And stop calling me child and married lady in the same breath, I think disagreeably, I can't be both. 'Can I put the radio on?' I ask instead. 'It's almost time for the News.' And I can listen to Ed Stewart in the meantime.

We're pulling onto the driveway and I'm saying my usual, 'Thanks, Dad,' when he interrupts.

'What is your mother doing on the doorstep? Why the welcome committee?' which actually translates as, 'Who is dead?' because Mum, sure enough, is never waiting for us, in her slippers and looking agitated, unless there's a crisis.

'What's wrong, Mum?' I call, hoping neither Laly nor the boys have done something stupid. Or that anyone has died.

'Why are you so late?' she scolds. 'Why should anything be wrong? Everything is right – look!'

As I step back to let Dad cross the threshold first, Mum comes at us both with what appears to be an offensive weapon.

'Madhu, what is this–'

'Mum!'

'Special delivery,' she announces. 'For you, Anoushka. So beautiful.'

So big. I take in the enormous bouquet of flowers that are shrouded in a whole forest of greenery and being thrust into my face. The cellophane wrapping crinkles in my tentative grasp and the thought, how tacky, steals across my brain before I can unthink it.

'Read the card. Read the card.' Mum plucks it from the arrangement in such a way that I know she's already read the card, and I'm burning with embarrassment.

'Let us in the door, Madhu first, It's raining out here,' Dad says mildly, but it's enough for my mum to regain her wits.

She stands there caressing – yes, really – the flowers while I shrug off my coat and hang it, and my bag, over the banister; she's so entranced she doesn't even tut at me to put them in the proper place.

'Welcome to our family, Anoushka Malhotra, from the Tilaks,' I read out loud. Oh, thank all the gods. Thank you Mata Rani. I smile broadly enough to please my mother, but it's in relief. This monstrosity has Dukkha (aka birds-nest perm) written all over it – Ravi doesn't have truly terrible taste after all.

'Such an honour! Flowers from the family,' Mum trills, as if she means the Royal Family itself. Then, 'Laly? Lalita? Come, bring that vase for your sister. Her hands are full.'

That's a turn up. As is Laly appearing at the kitchen door with a giant crystal thing. She holds it up like a trophy, her smirk distorted by the glass. 'D'you think this is big enough for the Triffid or shall we just plant it straight into the garden? Does Ravi have ancestors in the Amazon Jungle?'

The reference goes over Mum's head or she plain doesn't hear Laly. Happily, she can't wait to arrange the bouquet; all I have to do is admire it from time to time. When Ravi phones, she lavishes praise on him, so there's little I can – politely – add.

'It was very kind of you...of you all.' I cross my fingers and Ravi doesn't disappoint.

'It was my idea,' he admits. 'You deserve a bouquet,

Anou. But my mother chose it especially. Is it very beautiful?'

'Unique. I've never received anything like it. Please tell your mum.'

When we've talked about his day, I broach the subject of the PhD, paraphrasing my thoughts from the car. 'I could ask about opportunities in Bradford,' I suggest. 'There's no obligation–'

'Of course you should.' He responds so immediately that I can't understand why I'm being so diffident. 'In fact, I insist. My wife, the scientist: Dr Tilak. Sounds good, huh? Maybe I should study my doctorate too.' I can hear the pride in his voice, which he lowers slightly to say, 'It will give you a status until...'

'Until?' Surprised by his enthusiasm, I'm slow on the uptake. 'Until what?'

'Babies, Anou. The children we will have.' He laughs. 'You must have thought of this? All women want babies, right?'

I laugh too. 'Of course. Of course I do.' And I do, in theory, I think, as I put down the phone. I've always known I'll have children, a big family, but not right away. First a wife, then a PhD, then a mother, I decide. It's a plan that doesn't lose sight of the real Anoushka, and it's supported by my husband. What more can I ask? That his mother never, ever be let loose in a florist's again, I think, as I run lightly down the stairs to start on the ironing.

I soon realise this – the flower delivery – is just the start of a gift-giving extravaganza. Some are cute and thoughtful, like the Thorntons boxed chocolate heart ('There's the 'h' missing in Anoushka,' Laly points out, but that's a quibble; people often get the spelling wrong) and the Minnie Mouse keyring wearing a coy bridal veil. Others are funny – at least I hope Ravi means them to be funny, rather than it being Dukkha's hand – such as The Dummies Guide to Getting a Degree and one of those grot-shop Tam o Shanters, with red hair hanging down and a mortar board stitched on top. ('That's downright double racist.' Laly again. 'And where the fuck did they get it in Yorkshire?') The pièce de résistance is a gold pen, which I query, not because it's expensive for a pre-engagement present, but that it's engraved with his name rather than mine. I wonder if he got a matching pair and sent me the wrong one. But no. 'I thought you'd like it,' he says earnestly. 'My name next to your heart. A token of my love.' Kind of makes sense, I suppose – sometimes I'm too logical to be romantic. Since I've been brought up on It's the thought that counts, I save everything carefully into a shoebox and look forward to a safe and secure future when we can look back and smile over such keepsakes.

Meanwhile, in a folder I'm collecting PhD information and prospectuses from unis in England. Dr Moffat – Gillian(!) – has already sorted out Donald and he's guaranteed a placement right there with her, as long as he gets a 2:1, which he'll do even if he turns up late and works with his eyes shut. Now, she's pulling out all the stops to see what's available for me in the North of England. She's really hopeful about an autumn start, which gives me time to do my Finals (help, gulp, please Mata Rani, I'll need a First if I want funding; I don't want to assume Ravi will pay), get married, move to Bradford, be a successful newly-wed, and then re-start studying, which I'll do full time for three years, then start a family.

I look at the notes in my diary and go over the timeline again. It's all coming together – and see. There is such a thing as a romantic scientist. Mum, in the meantime, is planning equally hard for the engagement. She's rallied the Auntie troops and is constantly on to Auntie Sonu, who's now on a beach holiday in Kerala, apparently – something it's very hard to imagine. Dad is making daily mutterings about our phone bill, but Mum's answer is that she's never arranged a marriage before and needs to take advice. 'A mother's shoulders are broad, but she knows when not to carry the stress alone,' I've heard her saying to all and sundry. Laly says she got it off a fridge magnet, and every time she hears it, she replies, 'It's okay, Mum, this is the dress rehearsal, remember? So you get it right for my wedding.' I don't think she's joking, and Mum doesn't bother contradicting her. Whatever, she doesn't seem to need my help with the many fiddly ceremonies and traditions that I get my head down and keep studying; I speak when spoken to, offer the opinion she wants when told. Once the exams are out of the way, I vow that I'll throw myself into the wedding proper.

And then, the shit hits the fan. Big time.

If a Scottish person described there being weeping and wailing and gnashing of teeth, they would be exaggerating for effect, but we're Indian and that's what actually happens. I come home to a Council of War, the magnitude of which should only mean that Ravi has run off with Laly, Dukkha has dropped dead, and the wedding has been inexplicably mis-booked for the day of my graduation. Dad looks as mystified as I am (so I figure it's none of the above, or surely he'd have been phoned at work) but is clearly dubious about entering the all-female fray in the lounge.

'Bring me some tea, beta,' he whispers, then vanishes upstairs to change out of his work suit – which he never usually bothers to do – and I sigh, take my hand off the door knob and go into the kitchen; I'm sure I'll be summonsed when the coven sees fit. There,

I find my brothers sitting at the kitchen table, calmly doing their homework.

'What's happening?' I ask them. 'Aditya?'

Aditya shrugs, his tongue poking out as he concentrates on the maths questions in front of him. I know he's got a forbidden calculator on his lap but I'm not about to stop him. 'Dunno,' he says.

'Akash, then?' When I glare at him, Akash is slightly more forthcoming.

'Something about a hotel that has cancelled something,' he says.

'Oh, yeah, that. Your engagement one,' Aditya pipes up. 'It must be burned to the ground or got bombed, I think.' Mum cried.

Is that all, I think, but I bite it back; I should care more, I know. 'Oh, dear,' I manage, – in case the boys report back – 'but I expect we can book another one.'

'You can't.' Akash shakes his head. 'Every single hotel in the whole of Edinburgh that isn't a disgrace is full. Mum said so. She's going mental.'

'More mental than usual,' Aditya agrees. 'But not at me.' He looks supremely pleased about that. 'Anou? Will you get us some food? We're hungry.'

I set about doing that, bribing Akash upstairs with Dad's tea. 'You'll take it up if you want anything to eat,' I argue with him, pleased with my firm and fair hand. Akash just looks mutinous and probably sloshes it everywhere en route. And both boys have packed away their books and disappeared outside to play, ('Put your coats on,' I call to deaf ears) by the time the lounge door opens.

'Auntie Sonu!' I'm surprised to see her. 'Welcome home. When did you arrive?'

'In the nick of time,' she says grimly, but seems to think better of it, and pats my shoulder. 'But do not worry, beta, a little snafu, already resolved.'

All, it transpires, being far less dramatic than my brothers would have it: a double-booking (my mother's and Dukkha's insistence) or an unconfirmed, deposit-less booking (the hotel's) at the Bonnington. 'So, we're going to Bradford, after all,' Auntie Sonu finishes up. 'You need not worry, Anou. I, personally, will be confirming with the wedding hotel. Lucky it is not the same place, huh?'

'Um.' I'm looking at her blankly, because how are we all suddenly supposed to get to Bradford in a couple of weeks? I mentally scan my lab timetable, my revision classes, my mock papers...

'Take the frown from that face, Anoushka.' Auntie Sonu reaches over and tweaks my cheek. 'If your favourite Auntie-ji says all will be well, all will be well. Come, make tea and reassure your poor agonised mother.'

Chapter 13

And suddenly the 24th April, formal engagement day, in bloody Bradford, is here. I feel sick with nerves and just wish it were over, partly because this last minute change has buggered up my Finals plan, but mostly because I hate the thought of being the centre of attention and everyone cooing over me – or cooing over me to my face, that is. Behind my back I'll be compared to every other daughter who's been married off in the last five, if not ten, years. It's how it works. It's what I've done, and now, rigid in bed with the Travel Lodge pillow over my face, I mentally apologise to every girl I've ever judged for her dress, jewellery, venue, guests or choice of groom. I understand, this morning, that she probably had little say in any of it.

It was a nice trip down yesterday. Five car loads of Malhotras, extended family and various hangers on travelling in convoy reminded me of going on days-out when we were little: to the beach at Elie or North Berwick. This time instead of a roof-rack groaning with picnic provisions, Dad had the boys fill the car boot with twenty-one boxes of (even more) Indian sweets and four baskets of dried fruits. In the passenger seat, Mum kept fussing with her handbag containing a bracelet for Ravi – a price tag of £400 made me stop and stare – and a pretty engagement ring. It won't surprise me to hear she slept with the bag under her pillow, because she's also in charge of all the cash gifts for the Tilaks. It strikes me again how one-sided tradition is, that the girl's family has to add such sweeteners to seal the deal! All this, and potentially so much more if Mr Tilak hadn't stuck to his guns about not wanting a dowry. Mata Rani, is not it enough that the girl's family is giving their most precious possession, their daughter, away to virtual strangers?

'What–' I'm being poked.

'You can't suffocate yourself, Anou, it's impossible. You should know that, so get up–' The doughy white pillow is snatched from me by a grinning Laly, who's wide awake and perky in the double bed beside me, and thrown across the room at the hump in the small single bed tucked under the window '–and face the day. Shouldn't she, Sharmila? Hey, Sharmila, wake up. You're the one who's got to put my sister's engagement face on!'

'Ugh?' Our cousin Sharmila's bleary-eyes emerge from the duvet. 'Take a shower, Anou, then we'll start. What time is it?'

'Nearly nine.'

'We've got ages,' she mumbles and burrows down again.

By noon, though, we're all firing on all cylinders: ready and waiting to drive to the hotel to meet the Tilaks. Sharmila has pulled out all the stops; I never before realised how talented she is. I turn this way and that in the mirror, and while it's still clearly me, it's the Bollywood-Hollywood polished and painted version of me. Even Laly's impressed. 'You should do this every day, Anou,' she says as she tweaks the material of my new duskier pink salwar suit.

'What – get up at 5am, spend three hours making up, and then tie my hair back and put on a lab coat?'

'Well, you won't need to do that when you marry the Money-Bagses out there, will you? You can lounge till lunch.'

Needless to say, she thinks me pursing a PhD is nuts.

Sharmila has given my mum and the aunties and cousins a (quicker) makeover, too, and I can't help but wonder if Ravi's family are doing the same thing. The best beautician will have her work cut out with Dukkha, but maybe her own sisters are luckier...I curtail the thought in case being mean on my engagement day is an omen of bad luck, but not before thanking the stars that Ravi himself got the handsome gene from somewhere.

'Are you happy, Anoushka?' Mum asks, as she eyes me up and down – also tweaking my outfit. I twitch out of the way.

'Yes, I am.' For once I don't have to think about it, because I am. The fizzing uncertainty of the last few weeks has settled to not unpleasant butterflies, and while I'm aware it's transitory, the effect of homely lab-coated Anou replaced with her glamorous best-dressed self, I might as well run with it and enjoy the day.

And with that, we're off in a loud and proud crowd, everyone in Reception and the car park pausing to have a look at what's going on. Once in the car, Dad's leading the parade, with Mum clutching the written directions and muttering ominously about how we really should have had a trial run last night. But after a quarter of an hour of us driving the unfamiliar streets (me trying to imagine living here), Mum gives a little squeal.

'There, Dev, on the right. Look, the sign says, Manningham Hall. Look, girls.' Ever since the Bonnington catastrophe, poor Mum has remained suspicious of any venue that has availability, but somewhere with its own brown signpost makes her day. We're on the outskirts of the city, dotted between smaller villages, and the lane to the hotel is flanked by green fields where a couple of old-looking horses are grazing. Close up, the building is a detached stone house with mini-turrets; pleasant but not grand; with character, designers would call it.

'Where are all the others? Where are the cars parked?' Mum frets, fanning herself with her handmade map. 'We're to look for The Ballroom. Where is The Ballroom? Dev, where are you going?'

Ignoring her, Dad follows the driveway round to the back of the building – and Laly and I take one look, glance at each other, and will Mum not to point out how the rear of the hotel is a mish-mash of messy bins and steel fire-escapes, and it looks like a dodgy Children's Home.

'Fur coat and no knickers,' Laly mouths to me, which is so the thought I first had about Dukkha that I have to stifle a giggle.

There's a boy about Laly's age, in dirty chef whites, sitting on a step and smoking and without any prompting, he does a vague sort of pointing and flaps his hands. Dad gives him a half-salute and in lieu of any other option, carries on following the road round. Behind us – I look over my shoulder – the convoy follows. I hope we don't have to do a U-turn.

'Dev, why are we going this way? The Ballroom–'

'Madhu.' Dad lifts his finger from the steering wheel and points. 'Read.'

Ballroom Car Park, the notice says, and right beside it is a barn, that looks as if it's being converted into something, and at a guess, I'd say it's The Ballroom. In fact, I know it is, because I can see Dukkha and Kabir Tilak amidst the throng of brightly-dressed people, all clustered around the main entrance. When the penny drops, my poor mum looks cheated; I can see her mouth working, but she rallies well.

'A purpose-built hall,' she says, 'within the grounds of a…a traditional hotel. Hmm.' Already I can see her re-framing it for the distant relatives who aren't here. Laly reads my mind and nudges me. 'A magnificent barn conversion on the estate of a stately home,' she murmurs.

It looks fine to me, better than our house or Granton Village Hall would be for all these people I don't know. I can't see Ravi anywhere. Everyone looks our parents' ages. I don't have time to dwell on it though because Mum, encouraged by Dukkha pointing to our car, and hustling her friends inside, starts waving regally to the stragglers, and in a flash, Dad has parked and I'm going to have to get out and perform. In fact, the next few minutes are a blur. Dukkha, resplendent in a garish yellow and murky green sari, rushes over and pounces on me, dragging me away from Mum and Dad and Laly, as if I really am the daughter-in-law of her dreams.

'Anoushka, beta,' she croons.

'Hello, auntie-ji,' I reply nervously.

'No, no, beta.' Her talon-like fingers grip my wrist harder. 'Mummy-ji, now. Call me mummy-ji.' Luckily, it's rhetorical, as she goes on, 'How was your journey? Did you sleep well? You look so different, so beautiful. A good start. A credit to my Ravi.'

Er, thanks, I think. I don't say anything, though. I try to twist round to see if mum and dad are following us. I catch sight of them, still at the car, but Kabir is there, too, the car boot open, so I relax slightly. I mean, the Tilaks have done this before so they know the drill.

'Where's Ravi?' I venture to ask Dukkha. I glance round but I can't see him. The barn is one big space inside and it's gloomy. And chilly. There's been an attempt to keep some of the original timber, with rafters and beams across the ceiling but the floor is bog-standard grey concrete, cold and uneven. It's covered in places by strips of red carpet but not enough to add warmth or colour.

'Ravi?' Dukkha doesn't break her stride. 'All in good time. He's with his cousin, Anoop – like a third brother he is. Fortifying themselves against the day.' She giggles. 'You can't see him before the ceremony, silly girl. Now, Anou, I am going to introduce you to our most important guests – my family. You will remember to kneel and touch their feet, yes?' Her beady eyes slide towards mine and goes on, 'The charan sparsh, beta. A sign of respect to your elders.'

'I know what it means.' If I sound slightly nettled, I am.

'Oh. We wondered, that's all.'

What she means is, I didn't fall at her feet and kiss them when we first met. Should I have? Maybe, but it's not something we, as a family, go in for on a regular basis, and it was so informal at home, I honestly overlooked the greeting. Shite. I'm tempted to say something trite like, I can't think of you as my elder, Auntie-ji, you look so young, but that would need the guile of Laly to carry it off. I say nothing; Dukkha's smile widens.

'Nobody wants to be embarrassed on their engagement day, do they? Now, dear.'

There's a dais, a sort of narrow stage at one end of the barn, and just in front of it, a row of folding chairs, each one of them filled with a stout person of varying decrepitude: Dukkha's relatives, I guess from the raised eyebrows and sour expressions – except for the bearded old man on the end who gives me a wink. On balance, I'd rather concentrate on their feet. Dukkha doesn't introduce me, just lets the old folk continue whispering amongst themselves – in Hindi, sure, but do they think I can't understand? Like as if the language is different in Scotland – about my name, dress, height, skin colour. Oh, it's not about me, per se. Just another example of the gossipy bitching that goes on at these occasions; some of it's even kind: my salwar suit passes muster, as does my hair-do. They'd like a bit more height and lighter skin – that is, Laly – but that always happens.

Dutifully, and hoping Mum and Dad can see me, I bow down and shuffle along the line. Touching an elder's feet is a mark of respect, which in turn will bless me with everything from intellect and knowledge to strength and fame. I don't disagree with the respect thing at all, but I can't say I feel endowed with anything. One or two address a remark to me or pat me on the head, but mostly I feel like a family pet snuffling at shoe laces.

When I get to my feet, a bit awkwardly, Dukkha rushes me off again, opening the door into a dark corridor running the width of the barn. 'Now where is your mamma?' She tuts. 'Your sister and cousins? Is it all to be left to me to change you?'

'Change me? What–'

'Wait there.' Dukkha bundles me into what looks like a forgotten waiting room, that's bare of anything but two chairs and a broken blind at the window.

Instead of following her back out and demanding to know what's going on, I stand there like a bloody idiot and try not to bite my carefully painted nails. Okay, it's customary for the girl to be brought in once the priest has carried out all the religious aspects with the boy's family (mine hovering at the back, I just bet) but am I really going to make my entrance from this hole in the corner? I don't know whether to see the funny side or cry. Other than my beautiful salwar suit, the only splash of colour in the room is a swathe of material laid over one of the kitchen chairs and I run my fingers over it with curiosity – and a sinking feeling. 'Oh, please, no,' I breathe.

It's a sari, silk, yes, with an array of yellows and purples – a jazzed up version of Dukkha's turgid outfit, if I'm honest. I hope against hope that she's

114

going to change into it, but as I hear the main door of the barn swing open and the murmur of excited voices growing louder, I know it's my fate. And there's not a thing I can do about it: if this is Dukkha's choice of sari for me, then out of respect I'll have to wear it.

Laly and Sharmila tumble into the room, Mum and the aunties hot on their heels, and a glowing Dukkha closing the door after them. Laly gives me a cheeky grin of mock horror when the garish sari is held up reverently by my future mother-in-law, and I can see Sharmila mentally trying to work out how my nail colour will ever blend in. Mum carefully doesn't look at me at first, but when she does, there's mute appeal in her eyes. Even though she's bought me a second salwar suit that's only going to be worn for a couple of hours. I can see her thinking, It won't be like this when it's Laly's turn. Auntie Sonu actually seems to like the dress, and Auntie Deepti will always agree to keep the peace, so there are a lot of willing hands helping me step out of one and get wrapped up in the other.

I can't help but be glad there's no mirror in the room. If pride comes before a fall, I was so pleased with my reflection back at the Travel Lodge, I deserve it, but I'm sure I must look like a clown. I'm going to refuse point blank to have my make-up redone, but Dukkha doesn't say anything about that. Instead, she unwraps a paper parcel from her handbag and passes me something tied up in a scrap of old cloth.

'My mother-in-law gave this to me when I got married and now I'm giving it to you,' she says. 'Open it, beta.'

The necklace looks old rather than antique, right down to the bits of rust on it. The faded colours are not attractive now, and probably never were, even thirty years ago, but it's inoffensive, and so if it has sentimental value for Dukkha, I'll keep her – and Mum

– happy. What's one more thing? If I tell myself that this is their day, and the wedding will be mine, we'll all be happy. I still get Ravi, don't I? And we do love each other. He's said it to me daily since the Rokka, and I must love him to be putting up with all this crap with such good grace.

'Anoushka? Anoushka!'

I blink back to the present to see Dukkha snapping her fingers at me – which nearly undoes all my good resolutions – and holding out a tikha, the piece of jewellery you put on your forehead.

'You're all lit up like a Christmas tree,' Laly blurts out, before Mum can slap her arm to silence her.

'I'll touch up Anou's make-up,' Sharmila says quickly. 'You'll allow me that, Auntie-ji, my engagement gift to her. It is my profession.'

There's a second of hesitation, as Dukkha eyes up a tatty beige vanity case the size of a hat box – obscured before, under the folds of the sari – and then graciously concedes.

Sharmila turns her back on the others and gives me a conspiratorial wink as she does the bare minimum to my face. 'You still look beautiful,' she whispers under the cover of the idle chit-chat behind her – mostly Dukkha telling Mum how her own daughters got engaged and how The Ballroom was such a lucky find – 'The sari mightn't be your choice but it's really good quality and doesn't look half bad. Your man will still love you.'

But I just want the day over with now.

Chapter 14

When I'm sitting on a big throne-like chair on the stage, a matching one empty beside me (Did the Tilaks bring these specially? I find my mind wandering. Or is the hotel planning on specialising in Hindu marriage celebrations?) it doesn't feel real. It's like I'm in a school play all over again: so out of my comfort zone, not really cut out for acting, but given the role to encourage me, the little Indian girl. Thank goodness the change in venue means that the slim chance of Dr Moffat or Donald attending – after my spontaneous invitation – ground to no chance. Going through the motions, I allow a large red veil to be placed on my shoulders and follow Dukkha's orders to pull it onto my head. She then places some mehndi in the palm of my hand – to symbolise me becoming a new bride in the very near future. Then, together, she and Kabir Tilak put an envelope of money in my lap, a symbol of our new bond. My mum and dad follow suit. The Tilaks' envelope is fat and heavy, which should feel generous, but from now on, anything I receive goes directly to my groom's family, so it's hard to see it as such. It's mostly a repeat performance of the Rokka and I'm not sure why, even in the midst of it, why other than outdated tradition, we need both.

If I were to be asked now, on pain of death, how I feel…Honestly? It wouldn't take anything for me to cut and run. I don't want this. I don't want to be painted and paraded and paid for. But I'm not brave and this isn't a film, and I'm not expected to smile or look happy, so I stare at my lap and will it to be over. Heat steals over me, prickling my forehead and I'm suddenly glad that the multi-coloured sari will hide the sweat-stains under my arms. It's just nerves, I tell myself. A panic attack. Just a panic attack. I've never had one before but I understand the physical symptoms. Fight or flight. I'll feel better when Ravi is wheeled out to sit beside me. I will. Please, Mata Rani, I really will…

And –

I do.

He's impeccably dressed (unlike me) in a neat suit, not the fancy traditional garb I half-expected, his hair slicked back, and his jewellery understated. All in all, he's the chic city boy – and I can't say I'm not relieved – and I'm the village cousin. My lovely dark pink salwar suit would have been perfect, and I vow to change back into it for the party. But if Ravi's packaging is perfect, he looks even more nervous inside than I must. His thumb nail on the hand nearest me is scraping the nail of his middle finger, a small but frantic movement, like a dog scratching and his opposite leg is jiggling up and down of its own accord. I want to put out my own hand and steady him, but I'm frozen in place. Initially, we don't acknowledge each other at all, then he turns his head slightly and gives me a half smile and widens his eyes in an unmistakable, 'Shit, what the hell are we doing here' glance. It's fleeting but enough to return to me some semblance of control; it reminds me how we're equal pawns of both sets of parents. My mum and dad are sticklers for all of this as much as Dukkha is, they're just not as in-your-face tunnel-visioned.

The exchange of rings is mercifully quick, and we both loosen up as the photographs are taken.

'Are you alright?' Ravi asks me, giving my thumb a quick squeeze, as we hold out entwined hands for an arty ring picture. Before I can answer, he whispers, 'That ring is loaded with diamonds and emeralds and sapphires, and it cost an arm and a leg. Mum insisted. We'll put it in the bank and get you a simple one for every day. More like mine.'

'It is…' I am about to say, 'a bit bling for me,' but just in time change it to 'heavy', even though it's not really. I wasn't expecting costume jewellery, exactly, but neither did I think the Tilaks would push the boat out this far. In turn, Mum and Dad's choice for Ravi looks elegant at home on his long brown finger.

'I hope all this is not too much for you,' he goes on. 'My mother wanted something special, to take away the memory of Rohit's marriage – my brother, you know? And something different so that people don't compare it to my sister Heera's. Rohit's wife and Heera refused to wear the dress my mother chose, so I'm thankful you have.'

There's so much to unpack in those words, I'm glad we're distracted by two laden plates of food, brought to us to balance on our knees and nibble on, while the guests mingle and relax and stuff themselves. The noise level in the barn ratches up a level, and somebody switches on the music and a roof full of fairy lights. Did Ravi just let slip that I'm wearing a second-hand dress? And a discard from the first girl – is that better or worse? I'm suddenly sorry that Rohit's wife died, as we might well have got on very well. Except she's braver than me. And I can't get changed now, can I? At least I can spill bits of food on this bedspread of a sari, and wipe my greasy hands on the folds, without anyone noticing. It's hard eating from a loaded paper plate, sitting on a platform, when any guest might jump us at any second to say congratulations.

'I was very nervous,' Ravi confides. 'But now I see you, the nerves are gone. We will be so happy, Anou, when it's just you and me. I can't wait for the wedding.

I love you.'

'I love you, too,' I reply, and in that second, all this ring stuff, the half-converted barn, my dress tantrums…well, they all slot into place in the jigsaw. The important thing is that Ravi and I are in tune, one giant step closer to being a couple. The family stuff, well, that's just detail we can work out.

There's dancing and partying into the evening. Ravi gravitates back to his mates, Anoop leading him away, with a leer on his face; I can imagine the lewd remarks over in that corner. Laly and Sharmila gather me up into a circle of women, pore over the ring and take sides on whether my sari is one-off couture or a monstrosity. We have a really good laugh together, and for once I, Anoushka Malhotra, the loner, feel part of something bigger. Marriage is going to be good for me.

'Not a decent husband prospect in sight,' Laly complains in between sucking Coke up through a straw. 'For me, I mean. I'd thought about the brother, Rohit – yeah? But he's a miserable git, isn't he?'

'Ssh, Laly.' Sharmila puts her hand to her mouth. 'His wife died.'

'But he didn't, did he? You take him, Shar. Cheer him up.'

Laly hiccups suddenly and I grab the plastic cup and sniff it. 'If you've been topping that up with Bacardi, Mum is going to go mental,' I warn her.

'Chill, big sis. It was only one and your mother-in-law saw me and didn't say a word.' Laly grins.

'She's got her hands full with the real drinkers.' Sharmila nods to the rear of the barn, where the bar has been set up. It's a bit furtive, like a speakeasy, with staff back and forth from the main hotel with boxes of wine and bottled beer and spirits. 'They got their wires crossed and thought we were Muslim and wouldn't be drinking,' Sharmila confides. 'The mother-in-law soon put them right. They're dead scared of her.'

'Who isn't?' Laly says.

A small group of middle-aged men have pulled chairs into a circle in the shadows, and seem to be sharing cheap whisky – I might not drink much but I'm Scottish; I know my whisky – as if it's Pass the Parcel. They're getting louder and heads are turning. I can see Mum going off at Dad, presumably to Do Something, which is wander off and find Kabir Tilak. The two men stand with their heads together, looking as if they hope the problem will go away and pointing to their watches.

'The room is only booked till 8pm,' Mum says at my shoulder, making me jump. 'They're hoping there won't be trouble.' She scowls at Dad and Kabir. 'Sometimes I wonder how do these men run a company?'

'Dad only runs a department,' Laly corrects her, but Mum doesn't even bother giving her a withering glance. I follow her anxious glance; she's checking out who the potential troublemakers are. If they're all on the Tilak side, she'll put on an accepting front, well, what can you expect, it's a party, people let their hair down. If there's any of the Malhotra clan, she'll wade in and sound the fire alarm, if that's what it takes to avoid us being shown up.

'Rohit,' Mum breathes. 'I will kill him.'

My Uncle Rohit, Mum's brother, is a short, fat man, the mildest guy alive until he's had a bevy or two. He's a total lightweight when it comes to alcohol and gets belligerent like a man three times his size. He's raising his voice (and his near-empty bottle) to a Tilak I don't know, and who, to be fair, is in an even worse state.

Mum and Dukkha are the ones, mouths in matching thin lines, who hot-foot it over there.

'Rohit,' Mum says, 'I need your help. It's time to clear the hall.'

'Lalu, you too. Can you collect the empties, please?'

They're like a tag team, and the flinty orders aren't lost on the other men, who get up guiltily and melt away into the crowd. Even the innocent guests in hearing distance start discreetly gathering their belongings together and making remarks about it getting late. Rohit and Lalu glare at each other, mutinous.

'Get them out,' Dukkha hisses at Kabir, who has crept forward.

'Now,' Mum instructs Dad, who's beside him.

Then, all smiles, they turn back to us all, and taking one half each, proceed to work the room and pour oil on troubled waters. It's seriously impressive. I wouldn't call either of them charming in the general sense (sorry, Mum) but right now they are ambassadors. Only after the barn is starting to clear, Kabir and Dad on herding duty at the door, do they confront their respective relatives.

'I wonder what it's all about?' Laly says, nosy to the last. In her own words, she loves a bit of aggro – from a safe distance.

'Foolish men,' Auntie Sonu snorts, passing by. She's looking at Mum as if she can't believe her eyes, and makes a beeline for her.

Grinning at Sharmila and me, Laly follows. 'What? I'm grabbing a last Coke,' she protests.

Ravi and his cousin Anoop make their way over to where we're standing.

'I apologise for my relative's behaviour,' Anoop says.

'We apologise for ours,' Sharmila replies.

Ravi and I just look at each other. He reaches out and takes my hand. The moment is spoiled by Laly lurching back to us, a can of Diet Coke in each hand. 'Well, you'll never guess–'

'Laly–'

'Seriously, you've got to hear this.' Laly is undeterred. 'You, too, favourite brother-in-law to be.' She raises a can cheekily at Ravi. 'Apparently, Uncle Rohit and your one have met before. They didn't like each other then and now they're chucking dirt. Apparently, Anou, you're like the eighth match, the Tilaks have tried and Mum and Dad are paying a fortune to unload you into a seriously rich family. But the joke's on us, cos, you, dear Ravi were done for nicking money from your American Bank and your reputation's shot–'

'Laly!'

She shuts up straightaway. I've never seen Mum so incandescent. She looks horrified and furious in equal measure. So does Dukkha. Ravi and I are just horrified. We stare at each.

'Laly, how could you?'

'What?' Laly sounds sulky. 'I didn't say I believed it. They're drunken idiots. But it's funny because it's so stupid. Anou, you should hear the rest–'

'Lalita Malhotra, you are the drunken idiot. To think I should say that about a daughter of mine. On her sister's engagement day!' Mum throws her hands up. 'I turned a blind eye to one alcoholic drink, but you have taken advantage. Don't lie to me; Dukkha saw you. And Deepti. Even your little brothers…' Words apparently fail Mum. 'Take her to the car,' she snaps at Sharmila.

Mum turns to Dukkha. 'I'm so sorry. I hope such nonsense hasn't spoiled your day.'

'Or yours,' Dukkha reciprocates. 'Such lies.'

'Families.' Mum shakes her head.

'Families,' Dukkha echoes.

What a way to bond, I think. Ravi and I are still holding hands, it's like a little symbol of trust between us, and when he squeezes mine, I squeeze back. It looks like this is the end of the engagement, and apparently neither of us knows what to say.

Dad and Kabir Tilak, both looking mightily relieved, save the awkwardness. 'They've both apologised and we'll leave it at that,' Mr Tilak says.

'No harm done,' Dad adds. 'We thought, that is, Kabir here, has offered that we drive by their house on our way out of town. You'd like to see where you'll be living, Anou?'

'She'd love it,' Mum answers for me. 'What a kind thought.'

What she means is, she'd love it but of course I'm curious. 'Yes, please,' I agree. Tradition dictates that the bride can't go inside her groom's family home till after the wedding, but I'd like to have an image. If it's not as big and posh as they've hinted, then I won't look so disappointed on the day. And if it is, well, I'll know what I'm going to have to live up to.

With a hurried arrangement to meet the rest of the Malhotra convoy at the first services on the M1 North – Auntie Sonu and Auntie Deepti take some convincing because they're dying to get a view of the Tilak's house, but Mum semaphores that we've had enough embarrassment for one day, and everyone coming and gawping is not mannerly but she'll snap a picture if she can – we follow their Carina back past the hotel proper and out on to the side road.

'Where are we going?' Laly asks in a small voice.

'None of your business, young lady,' Mum snaps. 'And you're only with us because the other cars are full. You don't deserve a treat.'

'Sorry, Mum.' Laly sounds contrite, but nudges me, with a, 'What's going on?' hand signal.

I just shake my head.

A scant five minutes later, and the Tilaks' car, is already slowing down and indicating. They pull over into the opening of a huge gravelled driveway and wave us on. Clearly this is as near as we get; can't tempt fate. Dad gives a little toot of the horn and drives obediently, if very slowly on. The rest of us have discarded all attempts at sophistication and are craning our necks as we pass by.

'Bloody hell,' Laly says, and for once nobody cautions her.

There's a wide stone arch above the driveway, engraved with the words Hoxton Hall Estate. The road bends slightly to the left, and through a line of trees, I can just make out the walls of a sandstone house. It might be similar in size to the Manningham Hall we've just left, but it seems much better kept.

'You're going to be lady of the bloody manor.' Laly again.

This time Mum picks her up on it, with a stern, 'Enough, Laly.' But it's the only word uttered in the car until we pile out, still in silence, at the Services.

Mum must be about to explode.

I don't know what to think – again. Other than it's the fitting end to the most surreal engagement in history. I fiddle with my over-sized and over-jewelled ring and wonder if Laly can blag her way into getting another very large Bacardi and Coke, this time for me.

Part 3
Before the Marriage

Chapter 15

I can't decide if I'm getting in deeper and deeper or if I'm just skimming the surface. I mean, the engagement – what kind of a farce was that? Mum has just about forgiven (grudgingly, but that's our Mum all over) Laly for her contribution to the madness when my outrageous sister only comes home from school and says she's started to write it up as a play for her English Higher. I assume Laly is trying to wind us all up, but Mum goes mental. She's all but got her coat on to go and see Laly's head of year before Dad talks her out of it.

'Madhu, think. Even if she is telling the truth–' He pauses to glare at a smirking Laly '–which I highly doubt, it's just a made-up story, isn't it? If you go in there and complain, then they'll know it's true. Do you want that, hmm?'

Mum, with one arm still in her coat, concedes he has a point.

'Yeah, Mum. They already think Indian families are always going wild celebrating weird festivals. And Miss Dunbar thinks it's the best multi-cultural idea since haggis pakoras were invented.' That's Laly for you, she doesn't know when to leave well alone.

The swithering other arm goes in the coat. 'So we, the Malhotras, are encouraging racial stereotypes, are we? We are the ones single-handedly giving the school their quota of multi-culturalism?' Her lips tighten like a cats bum.

'Wow, Mum! Are you doing Open University on the telly?'

Laly says it, but all three of us look at Mum in surprise. It's not the kind of thing she usually comes out with.

'I'm not totally uneducated, thank you. Even if I'm not a company director or a first class honours student.' She looks wounded, and Dad pulls himself together first.

'That's enough, young lady,' he says to Laly. 'You go to your room and do your homework – your maths homework. Your mother is going nowhere.' He turns to look sternly at my mum, who pulls a face but takes her coat off, muttering. 'But, Lalita, if you do anything to bring shame to the Malhotra name, then I will send you to the Girls Higher School in Mumbai for the rest of your senior education. So help me, do not call my bluff. Do you hear me? Lalita!'

She's already half way up the stairs but half-turns back, with a sulky, 'Yes, Daddy.' Her slam of the bedroom door shakes the house.

My mother sniffs. 'Too much to expect a word of apology from that little madam.' She turns to me and snaps, 'Thank goodness we have your match to make the family shine. Don't mess it up.'

'I'll do my best.' I want to poke her righteously retreating back as she stalks off to the kitchen. Note how it's the match that's doing them proud, not my degree, not the Reid Biology Prize or the Vice Chancellor's letter of congratulations. Oh no, it's all…

'Anou?' Dad's tired face stops my internal rant. 'Give her a minute, then go and talk about the…the curtains or bedspreads or something you'll need for your big new married house,' Dad whispers. 'I cannot have another dinner with your mother and sister at each other's throats. She is proud of you, you know for all the studies,' he adds. 'But she never had an education. Marriage is what she can relate to.'

Gosh – Mum being intelligent and Dad being sensitive: a double turn-up. I swallow the mean thought back. It's funny being the favourite after years of Laly in the spotlight. I better make the most of it.

Mum looks up sharply when I enter. 'Oh, it's you. Make yourself useful and put this in the microwave. You probably won't be doing it much longer.'

I take the bowl of rice and shove it on 'High'; she's waiting for me to take her up on that comment, so I hide behind the hum of the microwave. Then I think better of it. 'Just because it's a big house doesn't mean there'll be a mountain of servants,' I say. To be honest, though, it has passed my mind. Ever since we saw that giant house – Hoxton Hall, for goodness sake – I've been trying to imagine daily life. I had a vague notion of somewhere like this, but (fingers crossed) with an extra bathroom so that I don't have night-time run-ins with Dukkha in her flannelette nightdress and curlers, or whatever she wears at home. Now it's looking like we might live in separate wings. Can't say I'm disappointed. As for staff, though…

'Of course they have servants.' Mum bangs down a tray of marinated chicken. 'There'll have brought over a harem of young girls from some godforsaken family village. They'll live in a couple of rooms behind the kitchen and do all the work. Back homes their families will get a postal order for a few hundred rupees a month and think their daughters are living the high life in Scotland.'

'You don't really think so?' I look at Mum in horror. 'They wouldn't do that, would they? A cleaning company once a week and a couple of Dukkha's widowed cousins is what I thought.'

'Well, maybe you're right,' she says, after a minute. 'I don't know. But whatever the arrangement, you won't have to wait heart and soul on your new mother-in-law.'

'It's "hand and foot", Mum. To wait hand and foot

on someone.'

'Just as well. That woman looks like she'd suck your soul with a slice of lemon.' Mum claps her hand to her mouth. Then we both dissolve into giggles. 'Ignore me, Anou. Dukkha has her faults but I have respect for the way she handled that funny business at the engagement.'

'I suppose.' I hesitate then, wanting to ask something but not wanting Mum's wrath swapping from Laly to me. 'Mum, it was all nonsense, wasn't it?'

She stops mid-stir to look at me, frowning. 'What do you mean? Of course it was. They were drunk out of their heads. I've no idea why Glaswegians are seen as the worst alcoholics at all…' She's heading into one of her full-on rants, when her eyes narrow. 'Why do you ask? Has someone said something? Ravi…?'

'No, nothing like that,' I jump in, before I'm forced to tell an outright lie. 'It's just well, no smoke without fire and all that.'

Mum looks sceptical. 'Call yourself a scientist, Anoushka Malhotra? I'd expect that talk of Laly but not from you. All the evidence points to Ravi being a good boy, doesn't it? Well?' She waits for me to nod; I can't argue. 'And Dukkha might be…eccentric…'

I have to hold my tongue there: when the woman was moderately well off, she was 'odd', now she's rich, she's upgraded to 'eccentric'. Right

'…but I don't think she's a liar. If she is she's a very good one. You worry too much, Anou. Here you are getting what every Indian girl dreams of, and you worry about the what-ifs.'

'What every Indian parents want.' I say it with a smile and Mum takes it in good heart.

'That, too, of course. It's a good match, enjoy it. Whatever they say about happiness, money does help.' She gives me a half smile. 'You won't have to push a pram around a freezing, dog-dirt ridden park while waiting for the Indian corner shop to open, at least.'

'No, I'll have a nanny to do that, while I get my hair done.'

'Exactly.' Mum looks at me brightly, totally missing the point, and in a way I'm glad; an enlightened mother is far too much to deal with on top of everything else: by which I mean my Finals, starting tomorrow. Eek.

'I'll need to leave early in the morning, Mum,' I remind her while I'm thinking about it. 'My first exam, remember.'

'That meat is tough.' Her attention is back on the food. 'What? Oh, yes… I'll be having words with that butcher.'

'It's a chemistry practical. Three hours.' I push for a reaction, whatever Dad says, I'm immediately miffed that a dead lamb is more important than my education.

'Well, good luck,' she says, 'not that you need it…'

That's better.

'…after all, the pressure's off now, isn't it? You must be so relieved.'

'What do you mean?'

'You're getting married.'

'So?'

'Your exams don't really matter now,' she explains. 'Of course, they're a nice bit of paper, but you don't need them anymore, do you.'

We each look at the other as if we're strangers, aliens, maybe, not mother and daughter.

Do we even live in the same world? How can she think that, let alone say it? She and Dukkha deserve each other. The sooner I leave this… this…narrow-minded family, the better.

I do a bit of a rant to Laly, who's delighted to fuel my indignation; anything to take the heat off her misdemeanours. Then, when she's bored, she gets philosophical.

'It's just Mum being Mum.' She shrugs. 'Screw 'em all and join the swingers is what I say.'

'Not funny,' I snap.

'So funny,' she counters, pulling what's supposed to be a come-hither-lover face and willing me to grin.

'A bit funny,' I relent. 'As long as it's not true.'

'Of course it's not true, you prat. I mean – Dukkha? She's got a face like the back of a bus and Mr, well, he's a human Mr Potato-Head. The Asian version.'

'It's not all about looks.' Even as I say it, I wonder why I'm even involving myself. This is part of why I asked Mum that question earlier – whether she thinks there's any truth in the allegations those men made at the engagement. According to Laly, the bit she didn't get to tell us on the day, is that the bloke accused the Tilaks – Mr and Mrs, not Ravi – of sleeping around at a secret wife-swapping club in Leeds. "Pampas grass on the lawn and keys in a lucky-dip", was the phrase he'd used. To be honest, both of us were mystified but a bit of research (Laly in the library, would you believe) said that in the 1970s, 'swingers' used to identify each other with garden plants and have parties in their houses.

Laly is enthralled at the notion, and now she's eyeing up all our relations over forty and Mum and Dad's friends, wondering if they did it. I just find the whole thing embarrassing, I mean – really? Each to their own, but it's embarrassing enough thinking of doing it with one person you know, let alone a bunch of relative strangers or your neighbours. And the idea of Dukkha…no, not going there. I've seen some revolting sights under a microscope but there my mind still boggles.

Actually, that it is so nonsensical it reassures me about the more – theoretically – possible gossip concerning Ravi. I mean, if he were a thief or had been accused of something, that would be story enough. Adding the rest stinks of drunken and jealous stupidity. I felt a bit awkward with Ravi, in the phone calls just after the engagement; not sure whether to bring it all up or whether he would – does he even know what was said? Laly says no. According to her, Ravi is his mummy's little soldier and she'd keep any nastiness from his tender little ears. I'm inclined to agree. I let it go, anyhow, and now we're back on track. He, at least, is interested in my exams.

'I'll be thinking about you especially at the right times,' he promises tonight. 'Chemistry practical at 9am tomorrow, right?' He asked me for the timetable and I read it over the phone; he must have copied it down. 'And Anou, I'm sending a special kiss now.'

'And I'm sending one back,' I whisper, my toes tingling, either at the kiss or the exams starting in twelve hours.

'Good.' He sounds amused. 'We'll share it for real on the day of your graduation.'

'We will.' If we can distract two sets of parents for the duration of a peck. 'You're still coming?'

'Of course. I suggested I come alone...' My heart lifts. 'But my mother wouldn't hear of it.' It sinks. 'She insists on coming along, and my dad will drive us. They're very proud of their daughter-in-law-to be.'

'I don't know if I can get four tickets.' I take a deep breath. 'Sorry. I'm panicking unnecessarily, I've not even done the exams yet. I might fail.'

'Of course you won't fail,' Ravi says. 'My wife will have her degree. And I, and my family will be there to see her honoured. Yes, Anoushka?'

'Yes,' I say, 'Yes,' glad he can't see my fingers crossed on my lap.

Chapter 16

And, I am delighted to say that my brilliant fiancé was right. The exams passed in a three and a half week blur: taking my white coat endlessly on and off, sitting at a rickety table with one leg shorter than another to write my papers, watching the clock and hearing real life going on outside, slowly emptying my brain of everything I've spent four years learning. I don't think I spoke to anyone but Donald during the whole thing. I refused to answer any questions at home, and I'd say they were all relieved anyway; absolved of having to show interest in something so boring and unnecessary (yep, my Mum's opinion still rankles). Ravi checked in with me at 9pm each night, and after a three minute call, sternly told me to get to bed and take sufficient rest, which I did. On the other hand, Donald and I spent every second between bells deconstructing and analysing and alternately moping and being exhilarated.

'Come on, Anoushka, you're getting a First,' he'd say, banging his hot chocolate cup down on the table. 'You can't not.'

'I can not. Even if I don't mess up, there's probably a quota, and if so, you get the First, obviously, and I'm downgraded.'

'A quota of one? That's mathematically insignificant and ethically a bit off,' he scoffed. Then, looking over his shoulder and lowering his voice, 'We'll both get the best marks, Anoushka, you have to admit that. It's not as if the competition is great, is it?' He winked to dull the sting, but it's true. He's by far the cleverest in our group and I work the hardest.

'A 2:1 is respectable, anyway,' we'd chorus, but the

is it respectable enough for a PhD hung in the silence.

Well, that we'll never know, because...because...both of us have got First Class Honours! The official letters came this morning in the post. I was watching the drive for the post, something I haven't done since about my ninth birthday and waiting for a frothy, lurid, tutu-like rainbow salwar suit promised from Auntie Sonu in Mumbai; not a thing you'd pick up down the Barras. (When it came it was too small and Laly got to wear it. I was heartbroken. Mum got me – oh, my goodness I'd forgotten this trauma till now – a Miss Piggy outfit from somewhere, because we'd seen The Muppet Movie for my treat. It wasn't the pig-thing that bothered me, actually, it was the pink-thing: Miss Piggy is pinky-white and has long blonde hair and blue eyes and I was too brown all over. What was Mum thinking of?)

Anyway, I survived that, I'll survive this, I was telling myself, when the postman cut across from next-door and I was down the stairs before the letter box rattled. I shoved the white oblong into my bag and shot out of the door, yelling I was getting the bus to college. Mum and Dad still haven't a clue about my timetable, or that it's not a college day, and everything is like the Marie Celeste this late in the term. Donald and I promised each other we'd open them together, before we joined the crush at the department noticeboard, and the milling tutors and students, congratulating or consoling each other as required.

I have to admit, I opened mine on the bus. It was burning a hole in my side, and I fiddled with the envelope flap, worrying at it with my nails in the depths of my bag. Then I read the letter through squinted eyes, just in case...the relief was immense. Not excitement or joy or pride, but just an acknowledgement that it was over and I'd done it. I'd broken free and done something on my own before I swapped one family-of-expectations for another.

Donald – also a First, the only other one – looked as shell-shocked as me. We sort of shrugged blankly, accepted the accolades – with genuine pleasure on both sides from Dr Moffat – and here we are now, with our celebratory chicken sandwiches from the cafeteria and hot chocolate made by a lady behind the counter rather than the vending machine.

Suddenly, Donald bangs the table. 'Anoushka, what kind of party-poopers, are we?' he announces so loudly, I wonder if he's had a wee nip of whisky to calm his nerves. 'Wait here.'

He picks up our mugs, goes back to the counter, and has an apparent heart-to-heart with the lady behind the counter. Then he comes back with a tray and a flourish. 'This is more like it!'

Donald has got her to spray cream from a can onto the mugs of hot chocolate, and there is a Flake, broken in half in each, to make a victory V sign.

'Anoushka Malhotra, BSc, congratulations,' he says.

'The same to you, Donald Johnstone, BSc.'

We pick up the drinks, make a Cheers clash, and grin like idiots.

It is the best moment of my life.

Mum and Dad are pleased for me, in an understated kind of way. Neither say very much to my face but I hear Mum on the phone doing the passive-aggressive boasting she's so good at ('The graduation and the wedding to plan…What? Yes, well, she has to go really, what with the First Class Honours being so rare…Oh, didn't I say?') On the other hand, Ravi gushes on for a good five minutes; it's nice of him, of course, but excruciatingly embarrassing at the same time.

'It's not a Nobel Prize,' I snap eventually, then immediately feel bad. I'm sure I can feel his hurt wafting down the telephone wires. 'Sorry, I–'

'So modest, Anou. Wait.'

The phone call gets muffled for a minute, then Dukkha comes on. 'Congratulations from Mr Tilak and myself,' she says stiffly. 'Ravi is very proud…Hmm?' More shuffling and voices off. 'That is, tell your parents we are all, our family, very proud.'

'Er, thank you.' But like a child who's been coerced to do their duty, she's already gone.

'I can come to your Graduation?' Ravi asks. 'I'll take the day off and we'll drive up. Take lunch together, our two families.'

'Yes, I suppose so.'

'Anou?'

'It's just I'm still not sure how many tickets I can have for the ceremony.' I'm madly counting up; it never occurred to me to imagine Dukkha there.

'You only need one for me. My parents will amuse themselves.'

Small mercies, I think.

I realise what a favour they're inadvertently doing me when I relay the conversation to Mum. She's about to start a full-on mutter about the fool who planned my Graduation two weeks before my wedding and the need to sacrifice the first for the second. When she learns that not only Ravi, but Dukkha and Kabir Tilak are going to make the effort to come north, she backtracks faster than a reverse rollercoaster and it becomes a free-for-all family jaunt. Yet I'm not sure I want any of them there; it's a weird crossover of three different bits of my life, so I resolve to let them fight it out over my allocated two tickets. Those, I'd give to Dr Moffat and Donald but they'll be there with me on the platform, so I fill out a form to be entered into the ballot for extras and leave it to fate.

Chapter 17

Mata Rani is on my side and the Graduation Saturday is the sunniest of sunny days. We're supposed to wear black and white under our academic gowns, which makes Mum and the aunties cluck their teeth and shake their heads – 'colour, where is the colour? So drab' – but I like my wide-legged trousers and long tunic, they make me feel serious and academic, and I can blend in with the surroundings.

I need to collect what Mum insists on referring to as my 'full regalia' so she, Dad, and me get an early bus into town, leaving Laly and the boys to follow with whatever aunts and uncles show up. I'm slightly – more than slightly – disconcerted to see Ravi and Mr and Mrs Tilak already there, sitting in a stiff line at the bus stop on Potterrow. I mean, there are hundreds of cafes round here. I wanted to be gowned up and ready to go before meeting them. There's a bit of back-slapping (the men), commentary on outfits (the women), while Ravi and I stand on our respective sides and smile when we catch each other's gazes. You'd never think we speak daily on the phone, and as for being engaged... I half despise myself – no, both of us – for not ignoring protocol or diffidence or whatever it is, grabbing hands and taking off for breakfast. But we don't. We stand ignored by the grown-ups, until I tug at Mum's sleeve (I know) and whisper that I need to go and pick up my gown.

'Go, go.' She waves me off.

'We'll find you for photographs afterwards,' Dad adds.

Dukkha looks at me as if she's just noticed I'm here. 'Oh, yes, Anoushka, you need to leave plenty of time

139

for these things.'

Well. I'd expected a bit more enthusiasm, but it appears they're keen to get rid of me so they can carry on the pre-wedding gossip. Good luck, Ravi, I think, but he's looking past me and his face has brightened. I turn, and there's his cousin Anoop.

'Bye, then,' I say to the air and wander across the square. I'm almost at the entrance to the hall when there's a shout behind me.

'Good luck, Anoushka,' Ravi calls, blowing an awkward kiss – or maybe he's got an itch on his lip.

Putting them all behind me, literally, I hurry into the building and follow the tacked up signs to the makeshift gowning room. It occurs to me that I don't know who will win the two tickets to watch the ceremony. I couldn't get any more, after all, and I'm leaving it to them to sort out. I take my place in a short line and am soon kitted out with a neat pile and I look around for a place to get ready.

'Was that your family and your man's family out there?'

I whirl around to see Donald, already resplendent in kilt and gown. It's funny seeing him without his lab coat or North Face jacket, and he's more Harry Potter-ish than dashing, but a friendly face is a friendly face.

'Yes, and yes,' I say. 'You should have come over to say hello.' It's safe to say that now he can't and I'm busy hiding my lying face in the folds of the black gown.

'I was marshalling my own folks over,' he says. 'Though yours look more interesting.'

'Interesting? How?'

'A bit them and us. You know Westside Story, the two rival gangs…' He breaks off, turning red. 'God, Anoushka, ignore my bad manners. I should never have said that. Put it down to nerves.'

But I'm already hiccupping with laughter, far more than is warranted, at the thought of the Tilak-Malhotra families starring in their own musical. Dukkha bursting into a dance routine…

'Sorry,' I say. 'If you're nervous, I'm clearly hysterical. Right. What do we do now?'

Donald looks at his watch. 'Hang around for an hour or so. We could go and meet our respective parents, that's what people seem to be doing. Or–'

'Or?'

'Or go and hide out somewhere round the back – hey, Anoushka, wait for me!'

There really isn't anywhere much to hide out so we end up loitering in the halls and wandering round. Nobody takes any notice of us, other than to say an automatic 'Congratulations' as they pass. We don't say much either; Donald and I don't really know each other beyond experiments and exams, but it doesn't matter. It takes me aback when he says, 'So tell me about the wedding. That's soon, isn't it?'

'My wedding?'

He looks amused. 'Who else's?'

'Are you really interested?' I narrow my eyes.

'Actually, I am,' he says, leaning up against the wall with his arms folded. 'When my sisters got married they talked about nothing else for weeks, months probably. They managed to get a mention in to strangers in the street, the bin-men and bus drivers. You've hardly even said anything since telling us you got engaged.'

'I've been too busy with my exams, I suppose.' I shrug. 'I've been working on this degree for four years. The idea of getting married has only been around for a few months. I've only met Ravi twice. I'll concentrate on that once today–'

'Woah, woah! You've met him twice?'

'You don't know much about Indian Hindu weddings, do you?' I'm smiling, on surer ground because this is everyone's reaction. 'We've talked a lot on the phone. I feel like I know him well…' Do I, though, do I really? The thought enters my head but I'm not giving it space today of all days.

'As well as you know the friends you've had for years?' Donald asks.

'I don't have any friends who aren't relations.' It's out of my mouth before I can stop it; it makes me sound even more odd. 'Except you,' I add. 'And Dr Moffat – though I'm not sure I can call her a friend.'

We both grin at that one, and to his credit, Donald doesn't comment on my lack of friendships. Instead, he thinks for a minute, and then says, 'Alright then, but you know him better than you know me, say?'

'Yes.' I hesitate. 'In some ways. I mean I don't know his views on hot chocolate, his favourite sandwich or…or if he has an opinion on the principles of molecular cell biology. But I know about his life and what he wants to do with it. And he's nice to me. Kind. He–' I'm about to blurt out the random gifts Ravi has showered on me over the last while but it feels kind of disloyal.

'Fair enough,' Donald says after a minute. 'If he's nice and kind, then everything else is workable, I'd say. Not that I know anything about relationships. My entire female family despairs of me. I can't even imagine feeling ready to get married.'

'Who says I can?' Whoops. That one does sneak out. 'But I couldn't imagine being here getting my degree until it happened – and here we are.'

'Speaking of which,' Donald pushes back the folds of his gown to look at his watch, 'we should get back before we miss it.'

We start walking back down the long corridors,

back to the bustle, and as we congregate with all the others, at last I can feel the excitement stirring inside me. I'm getting my Masters degree, my First Class Masters degree. I've done it. I've achieved something and I decide I don't care if it's naff, once I get that certificate, I'm framing it and putting it on my bedroom wall...Oh. Well, a wall in Ravi's home. In a residence that size, there's bound to be a bit of free space amongst his awards.

'Anoushka?'

I realise I've missed something Donald said. 'Sorry, I was planning where to hang my certificate. Seriously.'

He doesn't miss a beat. 'Mine's going above the bath so I can remind myself every day that I've done this. But I was asking, shall we...I mean, would you like to stay in touch? We could write to each other.'

I look at his face and see that he's not just being polite, he means it. He really is my friend. 'Yes,' I say. 'Yes, I'd like that.'

'Good. Good.'

And that's that, because we're called to get in alphabetical order, and after that, the degree ceremony is all a bit immense: a noisy, rustling, clapping blur.

An hour later, I'm pushing through the crowds, trying to avoid getting into other people's photos, looking for Mum and Dad or even one of the Tilaks. You'd think they'd be easy to spot because it's not like there are millions of brown faces, but I'm short, so I'm lost in a sea of black gowns.

Eventually, I see them not a hundred feet from where I left them near the bus stop – Mum and Mr And Mrs Tilak, anyway.

'Your dad and Ravi took the two tickets,' Mum says. 'Did you see them? What was it like?'

'No, it was too busy to see anyone. It was alright, good. There'll be a video we can buy, so you'll be able to see properly.' I jump when I feel a hand on my shoulder, but it's my dad, looking strangely serious.

'Congratulations, Anoushka,' he says, and then totally unexpectedly, he turns me round and pulls me to him in a fierce hug. 'I am so proud of you, my daughter. Your mother and I, we are both so proud of you. It was only when I saw you cross the stage and receive your scroll that I realised your achievement.' He looks over my shoulder. 'Madhu, our firstborn. Look how far she has come. Such a good example for her brothers and sister.'

Mum steps forward, and I swear it's the nearest thing to a group hug we've ever had. There might even be tears in their eyes. It's disconcerting. I know they're genuine and I've a lovely warm feeling that they are proud, after all, and I'll put it away and treasure it, but there's still the bit of me that wishes they'd acknowledged it sooner. I shake that thought away.

As we all step back and look at one another, I hold out the tube containing my degree certificate. 'This is for you both,' I tell them. 'I wouldn't have got it without you giving me a home and allowing me to study. Thank you, Mum. Thank you, Dad.' Mum awkwardly takes the black tube and Dad blows his nose, nodding.

Mr Tilak clears his throat. 'I would like to add my congratulations on behalf of the family you are about to join, Anoushka. We, too, are very proud of you.' He looks at Dukkha, who nods stiffly, and across at Ravi, who's still behind my dad. 'Son, have you something to give Anoushka, to mark the occasion?'

Ravi bounds forward like an over-excited puppy, the moment of Malhotra-bonding gone completely over his head, but then he doesn't know how unusual it is. He'll be used to praise and prizes and accolades from his adoring mammy. Grinning, he reaches into his suit pocket for a slim box, which he hands to me. 'Congratulations, Anou. You made me so proud. This is for you.'

With them all circling me expectantly, I take the gift and open it. It's a watch. One with a complicated gold bracelet strap and a cluster of little clear stones – diamonds? – surrounding the face.

'Let me help you.' Ravi takes it out of the box and fusses to get it around my wrist.

It's heavy, cold, against my skin, and quite unlike anything I've ever had before. I hold out my arm for it to be admired.

'Beautiful,' Mum breathes. 'Oh, Anou, you lucky girl.'

'22 carat gold,' Ravi says. 'Eight cut diamonds. Inscribed with, you make me proud, but you can read that later. I am too impatient to see you wear it.'

'My boy has great taste.' Dukkha smiles with satisfaction – is it only me who can hear the unspoken – and seriously dodgy – 'He takes after me' in her voice. 'You are very lucky.' She's only repeating my mother but there's a clear note that tells me she's talking about far more than the watch.

'Time for photos, I think,' Mr Tilak suggests.

'The day just gets better.' Mum beams around. 'This is turning into the perfect rehearsal for your wedding, Anoushka. Not a wasted day at all!'

And with that, normality is resumed.

Chapter 18

Life is strange without the framework of college. I'm
all out of excuses to leave the house and delay the
wedding talk. After a few limbo days, during which I
horrify my mum by suggesting I should get a summer
job or even go and help Dad out in the office or
Sharmila in the salon, it takes Laly to point out that
there are only days until my wedding and that I'd
better give in to the narrow-focused obsession that's
the only thing that will please Mum.

'You don't even have to do anything, Anou,' she
points out. 'She won't let you do anything because she
knows she can do it better, so just drift round and
throw out the odd comment.

'Like what? She's thought of everything.' It's true.

'Oh no, she hasn't. Just say things like, "I heard
about a wedding where they hired twelve turtle doves
from a farm in Fife to let fly at the end of the
ceremony", or "Cardamom fairy cakes with our
families' coats-of-arms intertwined on them sound
nice". She'll be on the phone for hours trying to out-do
those. Suggest a bridal-party line dance, too. It's the
latest thing in Bollywood romance.'

'Is any of that even remotely real?' I ask her – not
sure which answer would be worse.

'Of course it's not, you wally.' Laly looks at me and
shakes her head. 'I worry about you, Anou, living
without me. The point is, Mum doesn't know it's all
made up and it'll distract her from obsessing over the
thread count of your dress and the size of the cake bits
that are going to be smooshed into your perfectly-lip
sticked gob.'

I'm not Laly and I can't carry off such total

nonsense, so I compromise by throwing in innocuous questions about Mum and Dad's wedding, Auntie Sonu's, Auntie Deepti's. Numerous anecdotes later about all the potential disasters in every wedding she ever attended here and in India – not to mention how Scottish weddings are so bland and black and white – we get through the days.

With two days to go, she finally concedes that everything is done. Absolutely everything. We're at the kitchen table drinking tea, and Mum looks as if she's doing a triathlon: she's done the first two events (match, engagement, wedding prep) and is psyching herself up for the final event. She's between exhausted and exhilarated. The aunties keep popping up like cheerleaders and the men are nowhere to be seen. Me? I'm like the star of the show who's being kept in the dark so that she shines all the brighter on the day. No pressure, then. I just keep whispering to myself that I got my degree, I can do this, too. It's just one day. Then I'll treat being married like I did studying: a big project with lots of different hypotheses and experiments.

'Well, Anou, if this marriage isn't perfect, it won't be anything to do with me.' Mum eyes me over her cup. Nods and murmurs from the aunties.

'I know, Mum. Thank you for doing it all,' I say, topping up her plate of sweets. 'Why don't you take it easy tomorrow?' More nods and murmurs.

'There must be something else, something I've forgotten,' she frets. 'Deepti, Sonu, help me here?'

'Nothing, Madhu. The clothes, the food, the hotel–'

'The hotel!' Mum bolts upright, upending her, thankfully empty, cup. 'Anoushka, bring me my address book. I need to re-confirm with them. What if it's the engagement all over again?'

'Ssh, ssh,' Auntie Deepti soothes her. 'You confirmed yesterday, remember? All is well.'

'But...' Mum moans.

'But if it worries you, I will confirm once more right now.'

Auntie Sonu sweeps into the hall and closes the door behind her. I've no idea whether it really is the long-suffering hotel staff she's phoning or if she's talking to the complicated Ansaphone she's got at her house, but it mollifies Mum, when Laly bounces in and says, 'Auntie Sonu says stop worrying. It's fine. What's fine?'

'Everything,' I say. 'Everything is fine.' I'm trying to semaphore with my eyes, but I can tell from a mile off when Laly's in one of her wicked moods.

Sure enough, she smiles beatifically at me, and says, 'What if the wedding day weather's not fine?'

Mum gives a strangled cry, echoed by Auntie Deepti, and I swear I want to clock the two of them – as soon as I've done Laly – on the head. What does it matter? I want to yell. We'll be inside. I don't care. But I bite it back because they do care and I'll only have to put up with this trauma for two more days. Just two days.

'Laly,' I snap. 'You're upsetting Mum. Stop. Please.'

'Ah, but that's just it, I'm not. I have the solution to stopping it raining.' She grins around the room (including Auntie Sonu who slides her bulk back in), basking in the attention she's got.

'I was telling Mrs O'Reilly at number 26 all about the wedding,' Laly announces. 'She was very interested. She has got four daughters all married, and nine grandchildren. She's only fifty-eight. Did you know that, Mum? She's nice, you should make friends. They had great weddings, even though I think some of them are divorced now, but anyway, she told me the trick to make sure the weather is okay.' She stops for breath, and to check her audience is rapt; to be fair, even I'm curious as to what the fuck she's going to come up with.

Laly waits a good minute and a half and then proclaims, 'It's this!' From the bottom of her backpack she brings out what looks like a ratty old garden gnome that's lost its weight and all its colour but dumps it in the middle of the table as if it's an Oscar.

'What–'

'It's a Child of Prague statue,' Laly announces with a relish. 'If you put it in our garden tonight and tomorrow night and say a prayer, then it guarantees good weather on The Day. It never fails, Mrs O'Reilly says. Oh, and she'll say the prayers for you, Mum, on account of it being a Roman Catholic thing and us being Hindu. Isn't that great? I think we should invite her to the wedding.'

I pretend I'm sneezing so I can cover my mouth and hide a laugh. Of all the idiotic stuff Laly comes out with, this has to be the funniest. And doesn't Laly know it. She catches my eye and her grin broadens; she'd wink if it wouldn't spoil her moment. Mum and the aunties look aghast, but they can say nothing: they can't afford to diss a neighbour's religion or pass on a potential lucky charm just in case. Laly would have a hold over them forever. I'm so going to miss my little sister.

'No need to thank me,' Laly says into the silence. 'Call this my wedding gift to you, Anou. And Mrs O'Reilly's, of course.'

Chapter 19

The 22nd September 1993.

My wedding day.

The day my parents have had in mind since the day I was born: the oldest daughter well-married, uniting two good families, and securing my future.

I just want the day over with, and the marriage to begin. It's my big escape – which is both exhilarating and terrifying because I've got to get it right. I'm not stupid. I know outsiders will cluck their tongues and suggest I'm like a wasp going from the jam into the treacle (sweet but ultimately stuck in one or the other) but I'm making a choice here and I stand by it, whatever the unknowns. Dukkha might be a piece of work, but you see what you get; it would be far worse if the Tilaks were hiding their dirty linen. If I can live with my mum for twenty-two years, I can get my mother-in-law on side (as Laly says, with one word: "grandchildren".) Ravi and I can make it, I feel it. Like Donald said, if you've got nice and kind, you can work out the rest. And my bonus is that I'm not blinded by romance – doesn't mean I don't want a sprinkling of it but it's back to that core of me being a scientist. You get results by starting from nothing and working. Hard.

That objective part of me is having a little laugh at the rest of me that's still in bed on this auspicious day, doing a thorough internal audit before the rest of the house wakes and it's full-on frenzy time. And I want to get today right for Mum and Dad's sake, what they want, they get. Dad's paying for the entire wedding, which is customary, and he's been tight-lipped about the cost, just assuring Mum that she has free rein. I was guessing a few thousand, but it was Ravi who let slip that it was twenty-five thousand. Gulp. He was commenting on my parents' generosity and how much the marriage means to them, and he obviously thought I knew the colossal figure involved. I mean, catering for five hundred guests – family, their friends, business associates, social acquaintances, people who matter (though not, as Laly says, Mrs O'Reilly at number 26) – with every vegetarian delicacy and enough variety to please the most ardent vegan.

Mum is still lamenting the fact that we've not had opportunity to go to India for my outfits – we would have, of course, if I hadn't had exams and a graduation that I insisted on prioritising; Dad's shut her down on that one, thank goodness, by promising a lavish trip for Laly's 'trousseau' – but she's made up for it by spending more thousands by mail order on the finest silks and dress-making not to mention forays into Jenners and Frasers for all the 'going away' incidentals, including a stash of household items and linens that I'm yet to see. I told Mum I'd like to be surprised and she's in her element with that, sending it all ahead to Bradford. Then there is the jewellery, all reverently laid out, waiting, on my dressing table, Mum's and Laly's – an opportune thief would have had a field day in our house last night. I've got necklaces and earrings, rings and bangles, and so have they. And there's more gold for Ravi and his family, to be presented later today. Dukkha has to approve of the necklace and earrings my Mum agonised over choosing.

When I hear Mum and Dad's bedroom door open, I know it's Mum's tread padding across the landing, so I brace myself, take a deep breath and get out of bed. When she calls my name, and looks in, I'm already pulling the curtains back, to glorious blue skies. The Child of Prague may have worked its magic, but I decide not to start the day by mentioning that to my beaming mother. I'll leave that pleasure to Laly.

It's a surprisingly calm morning. I'm not expecting to enjoy it, but I do. Mum has assumed a resigned 'I've done all I can' air and life is all the better for it and Aunties Sonu and Deepti spirit her off to spruce her up, promising, good-naturedly, she'll look a million dollars and upstage the bride. Mum shouts them down but she's clearly delighted. Sharmila and Laly are left to help me dress into my deep red and gold costume. It is beautiful, fits perfectly and I love it, I even feel a bit princess-y. The effect is spoiled a bit – for me – when I'm loaded down with gold jewellery. 'Wish I'd weighed myself before and after,' I grumble. 'I must be carrying pounds extra.'

'Of course you are,' Sharmila scolds. 'What kind of wedding would it be if you didn't have gold things everywhere? It would be like going naked. You'd be the talk of the community. Poor Auntie Madhu.'

'Poor, my arse.' Laly is busy checking her own adornments. 'Our mother will be dripping with gold ingots, trying to keep up with Dukkha-the-dreadful.' She adjusts her gaze to me. 'You look really good, Anou. Not under-done or over-done.'

'She is perfect,' Sharmila agrees, standing back to admire her own handiwork in my ensemble. 'Don't let your mother-in-law talk you into changing anything today,' she warns. 'Promise? We don't want a repeat of the engagement dress horrors.'

'She wouldn't dare.' I've got the power today, I'm the one marrying her golden boy, and like an actor on the stage, in costume for a role, I can feel that power coursing through my veins with every piece of clothing, extra gemstone and gold trinket I add. 'Bring it on,' I mutter.

'Go, Anou.' Laly gives me a round of applause.

Ever practical, Sharmila is ticking off my 'just in

case' stuff in an overnight bag. I have spare everything, plus a suitcase all packed for afterwards. 'Passport?' she checks.

I nod, hoping I'll need it. Ravi is taking care of the honeymoon. He asked me where I wanted to go weeks ago, that the decision was all mine and he would move heaven and earth to arrange it – whatever the cost. Put on the spot, I couldn't think of anywhere or anything. The first exotic spot that entered my mind was the Caribbean, and it was inspired because Ravi said his friends had been to Barbados and had an excellent 'five-figure' time. 'Leave it with me,' he said. 'I'll book it tomorrow.' Ever since then he's been cagey, wanting to surprise me. I don't care if it's not the Caribbean but please, I beg the universe now, don't make it India with the relatives or somewhere wetter than Scotland.

'Then we're ready.'

The three of us hook arms and sit on the side of my bed, jostling position to see in my dressing-table mirror. It feels unreal, that this is the last time this will really be my bedroom – isn't that what every bride-to-be says, leaving home? But it feels good, even if I can't imagine what's to come. Get through today first, I remind myself. If you have to, imagine the promise of the PhD.

'At least I look the part.' I'm thinking aloud. 'We all do. Thank you, both. I'll do the same for your weddings–'

Auntie Sonu's, 'Yoo hoo, girls,' from the landing interrupts me. 'And there's our cue.'

The aunties line one side of the narrow space, and Laly and Sharmila the other, all of them giggling, as they choreograph me and Mum's exits from our respective rooms.

'Da da!' says Layla, as we catch first sight of one another.

I'm sure I'm looking as shy as Mum does, but she does look lovely – a younger, polished, radiant version of herself. From the look in her eyes, she's both aware of this, and surprised that I look good too. We don't speak, don't even touch for fear of messing up make-up or knocking a hair or a bangle out of place, but the aunties push Mum forward down the stairs, with me following her. The rest of them crowd down behind us, chattering. And this is how we make our big entrance into the little hall downstairs, where my Dad, the uncles and my brothers and cousins are all waiting in their finery.

Dad hugs Mum, and then me, as sincerely – if more carefully, as if I might break – as he did on my graduation day. 'Beautiful, beta,' he whispers this time. 'Be loved, be happy.' It means more than a long flowery speech. My mum and dad love me, they really do; I know it intellectually, but today is the first time I remember feeling it, seeing it. If they've kept me in an invisible cage, it's the only way they've known to care for me and protect me, and now they've got to open that cage door and let me fly.

All of this passes through my mind in an instant, a silent lucid moment as we all take stock– and then it all breaks loose! Everyone finds their voices, gives vent to their opinions on the monkey suits, the dripping diamonds, the scrubs-up-wells, and there's all the rowdiness that makes a wedding a decent Indian wedding. Akash is in charge of the video camera, but it turns out he hasn't got it switched on, so we all have to troop back upstairs and do the big bride and mother-of-the-bride welcome again. Then he has to film us leaving the house, having a few photos on the lawn, and fight over who's going in which car. The neighbours are all standing on their doorsteps wishing us well, and Laly bellows, 'Thank you, Mrs O'Reilly, the little saint man worked, and I'll fetch him back to you tomorrow. I fancy a sunny day tomorrow too.' Mum sends a regal wave in the direction of number 26 and gets a warm smile in return, so much so, I wonder if it's within the realms of possibility that they could become friends…a bit like me and Donald.

We drive across town to the Downfield Hotel. The traffic is slow but even Laly is quiet. It's not the wedding, for me anyway, it's the acknowledgement that this is me leaving them for good. When we return home tonight, it won't be my home anymore. I'll collect my things and go to live in Bradford. The excitement in my belly doesn't quite shrivel and die, but it's hit with such a splash of cold water, I let out a little gasp. Laly keeps looking straight ahead, but she reaches across and takes my hand. She doesn't let go until Dad is indicating into what appears to be a housing estate. We clearly both have a flash of déjà vu at the same time: despite the promise, is this going to be a back street venue, the engagement party all over again? Well, I can't blame anyone. I had every chance to come and check the place out myself and I told Mum to go ahead without me. It was on the impossible list – they were booked up till about the year 2000 – but they'd had a cancellation for the Orangery in the grounds and Mum snapped it up by insisting Dad pay outright in cash.

'They saw us coming,' Laly mutters. 'Again.' Which is only what I'm thinking.

Mum's bat-like hearing kicks in. 'Wait and see,' she says smugly. 'I do things properly.'

Laly raises her eyebrows as we follow signs down a long twisty drive and see a gorgeous, perfectly renovated and tastefully extended house ahead of us.

'Queen Anne,' Mum pipes up. 'Down the side to the left, Dev.'

And we give Mum her moment. Dad parks in a neatly hidden 'VIP' bay at the rear of a huge glass summerhouse ('orangeries,' Mum corrects) and a man in a tuxedo hurries across to open the car doors and welcome us to The Downfield orangery. He leads us, and the approving and gloating family in tow, towards the glass house, where waitresses with silver trays offer drinks and we're led to a front row of garlanded white seats, bunting and flowers, even a dais with the God of Fire in place. The rest of the room is decorated with tables, set for the feast.

It's all just lovely. My excitement bubbles up again.

Mum settles herself importantly and pokes at bits of me: hair, dress, jewellery, until they're sitting to her satisfaction. 'Now all we have to do is wait for the groom,' she says.

I'm winded by a sudden cramp, what if he doesn't come? What if Ravi – or Dukkha – has second thoughts and I'm left stood up in front of five hundred people? That I don't know most of them is cold comfort; the ones I do know will add me to their fabled list of wedding disasters and dine out on me for years. It will be worse than the engagement, much worse. It will...

'Breathe, Anou,' Mum says briskly. 'I know what you're thinking, but the Tilaks are honourable people. They'll be here soon enough. Breathe and look pretty, beta.'

How can someone reassure me and annoy me in the space of one sentence? But it works. Of course Ravi will be here; the fall-out for the Tilaks would be even greater than for us once the news got out. He'd have to go to India to get another decent match... No, no, no, Anoushka. I try and stop this runaway train of thought, too; deciding your groom will marry you because it's too embarrassing not to, is no way to start out.

Akash is prowling the perimeter of the room, getting 'action footage' on the video, with Aditya his shadow, desperate for a go. As they pan past me and my painted smile, I catch Aditya and bribe him with sweets to keep a look out for Ravi and co.

'Well, I will,' he says, 'for the sweets. But you can already see everything out of the windows, silly Anou.'

My little brother is right, although it's hard to pick out any specific person in the milling around. I'm seeing what five hundred guests looks like, and it looks like more than my graduation. Far more than the engagement… Help. I wonder if the drinkers are here and someone is keeping them in hand? That makes me think of Dukkha and the swinging allegation and I give a hiccup of laughter. Mum's head nearly does 360 degrees to see what's going on, and 'Tickly throat,' I mumble. She sends Dad off for some water. She's as nervous as me at this point.

Dad comes back with a proper glass of water – not a paper cup in sight – and news. 'They're here,' he says. 'Ravi is just getting sorted out at the stables, apparently. Five minutes, Anou. Alright?'

I gulp down the water in utter relief. Then I catch on to the detail; Mum's there before me and her eyes are gleaming.

'He's coming in on the white horse, then. Dukkha was very cagey about the entrance, I had to leave it to her. You didn't know?' she asks me – as in, 'If you knew and didn't tell me I'll throttle you, married woman or not.' But my conscience is clear. Like the honeymoon, I'd been happy to leave the groom's arrival to him.

The man in the tux throws open the front doors to the summerhouse. They lead on to a garden area, and it makes the inside outside, if that makes sense. With Mum on my left and Dad on my right, we go forward:

front row to see the groom riding in. It's a Hindu thing, this, the groom arriving to the ceremony on a decorated white horse, his family behind him in a sort of carnival procession. They're called the barati, come to be greeted by the bride's family.

There are oohs and aahs behind us as the Tilaks appear round the corner. There's Ravi, resplendent in red, white and gold, on an elegant horse in matching colours. At a decent distance, the Tilaks, led by Dukkha and Kabir, are equally brightly dressed, and with the blue, blue sky, it's like a little slice of the best of India right here in Edinburgh. Over my shoulder, Laly whistles through her teeth.

'He scrubs up very well,' she says in my ear. 'Look, even the peacocks are out. You didn't need those homing doves, after all.'

And sure enough, the birds belonging to the hotel, left to wander the grounds, are out, two of the males flaunting their intricate blue and green tails. It's all like something you'd watch on the telly and I can't believe I'm part of it. My heart goes out to Ravi, out there with all eyes on him – and I'm glad it's him on show, not me. Glad I don't have to walk down the aisle of a Church like a Scottish bride. His face is set in concentration, and the horse handler is walking very closely, holding the reigns; I gather Ravi isn't a natural horse-rider and it makes it all the more special. The tradition comes from centuries ago, when the groom had to ride for days to reach his bride – an arduous and humbling journey. He's putting a front on, but five minutes up the incline here looks like both things for Ravi.

As Ravi's getting down, the family surging around him to assist, we move back and settle in two separate areas – one for the bride and one for the groom. As Ravi, with Anoop beside him, Dukkha and Kabir on the other side, takes his tea, our family showers them with wedding gifts: the gold rings, jewellery, sarees and fancy shirts. I'm just deciding if I can discreetly nip to the loo, when some tacit sign moves us on to the actual ceremony. I don't really have time to get my head around it. I'm pushed forward, as is Ravi, and we are led in taking our vows in front of a priest I don't know and the God of Fire – the Agni Deva, I should call it. Minutes, I think it's just a few minutes, later, Ravi's father is coming forward, and before God he makes his promise to look after me and love me like a daughter, and to respect me in all things and for all time. Funny that this is the bit I remember clearly; it feels like a safety net in the unknown. It's what dads do, protect.

And after that, we do what Indian weddings are famous for: dance a lot and eat a lot. It's everything that the engagement wasn't, and I keep trying to catch my parents to tell them that, and to thank them, but both are whirling round the floor as if they're twenty-five again. It's good to see. Ravi and I have the odd moment together, swap smiles, but we're each taken up by family, friends, people we've never seen before and may never see again, wishing us well.

I catch Mum's eye as she takes a breather, downing a glass of juice like a seasoned drinker. 'Happy, Mum?' I ask her.

'Anou, I am very happy,' she says. 'Isn't it the perfect wedding, hmm?' She pans the room, taking it all. 'How will we top it for Laly?'

in

Chapter 20

The party pauses to wave off our newly-joined Malhotra-Tilak clan, before the extended families stay to make the most of the hospitality and the long summer evening. In one sense, I'm not sorry to be leaving: my feet hurt, my mouth aches from smiling, and I've got that heavy-head feeling that comes with an intense few hours on show. But another part of me wants the day to go on forever. That realisation I had this morning, knowing it would be the last time I'd get dressed in my bedroom, it's just hit me again like a ten-ton truck. Once I've been back to collect my things, there's no going back. I know people might shrug and ask what's the big deal at my age, I'm not a child being sent away to boarding school or to work in service like the little girls Auntie Sonu keeps in the village near Mumbai, but I've been so sheltered, I've never even spent a night away from home on my own. Not an overnight school trip or uni field-trip, nor a visit to a friend. I'm trying not to panic.

Mum is crying silently in the front, all the exhilaration of a perfect day gone – Laly is kicking the back of the passenger seat and sniffling, and Mum doesn't say a word – while Dad's shoulders are ramrod still, his cautious driving slower than I've ever known it. My brothers have stayed behind with Auntie Deepti, for which I'm glad, as I want this to be a happy day for them. Back at the house, I've no idea how we're going to say goodbye; I dread Dad making a speech, or Mum throwing herself on me in a funeral-pyre sort of way.

In a way, it's Dukkha that saves us. The Tilaks have tail-gated us all the way home, so as we pull on to the drive, their Toyota headlights are right behind us.

When we get out of the car, they get out. Mr Tilak opens the boot and Dad hurries in to get my bags waiting in the hall. Mum so half-heartedly offers tea, I understand she's as keen to get this over with as I am, and when Dukkha declines with a comment about how long the drive ahead is, we all nod our heads. Not even Laly has any smart remarks – truly a first. Poor Ravi looks anguished as he hovers between me, his mother, and the dads doing the fatherly practical tasks.

'I will take good care of Anoushka, Mrs Malhotra,' he blurts out at one stage.

'We all will.' His dad comes up and claps him on the shoulder. 'Madhu, Dev, you need not worry, she will be well looked after.'

'She will never have any complaints from us,' Dukkha chimes in. Then before anyone can respond, my mother-in-law thrusts a brown paper package at me, and says, 'Here, beta, a gift from your new family. Run upstairs and put it on.' She looks round all of us. 'A tradition I began with my oldest daughter-in-law. Each of my son's wives have allowed me to choose the first outfit they wear into my home.'

That almost goads Laly into words – I can see her mouth working – but I surreptitiously shake my head. The wedding is over. Let Dukkha pull rank and dress me in any monstrosity she wants to; it's not like Akash is here with the video camera.

With a quiet, 'Thank you, mama-ji–' I avoid my Mum's gaze as I say that, I accept the parcel and go towards the stairs. Laly and my mum make a move forward to help me, but Dukkha is ahead of them, one hand already on the banister.

'No!' I say. Politeness is one thing, but I draw the line at having Dukkha be the one present when I leave my room for the last time. 'I don't mean to be rude, but I'd like to get changed alone. Please. It's a big moment.'

Nobody can argue with that, or at least I run upstairs before they try, and shut my bedroom door thankfully behind me. I stand there for a minute, just looking around, waiting for a wave of terrified grief to wash over me.

And it doesn't.

With the magic of necessity, I can see the shabby curtains and the saggy single bed, the marks on the wallpaper where I'd hung posters of the Periodic Table and an annually changing study calendar. It needs a makeover, and I'm sure Mum will have Dad start tomorrow. That makes me feel good, rather than sad, it's as things should be. The room belongs to a girl, a student, not a married woman – the phrase sends a frisson through me – and this is my time to move on. Downstairs, my husband is waiting…I hold back a hysterical little giggle. Downstairs, my new improved life is waiting.

'No pain without gain,' I mutter, and with that I rip open Dukkha's parcel, intending to be magnanimous and patient. Instead, the wind is taken completely from my sails. The salwar suit I shake out is pale pink and lace-edged. It's linen, I think, but the tissue paper it's been folded in has kept it crease-free, and the filigree detail is delicate and pretty. Of all the things Dukkha could do to surprise me, this is top of the list. I can't fault her taste or her knowledge of what I'd like, and it would be churlish to worry that the smooth material will hardly survive a three- or four-hour car journey. 'Well, well, mother-in-law,' I say, as I take off the warm silk wedding dress and lay down my necklaces and bangles one by one, leaving the minimum to complement the new outfit.

It's the best start to married life I could possibly expect.

Suddenly I just can't wait.

Part 4
The Honeymoon

Chapter 21

We must be at least twenty miles south of Edinburgh before any of the Tilaks – it's going to take a bit longer than this for me to think of myself as one of them – say a word to me. I don't mind. It's not an uncomfortable silence, and it's punctuated with Dukkha making random observations about the wedding: 'Asma has put on weight again. She blames her thyroid. Hmm' and 'Palo isn't looking well. Apparently, the diagnosis is not good, but they're not saying anything. Pity', accompanied by a lot of tongue clicking and head shaking. She doesn't seem to require an answer and taking my cue from the men in the front – she and I are cocooned in the back but it's a big car and I can legitimately face the window and look as if I'm dozing – I just let the words fall. Ravi and his dad carry on an intermittent conversation that's about the route we're taking and whether Ravi should take over the driving. I let my mind wander back over the day. It's been a good one. A good wedding; the best I could have hoped for given it was the hard work of my mum and Dukkha that carried it off.

'Thank you,' I say suddenly – it's spontaneous enough to surprise even myself and my voice sounds loud in the car; I'm sure Dukkha jumps. I turn to her. 'Thank you, mama-ji, for arranging such a beautiful wedding day. I…I really enjoyed it…' I feel there should be more, but I haven't planned a speech and don't know what should come next.

Dukkha's eyes meet mine with what seems to be equal surprise, but she recovers well and nods graciously. 'You are most welcome, beta,' she says. 'We have only the best for our son – and his bride.'

If that bit sounds like an afterthought, I can forgive her; I'm sure my mum and dad are currently congratulating themselves for giving me such a good send-off, and the thought of Ravi is bringing up the rear. Although maybe not; I've heard Mum say several times that marriage – and particularly marriage to a man like Ravi Tilak – will be the making of me. Me, married. A married woman. It's going to take a lot of getting used to. Starting with tonight, a little voice in my head, one that I've been batting away since we left the hotel, reminds me. I tell myself firmly that I don't need to go there, that we're hours away from Bradford, there's no need to worry about anything yet. But it's no good. The married thing is looming like a spectre. I can't…I mean, I've never…I take a deep breath. Sleeping with a man, with Ravi…Call it what it is, Anoushka, I tell myself, you're a bloody biology graduate – first class. Sex. Sexual intercourse – I make myself think the words – well, I've no idea what to expect. How could I? I'm curious, of course, and I like Ravi but mostly? Mostly I'm so afraid it will be really, like really embarrassing.

I shift uncomfortably in my seat, and fiddle with the seatbelt, realising that Dukkha is still looking at me, a funny little smile playing at her lips. She knows. She knows what I'm thinking. My cheeks flush pink, I can feel the heat, and I'm mortified.

'Oh, Ravi, son,' she says in a sort of singsong voice but still staring at me – and I could die. 'Ravi?'

'Yes, Mum?' He twists awkwardly round to face us, giving me a quick smile, while my face is burning.

'I think,' Dukkha says, looking at him greedily or gloating or something – I can't pinpoint what it is except that it's weird and I brace myself. 'I think that now would be a perfect time for you to tell Anoushka,' she glances over at me again and I let my eyes drop, 'all about your surprise.'

'Surprise?' Not what I'm expecting.

'Well, go on. Ravi.' She gives an impatient jerk of her head and Ravi jumps to attention.

'We won't be going home tonight,' he says. 'We're going to stay in a hotel. That's the first surprise...' I can't think of anything except a pointless echo of, 'Hotel?' to fill the pause but he doesn't seem to notice, just adds importantly, 'And the second is that we're going off on our honeymoon tomorrow.'

'Honeymoon, tomorrow? That's good,' I manage. Is it? I'd thought we were going in a week or two, once we'd settled in together in what Laly started calling 'Tilak Towers' but my brain working at a hundred miles an hour tells me it really doesn't matter either way.

'Yes, it is.' Ravi nods. 'We're flying direct from Manchester. This time tomorrow we'll be in Barbados.'

Now, that does sound good. But–

'Wait. What about my suitcase? I'm not packed for Barbados. All my things have gone to your house.'

Ravi and Dukkha give me eerily matching beams.

'We thought of that,' he says. 'Mum?'

'Yes, we did. Of course.' She sounds as if I'm an idiot to think otherwise. 'We've packed for you.'

'You have?' I can't help myself, adding, 'Who has?'

'Me.' Dukkha raises her eyebrows. 'Your mother and sister helped.'

'Thank goodness.' I relax. 'I mean, great. That's great. Very good of you. Thank you.'

'I almost packed a case for Kabir and me, didn't I, dear?' Dukkha's eyes glint and she gives a tinkling little smile. 'Ravi said you wouldn't mind...'

Please, Mata Rani, no, no, no. Too late, I hope the horror doesn't show. 'Of course not,' I stutter.

There are a few seconds of silence, then Dukkha

says, 'Just my little joke, dear. A honeymoon is a private affair.'

'We'll have many other holidays together, I hope,' I say desperately.

She puts her lips together and smacks them. 'Yes, Yes, we will,' she says.

And that's that, until we see the signs for Manchester Airport.

We're still a good ten miles away from the actual airport when Mr Tilak turns on to a slip road and then a few miles later pulls into the car park of a Travel Lodge. 'What? Have they got shares in those places? It's your wedding night, where's the Radisson or at least a Premier Inn,' I hear in Laly's voice and have to contain a giggle – that dies of its own accord when it occurs to me that my parents-in-law have driven us here, miles from anywhere, and are choosing a parking space with sufficient care to show that they'll be spending the night here too. 'A family room?' That's the echo of Laly again and I have to close my mind to the vision of Dukkha in an adjoining room with a glass between her ear and the flimsy party wall.

'Are we all staying here?' I blurt out.

Dukkha sighs. 'On your wedding night? I don't think so, dear, do you? That would be a slightly strange arrangement, where I come from.'

Thus taking the wind out of my sails again. What do I make of this woman? I look to Ravi, but I don't think he's even noticed the exchange; his Dad is busy ordering him to deal with the bags in the boot.

Entering the foyer of the hotel, Ravi and I are behind Mr and Mrs Tilak, dragging our combined luggage, and I feel like a teenager going on a reluctant family holiday. I wonder if Ravi feels the same, but the question dies on my lips – as I realise that I don't know him well enough to know if I'd be sharing a joke or offending his family. It puts the lid on my rising hysteria, anyway, and I'm subdued as Kabir checks us in, haggles over breakfast – that isn't included but Dukkha says should be – and then leads us to the single lift. When the door opens, it's a capsule, barely big enough for the four of us.

'You don't have to come up with us.' I glance between Mr and Mrs, wishing Ravi had been the one to say this. 'You must want to get to…wherever you're staying,' I peter off lamely.

'Your mother would never forgive us if we don't see you safely in.' Dukkha leaves me unable to argue with that. She grabs my case, shoves Kabir, and makes sure we're all crammed in to the groaning lift. My nose is pressed against Ravi's shoulder and as the lift moves, he jerks away, sniggering like a little boy. For a second I want to slap him – not the ideal feeling to have for your new husband hours into your marriage – because he reminds me of Akash snatching his hand away and giggling when he was told to hold hands with a girl in his P5 school concert. Then I give him the benefit of the doubt; if this is the most uncomfortable thirty seconds of my life, it's probably the same for him.

On the second floor, he and I drag behind again, while Mr Tilak unlocks our bedroom for Dukkha to step in ahead and check it over. We huddle in the doorway while she pokes around, commenting on the wall-mounted TV and fingering the towels. 'They're the same as every Travel Lodge in the country,' I want to yell, but I don't. I'm too busy praying she doesn't make any reference to the double bed that dominates the room.

'We'll be fine now, Mum, Dad.' Ravi catches my eye, and I want to cheer. 'I'm exhausted and I'm sure Anou is, too.' I nod, far too vigorously. 'So, the two of you must be dropping on your feet. You head off now. See you in the morning.'

His words are more than enough to make up for his lift-giggling, especially because his parents meekly agree and with a final hug (for him) and matching pats on the shoulder (me) they disappear off like lambs.

I rearrange the obstacle course that's our luggage, Ravi locks the door behind them, and with that, for the first time ever, we're properly alone.

Chapter 22

'What do you want to do first?' he asks. 'How do you usually do it?'

'What?' Now, I'm all for being direct but it's our wedding night, a bit of romance wouldn't go amiss–

'Unpacking.' Ravi gestures to the over-large suitcases and it fleetingly crosses my mind to wonder what on earth is in mine, before I go back to being mightily relieved he interrupted before I could announce that I didn't usually do it; I'd never done it; and why else had he made a play for an Indian bride-to-order? 'I usually just take out and hang up the things I need for the night, when it's one night and I'm travelling on – you know, on other holidays or business. But if you'd rather unpack everything, there's plenty of hangers, I'm sure. We can ask housekeeping for more…' He turns away to open the clothes cupboard. 'Plenty of hangers,' comes his muffled voice, 'and an iron. Do you want to iron something?' When I don't answer immediately – I haven't even had time to draw breath, let alone work out what to say; Ravi always looks well turned-out but this level of…of care isn't something I imagined – he shuts the wardrobe and moves to the bathroom. 'Lots of little toiletries here,' he calls. 'There's soap, too–'

'I'm fine with doing what you do,' I get in before he can give me a run-down of spare toilet rolls and, oh help, those little bags to put sanitary towels in. 'I'll make a start.' I haul my case onto the narrow sofa under the window.

'Right. Right.' His head pops back. 'Good. Then I'll er…'He clears his throat. 'That is, if you don't mind…'

'Mind?' I'm trying to balance my teetering case,

vaguely irritated that he's not bounded across the room to help me. 'Mind what?' I look up and he's pulling an agonised face. What the hell does he want to do? Run after his mum and dad for a night-night kiss? Ask me to unpack for him too? I mean, should I? I want to be a good wife but more in the supportive, loving kind of way, not sorting his laundry for the next forty years.

'It's just that, I need to…use the bathroom,' he mumbles.

I laugh out loud, I can't help it. He grins back, sheepishly. 'Oh, Ravi,' I say, 'you're going to be using the bathroom millions of times in this marriage, so am I. Let's get the first time over and not make it a weird thing. Go on. I'll go right after you.'

'Er…okay.' He looks slightly nonplussed but disappears, with a snap of the bathroom lock, and obviously turns both taps on full pelt.

'Hey, Ravi?' I yell. 'Do you want me to unpack for you?'

The rushing water calms a bit. 'No! No – I wouldn't dream of it,' comes back.

'Good question. Good answer,' I mutter to myself, pleased that the first – I look at my watch – ten minutes of husband and wife alone-time has shown us both in a decent light. The fact that his nerves are so strung out, that the suave Ravi, Prince of the nightly telephone calls, is worried about me hearing him in the loo, gives me confidence and with it an upper hand. And – 'I'll need it,' I mutter some more as I pull the zip and rifle through the outfits my Mum, my sister and my new mother-in-law find appropriate for my honeymoon. I say that, but this…this selection has to be all Dukkha. Half of it I don't recognise: loose linen tops and drawstring trousers in cement and muddy grout colours and a couple of pairs of orthopaedic-looking sandals that say Dr Scholl on the soles – surely they went out when I was a kid? I'm not much like a clotheshorse, but even I can see how drab and middle-aged I'll look wearing them. Where the hell was Laly in this? There's some of my summer things at the bottom: a long red wrap-over skirt I like and snuggled inside, some jeans and a silky tunic – now that's Laly's hand because Mum hates me wearing jeans and Dukkha would probably faint at the thought.

There's a note tucked into the lining of the case, my name on it in spidery handwriting: Anoushka, beta, your Scottish clothes won't do in the Caribbean, will they? I've chosen some new ones for you. Look nice for Ravi. I will expect photographs! Mama-ji.

Did she go out and buy them, or are they actually hers, I wonder. I mean, she has a point, most of my stuff is good for an Edinburgh summer i.e. warm and woolly, and the times we've been in India, we just buy things there, but I'd had half a mind to go shopping between the wedding and the honeymoon. Ravi said Leeds is really good for shops and he would come with me. Maybe I can get something in the airport in the morning. And meanwhile, I shake out my faded tartan pyjamas, these are what I'll be wearing tonight. I decide to find it funny and work out how I'll make a joke of it to Ravi. When he emerges from the bathroom; I might think he's avoiding me – if he wasn't a man at the start of his honeymoon. Maybe he's prettifying, I think. Let's hope Dukkha didn't do his packing too, or he'll probably be in Superman jammies and a grandad dressing gown.

I'm hanging up the least offensive beige trousers and my silky top – I won't look terrible on the flight, especially if we're in first class, as Ravi hinted all those weeks ago when I randomly picked Barbados – and can't help letting out the largest yawn, when, of course, he reappears. I clap my hand over my mouth, but I can't hide it, and that thing happens to him – he takes one look and falls into a sympathy yawn. When we can, we smile at each other. Then he takes my hand.

'Come, Anou. Let's talk for a minute.'

Actually, I'm desperate for a pee now, but for all my bravado, I can't go through the whole bathroom rigmarole again, so I squeeze my pelvic floor and join him on the end of the bed.

'It's midnight and our flight is at 11am,' he says. 'We are both tired, yes? I think we should er…start our honeymoon er…activities tomorrow night. Do you agree?'

I look around the nondescript room with the scuffed skirting boards and then ease my shoulders, stiff with the tension of the day. I can't pretend this isn't a relief. Who wouldn't like to start their honeymoon proper in a fancy hotel with a view of the sea, rather than a budget room over-looking the car park?

Ravi's looking at me anxiously.

I squeeze his hand. 'That's a great idea. Very thoughtful,' I tell him.

'I'm glad.' He lets go of my hand and stands up. 'I like to get some air before bed, so I'll leave you to get your night-clothes on and tucked in. I'll be back in ten minutes – is that long enough?'

'Plenty. Don't forget to take the spare key card.' I bite my lip; I sound like a wife already.

'Of course. Right, I'll give you some privacy.' He leans over and kisses me quickly on the cheek and is out of the door as if I might start undressing right away.

I look at the tartan pjs fondly; anything else would have been really uncomfortable tonight. Then I jump to attention: within about three minutes, I'm changed, my teeth are brushed, and I'm in under the covers, clinging to the far side near the window. I've shared out the pillows equally and made sure the lamp on the other side – Ravi's side – is lit. Then I roll onto my side, away from the door, and practise how he should find me when he comes back: propped up, reading or watching TV? No, that would suggest I'm waiting for him. Do I sit up to wait till he climbs in beside me, then sit up for a chat? But what would we talk about. The easiest thing is just to feign sleep, but I don't want to seem rude. Honestly, why hasn't someone written a rule book for this; The Indian Guide to Wedding Night Etiquette would be a guaranteed bestseller. And I can already think of half a dozen spin-offs: Honeymoon, Living with the In-Laws…

It's more than ten minutes, now, surely. I'm just planning how long I should wait before I go looking, or at least phone reception, when there's a noise outside and door eases open. I freeze, close my eyes – and wait. Rustling. Bathroom door closing. Silence. Bathroom door opening. More rustling. Then the light goes out and the bed cover is lifted slightly as he creeps into the other side of the bed. I can sense him trying not to wriggle because it's what I'm doing too.

'Anou?' he whispers across the great divide between us.

'Yes?' I whisper back.

'Goodnight.'

'Goodnight, Ravi.'

I'm fairly sure we both lie there wide awake and unmoving until the early hours.

I must sleep at some point because when I wake it's properly light and Ravi isn't there. The shower's running so I figure he's got up so as not to face any, 'After you, no, after you,' conversations. I get up, too, checking in the mirror that I don't look a total fright, when he bounds out of the bathroom, fully dressed and all his confidence returned.

'Need anything ironing?' are his first words, indicating the board pulled out from the cupboard. 'I've done mine. I can do your outfit while you're washing.'

'Okay, thank you.' I nod. I wonder if I should go over for a morning kiss, but I'm not sure of my breath, so when Ravi shrinks back to let me through to the bathroom, I scuttle past. It seems funny to think that in a few days or weeks we'll be as used to each other as I am with Laly or my brothers. Right now, it's awkward. I don't know why I thought that would magically melt away with a marriage licence.

I'm out of the shower and drying myself when I hear Ravi shout my name.

'Nearly ready,' I call back.

'I'm going down to breakfast,' he says through the door. 'I'll see you in the restaurant, okay?'

'Okay…' I echo in the wake of the accompanying slam. He's left my clothes across the ironing board and to be honest, I've never seen anything so crease-free, ever. I put them on, and then sort out my hair: up or down? I leave it down for now, I can tie it out of my way on the flight if I want to. I'm just grabbing my bag when there's a knock at the door, which I open with a big smile, expecting it to be either housekeeping or Ravi back to take me to breakfast. It's neither.

It's Dukkha, large as life and grinning all knowingly at me. You know nothing, flits across my mind – and gives me great satisfaction as it does so. I muster enough courage to say, 'Good morning! Thank you for coming to get me. Ravi's gone ahead – with his dad, I expect? Did you have a nice evening?' And all the while I'm saying it, I'm locking the door behind me and marching along the corridor. I ignore the lift and take the stairs. That stops her in her tracks. The mole at her mouth wobbles as she trots along behind me. I smile determinedly and stay just ahead enough to hold the restaurant door open for her. 'After you, mama-ji,' I say sweetly.

My mother-in-law can't fault me as she stalks over to the table for four where Ravi and Kabir are already drinking orange juice and eating toast. Kabir, his mouth full, gives me a half wave, and Ravi manages a lopsided smile. Nobody says anything for a few minutes as we eat the frankly disappointing breakfast, then as we're all staring into our coffee cups, Dukkha says loudly,

'Well, did you have a good night? Did everything work alright?'

Ravi and I avoid each other's eyes and both nod like naughty school children, caught out in something a bit silly. It is on the tip of my tongue to turn around and say that they might as well have stayed; nothing happened, but of course I don't. I smile determinedly and remind myself that a few hours from now I'll be on a gorgeous beach with my gorgeous new husband – the perfect gentleman, whatever his mother is – and we'll work on getting our gorgeous marriage off to a fine start.

Chapter 23

I don't think I'm a high maintenance kind of person –
someone like Laly, or maybe Donald would laugh if
you suggested it – but my resolve is tested over the
next twenty-four hours. First of all, Ravi's parents
delay us so long this side of the security gate with
stupid travel tips and warnings and stuff that we have
to rush straight to the departure gate, and I don't get to
do any shopping. Then the plane isn't even boarding. It
turns out that Ravi likes to be early for his flights; for
someone who travels so much for work, he's incredibly
nervous. It must be the whole honeymoon thing again,
so I don't say a word, just sit on the plastic orange
chairs for far too long, waiting. When it occurs to me
we should be in the business class lounge, Ravi
explains that we're flying economy, after all. When he
changed the honeymoon dates to surprise me and to fit
better with his time off, it was all he could get. I'm
disappointed but don't show it; we'll get there all the
same, and it's not like I've ever travelled anything but
economy to India. But I was looking forward to the
pampering and honeymoon special-ness beginning.

'Did you have to change the hotel too?' I figure I'd
better manage my expectations, just in case.

'Oh, no,' he assures me. 'Everything else stays the
same. And where we sit on the plane doesn't really
matter, does it? As long as the seats are together.'

He's right, of course, and I tell myself to stop being
ungrateful. I mean, we're going to Barbados;
Sharmila's best friend got St Andrews for the weekend.
My mum and dad didn't have a honeymoon at all.
However, Ravi's words come to nothing when we
finally board the plane (two hours late), and I turn to

him expecting we'll talk to find him already looking at the TV screen ahead.

'If you don't mind, I'd like to watch the film,' he says. 'But only if you don't mind.'

'Of course, I don't.' I sigh and watch it with him but it's all James Bond and action and I can never keep up with the plot of those things. I've got a book to read, a Marian Keyes book that Laly says is hilarious and clever, but I'm so used to having to study I can't get going with it. When I find myself wishing I still had some revision to do, I take out the in-flight magazine and read that from cover to cover to make a point to myself. Then I start the novel, and I'm just getting into it when my tray-table has to come down for lunch. Ours comes first because it's the vegan option, which means limp blobs that were once roasted vegetables and some brown rice. I can live with that, as I know airline food, back here in the plane, isn't gourmet ever, but the dessert is an orange and the 'treat' a mini box of raisins. When the woman on the other side of me finally gets served with some sort of trifle-thing and a single chocolate in a box, the stewardess must see the gluttony in my eyes as she offers me both. I hesitate but shake my head; I don't want to offend Ravi. He's glued to the car chase on-screen, eating his raisins – and mine; I don't want them – one by one and dutifully peeling his orange but even if he's open to not being a hundred per cent vegan, I don't want to look as if I'm complaining about the travel arrangements he's made. Mind you, when tea comes round later and it's a lentil spread and a bread roll with more raisins, I'm all ready to grab the standard cheese toastie and blueberry muffin but it's a different stewardess and this one apologies for potential cross-contamination.

I'm not at my best then, grumpy and hungry, when the film show comes to an end an hour before landing and Ravi decides he wants to talk. Luckily, as long as I smile and nod in the right places he's happy. It's something I'm good at, having lived with Mum for all these years but I'm a bit disgruntled I'm already doing it with my husband. But this doesn't really count, does it, I convince myself, like we agreed last night, we start the honeymoon in Barbados; long-haul flights are just something to get through as best you can. Anyway, the woman on the other side of me is drinking it in. Ravi's talking about the price of the honeymoon, how it cost him an arm and a leg, 'Four figures, Anou,' he says. 'Only the best. A five-star hotel and a private transfer. It's a shame about losing the business class flights but maybe we can upgrade to those on the way home. This is going to be a trip of a lifetime.'

I hope so, I think, as long as it's for all the right reasons. As the cabin lights are dimmed, I find myself unexpectedly nervous. 'I've never been abroad before without my mum and dad,' I confess to him. 'And then only to India where it's all family all the time.'

Ravi likes that, I can see. He pats my hand and promises to look after me. 'Knowing what's what does take practise,' he says. 'That's what husbands are for.'

It's the middle of the night when we finally disembark. It's a warm, balmy night, and sort of moist-hot as we wait for our passports to be stamped. It does remind me a bit of arriving in Mumbai, but this airport is small and relaxed, there are no clamouring crowds. I expect us to head for a taxi rank, but Ravi points at a woman with a sign saying Masood Holidays, and she points us to a cluster of buses. The drivers are hanging in a group, smoking, not rude but not friendly; indifferent. One of them looks at our papers and nods at Ravi to throw our cases onto the roof-rack of a rundown minibus, and ushers me inside to a torn seat and windows that are jammed open.

'Are you sure this is it?' I whisper to Ravi – it's not screaming four figure amounts, and I don't want him to be cheated out of his hard-earned salary; airports are notorious for scams, even I know that. But he shrugs.

'It's authentic,' he says after a minute. 'Not everything will be the same as at home, you know.'

'I know that.' I'm stung but I don't want to appear unsophisticated and naïve. 'It's an adventure,' I add in a jolly voice, that goes somewhat off the rails as the minibus takes off with a jerk and bumps through an obstacle course of potholes. 'Oof. Ow.' I try not to grunt as I'm launched almost into Ravi's lap, and he has to grab me to stop himself falling into the aisle. The absurdity makes us both laugh, and by the time the hair-raising ride has come to a squealing halt, it's really broken the ice between us.

It's just as well because the beachfront luxury hotel in which we're supposed to have the palatial honeymoon suite, is a dump, a crumbling two-star guesthouse at best. Ravi takes on the monotoned driver but he's adamant we're in the right place.

'Don't worry, I'll sort it out. Wait here.' Ravi rushes alone into the reception, leaving me on the smelly pavement, wondering where the beach belonging to this 'beach front' hotel could be. I'm not venturing into any dark corners to find out. We seem to be in the middle of nowhere, there's not a soul about, just rustling trees and what sounds like a bull frog. There's a vague whomp-bump, swish sound that I can't quite make out but is hypnotic if I tune in. It must be a mistake, I convince myself, eyeing up the minibus driver, who's sitting on the kerb, sucking yet another cigarette. He's probably trying it on, like they do in Indian tourist resorts – you'd want to hear Auntie Sonu on this scourge (her word) – when taxi drivers insist your booked hotel or restaurant is no good, but their brother or cousin has a far better place. You can argue till a buddha turns blue but get in their car and you'll end up at their brother's place.

The driver catches my eye and offers me a cigarette. When I shake my head, he passes over a tube of mints instead, and mimes that I should take the packet.

'Thank you,' I say. I'm hungry. Hangry, as they say.

'Welcome,' he replies. Then, 'First time on our island?'

'Yes. We're on our honeymoon…' Why did I say that?

But he just nods slowly and indicates the hotel. 'So why you staying here, then?'

So, he's not being a chancer, after all. 'I think it's a mistake. I think, I hope, my husband is sorting it out.'

He's gone ages; I don't know if that's good or bad. When Ravi finally emerges, he's running his hand through his hair in a harassed way. 'There's some kind of mix-up,' he announces. 'It seems we are booked in here, not in the place I chose. Nobody seems to be able to explain it. I suggest we spend the night,' he glances at his watch grumpily, 'or what's left of it here, and sort it out in the morning. I'll get on to the travel agent first thing. Sorry, Anou.'

'It's okay.' What else can I say? 'As long it's clean…ish.' Just in case.

Ravi's face brightens. 'Oh, it's clean. They showed me. And there's a TV and a terrace with a little garden. They said they'll bring us breakfast there.'

I'm about to ask who 'they ' are, when a girl about my age appears in the doorway. She's wearing cut-off shorts and a sweater and has the best long braids I've ever seen.

'You must be exhausted, Miss Anoushka,' she says cheerily. 'Your husband explained you're just married and have travelled day and night. Welcome. We're not splendid but we have a beautiful beach house for you and the warmest welcome on the island. Come.'

It takes her all of that ten second speech to win me over. She has the driver deal with the bags, Ravi loaded up with two tall glasses of deep red juice and is weaving around the side of the falling-down hotel building and across a sandy square that might be a bar area at other times of day. Then, through a lopsided wooden gate – is the beach. And farther out, slapping on the sand and a narrow line of rocks, is the sea: the curious whomp-bump-swish I heard earlier. It's lit by four very faint lamps, each coming from the porch of a squat square hut.

'Here is your home, Bungalow 2,' the girl says, taking the key from the lock and handing it to me. 'No air-con, no bathtub, no electricity – just TV hook-up – but everything else you could need for your romantic getaway.'

She beckons me in, and it is quaint, in a rustic way. It's like one of those beach huts along the sea front in English holiday resorts – they have brightly painted doors and jolly sea-faring names and cost about twenty thousand pounds – with a toilet tacked on the back and an outdoor but enclosed shower. It could be much worse.

'Stop!' commands the girl, addressing the driver who's about to drop my bag onto the end of one of the beds – one of the single beds. 'Leave those at the door and help me move this furniture, man. We need to make up a double bed for our honeymooners.'

My face, and I bet my whole body, blushes scarlet, and I look everywhere except at Ravi, but nobody else seems remotely discomforted. The three of them heft and heave and shove the beds together. The girl stands back, hands on her hips, and surveys the result. 'Not ideal but who needs a bed when you have the beach and the ocean, hey?' She looks between the rest of us, with a shrug and a smile, until I feel I might die of embarrassment. While Ravi goes outside with the driver and sorts the tip, the girl fiddles with the bulky TV and manages to get a picture on the screen – the kind with buzzy snowy interludes that's the result of an old-fashioned aerial – and flicks through half a dozen blaring channels to a David Attenborough documentary – the one we watched at home before the marriage match. I reach for one of the pink fruit drinks Ravi's left on the table and take a big gulp, and another, before I realise there might be fruit juice in there somewhere, but it's laced with a lot of alcohol. I cough, as the taste hits the back of my throat, and then down the rest. What the hell.

'Rum. With pomegranate and cranberry,' the girl says. 'Our speciality. Take it slowly, until you've acclimatised.' She crouches down and pulls back a frilly, under counter curtain. 'Bottled water here. Don't dehydrate.'

'Thank you,' I say faintly, suddenly totally overcome – by her motherliness, the travelling or the rum, I'm not sure which.

She sees it. 'Sleep. And I, personally, will bring you a full and hearty island breakfast tomorrow at noon. Then I will help you unpack your bags and show you the shaded swimming spots and the best fish shack along the shore.'

'But…' It would be churlish to point out that we'll be leaving for the correct hotel in the morning; she's too nice. 'Thank you,' I say again.

'Good night, Miss Anoushka,' she says. 'If you need anything, send that man of yours to tell me.' She winks.

'I will. And call me Anoushka, not Miss, please.'

She waves a hand over her shoulder as she goes to

leave. 'I'm Darina. Sleep the sleep of the good, Anoushka.'

I see her have a quick word with Ravi, who saunters back over a few minutes later. 'Alright for now,' he says rather than asks, but I nod. It is nice, not five star, but nice. And I just want to lay my head anywhere; the alcohol has gone straight to it. I really hope Ravi doesn't want to –

'Let's rest,' Ravi says, as if he reads my mind. 'Sleep. Breakfast. Talk.' He pulls me into a warm but brief hug. 'What's another day? Our honeymoon can start tomorrow.'

That makes us both laugh. For the second night of my married life, I pull out my tartan jammies – far too hot but I'm shy about sleeping in just the top and my knickers under a single sheet – and get ready for bed. Tonight, though, there's no anxiety over how to sleep and what to say or do. I know I'll be asleep before Ravi's even stopped watching David Attenborough and the penguins.

Chapter 24

In the morning, I sense Ravi getting up and moving about, but it's too early for me to care about what's he's actually doing. It's going to take a while to get used to sleeping in the same bed as him and wake up with him. I've only ever shared a bed with Laly before, sometimes Sharmila too, or my mum when I was little. Snoring, wriggling, farting or drooling, I wonder what he'll do? I was too drunk on my single cocktail to take stock last night. Laly says I talk in my sleep; mostly mumbling but that once I sat straight up and said, 'It's the double helix.' I've no recollection if I did, or why I'd say that.

After a while, I hear the door creak open and then close, and then he's whistling as his footsteps disappear into the sand. I sneak a look at my watch and it's only 8am and very quiet so I decide to have another ten minutes, then get up and have a good look at the sea before we leave. My stomach rumbles and I hope Darina's noon breakfast is negotiable.

The next thing I know, Ravi's hand is on my shoulder, and he's saying, 'Wake up, sleepyhead. Come and eat.'

'Huh?' I blink him into focus and try to untangle my hair from my face. Not the movie-type newly-wed moment you'd want on a Caribbean island.

Ravi laughs. 'Darina has set up breakfast outside. Hurry up.' Rather than a lingering morning kiss, he gives me the kind of brotherly peck I'd expect from Akash and bounds out of the room. Just as well, as I've kicked off my pyjama bottoms in the night and I'm not ready for him to see that without planning it.

It is the breakfast fit for a King, the equivalent of a

full Scottish fry-up, a Continental bakery and an Indian Auntie; the table is groaning, even though Ravi has clearly been tucking in (I see he's full dairy yoghurt, goats cheese and butter, so I say nothing and follow his lead, kicking myself for being too polite yesterday) and it all looks heavenly.

'I didn't know what you like best for breakfast, so I told Darina to bring everything,' he says as I pull out my chair and sit opposite him.

I don't care if I look greedy or, as my mother – and I'm sure Ravi's – would say, unladylike, I pile up my plate and guzzle (after sniffing it first and taking a cautious sip) pure orange juice.

Ravi clears his throat importantly. 'I've been thinking,' he says, 'that we should just stay here for our remaining six days. Look, the view is picture-perfect, yes? The accommodation is comfortable and unusual, and Anou, we can have all the ordinary five-star luxury hotels you want in our married life. Maybe Dubai? Or Monte Carlo.' He drifts off for a second, as if he's picturing lavish villas and butlers in the company of a sheikh or two.

'Yes?' I prompt him eventually, taking the opportunity to spear some more pineapple and what looks like a savoury cheese dumpling but is actually filled with sweet cream.

'There are two restaurants along the beach that don't look up to much from the outside but have fabulous reputations to those in the know.' He looks pleased to be one of them – like Laly did when she brought that Child of Prague statue to me and Mum. But less ironically. 'And the staff here are the same. Scruffy, maybe and,' he lowers his voice, 'Darina was wearing a bikini when she brought our breakfast, but she and her brother are efficient and attentive.'

'Friendly,' I mutter, through crumbs.

'Hmm?'

'Darina is friendly and very pretty,' I say more clearly. 'I like her casual clothes. It's hot, Ravi.'

'Well, yes, but she's…'

'She's what?' I wait to hear exactly how he's going to say what he's going to say.

He looks uncomfortable but to give him his due he doesn't wimp out. 'She's fat, Anou. She jiggles. I'm not used to it.'

The face he pulls makes me laugh. 'I shouldn't think she cares what you think, Ravi,' I remind him. 'And she's not fat, she's just curvy. Well, curvier than me. I'd look awful in a bikini because I don't jiggle.'

'Well, I like slim women, and I like them covered up,' he says primly.

Which translates as, I don't like my manhood threatened by strong, confident women. Him and half the men I know; I expect my dad would slap Ravi on his back for his moral stance. Maybe I should challenge this attitude right now but I'm not Laly, I'm more for the softly softly approach.

'Of course, you are lovely, Anou,' he adds somewhat hurriedly.

'So are you, Ravi.' I let him off the hook. 'Anyway, you're saying we should stay here? Not move?'

'Well, yes, I am. But it's up to you totally. It's not a problem to contact the travel agent. We can re-pack–'

'Re-pack?'

He's discomforted again. 'Yeah. I, well, I woke early and thought it was nice here and we don't have long and moving to the Hilton will take another day. I should have asked you, but I'm used to just making decisions…'

'It's alright, Ravi.' Because it is. I feel relaxed for the first time since, I don't know, before the wedding, probably before my graduation. And we're only away for a week, all-in, Ravi couldn't get longer away from the office because of some big trial they're all involved in preparing for. He's taking depositions and gathering evidence next week and it seems like it's a big deal for his promotion prospects because most of the lawyers don't want to work in August. 'I don't want to move either. All's well that ends well. Are you sure the room – bungalow, I mean – we're in is free all week? And that the other hotel, the Hilton, you said, is fine about it? You should get some money back, at least.'

'What?' He dismisses all of that with a quick head shake. 'Oh, yes, that's all no problem.'

'Then we're all set.' I push my plate away, regretful but sure I can't manage any more – until tomorrow. Hopefully lavish breakfasts aren't Darina's way of placating lost and possibly litigious overnighters. 'Did you mention you're a lawyer?' I ask.

'Why would I do that?' Ravi appears genuinely surprised.

'No reason.' Folding my napkin, I gesture along the coastline where the water is catching the sunlight and sparkling like a diamond cluster. 'Can we go for a walk? It looks lovely right here but what if there's a building site next door or a line of Club 18-30 nightclubs?' Laly would love either, me not so much.

'There isn't,' Ravi says. 'And yes, we can, but look, Anou, there's one more thing.'

'Go on?'

'I know it's our honeymoon and we'll do lots of things together and have a great time, but there's this one thing I really want to do.' He's bubbling with enthusiasm suddenly. 'I've wanted to do it since Anoop tried it, and a few of the guys from the office. It's a sort of rite of passage in the firm and the further away and the more exotic the better. This could get me a lot of Brownie points, Anou.' He takes a deep breath and turns puppy-dog eyes on me. 'What do you think?'

'About what?' My mind boggles.

'Huh?'

'Ravi, you need to tell me what it is you want us to do!'

'Oh. I'm an idiot.' He slaps his forehead, dislodging his sunglasses, and has to catch them before they drop into the remains of his eggs. 'Diving School. Advanced PADI certification. This is the perfect place. Matteo – that's Darina's brother – was going out this morning with all his gear and we got talking.'

'Diving?' I'm not even a strong swimmer. 'Ravi, I'm not sure that's for me. I mean, I'll give things a shot, but I'll hold you back. I didn't know you were a diver. We've so many things to learn about each other, hey?'

About ten different emotions cross his face. 'No, no, sorry, I'm not…When I say, diving, I mean me. That is, both of us, of course, but if it's not your thing, if you'd rather go shopping or read a book or…or make jewellery, then just me. It's a few hours a day but we'll have the evenings.'

Make jewellery? Random. It's occurring to me that it's going to be a while before I understand Ravi's thought processes. He does do a lot of blurting out when he's nervous or excited. I pick through what he's said, considering it – and letting him know I'm considering it. I'm not stupid. The 'both of us' isn't an option, this is something that Ravi alone wants to do, and I could wager a guess, will do whether I throw a tantrum and play the honeymoon card or not. If I disagree and he gives in, he'll probably be a martyred sulk (living with Laly and my mother has made me party to the finer points of passive and not-so-passive aggression) all week.

'Can I do whatever I want while you're diving?' I

say.

'Yes, of course–' His smile turns into a frown. 'Like what?'

Wander around jiggling in a skimpy bikini, is on the tip of my tongue, but I resist. 'Oh, I don't know, but I might want to go out and see things. And, well,' I'm not sure how to phrase this because it is a bone of contention, but I've shoved it to one side, 'I haven't got much money, Ravi,' I say in a rush. 'We've not really talked about it yet, and I don't want to presume, but I've been too busy studying to earn anything, and Mum and Dad spent a lot on the wedding and the dowry, so they assume...you know.' That you, my new husband, will take care of me financially, as well as in all other ways, is the unsaid; I'm not sure why I'm bothered about saying it aloud.

Ravi's face clears. 'Anou, why would you even ask? What's mine is yours. My money is your money. My home is yours. My father promised you, remember? Here–' He stands up and roots in the pocket of his long khaki shorts, pulling out a wallet. It's stuffed with a wad of notes, half of which he holds out to me. 'Take this. I can get more.'

'Stop.' I flap the money back at him, but I'm laughing, relieved. 'I don't need it now, I just thought I'd better bring it up. I might be happy lazing around here, reading and swimming, but I might not. That's all.'

'Then...?' His eyes light up.

'Of course you should do your Advanced PADI certificate and impress all your colleagues,' I say. And I'm not just being nice. This marriage lark is exhausting; we've only had breakfast and I'm worn out from the conversation. 'I'm going to rest and feed my inner hermit,' I tell him. 'I want to be married, Ravi, but I'm used to being alone. I like it. And I don't much like the idea of diving myself.'

He leans in and drops a sloppy wet kiss on my forehead, and hand in hand, we take a few steps towards the vast, empty beach.

There's just one thing that might rankle–

'The diving school, Ravi. Had you planned it all along? Is that why we came here – to Barbados, I mean?' I try to sound neutral rather than suspicious.

He gives a hearty laugh, picks me up under the shoulders, and swings me around in a wide circle. 'Don't be a silly goose, Anou. Of course not. It's just the icing on the cake of the best honeymoon with the best wife ever. Wait till I tell everyone all about it.'

It's not the honeymoon I envisaged, but as these things go, I think it's up there with the good ones. At least by mine and Ravi's standards – and nothing else really matters, does it? Not what Dukkha or my mother, or Laly thinks. For five more days – the length it takes to get the PADI qualification; in the end not the advanced version as that would take longer, Ravi says, so he's looking on this as a refresher – we have an early breakfast together, then he goes off with Matteo in a battered old jeep, and I walk along the edge of the water and watch the jewellery makers (now it makes sense) and the artists set up their stands on the sand. It turns out we're at the tip of the island, the quietest part and there's some sort of creative colony or retreat a little way along. Occasionally, I stumble into their morning or evening meditation, which the leader always invites me to join, and I always respond with a vague Namaste greeting, and once a game of volleyball, but mostly it's just me and individual fishermen, gutting their catches on the rocks. For the rest of the day, I read and doze in a hammock under the trees, swim when I'm hot, and talk to Darina

whenever she's passing. It's my own retreat, I suppose
– and I hadn't realised how much I needed it. I've
studied and helped out at home and done all the
family activities and cultural stuff demanded of me for
so long – not to mention the match, engagement and
wedding, that I've forgotten how nice space is, how
caged in I've been. I'm not going to do it again, I think.
Freedom is intoxicating.

'You want a massage, girl?' Darina asks me one day.
She's brought her lunch of fish and pineapple (not
together) out to eat, an extra plate for me. 'I know a
good masseur.' She wriggles her shoulders. 'Can she
get those knots out or what.'

'No, thank you,' I say. 'I don't like people touching
me. I never know what to do or say so I don't relax,
and it defeats the object. I'm happy, honestly.'

'Sure? Then I'm happy.'

But she doesn't believe me, I can tell by the way she
looks at me, dying to ask why Ravi and I aren't
wrapped around each other all day and night, barely
with eyes for anyone else. I've told her how our
marriage has been arranged and that we're taking it
slow, getting to know each other, but can see her
holding in even more questions. The big one of course
is whether we've slept together yet, and the truth is, we
haven't. We haven't even tried and even though it's a
mutual decision, I'm not actually sure how I feel about
it. I'd come out here expecting Ravi to be jumping on
me morning, noon and night; assuming there would be
pain and messiness; praying for some tenderness; and
hoping that I could translate my quite theoretical
desire for him into something real. Deep down, the
truth is that I hadn't – haven't – a clue what to expect.

Ravi came back from that first dive session all
macho and pumped up and spilling adrenaline. We
had a lovely fish dinner along the beach, and walking

back had our first real, long kiss. I was ready to take it further when we got back to the room, and I could feel that Ravi was, but he hopped straight into the outdoor shower. When he came out, wrapped in a towel and still glistening wet, I braced myself for him to make his move and I was determined to go along with him, do whatever he instructed. After all, it's not like he would expect me to have any experience. I have to admit, too, that a bit of me just wanted to get the first time over with.

Instead, he sat down beside me and took my hands and told me that now he had me, he would never ever let me go, and that we had all our lives to get to know each other. 'I don't want to rush you, Anou, you know – in bed – I know it's a big thing for a woman,' he said so earnestly I wondered if he'd practised the speech in advance. 'I want it to be right, to be perfect. I want to perform well and for you to be happy. I want to worship your body, Anou.'

I didn't like to interrupt him to say I don't want to be worshipped, just loved, he was so in his stride talking about honour and respect and sanctity of the act of love. Half of me was – is – touched, the other half of me thought – thinks – he is. I was relieved when he finished up with, 'And it's probably not a good idea to over-tax my body, you know with the stress of the diving.'

So, the upshot is, lovemaking is something we're saving until we get home and can take our time at. 'Weeks, months, years, if we need it,' Ravi said. Well, yes, I thought, but even my BSc only took four years and that was going at it full time. I couldn't – can't – work out yet if Ravi is an extraordinarily thoughtful man or just as scared as me of having our first sex as a married couple. Probably both.

But I'm not sharing any of this with Darina, or

anyone else for that matter.

What I do say is, 'I'm so glad we ended up here, that we didn't move to the right hotel. That travel agent really did us a favour, even though I didn't think so at the time...' I put my hand over my mouth as soon as the words are out. No wonder Darina is looking at me oddly, I've just totally dissed her hotel when I meant it as a compliment. Shit. Shit. I try to explain, but she just sucks pineapple juice off her fingers and waves my apologies away.

'Anoushka, we are not everyone's cup of tea but if you like us, you like us. And you, girl, like us. I know it. Your husband did you both a favour.' She narrows her eyes. 'Just you make sure he keeps doing you favours, alright? And if you need to, you arrange them.'

'Oh, I will.' I laugh. I'm pleased that because of staying here and Ravi's diving, I've made a new friend, my first one since Donald.

She nods at me. 'You'll do, girl. You'll do.'

I don't say anything, but I know she'd approve of the PhD part of my marriage plans.

Part 5
The Marriage

Chapter 25

Sexual intercourse or no sexual intercourse, on the plane going home, I think about how far we've come in a few days. We know each other better in lots of silly little ways: he sleeps without pillows, I like two; he drinks milky coffee loaded with sugar, mine is black; our TV tastes are way apart; at heart he's no more vegan than I am. Ravi has some strange habits too – he probably would say the same about me but I'm not asking him – like painting his finger nails. He's very particular about taking care of his hands. He also irons every piece of clothing before he wears it, even if it's his swimming shorts and even if it means waking up half an hour early to do it. The first time he said, "I can never wear anything that's creased," I thought he was joking; I don't care if my clothes are creased or not folded in a certain way.

There's a vanity to him that was evident the first time I met him, but back then I figured that was Dukkha's doing, that she (or the servants, as Laly would say) looked after him like a little boy. If anyone caught me standing in the mirror admiring myself, I'd be embarrassed but Ravi is a bit of a peacock, and if he catches me watching, he just says, 'How do I look? Do I look good?' My dad and my brothers have never asked me that in my life. But I suppose – and I'd never say this aloud – the men in my family are nice enough looking, but not in Ravi's league. I'm fairly ordinary in comparison, when I'm not done-up for meetings, and engagements and weddings, although he's said nothing, and it's too soon to say if it's going to be a bonus or a problem.

On the other hand, he's kind and protective of me,

and gentlemanly – overly so – but of course he's on his best behaviour. So am I. There's a short fuse to his temper for trivial things, like there being no vegan food on the flight home. I wouldn't mind if he was a genuine vegan, but getting into a sulk (even after the stewardess apologises several times and brings him salad and some fruit from business class) and threatening complaint letters when he's spent a week guzzling ice cream and butter-cream cakes is a bit off. I point this out to him, nicely, and for a minute I don't like the dark flash in his eyes, but he apologises charmingly to the stewardess and says to me, 'It's the lawyer in me. We have expectations of all contractual arrangements, however minor.'

It's late afternoon on Saturday when we get back to Manchester, timed so that we have all of tomorrow to settle into the Tilaks' home as a married couple before Ravi has to throw himself into the sixteen-hour days that his Court work demands. He's warned me it will be hard going for a few weeks but that his mum will 'show me all the ropes'.

Can't wait.

She's waiting at the Arrivals barrier, clutching a hanky and all teary-eyed at the return of her big boy, 'A married man, bringing his little wife into my home. Come here, Anoushka, dear, and kiss my cheek.' She accepts my gift with good grace; a pair of topaz and silver earrings from one of the jewellery-makers on the beach. They're inexpensive but unique, and I was double-sure to check her birthstone with Ravi. Kabir is more expansive about his leather wallet, and Ravi and I look at each other, smiling, the homecoming off to a good start.

She doesn't ask anything about the honeymoon, she just witters on about her busy week and people I don't remember meeting, while Ravi and his dad are back in their silent roles in the front. My spirits dip when she gaily reminds us that 'everyone' is waiting for us back at the house. Hindu tradition involves various rituals and games meant as an icebreaker for the nervous bride approaching her in-laws' home for the first time, and the intervention of our honeymoon hasn't spared us. Will this bloody wedding stuff never end, comes into my head, but I make sure my dutiful smile in as set in place as Dukkha's hair, even when we stop at the M68 Services to 'freshen up' and she makes me get changed into a gaudy rainbow salwar suit.

'Your sisters-in-law have come home specially to see you into our home,' Dukkha says, eyeing my red wrap-over skirt and white blouse. 'They have made such an effort to dress up, I don't want you to be embarrassed in your old holiday clothes.'

I lock myself in a cubicle for longer than I need, sitting on the toilet seat in the party outfit and rapidly applied make-up, and digging deep for my inner cool. I'd begun to feel grown-up in Barbados, but the instant I'm back I'm a sulky teenager all over again, I can feel the sunshine slipping though my fingers.

'Anoushka, we're all waiting for you,' Dukkha trills, rapping on the door. 'What are you doing?' There's a pause and her voice changes slightly. 'You're not feeling sick, are you, beta?'

And so it starts: we're married a whole week, now let the pregnancy hints begin. 'Not sick at all, mama-ji.' And if I were it could only be of the travel variety. I emerge from the cubicle so quickly she stumbles backwards to get out of my way and make a meal of washing my hands. I feel better when I see Ravi has changed too, even accepting his lie that I look lovely.

It's probably half an hour later when I recognise the road up to their house, and the archway proclaiming the Hoxton Hall Estate comes into sight. Tonight, we drive straight through, along a road that winds round slightly, and I hold my breath, feeling like the second Mrs de Winter approaching Manderley – I've loved that book since the time my S4 English teacher recommended it – for the first time. And then…

Then the similarity ends, and I realise what a colossal fool I've been. That my whole family has been. There's no vast Hoxton Hall manor house ahead of us, rather a sort of stone gatehouse, with pointed chimneys and a stained-glass window above the door, and beyond that is a common or garden housing estate. We drive down Spruce Road, past Fir, Oak, and Willow Streets, full of open plan semis, and then into Chestnut Close, where we pull up outside one of half a dozen identical boxy detached houses.

We've been had, is my initial thought. Cheated. But hot on its heels is the revelation that no we haven't, we made assumptions. We put two and two together and made Hoxton Hall Estate into a fairy tale. I rack my brains, but not once did Ravi or Dukkha or Kabir suggest they lived anywhere remarkable. Did they mean to imply it by driving us to that archway? I can hardly ask.

All of this rampages through my head like lightening, along with half a dozen quickfire questions, and all the while, I'm getting out of the car and smiling without really seeing the crowd of people on the lawn, in the porch, along the drive. Do I mind a bog-standard house? No. It's still madly superior to ours in Granton. Would I have married Ravi if I'd known? Yes. I didn't even think he had a big house until after the engagement. Do I think any less of Ravi Tilak and his family? Not for failing to be mega rich – but I might if they deliberately set out to mislead us. And, most of all, what will my mum say when she finds out? She'll be devastated.

Oh well. At least I don't have to work out how to live with servants. Then again, Ravi and I won't be living in the West Wing miles away from Dukkha either.

On either side of me, my new sister-in-law and a woman I don't recognise are unwitting supporting actors to my Oscar-winning performance towards the front door of 3 Hoxton Close. Ravi is behind me with his brothers and Dukkha has zoomed ahead to anoint the doorframe with oil, a sign of good luck. She slaps it on like emulsion, then darts back, to put the red tilak spot first on my forehead and hands, and then on Ravi's. The ritual is that I go ahead and place my hands on the door to symbolise entering my new life in a new house as wife and daughter in law, and the assembled family and friends are lapping it up. Someone, it sounds like Anoop, but I can't be sure, shouts out, 'Auntie Dukkha, it's a back-seat for you now the new and final landlady is entering the house.'

'This is my house, it always will be, shame on you for interrupting our tradition.' Dukkha, without hesitation, scolds the heckler and reminds me of my place.

I take a step forward, hands raised, when she grabs my wrist from behind, and shrieks, 'Stop! Have I yet told you where and when to place your hands?'

I turn to face her, shocked by the tone; even a ripple runs through the crowd, but Dukkha gives a loud laugh and waves away the comment, with, 'Me first, or it's bad luck, remember.' Maybe that's true, maybe not, but I'm the only one who feels my mother-in-law's pressure on my wrist and she whispered, 'You will do well to wait for me and to curb that impatient streak, beta.'

I step to one side to let her place her hands squarely on the door, then wait – pointedly, although nobody but me probably notices that – to be invited to copy her.

'Now it's your turn,' she tells me graciously, and obediently I do as I'm told. I'm under no illusions as to who wants to be in charge here.

A spontaneous round of applause accompanies the echoing chorus of 'Congratulations!' as everyone crowds around Ravi to shake his hand, and Dukkha, all smiles now slips her arm through mine, with a 'Good girl. Come,' and escorts me into the house.

New brides are expected to keep their heads down and walk quietly as they tour their in-laws' home for the first time. I can't help but tilt my head up for a second here and there and take in snippets of my surroundings. Tatty is the word that comes to mind. The wallpaper is a uniform deep yellow, faded in places, plastered with photographs of spiritual gurus in others, and all the woodwork could do with a fresh coat of paint. At my feet, the seventies-style beige colonial carpet is worn, even threadbare at the edges. We don't go upstairs, but through the gadget-crammed kitchen and out into a square of garden that's all lawn. The ornamental water-feature dominating the middle would definitely be more at home in the Hoxton Hall of my imagination.

Someone has erected a gazebo to run the length of one half of the garden, and Dukkha ushers me there, where I'm given a chair and it's my turn to be greeted and offered blessing for my future as a wife and daughter-in-law. Everyone is perfectly nice and they seem genuinely pleased to see me, and beside me, Dukkha is lapping up compliments like a cat at the cream, but nobody is mine: no family or friends from Edinburgh, no familiar face – I search for Ravi, but he's nowhere to be seen – and I feel alone and far away, much more isolated than I did a continent off in

Barbados. This is my life now, I think, and I have to swallow a second of panic. I can visit Edinburgh any time, I can phone them any time…and anyway, you were always complaining how annoying they all are, I tell myself. To mask the loneliness, I throw myself into the newlywed games that tradition demands Ravi, and I lead – probably too well, because I keep winning, which clearly irks my new mother-in-law who is, as Laly would put it, 'Damning in her faint praise.' I'll probably regret it, but I don't care, with Ravi – thank goodness he suddenly appeared again – egging me on, I keep playing to win, only giving in when she says brightly but gimlet-eyed, 'Well, somebody else will have to win before we stop the games.'

Game, set and match, Dukkha, I think, as I sit back and let Ravi come out top on the next round. But it works, and the interminable game-playing comes to an end and the guests split into those who like their comfort and so are going home, and the die-hard remainder who are seeing custom through and staying the night, joining the household – including the bride and groom – in sleeping on the floor. I curl up beside Ravi, still fully dressed in a sleeping bag that's some barrier against the well-trodden carpet and will the night away. It's hot and noisy with the sound of so many people sleeping, and for some odd reason, Ravi keeps squeezing me and giggling. If I didn't know better, I'd think he was taking drugs, but I've already had his lecture about that kind of misdemeanour being the end of his career. I suppose he's as nervous as I am, it's just coming out in a different way.

After all, the honeymoon is over.

Chapter 26

Never have I found time more elastic. If seven days in Barbados flew by, the next seven don't even crawl, they shuffle. Forget all my high and mighty grandeur over my degree, being a daughter-in-law is the steepest learning curve I've ever been on.

Contrary to what we'd planned, Ravi is absent most of Sunday running undisclosed errands – though I don't blame him for that; if I arrived home now, my mum would have half a dozen jobs just waiting for me, no excuses – and anyway, it takes half the day to feed and then get rid of the guests who stayed overnight. I help Kabir take the gazebo down, although he protests that I should be doing something more 'gentle'. There's nothing gentle about a hot kitchen and that lot in there scrabbling for more food, just another morsel, Dukkha, for the road, after all it's the last wedding you'll see in this house…Left to himself my new father-in-law is good company, well, he's polite and virtually silent, and that counts. I get satisfaction in rolling and folding and packing the material away – and an attack of the giggles at one point, imagining Ravi wanting to take it out and lovingly iron it for next time.

Mid-afternoon comes and goes before I realise that Dukkha, Kabir, and I are the only people still here; the house, downstairs, at least, is so cluttered with furniture and pictures, gadgets and general stuff, that it's busy when everyone's out. I wonder if now is a good time to ask to see mine and Ravi's room and then have a shower; we slept down here last night, where there's a tiny cloakroom off the hall, so I've yet to have the upstairs tour.

'Of course, of course. Why didn't you say?' Dukkha

is still buzzing from her successful hostess duties. 'You'll be taking the double room at the back. There's plenty of space for two and bedrooms are only for sleeping anyway, aren't they?' She motions me up the stairs ahead of her. 'That door there…No, not that one.' Tsk tsk, she goes, shaking her head when I reach for the wrong handle. 'That's it, that one.'

You'd think the hotel in Barbados would have taught me not to make snap judgments, and I try, but there's not much here to be cheery about. A saggy double bed dominates the room, it has a frilly valence, but no headboard and it needs making up. Dukkha nods to the chest of drawers under the window. 'Sheets and pillowcases are in there. I have a bad back, so I try not to do too much domestic work. I'll leave that to you young things who need the exercise.' I smirk, wondering if Ravi will need to iron it before he sleeps in it? There's a third bed, a single, against the wall, which seems to double up as a sofa and makes it an obstacle course to squeeze round, and no wardrobe other than one of those moving clothes rails you see in shops with a jumble of hangers on it. Homely, it isn't. It makes Mum and Dad's neutral spare room look like a warm and fuzzy cocoon.

'It's not Ravi's old room, then?' is the politest thing I can say. If it is, and he's just cleared it–

'Heavens, no,' she clucks. 'Ravi still has his own room at the other end of the landing, a cosy little bolt hole just in case he needs it.' She pauses for a beat. 'For work or study.'

Not much faith in me, mother-in-law, have you? I think, turning the words that emerge into a cheerful, 'Good idea, mama-ji. While Ravi is working in his old room, I can use this one to study.'

'Quite,' Dukkha says.

'You won't mind if I paint it,' I ask sweetly, 'to save

your poor back?'

'We left it for you.' Her voice is stiff. 'I doubt my taste is yours and you must treat this as your home.'

'I will. I...oh!' It's taken me a minute but now I know what's wrong. 'My things from home, Edinburgh, I mean. And our wedding presents. Where are they?' I glance around as if they could be under the bed or on a hidden shelf or something.

'Garage. It seemed best to leave them to you to sort out.'

Welcome to your new home, Anou, I mouth to myself as she stomps to the door. To my surprise, Dukkha stops there and looks back over her shoulder. 'I expect you would you like to see the burrie,' she says.

It's not a question. I trail after her to what I think is a cupboard on the landing but find it opens to a very narrow and steep flight of stairs – this house is like a Tardis and it's sucking me in – into some half-converted roof space, with an odd smell – damp? Mould? The far end is like a second-hand shop that specialises in decrepit house clearances, but someone has tidied an alcove right inside. It's here that Dukkha has laid out space for the burrie, the gifts given to the bride by her in-laws as a token of their love. It usually comprises beautiful Indian outfits in an array of colours, accompanied by more mundane necessities: shoes, shawls, cardigans, make-up, anything a new bride might find useful in her new home. Mum and the Aunties have very strong feelings on the quality of the burrie, so it's something I'm keen to see.

'Sit there.' Dukkha nods to a carpeted section of the floor. At the same time, she pulls forward what I thought was a coffee table but is actually an old-fashioned cruise liner trunk and lifts the lid. I'm more excited than I thought I would be, but who doesn't like a pile of presents? And Dukkha did come up trumps with my 'going away' outfit, so she knows what she's about.

I should have known better. The Indian outfits aren't terrible, they're just cheap and poorly-made to the extent that even a non-seamstress like me can recognise the shiny material and printing rather than stitching. They're the kind of clothes made in India or China or Bangladesh that never see export, they're sold in crowded bazaars for a few rupees, and the village girls are glad to have them. That thought makes me feel bad about my snobbishness – but not bad enough to want to wear these things. There are hand-knitted cardigans and some bangles, Ponds Cold Cream, sachets of shampoo and a jumbled pile of hair accessories.

'These are pretty,' I say weakly, thinking they would be if I was ten, but Dukkha's not listening, she is rooting in the bottom of the trunk as if she's lost something.

When I think of the money my parents have spent on this marriage, the gold, the jewellery, my fine silks...I feel sick; really, actually nauseous as if I might throw-up. I swallow the bile, not wanting to give Dukkha the satisfaction of looking me up and down again to see if I'm pregnant.

'Take what you want to your room now.' Dukkha says. 'You can come up for the rest anytime. That's what my other daughters-in-law did. I'd forgotten there wasn't–' She stops suddenly, as if she's said something wrong, and bears her teeth at me in a smile instead. 'It doesn't matter. I'll tell Ravi and Anoop to bring up your things from the garage first, hmm? Now do you want to phone your parents?'

It only occurs to me when we get downstairs that in being nice, she's distracting me – and why. The burrie isn't a collection of gifts chosen for me at all, it's the leftovers that Ravi's brothers' brides picked over and discarded. Dukkha didn't remember what was there and now she's found out, even she's embarrassed. I chuck the hair-ties in the chest of drawers, determined that the tat can stay in the loft; I defy Dukkha to say a word.

I take the opportunity to phone Mum. She's sniffy because she's been waiting for my call since last night and it's taken me till now to bother – and right when she's busy. 'Okay,' I say briskly, 'Give me a time during the week and I'll phone back then. Is Laly there? Or Dad? I want to tell someone about the honeymoon.' She changes her tune quick sharp and is soon grilling me about the flight, the hotel, the activities, the food, did we meet any nice people? I give her the edited highlights she wants to hear, conscious, too, that Dukkha, in the lounge with the door wide open will be earwigging like mad. I don't know why she hasn't asked us outright, unless she's got the lowdown from Ravi already.

'I don't want to tie up the phone,' I finish loudly. Dukkha has developed an attack of dry coughing, which might be coincidental with my speaking for ten minutes, but might not. I ask Mum to tell Laly to phone me in the week and I promise to go home for a visit soon. Then I get a glass of water from the kitchen and take it to the now-silent Dukkha.

'I heard you coughing,' I tell her. 'It's horrible having a dry throat, isn't it.'

She sets it, untouched, on a lacy coaster and says, 'You'll want your shower, dear. And dress for going out tonight. We're invited to friends of ours in Drighlington who couldn't make the wedding. This is their only free evening, but they adore Ravi, so make a good impression.'

'I'd quite like us, me and Ravi, I mean, to stay in tonight, mama-ji.' Well, I've got to try, or she'll walk all over me forever, and I do want to spend some time alone with my husband.

'Really. Well, you can do as you wish,' she says as if it's not a big deal – which is not what I'm expecting.

'Er, thank you.' I turn to leave the room. 'I'll go for that shower, then, if nobody needs the bathroom, and plan for an early night.'

'I'll pass on your excuses,' she calls after me. 'Ravi can collect your wedding gift. I expect he'll come with us…' She lets that hang, and although my step falters, I hold my tongue and carry on up the stairs. In the bathroom, I lock the door and plan on using up all the hot water. Witch. Bitch. Cow. Poor Ravi, facing a tug-of-war this early on. Well, he must do it alone – and we'll see where his colours are nailed. Doesn't mean I'm going to play fair though.

'I want us to make love tonight, Ravi.' I accost him as he sticks his head around our bedroom door a couple of hours later. 'Can we? It's been eight days since we got married.'

'Anou, shh, they'll hear you.' His scandalised expression suggests I've stuck it on a placard and picketed the housing estate. He comes right into the room and shuts the door firmly behind him.

'I love you, Ravi, I want us to make love.' I feel like I'm acting a part in a play, taking such an initiative. It's quite exhilarating, actually. 'Don't you?'

'Yes…yes, of course.' When he sits down beside me on the bed, it sags and squeaks ominously; he jumps up as if the springs have poked him. 'They'll think we're…now…' he stutters.

'Open the door and we'll talk in whispers, if it makes you feel better.' I sigh.

'No. No, it's fine.' He sits down again, gingerly, and

takes my hand. 'I want to do it, too,' he says. 'I do, Anou. I've been thinking about it all day, all week.' A little shiver goes through me at that, and we smile at each other shyly. 'But, you see, there's something – wrong.'

'Wrong? What's wrong? Are you ill?'

'No.' It's his turn to sigh. 'Maybe it's complicated rather than wrong. Men…men are supposed to be experienced, aren't they? And I'm not. I haven't…you know…before.'

'Ever?' It pops out before I can stop it and he won't meet my eyes, just shakes his head. So that's why he's been putting it off. 'Neither have I, but you know that,' I say. 'So we're just going to have to try. Tonight,' I add firmly. Because the next thing is he'll convince me to wait till after the big stressful court case and that will take weeks – it's not actually in the court itself till the end of September. I'm going to have to work bloody hard at being a wife, I'm not being a virgin version. I would like some orgasms – I'm blushing thinking that, so obviously don't say it aloud; Ravi would faint. I've got to come clean about something though. 'Your parents are going out later and they asked us to go. I've told your mum I'd like us to stay here, to relax before you start work. She said you'll want to go…? But if you don't, we'll have the house to ourselves.' Am I being manipulative? Yeah. But with just cause and good reason, your honour; I think of Ravi in court proving his case by skewing the facts – of course he does it, all lawyers do, I've watched Kavanagh QC – and refuse to feel bad.

'They'll be out?' I can see Ravi's mind working – and hope he's less transparent in front of a judge. 'Alright, then. Yes. I'll tell Mum, we're watching TV up here and getting over jet lag. She won't mind.'

And I know she won't mind, what Ravi does,

anyway. He's her blue-eyed boy. I'll probably live to regret it though. Hey ho.

I want to say it's movie-magical, that everything about us physically works perfectly and fits like a dream. It doesn't though. Obviously both of us know the mechanics of sex, but I don't think either of us has a clue what lovemaking is all about. We are trying so hard that it's more about grim determination than any momentum. I'd thought it would be painful, but the pain of Ravi's uncontrollable and insatiable lust, not the discomfort of trying to shove a floppy flannel into a dry hole – which I know is TMI, but it is what it is. I can suddenly see the value in sleeping around a bit before marriage, though how couples meet up, snog a bit and have a one-night stand. How is it not excruciating in all senses?

If Ravi were the right one…My disappointed heart can't help doubting us, but my head knows better; intimacy has to be worked at. My body just wants to be left alone until another day.

Chapter 27

Ravi's up and gone long before I hear anyone else in the house stirring. I'm tempted to get up and go out with him but how would I explain why, and where would I go? If I'm living here, I've got to live here. I do need to crack on and sort out my PhD, but the academic summer is longer here than it is in Scotland; Laly and the boys are already back at school, but English terms don't start till September. I can contact Donald though, can't I? And Dr Moffat. I'll write to them both this morning. I'm waiting for Dukkha (and my Mum) to start banging on about thank you cards, so I can keep them happy and slip my personal letters in–

Wait a second. What am I doing? Part of the marriage deal, with Ravi at least, was that I do my PhD. All those phone calls when he was really enthusiastic about it – 'my wife, with the doctorate' and how he'd pay my fees in full. There's nothing cloak and dagger about any of it. I just can't convince myself that Dhukka will approve.

I've had my breakfast, tidied up what I can, and am sitting at the kitchen table writing to Dr Moffat, when my parents-in-law make an entrance. Neither is dressed; she's in a hairnet and he's still removing ear plugs. I thought Kabir would be going to work, but I suppose you don't own the factory and do the daily grind yourself. He probably goes into the boardroom mid-morning to sign mega deals and fire people. Not that I can imagine him doing either. Dukkha, I assume, 'runs the house' and goes out to lunch or does some charity work.

They both plonk themselves down at the table and

look at me expectantly. I am my mother's daughter, so I'm on my feet making tea before they can ask for it and offering to make them whatever they prefer for breakfast.

'Have you had yours?' Dukkha raises her eyebrows. 'In future it might be nice if we all start the day together, Ravi, too, when he's working a normal day.'

'Yes, of course.' I'm too flustered to bother with the implied rebuke. I'm opening and closing cupboards and drawers to find ingredients and utensils, while they sit there as if it's a restaurant. It doesn't occur to Dukkha to tell me where anything is, or to get up and help, and I doubt Kabir knows where anything is outside the garden and garage. I might as well be back in the lab doing a practical exam - and then it occurs to me that's exactly what I am doing. If I were a Brownie Guide, then this would be my Daughter-in-law badge.

'I thought I could get started on our thank you cards today,' I say as they eat. I'm steeling myself for feedback on the food; it's hard to make things taste nice when you can't chuck eggs or chicken in the dish, but they're fuelling up as if preparing for a marathon.

'Oh, beta, really. They were done and sent while you were off sunning yourself in the Caribbean. We couldn't have people waiting so long.' Dukkha wiggles her head and looks smug.

'Oh, mama-ji, really?' She doesn't know I'm mocking her. 'That's great. I was dreading doing something so tedious.' The best thing is, I mean it.

'But I see cards on the table.' She nods at my writing case. 'Who are they to?'

The cheek of her. 'My university tutor and…a colleague. I'm enquiring about my PhD studies. Ravi is keen I get started quickly. So am I, of course.' I hold my breath.

She slows down her chewing and starts to nod in

time with it. 'Very good. That is a good idea, beta. I didn't know you were so organised.'

And yet again, I'm wrong. Will I ever get the measure of this woman?

But she's going on: 'We, too, are organised. Kabir and I have taken this morning off work to talk about house and family rules. We can get to it immediately once you've cleared the table and seen to the dishes.' She gets to her feet and motions to her husband to follow. 'We'll get dressed.'

I'm so flabbergasted by the entire speech that I do exactly as she tells me. What the fuck, rules? Am I getting a job description and a curfew? Take baths on Tuesdays and Fridays and turn off the TV before the watershed? Come to think of it, knowing those sort of nit-picky details might make life easier.

This time, the two of them sit one side of the table and Dukkha points at me to sit across from them, just like an interview. To be fair, Kabir looks more miserable than I've ever seen him, so I'm guessing these are my mother-in-law's rules and he's here for back-up.

Sure enough, she launches in, but it's more a...a manifesto than a framework. In order to gain their respect I have to do whatever I'm told without questioning it; I'm to think before I speak so as not to offend anyone in the family or lose their respect in the community; any actions I take must only be after consulting them and taken with the best of intentions in respect of them. 'If you love and respect us, Anoushka, then you will get the same in return,' Dukkha concludes.

Po-faced and entitled old hag. What gives her the right to say these things to me, to anyone? I am, literally, speechless, which she must take for acquiescence, because she waits for a couple of beats and then nods her birds-nest hair and self-righteously quivering mole in apparent satisfaction.

'Have you anything to say, Anoushka? We do want you to be happy here,' Kabir pipes up, which from the daggers look his lovely wife shoots him, is not in the script.

Oh, I've plenty to say, I think – but I haven't. Not now, at least. 'I think you've made everything very clear,' I say stiffly. 'Thank you, mama-ji.'

They go off again to 'get ready for work, some of us have to earn a living, ha ha,' leaving me too stunned to finish writing to Donald, and brushing away angry tears before they can fall.

'There's one more thing…' Dukkha's head peers around the doorway, and while Kabir sits in the car, periodically tooting the horn, she proceeds to list my contribution to keeping the household running. As far as I can tell, it's the cooking, cleaning, shopping, laundry and looking after Ravi. 'We'll be home for dinner at six,' she adds.

'And there was I, thinking marriage would give me independence,' I mutter to myself when I hear the front door shut, 'allow me to make some decisions and choices, at least.' Instead, it's do what we say and we'll love you. Control, control, control. They might as well have got a maid. Or a Labrador puppy.

I allow myself a little cry – me, who never cries – and then a few minutes of banging things around aggressively. It brings enormous clarity. I can go either of two ways in this moment: give in and go running home to Edinburgh, beg for mercy, annul the whole marriage experience and see if I can get a PhD supervisor back in the university. Or I can stay here, work on my marriage and learn to manage Dukkha, until Ravi and I can make a proper life together. Ever the scientist – so sue me, it's the way I cope – I push my letters to one side and make two lists. By the end, it's clear that I need to stay here: I love Ravi. The only bad thing is Dukkha – only, right, and I know she was a piece of work before I took on this gig. I'll either have to charm her, ignore or put poison in her tea. I'll log my results and then revisit my hypothesis in one month, then two months ad infinitum.

Feeling brighter, I address my letters and then put them in my bag; I might have made my adult decision but I'm not giving them to my mother-in-law to post; why do I think they might never get there? Though she does sound strangely pro-PhD…I help myself to a couple of biscuits and prowl around the empty house, just because I can. Other than the kitchen, the rooms are all gloomy. They have nice proportions, but they're over-filled with furniture that's far too big, ornate but scruffy. It's as if the Tilaks shipped their entire family's belongings over from India in the 1970s, used this house as storage and have been adding to the stash ever since. And none of it's nice. The sofa is covered in a throw that looks suspiciously like the Indian flag – it can't be, can it? I take one of the edges to have a better look and it slides off; the plastic is still on the horrible chinzy cushions underneath. That just about sums up the whole place.

As I'm sorting the throw out, giggling as I realise it's actually the green, white and gold of the Irish flag, not the orange, white and green of the India flag (and wondering, evilly, if Dukkha knows that!) I drop my fistful of biscuits and while I'm tempted to grind them into the junk, I can hear my mother saying, 'I brought you up better than that, Anou, don't lower yourself,' (although it's true she'd be more likely to say it to Laly) so I bend over and scoop up the crumbs. There's a wastepaper bin under a side table, so I go to drop them in there – and do a double take. There amidst the balled-up chocolate wrappers and crisp bags (it passes my mind as to who's the muncher: Kabir or Dukkha, and why are they eating Dairy Milk) is the box containing the earrings I brought Dukkha from Barbados, the earrings still nestling inside. I rescue them and in a second of (admittedly) childish rage and glee, I take out the biggest chocolate wrapper as well, grab Dukkha's spare glasses – from the side table on top of the Radio Times – and chuck them in the bin instead.

I've never been one for mind games, but I was brought up watching my mum and Laly battle wills and play each other off, so if Dukkha wants a battle, I'll take her on. In between doing my PhD and being the Hoxton Hall skivvy.

I run upstairs, all set to have a nosy in my in-laws' bedroom, but my bluff is called because the door is locked. She's locked me out deliberately, I know it. None of the other rooms are shut off. The one next door must be Ravi's old room; the single bed is made up with pyjama-holder neatly on the pillow and the picture of a football team – I squint at the small print and see it's Leeds United 1984 – on the wall. There's an empty desk and a shelf that holds nothing but a few Business Administration textbooks. I'm tempted to go through the drawers – more than tempted, my arm is reaching out to do it – when there's a bang downstairs and I jump a mile. I dart out of the room, down the stairs and come face to face with a pile of post on the front door mat. Guilty conscience, or what? Even though I tell myself it's not badness, looking at Ravi's things, I'm just curious about the boy he was. Another day, I tell myself, and I'll ask Ravi first. Probably.

I look around to see if there's an obvious place to put the post, but there isn't so I take it into the kitchen, glancing through the bills and official letters in case

Mum or Laly has happened to write to me. They haven't – but there's an envelope from Donald; I'd recognise his scrawl anywhere. I rip it open, expecting the standard wedding congratulations card but laugh when I see the old lab joke: Why did the biologist break up with the physicist? And inside, Because they had no chemistry. 'Ha, ha,' I say aloud, but it's cut off with a 'What…?' at seeing a fifty-pound note flutter to the ground. I catch it with one hand, holding the card with the other, and reading Donald's words:

Dear Anoushka, Congratulations on your marriage. I hope you'll be very happy. I asked my (also married/divorced) sisters what to get you for a wedding present and they said, 'Running away money'. It seems counterintuitive to me, but what am I other than a bachelor scientist? Apparently, it's good to have a bit of spare cash that only you know about. Just in case. Sister 2 (she's the still married one) hastened to add that you don't literally have to want to run away but if you wanted to buy someone – Mr Anoushka, I presume – a secret present or something, you can. Oh, and the deal is, if you use it, you have to let the donor (i.e. me) know as it's the law it must always be replenished. Bestest, Donald.

I read it twice, enjoying a rush of nostalgia for the hot chocolate vending machine and the washed lab-coats smell, and harbouring regrets that I don't know Donald's sisters; I like the sound of them. Then I run upstairs again and slip the card between the pages of my tatty old Campbell Biology and fold the banknote into a tiny square and hide it in one of the compartments of my purse. I leave the earrings on the table on top of the empty Dairy Milk bar, with a note saying, 'I found these in the bin. The earrings must have fallen in by accident – lucky I looked! And just a reminder that milk chocolate isn't vegan.' I even put little hearts above the i's.

A little while later I think better of it. I take away the chocolate paper and the note and leave the earrings to speak for themselves.

Chapter 28

I keep my mouth shut and carry out my mother-in-law's orders to a T for the rest of the week. A more subservient daughter-in-law couldn't be found in the most remote villages of Uttarakhand – not that I've ever been there or ever intend to go, but it's like the Girls Higher School in Mumbai, the places my dad threatens us with (well, Laly mostly) when we don't behave like 'the good girls we are raised to be' – and Dukkha is revelling in it. Some people are easily taken in. I cook their vegan food. I clean their cluttered house. I stuff their dirty laundry into the washing machine. And I keep a precise log of all the telephone calls I make, when, to whom and for how long, in pursuit of my PhD. An egg-timer miraculously appeared on the telephone table directly after I'd asked permission to use the phone. 'It's not personal, beta. We all use it,' Dukkha trilled untruthfully before sitting for hours with the cord twiddled around her fingers and yattering on in loud and gossipy Hindi. By Saturday, she's fawning all over me and I'm exhausted. It's not the housework, it's the effort of aspiring – or at least pretending – to do it with good grace and a rictus smile. I don't say a word when she 'forgets' to take me to the temple and instead we go to their weird cult-y prayer meetings in the local secondary school hall.

'My mother is very pleased with you, Anou,' Ravi says to me as we lie in bed early in the morning. 'She says you are a bright girl and capable.'

What is this, my first week's formal appraisal, I think. Am I here on appro? Does Dukkha have a behaviour chart in her knicker drawer…I rein in the thoughts and don't rise, annoyed as I am that Ravi is clearly pleased with me on his mother's behalf. I'm tempted to mention the earrings that he paid for and were tossed aside – the box quietly disappeared without a word – but I don't want to argue; we've barely seen one another since he scampered off to the office last Monday. I've left him food at night, gone to bed at ten – bloody knackered – and hardly registered him slipping in beside me and then leaving again a few hours later. He must eat the food though, because the dishes are rinsed and neatly stacked in the sink, unlike his mother's which are left wherever she finishes. I'm longing to know if she's always been a lazy slob or if my brightness and capabilities have encouraged it. I wish it were the kind of joke I could have with Ravi, but maybe in time.

'I'm taking you into town today,' he announces. 'We need to set up a joint bank account that I'll pay money into each week.'

'Thank you,' I say, thinking of Donald's fifty, which is all I have of my own right now. 'Will we have time to see a bit of the city? You could show me round.'

'Bradford is very small. Wait till my court case is finished and we'll go to Leeds. There's far more life there.'

'But the Museum of Film…and Photography, is here isn't it? I read about it.'

Ravi is rubbing my thigh absentmindedly and I wonder for a minute if he's got something more intimate in mind. Unobtrusively I inch slightly closer towards him. 'Not really my thing, Anou,' he says. 'But you can get a bus timetable and go in during the week, if you like. Mum might like to go on her day off.'

Like hell. 'If we started my driving lessons, I could soon take myself,' I suggest.

'Ask me tomorrow.' His hand comes to halt on my leg, pausing near my groin, it's as if he's trying to work out where to go next. I wish I was brave enough to show him, but instead, I lie here, waiting. Suddenly, he snatches his hand away, sits up, and throws the cover off. 'We'd better get up. The building society is only open until twelve. I checked.' He gives me a dry kiss on my forehead, then moves towards the wardrobe. He stands looking inside and frowning, before selecting a pair of black jeans and a black t-shirt, and spending ages going through his socks and pants. 'Do you need anything ironing,' he asks over his shoulder. When I shake my head, he makes for the door. 'I'll just do these while you have a shower. Breakfast in twenty, yeah?'

I nod, only realising too late that I'm the one who will be serving breakfast in twenty – unless Dukkha has it all in hand downstairs. Right. 'Ravi–'

'Yes?'

'Oh, nothing.' I get out of bed, too. I was going to ask if he was going to iron his underwear as well as his jeans and t-shirt – none of which I'd do – but I can guess the answer and I really don't want to hear him say it out loud.

My heart sinks as we head out to the car a little while later and there is Dukkha already in the back seat with her handbag on her knee, and Kabir is wiping the windscreen.

'Oh. I thought it was just you and me going.' I turn to Ravi, keeping my tone upbeat.

'Well, how would that work?' He looks at me, clearly puzzled.

Equally puzzled, I don't know how to reply. I mean, we are married now, we should be allowed out on our own, without chaperones. I don't want to offend Ravi, but even less do I want to set the precedent of going on jollies as a foursome.

'Anyway, we need Dad's car.' Ravi locks the front

door behind him. 'I can hardly tell him he can't come, can I?'

'No,' I say, thinking Kabir should have enough insight to offer us the car – if he doesn't want it, and he seemed quite happy doing unspecified things in the garage till a few minutes ago. They won't all bloody insist on coming on my driving lessons, will they? Shite. Which reminds me: 'Where are your cars, Ravi? I haven't seen them yet. Can't we take one of those?'

'My cars?'

'Your Audi...er something or other. The one you told me you were buying. Before we got engaged. You said I could have your old one...Have I got the wrong end of the stick?'

But his face clears suddenly. 'I forgot I'd told you that. The Audi's on special order, although it's taking so long, I'm wondering whether to cancel that and go for a Maserati instead.'

'Oh. I can't help you there, I don't know what either of them is like,' I say. 'So, where's the car you do have?' I glance around as if it's going to magically appear but there are no random cars parked in what Dukkha refers to as The Close, they're all neatly parked on driveways.

'What is this, twenty questions?' Ravi motions me to the spare back seat, before leaning on the passenger door himself. 'In the garage getting work for its MOT. It was supposed to be done while we were away, and I'll be having words if it's not finished soon.'

'Right.' The word gets lost in the flurry of getting into the car, but I can't help but feel I've touched a nerve; maybe it's not macho to have a car fail its MOT.

I wouldn't be able to recreate the drive into the city, but I do take note of the bus stop just along from the arch that says Hoxton Hall (that also reminds me I haven't told my mum yet that the Estate is an estate;

she was so geared up to talk honeymoons I've got away with it so far). Ravi must remember too.

'This side of the road for Bradford, that side for Leeds.' He looks back and smiles. 'Which university is giving you the best offer?'

'It doesn't work quite like that,' I say. 'It depends on my research topic and the best supervisor. I'll speak to both during the week, fingers crossed.' I feel a little spark of pleasure at the thought of getting back to study between cooking cauliflower and Hoovering up pistachio shells and fluff. I'll get what lessons I can on CD-ROM and listen as I do my chores. It might have only been a week but I'm proving a point; I'm already clear I'm not cut out to be an undistracted housewife.

'Good.' Ravi nods. 'Keep your options open and be strong in your negotiations. You have a first-class honours Masters degree.'

Me and most of the others looking to do research. But it's nice he's so supportive.

'Surely Leeds is the more distinguished place,' Dukkha butts in snootily. 'Bradford "University" is only a step up from a polytechnic.'

She says 'polytechnic' as if it's on par with borstal, which immediately makes me favour it. That's how I chose biology in the first place; ages before I picked my Highers, I overheard Mum telling the aunties that I was bound to read History and become a teacher, so in a contrary fit, I chose science subjects. Edinburgh Uni was a foregone conclusion. I'd fancied St Andrews (for the History direction), but no way were they letting me live away from home. Now, Dukkha looks slightly miffed that I don't reply one way or the other, and Ravi is oblivious.

'The bus won't be forever,' he assures me. 'Just until you can drive.

Dukkha tuts loudly. 'I manage quite well without a

driving licence.'

'You're a different generation, Mum. Anoushka needs to be independent.' I could kiss him for sticking up for me, until he adds, 'I'm busy. I've an important job. I can't possibly be chauffeuring her around all day like Dad does you.'

It shuts Dukkha up, if nothing else. She spends the rest of the journey sitting ramrod straight like she's got a poker stuffed up her bum, not even interfering when Kabir makes a hash of parallel parking round the back of the Interchange. I don't get much sense of the city centre because Ravi looks at his watch and says we need to hurry. I am pleased, though, that it looks small enough to find my own way round. Edinburgh might be the Scottish capital but it's basically Princes Street flanked by a castle and the railway station, so I'm nervous at the thought of a big city. Hmm, maybe another tick for Bradford Uni. If I get a choice.

When we get to the plate glass door of the Skipton Building Society, I expect my parents-in-law to say they'll meet us in a café or back at the car in an hour, but no, not only do we all pile in, Dukkha pushes past me as if she's got an important appointment. The staff all look up at the influx and I couldn't be more mortified if I'd brought my whole family to a job interview. 'She's not related to me,' I want to yell. 'Don't judge me.' Instead, I put my head down and hope the floor will open up. Thank goodness, Ravi takes charge, speaking in a low voice to a woman with the name-tag, Diana – Trainee. Then she looks us all over, frowns and pulls two chairs out. I sit in one and wait confidently for Ravi to take the other, But he pushes Dukkha forward. What the–

And then I am hit, repeatedly, by the same sense of disbelief and disappointment I felt when learning the truth about the Hoxton Hall Estate. Why? Because twenty minutes later, I emerge from the building society the proud owner of a joint current account – with Dukkha. She's beaming with pride – or maybe its crowing with one-upmanship – and Ravi, oblivious again, this time to my silence, is congratulating himself on a job well done.

'It makes perfect sense, Anou,' he says earnestly. 'You can share the budgeting and always have enough cash to hand. I've started it off with £100 and set up a standing order for a weekly payment.'

I know all that, we've just been through it – except that your dad paid the hundred because of some convoluted reasoning I didn't get – and except for the fact it makes no sense at all. I've married you, not your mother. This is what I want to say, what I'm semaphoring with my eyes, but am despising myself because I'm too weak to say it aloud. 'We never wash our socks in public,' is still one of my mum's misquoted but frequent sayings, and old habits die hard. Especially when the trio with me now would fervently agree with her, I'm sure.

'It's just…'

'Yes?' Ravi is looking at me like a cat that's deposited a half-chewed mouse trophy at my feet and isn't getting approval.

How to say this feels like a breach of faith in me? That his wife is not equal to him and barely equal to his mother. 'Nothing,' I say. 'Nothing.' And this time it's less weakness than the full and certain knowledge that however hard I do try and explain, we'll be at cross purposes. This hurts far more than any prevarication about his family home, yet my husband just won't get it.

Chapter 29

For me, the rest of the weekend is a disaster, or a disappointment anyway. Everyone else seems happy enough, so maybe it's my fault for having expectations I don't adequately share. Ravi decides that as we're a stone's throw from his Bradford office, he'll just call in.

'The senior partner is bound to be doing an all-weekender and it won't hurt my promotion chances to be in the thick of it,' he says. 'I'll make my own way home.'

'Could I come and see where you work?' I ask. 'We could walk back to the car that way.'

'It's over that way.' Ravi waves his hand in an unspecified direction. 'And they'll all be up to their necks in it. How about we wait until this trial is over and then you come in properly, to meet everyone?'

'I have to go to the optician now and get new reading glasses,' Dukkha chimes in. 'I can't find my good ones anywhere. You can help me choose new ones, Anoushka. I blame the cleaners in the factory. Stupid women.'

No, stupid Anoushka, I think. It hadn't occurred to me where she'd put the blame, and now I've got my comeuppance. Hours in Specsavers looking in mirrors.

'Then we must shop for groceries. We can beat the Saturday afternoon rush at Morrisons'.'

Oh, joy. 'Alright.' I agree because it's what expected, but Donald's fifty-pound note is burning a hole in my purse. As Ravi rushes off and I trail after Dukkha and Kabir back to the Interchange, the thought of jumping on a train north is tempting. As is blowing it on a fancy lunch at the Victoria Hotel but I'm not used to eating out alone and I'm not undergoing the torture of treating this pair and inflicting their vegan pretentions on a perfectly innocent chef.

It means we inflict it on a giant Morrisons supermarket but this way I'm the only one who suffers. As Kabir and I wrestle with a family-sized trolley, Dukkha is standing aloof, eyeing up the café and I wait for her to give me a list and say, 'See you later. Don't be long,' but she follows us without a word. I expect it's her desire to make sure I shop properly winning through. It's just as well, because Mum and Dad have always bought things at the smaller shops or from specialist butchers, friends of friends, so I'm a cross between overwhelmed and drunk on choice. Dukkha pats me on the arm as if I'm on day release from some institution, and promises that, 'We'll soon have you in the way of things, beta,' and it's an otherwise harmonious outing. Kabir's role is to keep up the rear and pay (until our new bank cards arrive) but I can tell he's more at home on the golf course and I wonder who usually takes Dukkha shopping – or does it for her. I add it to my mental job description.

It's all topped off with a tedious hour in a garden centre before I spend the afternoon unpacking and cooking while Dukkha 'rests', also known as talking on the phone – I can hear the occasional burst of affected laughter or exclamation of mock outrage – then after all that, she and Kabir appear all done up and swanning out for 'dinner with dear friends. You would have been welcome, but you made it clear last time you would stay at home with Ravi.' I wave them off, thinking that yes, I would, but there's no sign of Ravi. I've eaten my dinner, packed the copious leftovers away and have gone to bed when he finally comes home.

He staggers into the bedroom, pulling off his jacket,

all bleary-eyed and stinking of cigarette smoke.

'Nice time?' I ask, putting my book down. His eyes aren't focussing on me, but they're bright, the pupils dilated, and it occurs to me that he's been taking something more than alcohol.

'The social club with the lads from work,' he slurs. 'Cards. I didn't win but I didn't lose. Keeping the boss on side. Is that alright, Anoushka?' He sits down to kick off his socks and stands again, unsteadily, to unzip his jeans. 'The post-room boys said the missus wouldn't like it, but I said, nah, she's cool. You cool, Anoushka?' Then in a stage whisper with his fingers to his lips, he adds, 'Shh. Shh, Anou. Don't tell my mum. Don't tell her, Anou.'

'I won't,' I say. 'Do you want some water?'

'Yeah. No.' He drops down beside me and squints suspiciously at my face. 'Hey, why you laughing at me? What's funny?'

'You are.' Because he is. I've never seen him so unbuttoned, and a silly drunk is manageable, a belligerent one a different story. 'Come here.' I pull the covers back. 'And sleep it off.'

'No sleep.' He heaves himself over to me. 'And you come here.'

Suddenly he's rolled on top of me, nuzzling wetly at my neck and is pulling at my pyjamas and wriggling himself out of his underwear. Before I can even think to decide if this is what I want – or how to make it more civilised – he's shoving himself between my thighs and grunting. 'Open up, wife,' he mutters and shoves harder, using his penis like a battering ram. It's uncomfortable rather than painful and I'm not exactly sure he's in the right place, but I can't move because he's a heavy weight.

'Ravi,' I whisper, but it's too late.

'Oh Anoushka, yes,' he says into my neck and with

a few muffled snorts, goes rigid, then collapses sideways onto his back, eyes closed.

I wait a few seconds, then a couple of minutes, but it's clear that the heavy breathing is now snoring and he's out for the count. I'm left damp and sticky and with my hair trapped under his arm. I extricate it so as not to hurt me – he won't notice – and get up slowly for the bathroom. 'Well,' I say to the mirror, 'at least it's done, and it can only get better.' And washed and changed, I get back into bed, feeling a really stupid sense of achievement.

Maybe it's the shock on my body – or the alcohol fumes wafting from Ravi's open mouth – but I fall asleep before Dukkha and Kabir come home. I only know they're back when I see the Carina on the drive in the morning and the cups and dishes of a midnight snack dumped on the kitchen table. None of the three of them get up before noon, so I sit in the garden and read my book. The outdoors is by far the nicest thing about this house, and I have the company of a tortoiseshell cat, presumably a neighbour's, that sits on top of the fence, basking in the sun and occasionally looking my way. It's as restful as the days in Barbados and only broken by the loud beep-beep-beeeeep of a car horn out the front. I get up slowly to check it out, and see Anoop, parked at the top of the drive. I'm just opening the front door when Ravi swoops down the stairs, all in white, and flipping sunglasses onto his head.

'Cricket,' he says, giving me a quick hug. 'Last match of the season. I might be late.' And with a 'Hey, Anoop, mate,' he strides to the revving car and doesn't look back as they screech off.

There's a beat of silence and then from inside the house, I hear Dukkha's honeyed tones from the top of the stairs. 'Anoushka, dear,' she calls. 'I think some brunch would be nice, don't you? In the garden. Nothing fussy.'

'Yes, mama-ji. No, mama-ji,' I mutter, closing the front door and leaning on it for a moment. I'd like to say that I never thought that marriage, two weeks in, would be quite like this, but maybe I did. It's exactly what I feared, anyway.

'Can I go to the temple today?' I call.

'Oh, I don't think so, dear. Not today, we're expected in our own group.'

I bit back, but you promised...

Roll on the PhD.

'Unless,' a little voice breathes in my ear so unexpectedly that I almost jump, 'unless last night means you're pregnant. It's possible, you know.'

Ravi makes it twice as possible by coming home for the second night running, with the same unnatural light in his eyes, the same level of drunkenness and the excuse that his team lost and they had to drown their sorrows. His amorous intentions are almost identical to yesterday but this time I'm more prepared and manage to encourage him into a more comfortable position. It's equally short-lived and most certainly not earth-moving, but I feel as if I've had something to do with it this time. Another first – and second – ticked off the marriage list.

It's quickly clear that I'm not pregnant, as my period arrives with monotonous irregularity of cramps the next day, and I'm relieved. Partly because I don't want his mother, my mother and all the aunties, with glinting eyes and coy smiles, commenting forever more on honeymoon babies, and partly so I can legitimately say no to Ravi and meantime work out how to make the next time better. That said, I'd hazard a guess that lovemaking comes under his leisure pursuits and will be a weekend pleasure. Better that than a husband's right, I tell myself. We'll see.

Over the next few weeks, we fall into a sort of general routine in all things domestic and conjugal, in fact. They – by which I mean Dukkha, mostly – treat me like a child, or maybe a maid-in-training, eyes raised at the way I do things, quick to show me the correct way and silently but obviously wondering why my mother didn't teach me better. As if my mother-in-law can claim being houseproud! Dukkha and Kabir work a very boring 9-5 for people who own their own company. The people my dad works for are either there all day and night troubleshooting to outdo Sir John Harvey-Jones or calling in long distance from their luxury yachts moored off St Tropez. But what do I know about business? Dukkha more or less asked me that the other day; I was only trying to show an interest in what they do – actually, I was just trying to think of conversation while we were stuck in traffic after a second fun Saturday food-shopping (Ravi at work, again) – and suggested, without meaning it, that I'd like to look round their factory. Well, you'd think I was indulging in a spot of industrial espionage the way Dukkha clammed up and even Kabir looked at me like a startled rabbit through the central mirror. Idle visitors are not encouraged, apparently, which I can understand because it's a nightmare of paperwork showing someone round a laboratory, but the way Dukkha put it it's less Health and Safety than cheating competitors lining up to steal their ideas.

'You'd be going some to marry their son just to get your hands on some cheap material or whatever it is they actually manufacture,' Laly says, when I relay it to her the next time we talk on the phone. She was asking me if the mother-in-law had lightened up yet. 'Unless,' she adds, 'it's really a front for drugs. And if so, they'll

recruit you soon enough. I wonder why Ravi doesn't
work there?'

'Cos they need a lawyer, just in case?' I say, off the
cuff, and we both snigger, while the egg-timer runs
down for a third time.

'Has Mum got over me not being Lady of the Manor
yet?' I ask. We haven't mentioned it since I broke the
news to her and Dad that the original Hoxton Hall
Estate land was sold off to build a warren of homes for
people moving out of the city. It got quite confused
when Mum, no doubt unable to let the dream go,
thought the Tilaks had owned the original estate and
made a mint on the sale.

'I suppose.' Laly pauses to consider the question.
'From what I overhear, she's concentrating on them
being global industrialists, you know: New York,
Mumbai, Bradford.'

We giggle again. 'You should come and stay in half
term. We could escape the mother-in-law's clutches
and rampage round West Yorkshire.' I'm hit with a
pang of missing Laly and that comes out impulsively,
before I remember how much easier she is to live with
when we're in separate houses a few hundred miles
apart. 'Or after Christmas would be better,' I backtrack
hastily. 'I'll only be a couple of weeks into the PhD in
October, so I mightn't have much time.'

'That sounds crap, Anou. Why on earth do you
want to learn more stuff?' she complains.

'I do it so you don't have to.' I'm laughing but I
wonder if there's some truth in it.

'Doesn't work one bit. Mum and Dad keep banging
on as if you're Einstein and I'm, like, I dunno, well…a
total thicko.'

'Don't be a total thicko, Laly. They've got the perfect
Indian family, haven't they? The clever one, the pretty
one and two boys.'

My sister's voice brightens. 'Hey, you're right. They don't know how lucky they are. Don't worry, I'll remind them.' I bet she will. 'And can I really come and visit? Will old haggy mole-face let me?'

'Laly, stop.'

'Why? Has she got the phone bugged?'

I look at the pink sand in the egg-timer, hold it up to the light and flip it over. 'No. But have some respect if you're going to come and stay in her house. She's not all bad.'

'Yes, but what's the tipping point? Fifty per cent bad, seventy-five? You're a walkover, Anou.'

'No, I'm not.' That stings. 'I'm being cool and calculating.'

'You're a walkover,' she insists. 'Look at you and Mum. Didn't you learn anything living here for twenty-odd years? I thought marriage to swoony wonder boy was your escape.'

'Escape needs planning…' I shake my head and stop. This is a conversation that will go nowhere, it never does. She has a point and it's a sore one, but… 'Divide and conquer,' I say instead. 'Me and Ravi against,' I lower my voice even though nobody else is home, 'haggy mole-face. You can join our gang.'

Chapter 30

'How do I look, Anou? Handsome and clever? Hey, Anou?' Ravi pokes my leg under the duvet, and I sit up and squint at the clock. 5.45a.m.

'You look great,' I tell him, taking in his suit, shirt and tie, and realising it's his wedding suit. Or his wedding suit was his best work suit. I suppose it doesn't matter. 'Not a crease in sight or a hair out of place.'

'Too much gel?' he frets, turning his dark head this way and that.

'Ravi, you're immaculate. Like an advert for the perfect lawyer.'

He knows it. He just wants to hear it, and that has him preening. 'I think so, too.' He nods in satisfaction.

'Good luck. Break a leg, whatever they say at the start of big trials. I hope the rest of your team live up to you and the judge is impressed.'

'It's the jury we need to impress,' Ravi says seriously. 'There are millions of pounds at stake.'

'Better money than lives,' I say, and get a disinterested, 'Huh,' in response. He's given me the barest bones of the highly confidential and political case, all to do with commercial shipping lines, which I said I wouldn't have thought there'd be call for in landlocked West Yorkshire, but Hull is apparently the centre point. He's very cagey, saying their office is a subsidiary – but crucial. Naturally. 'You'll bring in a nice bonus then,' I add smiling.

'Eventually.' He frowns. 'I need my promotion, Anou. A lot is running on this. I might not be home much at all.'

'Nothing new there.' I'm cheerful about that

because: 'As it happens, I have my own news...I wanted to surprise you.' I hear how that could be interpreted and go on hastily, in case he mistakenly hears the patter of tiny feet. 'I start my PhD this week.'

'What...? Why didn't you tell me before now?'

That slight pause before he responds makes it clear I've misjudged the timing and stolen his thunder.

'I wanted to surprise you,' I repeat, lamely it has to be said. 'Sorry.'

'Don't be silly. That's great. Really great. My wife with the PhD.' He turns to me and gives me his best smile, before altering his gaze to his watch. 'But I have to go, Anou. I'll be late. See you sometime.'

'See you,' I echo, as he scarpers out of the room, keen as a kid to join his gang. How can he even contemplate being late at barely six o'clock in the morning? It's only a half hour drive at most... 'If you have a car,' I say aloud. Ravi's car is still in the garage, awaiting some mysterious engine part, so Anoop has been his unofficial taxi service, but at this hour on a Monday morning? Why have I never thought of this before? I get out of bed and run downstairs, pulling back the lounge curtains just in time to catch Ravi cycling off down the street. On his bike. Why not? But it makes me laugh; hotshot lawyer peddling to promotion.

As I pad around making breakfast, I think about his question. Why didn't I tell him before now? Mostly because I wanted to sort it all out myself – little Anoushka, beta, isn't a total moron even if she doesn't chop the carrots or wash the rice quite the way we do it in this house – and present it with a ta-da! For what I can only assume is some weirdly snobbish reason, they all three like the idea of me doing a doctorate, whereas despite their big talk and pre-marriage promises, I'd have had them down as far more conservative. It might all unravel if they don't continue to get the creature comforts they've come to expect...Shit. 'Not so clever after all, are you?' I mutter to myself, as it occurs to me, stupidly late, that I might have been hoist by my own petard. Or whatever that saying is. Doesn't matter anyway, if I can get a first class Masters while doing the household bidding of my critical and exacting mother, I can do a research postgrad under the eye of my critical and slobbish mother-in-law.

I'm going to be based at Bradford University, where I've got first and second supervisors, researching protein biomarkers to identify prognostic signatures and predict outcomes in breast cancers. It's part funded for three years, and Dr Moffat is a third distance supervisor in Edinburgh. It's not actually an area in which I saw myself at all, but everything has fitted together in timing and location and supervisors, and all I need to do to get up to speed is some training in proteomics. And that's where I'm starting this week; that and finding my way around a new city, department, library and laboratory – for which I have a secret weapon: Donald. He's a month or so ahead of me and is coming down on Wednesday to fill me in on what to do and what not to do for getting started. I think Dr Moffat has asked him to, because why else would he trek a few hundred miles south to give me the benefit of his wisdom? I'm not complaining, and he says he's looking forward to being let out for the day. Laly would say Donald secretly fancies me, but he doesn't. He's just plain nice.

So nice, in fact, that he phones me early on Wednesday morning with a change of plan. Ravi's already left and neither Dukkha nor Kabir have made an appearance but when the phone rings, I hear their bedroom door crack open – and when the call is clearly for me it doesn't shut.

'I've bagged a car and got away early,' Donald says. 'I've looked up your address and can easily come and collect you. Before you argue politely, it's hardly a detour at all, I'll just stay on the M62 another junction…if that suits you?'

'I…' My first thought – and I'm cross with it, even as it comes – is what Dukkha will say about me going out with a strange man and how she'll sell it to Ravi.

'If it's easier to just meet you at Bradford Interchange, no worries,' Donald says easily. 'Your call.'

'No. I mean, yes, please, a lift would be great.' I raise my voice slightly, suddenly decisive. I have been a heaven-sent daughter-in-law and Dukkha needs to trust me – which she clearly doesn't do because she's listening at her bedroom door. And all my work inside this house is to make sure that I get a decent life outside it. 'What time?'

'Excellent. See you about half nine then.'

'I'll be ready.' As I put the receiver down, the bedroom door closes with the synchronicity of a bad spy film, and part of me is a wee bit pleased to be doing a bit of passively-harassing my mother-in-law.

'I'll be going in to work later today,' she says when she finally comes down. 'Kabir will come home for lunch and collect me then.'

Of course you are. Of course he will, I think. She pronounces the statements like questions, as if I've answers to rush in and give her. I smile and nod and chatter on pointlessly about proteomics prior to going off to get ready. It's no accident that Dukkha is hovering in the hall as nine-thirty comes round: let her. I'm not fighting her to get the door and I've nothing to hide. In fact, when I hear a car pull up, the door slam, and there's a ring on the doorbell, I call out to her before she can snatch it open.

'Can you get that? It's a colleague of mine.'

In profile, I see her face tighten; no doubt she and Kabir have colleagues and so does Ravi, but the drudge-cum-student shouldn't have those kind of notions. Nor does she like being the doorman.

I put on my jacket and make sure I've my keys, purse, notes before I emerge into the hall. She's only just opening the door.

'Ah, Anoushka,' Dukkha says. 'You can introduce me to your...friend.' She gives Donald an exaggerated smile. 'It's so nice to meet one of my daughter-in-law's friends. You weren't at the wedding.'

'Dukkha, this Dr Johnstone.' I intervene quickly. 'Dr Johnstone, Mrs Tilak. I'm sorry we have to run, there's a full day's programme. Goodbye.' My smile to her is even more exaggeratedly brilliant.

I practically hustle Donald to his car, leaving Dukkha with her gob open on the doorstep. She pulls herself together and affects a regal wave in response to Donald's friendly hand raise, and I hide my face, messing with the seatbelt.

'Sorry about that,' I say. 'You really don't want to spend half the day being interrogated by my mother-in-law. Er, hello, by the way.'

Donald laughs. 'Morning, Anoushka. It's good to see you. But...Doctor?'

'Yes. I promoted you. I'd have said Professor, but you look too young to carry it off.' I squint at him. 'I think. Anyway, if she thinks you're just another student she'll sneer and draw all kinds of conclusions about me going out alone with 'strange' men. But if you're staff, then there's kudos.' I shake my head. 'Or something.'

'Well.' There's a pause. 'My obvious question would be how is married life treating you...but...' Another pause, light-hearted, but also an invitation to speak if I want to.

'Married life would be fine if I were married to Ravi.' Well, mostly. 'Shame nobody told me it was actually his mother I was marrying.' I don't realise till I say that how true it is. I look across at Donald out of the corner of my eye; he catches mine and we both burst out laughing. With tacit agreement, we leave our families behind and revert to what we know: biology, PhD plans and how everything is going in the Edinburgh department.

Chapter 31

We have a really good day; I'd started to forget the comfort of science, with its absolutes and the peace of mind that comes with a right and wrong instruction book. It's so easy being with Donald, too, no need to plan my conversation and calculate any hidden meanings in his replies. As with Laly, what you see is what you get – except he's knows the meaning of tact and thinks before he speaks.

Around three, we're technically finished, and I'm about to suggest we grab a hot chocolate from the cafeteria at the top of the Richmond Building, when he says,

'It would be a shame not to see something of the city while I'm here. Fancy a wee wander down? We could go to the Film and Photography Museum or whatever it's called. Unless,' he shoots me a neutral look, 'you need to get back to cook the tea.'

'There's a fridge full of food,' I say. 'And nobody really eats till late, so I'd say I'm safe. And I've been wanting to see the museum. Let's go.'

We wander down Great Horton Road, past the curry houses and kebab shops and turn right, me telling him about the huge IMAX screen that shows a really early 3D film '…it's called This is Cinerama. It's supposed to feel as if you're flying over 1950s California and joining in with the Vienna Boys' Choir–'

'What?'

'Something like that anyway,' I amend. 'I asked Ravi if we could go when his court case is finished. I'll report back.'

'Please do. Very much more sophisticated than the Pictures in Scotland,' Donald says. 'And how is Ravi's court case going? Or is that top secret?'

'Pretty much. It only started on Monday. The whole system is totally incomprehensible to me, but then so is biology to him.'

'Who does he work for?'

'Kendricks, Patel and Leigh. One of the roads of Cheapside.' I nod my head to one side. 'The main branch is in Leeds, I think, but there's a few of them over West Yorkshire. Ravi's working on being a partner soon.'

'Good for him.' Donald frowns as if he's thinking. 'You know, that name sounds familiar. Kendricks, Patel and Leigh…Hmm, I think a cousin of mine works in one of the branches. Small world.'

We have a quick wander around the museum, knowing we need to do it justice another day, then settle in the café, quickly reverting to type and talking through papers and research proposals and how Donald is already getting to grips with his book lists.

'It's going to be murder.' He groans. 'The practical side is one thing, the interesting thing. Having to do a literature review and actually write a whole chapter, you're so much better suited to that, Anoushka. I'm just a poor country boy who has an affinity with test tubes.'

'You need a research assistant, Doctor Johnstone. One day.' I smile.

'We'll share one. We'll share a whole team when we're famous for our contributions to the eradication of cancer and globally feared as reviewer number two.'

Donald offers to drive me home, but I point out that we're minutes from the Interchange and he's going to hit traffic. In a different life – no, in my future life – I'd offer him dinner and a bed for the night but even if I was confident enough now, I couldn't put him through an evening of the Dukkha and Kabir Show and sleeping in Ravi's old, unchanged bedroom. Instead, he walks me to the bus station.

And there, part of a group of four, all dressed in black and carrying briefcases, is Ravi. They must've all come out of the main railway station entrance and are half blocking it, the other three rifling through their bags and piling files into a legal box that Ravi is carrying. It's definitely him and the most natural thing in the world would be to call out – but I hesitate. I don't know what to do; what would Ravi want me to do? He's a stickler for etiquette, when and how I should meet his colleagues and the senior partners, and I don't want to put him on the spot, but it would be more weird to walk right past him. Wouldn't it? Then they make the decision for me: the other three go into the Interchange, leaving Ravi to balance his cardboard box and hoist a bag over his shoulder, and he's coming this way.

'Ravi? Ravi, hello,' I call, and to Donald, an unnecessary, 'That's Ravi. Come and meet him.'

Ravi's head jerks up as he searches through the commuters and finally clocks me. For a second, there's an odd look on his face, guilty – fearful, even – as if he's in the wrong place at the wrong time, before I register and he comes over, shifting the box awkwardly. 'Anoushka, what are you doing here?' Then he takes in Donald and nods.

'We've been to a training day for PhD research students.' I turn fractionally. 'This is Donald, he's in Biology too.' It flashes through my head that lying to Dukkha about his status might not have been a great thing to do, if she and Ravi swap stories. But then they've no need to. 'We're both heading home. Oh, sorry – Donald, this is my husband, Ravi.'

'Nice to meet you, Ravi,' says Donald. 'Er, can I help you with that box? You've been left with everyone's work by the looks of it.'

'My turn,' Ravi says. 'We take it in turns to get the papers back to the admin office. The others are off to Leeds.'

'Shall I come with you?' I suggest. 'We could go home together if you're not going to be long?' I don't mention the bike.

Ravi shakes his head. 'It'll be a late one, Anou. There's a debriefing in an hour. My notes are essential.'

'You're with Kendricks?' Donald says affably, it being obvious that Ravi and I have run out of small talk – it's weird seeing him, Ravi, I mean, out of context. 'I was telling Anoushka, I have a cousin who works for them. She's in Leeds. Helen Pritchard?

Ravi hesitates. 'I don't recognise the name.'

'She's not a lawyer, she does something in the conveyancing office. I think,' Donald adds.

'Ah.' Ravi's face clears again. 'Different department, different city. It's a big company.' Then to me, 'I must get off, Anou,' and to Donald, 'Nice to meet you. Sorry to run.'

And he runs. Literally. Cardboard box notwithstanding.

I'm still thinking about the encounter as I get on the bus, Donald waving me off. Was Ravi acting strangely – or would he say the same about me? Both of us were probably a bit embarrassed to bump into each other, after all, all of our other meetings to date have been carefully orchestrated or expected. Oh, well, another first ticked off the list. I'm tired but happy as I let myself into the house this evening, not even Dukkha's indelicate probing about Dr Johnstone or digs about the inferiority of Bradford as a university bothers me.

'We met Ravi in town,' I say, thinking that will please her. It stops her in her tracks at any rate.

'Where?' she asks – sharply doesn't cover it. 'What

was he doing? Who was he with? What did he say?'

'He was on his way back to the office after court. He didn't say much, just that he'd got a meeting and would be late.' For god's sake, he's a grown man, I want to add, what's with the questions. But I let it go; that's an issue for Ravi and his mother, not me. Though it doesn't bode well if she's not going to let go of her darling baby boy.

Dukkha sits back and advises me – as she does every night – how to clear the table, plate up some food for Ravi and put it in the fridge, wash the dishes and wipe down the counter space. I tune out, thinking over what Donald said about literature reviews and how I kind of like the idea of collating all that secondary research. It's only when I hear her say, 'India' and 'Christmas holidays,' that I catch up with her monologue.

'…that's why we thought you'd prefer to go to your parents for the holidays,' she's saying.

'That's instead of coming to India with you?' I try to patch it together without showing I wasn't listening.

Dukkha sighs but manages not to sound impatient. 'Exactly, dear. Our business concerns really aren't of any interest to you, and it will be…hmm, four months since you saw them last. Such a shame they haven't come down.'

I ignore the implication that they can't be bothered; Mum insists that they have to be invited properly, which is codswallop; she would have been here like a greyhound off the starter if I were mistress of Hoxton Hall. But the Christmas holidays will be ideal; the Tilaks in Mumbai, Ravi and me in Edinburgh–

'Is Ravi okay with this?' There's no point in either of us pretending she hasn't told him what we're all doing. I can't hear what they talk about late in the evening when he comes home, but I know Dukkha lies in wait.

'Would I suggest it if not?' She gives a little laugh. 'It was his idea. Dear, thoughtful boy. He's already booked his annual leave. You are very lucky, beta.'

She's almost purring, so I make the most of it. 'If we do that, can Laly come back and stay here for a few days?'

'Well, of course,' Dukkha says. 'I'm surprised none of your family has been down already. Anyone would think they didn't feel welcome in our home.' She sniffs; I ignore the barbed repetition. 'Why don't you go and phone them now?' When I don't immediately move, she flaps at me with her hands. 'Go on, dear.'

What's her rush, I think, it's barely October, and it's late; my mother will assume somebody is dead or in disgrace. Then again, if Ravi's got the time off, I don't want Dukkha thinking I'm not keen on going home and dragging us off to India instead. I do as I'm told, and Mum is thrilled, though she hides it well.

'It would be too much to hope for Diwali, I said that to your father. I said you'd have to spend that with the Tilaks.'

'None of us really gets time off for Diwali anyway.' I'm irritated with myself for placating her even as I do it. I feel guilty too. Despite my asking, Dukkha has never once taken me to the temple, we just go to her weird meetings, and Diwali isn't a big thing there. 'We'll have, I don't know, maybe a week in the Christmas holidays. Or, a long weekend, anyway,' I backtrack rapidly in case Ravi's annual leave ends up as being public holidays only. 'Then Laly can come back with us for a few days before school starts again.'

'If you think you can cope with her.' I hear my mum clicking her tongue and can picture the head shaking. 'Where did that girl come from? You were always such a good girl, Anoushka, head in a book too often, but a good girl. Your sister, though, she was sent to test us.

What will become of her? Wayward doesn't begin to describe her...' She laments in this vein for a while and I let her, smiling to myself: how I've been upgraded now I've gone.

As usual, I'm in bed before Ravi gets home. I must fall asleep because I'm woken with a jolt. I'm used to the hum of voices downstairs, but this seems to be some sort of argument: muffled shouting, then a sharp cry, followed by silence. After a minute, there's stomping up the stairs, which I recognise as Dukkha's angel tread. I can't make out if it's Ravi or Kabir downstairs or both; there's no more talking, just the dull thrum of the microwave. I'm not sure...should I get up? I don't want to walk in on the aftermath of a fight, but I do want to know who was fighting. That cry – my stomach shrivels. Surely neither of the men would hit Dukkha? I don't like her and many a time I'd like to give her a slap across her jowly cheek but surely her husband or son – my husband – wouldn't use physical violence. I might be a bit of a pushover at times, but that's a deal breaker for my marriage.

I go down to the kitchen, smile on my face and empty glass in hand, on the pretext of filling it with cold water. Ravi's there alone, eating. He's sitting in the half dark with only the under-counter lights shining a spool on the table.

He jumps when I poke my head round the door. 'Anou! I thought you were sleeping. It's late.'

'Dry throat.' I nod at his plate. 'More spice in the aloo gobi than I thought. Be warned.'

'It's good,' he says automatically as I turn my back and fill the glass, drink from it greedily.

When nothing more comes, I say, 'Is everything okay? Something woke me...voices... maybe I was dreaming.'

He clears his throat. 'Mum told you about going to

India? About the Christmas holidays?'

'Yes. I already talked to my Mum. She's pleased.'

'And are you? I thought you might want to go to India.'

'Not really,' I say. Not at all. 'The air, or more likely the lack of it, starts off my asthma. I know I'm supposed to think it's home but it's too hot and dirty. I'm a Scottish girl at heart. Or a Yorkshire one.' Whoops. Nice catch. 'And we can bring Laly back here.'

'What? Oh, yeah. Laly. Good.' He's still got his head down, shovelling food as if he's starving.

'Are you alright, Ravi? Is there–'

'I'm fine.' There's a flash of temper that makes me flinch, and he apologies immediately. 'Sorry, Anou.' He sits up and looks me straight in the eye. 'Does my mother ever really piss you off?'

I'm so shocked I'm able to bite back the 'Well, not all the time,' that springs to mind and it's lucky I do, because he holds up a hand and adds hastily, 'Unfair question. Don't answer that. I'm tired, that's all.'

'I'm not surprised,' I manage. 'You're working hard. It was nice to bump into you today. At the station, I mean.'

'Yeah.' His shoulders slump again.

I wait another minute but he just finishes his last couple of bites and pushes his plate away. 'Well, I'll go back to bed,' I say.

'I'll be up in a while. I'm waiting till Dad gets home so don't stay awake.'

I step forward to kiss his cheek, veering away at the last moment. There are two things playing on my mind as I go slowly back upstairs. First, the utter venom in Ravi's tone as he said, 'Does my mother ever really piss you off?' and secondly, the watery eyes and bright red mark all down one side of his face. Like tears and a hard slap.

If anyone was hurt here tonight, it was Ravi, not Dukkha.

And I need to think hard about that.

Chapter 32

There's a saying, isn't there, about giving with one hand and taking away with the other; well, there you have my mother-in-law in a nutshell. In the days after she bestows on me the gift of spending the Christmas holidays with my family, she informs me that her eldest daughter, Heera, is coming to stay for Diwali.

'Heera is Ravi's favourite sister; he is her darling little brother. The jewel of my precious daughters.' Dukkha gushes so much I have to work hard not to dislike this paragon before I meet her.

'It's a shame she couldn't come to the wedding,' I say.

Dukkha's eyes flash. 'She has a family, a big house, a business to run. She is indispensable. This visit is her wedding gift – a whole week with us.'

'Lovely.'

'But such high standards, so much for us to prepare.' She's a masterpiece of humble bragging as she lists the 'extra special bits and pieces' I should add into my weekly chores, including re-designing and re-furbishing Ravi's old bedroom fit for a queen.

'It might be easier if she stays in Ravi's and my room. We can camp there,' I snap, when she's finally bored of supervising me hunting through cupboards and drawers and packing boxes for 'Heera's treasures' that will make her feel at home.

'I thought of that,' Dukkha says, seriously. 'But this is a good chance to upgrade Ravi's room for future guests. Or if Ravi needs to move back–' She catches my eye and adds smoothly, 'When you have little ones, I mean. You'll want the babies to sleep with you, of course and the breadwinner will need his rest.'

I let that pass. 'And Heera is definitely coming alone? She's not bringing any of the children or her husband?' I'm checking because I wouldn't put it past Dukkha to 'forget' an entourage of kids, sisters-in-law, a maid or two. There's no implied rebuke – why shouldn't the woman travel alone – but Dukkha huffs.

'She would happily bring them all for a month and rent a house.' Her tone is withering. 'If we weren't going to Mumbai in December, where she will receive and cosset us like royalty.'

'Fair enough,' I say cheerfully. I've worked out that Dukkha gets a kick out of me presenting any downtrodden Cinderella sighs, and she has to grit her teeth if I breezily follow her instructions. 'I'll get cossetting from this end, too. I can't wait to meet Heera.' That much is true – will she be a young Dukkha or the ally of her favourite-little-brother's new wife?

'Oh, Anoushka?'

'Yes?' I pause but can't help looking at my watch because I need to get the bus; they only go every hour and aren't a hundred per cent reliable then.

'You'll need to bring some money in,' she says abruptly. 'Our expenses have been excessive what with your wedding, having you to live here, and facilitating your studies. Ravi needs support with funding the housekeeping account. There's barely enough being paid in to cover our outgoings.'

I stare at her, confused. Not only has she gone from simpering mother to Scrooge in the blink of an eye, where has this come from? As far as I know, there's enough money in our embarrassingly joint account. Ravi mightn't make a fortune until he's a partner but he's always making a thing of having a plenty of cash. In fact, he leaves me a handful of notes from his pocket whenever he thinks of it, and while at first that bothered me – it smacked of pocket money for the little lady – until I realised why not? We each put in to our relationship what we can: he the money, me the payment in kind: we both work equally hard, even if my housekeeping is undervalued. And it won't always be that way. But I wonder now if Dukkha knows this and is mad that I'm getting 'handouts' for myself. Which is stupid as she and Kabir must be comfortable, if not loaded…unless their business isn't doing as well as she boasts. Hmm.

'Stop gawping at me, beta. Like a gormless fish.' She sighs. 'For a clever girl you can be so slow in practical matters.'

'I didn't realise there was a problem.' I ignore the insult. Fight your battles, Anoushka.

'Now you know. I'll leave you to think of a way to solve it,' she says.

I feel like a charge-hand on her factory floor, being threatened with the sack if I can't come up with a contingency. Except in this case, I can, and I don't hesitate. 'I've been offered paid lab work alongside my PhD,' I tell her. 'Assistant Scientific Officer, to give it a formal title. It's part time but a fair wage, probably about £30 a week and it will help my research. It just means I'll be out of the house a bit more. Still time to do the chores though.'

'Well, alright. Teaching would be better but, yes. Fine.'

Now whose mouth is flapping open like a gormless fish? It's a buzz getting the upper hand. There's absolutely nothing she can argue with there, and I take the opportunity to grab my keys and coat and flash her a brilliant smile. I'll still make my bus if I run.

In the city centre, I check our account at the hole in the wall machine and sure enough there's only a few pounds left in it. I detour via the Skipton Building Society and ask them to print off a mini statement. Apparently, I should really have Dukkha's agreement to do this but Diana, the teller, is the woman who opened our account, and she remembers me. It works in my favour even if I do have to weather a sinking feeling of being notorious as the wife who has a joint account with her mother-in-law. Actually, I get the feeling Diana is sorry for me – don't like that either – but is enjoying helping me put one over on what she sees as my husband's overbearing family but can't say as it's unprofessional and possibly racist. Well, if it's either – or I don't believe it is – I'm happily colluding.

I read the transactions there and then and it is odd. Ravi has obviously been in sometime in the last month and changed the amount he said he was paying in every week because it's halved, but the amount being spent is double what Dukkha said we needed for groceries. Either she's been filching it, or we spend and waste far too much. I feel an idiot for not keeping an eye on this and I will from now on. Ravi's contribution though – why? Why say he can afford that much but then change his mind. And not tell me. Anything.

Out of a thought I push my luck with Diana, who's sitting opposite me pretending not to watch me. 'I don't know if I'm allowed to ask this,' I say and her head jerks up as if to say, ask away, please, 'but does my husband have a personal account here? Ravi Tilak.'

She looks at me for a second, then taps away on her computer keyboard. 'Same address, Mrs Tilak?' An image of Dukkha at my shoulder almost makes me turn, but I realise she means me. Nobody else has called me that yet. I signed up for the PhD as Anoushka Malhotra – it never occurred to me not to. I nod and she nods back.

'Well, Mrs Tilak,' Diana says (I jump in with, 'Call

me Anoushka, please!'), 'obviously I couldn't share any confidential financial details…' She gives me the impression she regrets that very much.

'Of course not,' I murmur.

'…But there is no record here of anything but your own account.'

I can see she's bursting with curiosity, and I'm not surprised. I don't know what I was expecting her to say. 'Thank you.' I smile at her. 'You should get Employee of the Month.' I don't want her left feeling sorry for me.

She grins back. 'Hear that, Mr Woolford,' she calls to the middle-aged a desk over. 'This customer says I should be Employee of the Month.'

'Tone it down, please, Diana.' He looks at her over his half-moon glasses, then transfers the gaze to me. 'But duly noted. We aim to please.'

I leave feeling I've made a friend.

It's all ticking over in my mind as I walk down the hill to the Richmond Building. The Tilak family, of which I am, for better or worse, now legally one of them, just has pockets of secrets. Of not quite adding up. Are they en masse eccentric or trying to hoodwink me somehow? I'm sure they're not criminals but they have their own little world of weird habits that I'm only on the fringe of. Maybe all marriages are like that, arranged or not; maybe all families are like that, extended or not. And still niggling me is the fact that Dukkha might have physically hit Ravi – and I'm too scared to ask either of them outright. 'Mata Rani, who would be a grown-up,' I mutter to myself.

On campus, I go straight to the admin office and check that the ASO job is still available. It is, and I take it, filling in the paperwork there and then. Sixteen hours a week, but term time only and on my own schedule; I can do that and keep Dukkha happy at home. Truth is, I don't need to spend half as long on cleaning and cooking – none of the Tilaks are connoisseurs, they won't even notice – I've just done it to fill my time in. It goes against the grain to give my bank account details, knowing that Dukkha will know exactly how much is going in and be able to draw it out, but it only puts me on a par with Ravi.

I collect a pile of internal memos and some external post at the same time and am about to shove it in my bag and head for the lab, when I read the Post-It on top. 'Please phone Donald Johnstone, Edinburgh Uni, Biological Sciences Ext 4521'. I don't like to ask if I can use the office phone, I'd guess I'm not important enough, but there's a payphone at the end of the corridor, and I've still got half an hour before the meeting with my supervisors, so I try him straightaway. You know where you are with Donald, and I'm increasingly seeing how unusual that is.

It seems like I'm fated to be in the Twilight Zone today though. Donald doesn't seem to be himself today. 'Och, I'm a bit out of sorts,' he says.

'Sick?' I ask.

'Chickenpox,' he admits. 'Never had it as a kid and now I've caught if off my nephew. My sister thinks it's very funny.'

'Calamine for the itch,' I remind him, sympathising, before remembering, 'Oh – you won't be able to come down this week.'

'It's a bugger,' he agrees. 'Especially…'

'Especially what?'

'Look, Anoushka, this might mean nothing and it's none of my business.' He sounds really awkward and goes on at nineteen to the dozen, not like Donald at all. 'But have a look at the brochure I sent you. Have a really good look and see if anything strikes you as odd. I hope it doesn't.'

I take a second to process that. 'You're very cryptic, Donald. Wait a minute.' I hook the phone receiver under my chin and rifle through the post till I find the A4 envelope with Donald's handwriting on it. 'I've got it here–'

'Don't bother now. It's just something silly, Anoushka, and it's probably my varicella-zoster spotted brain drawing curious conclusions.' I can hear a second voice in the background and his hand cover the receiver. When he comes back he says, 'I've reverted to ten-year-old me and that's my mum with my medicine. To save further embarrassment, I'm going now. Talk soon. Take Care. Keep the biology banner blowing.'

'Bye.' Poor Donald, but better chickenpox than Shingles. I'll send him a Get Well card on the way home.

I do exactly that, finding the least rude card in the Union shop, and post it on my way back to the Interchange. I keep an eye out for Ravi, but there's no sign this time, and anyway, it's earlier in the day, he'll still be cross-examining witnesses or whatever. On the bus, I take out Donald's envelope and rip it open. I don't know what I was expecting – journal articles or a conference programme, I suppose – but it's not. It's nothing to do with me, or with him, it's a lavish, laminated colour brochure advertising Kendricks, Patel and Leigh, Ravi's firm of solicitors. A loose-leaf page headed AGM 1994 Invitation falls out, but the rest is very slick. I'm just not sure why or how Donald would send this to me…His sister-in-law, of course, that's the how, but the why? It's brand new, put together earlier this year, and all I can think of is, he sent it to me because it shows Ravi and his firm off?

It's full of glossy photos of premises and events and

black-tie dinners. The staff from all three offices are pictured too, seemingly hundreds of them. The senior partners, other partners, lawyers, solicitors, paralegals...As I flick through, I watch the photos and by-lines get smaller, until they disappear, and the final few pages simply list the admin and support staff. I turn back to the Bradford pages, grinning, aware now why Ravi needs to look so well-turned out amongst this bright and shiny lot and wondering if he approves of his photo – and there lies the anomaly.

He's not there. There's no photo of him. They're alphabetical within role but the images go from Richard Tait to Alan Taylor, no Talik or any variation of Talik. I check Leeds and Hull, in the unlikely (given the high spec of this brochure) event that he's been mis-placed – nothing. And then the paralegals and all-encompassing 'advisors' – still nothing. It doesn't make sense. I remember Donald's sister-in-law...Helen something...Helen Pritchard! There she is, no picture, name in small but not the smallest letters. Idly, I run an eye over the rest of the names, and that's when I see it. Him. Ravi.

In the final column, midway down, but above the office juniors, one minute invisible and the next flashing neon in front of my eyes, he's there:

Ravi Tilak, General Administrative Assistant.

Chapter 33

There's nobody in when I get back to the house. Good, because I don't want to see any of them until my brain is clearer, and to do that, there's some research – some might call it snooping but I'm sticking with research – to be done. Never rely on one set of results; never fail to test, test and re-test a hypothesis; always back up your data. I keep repeating that like a mantra. I double lock the front door and turn the key in the lock of the kitchen one, so that nobody can catch me unawares, then run upstairs. Even though the house has that unoccupied feeling, I tap on Dukkha's bedroom door in case she's napping at home – it has been known – and waiting to pounce on me like the wolf on Little Red Riding Hood. I stick my head round but it's empty of everything except a fusty smell arising from the closed windows and curtains and the unmade bed, clothes strewn across it. How did Ravi get so obsessed with tidiness and ironing, I think – or is this mess exactly why? Wrinkling my nose, I close the door and check my watch: two hours before I'm likely to be interrupted, but I'll play safe with one.

I stand in the entrance to Ravi's room, hands on my hips, and surveying the space. Nothing has stirred since I peeked in here the week after our honeymoon. Technically, I'm doing nothing wrong. I've been asked to sort out his teenage room to house Heera, and I'm making a start; it's only because I know what I'm about to do that gives me a guilty conscience. Methodically, I start with the bed, a divan, with storage space underneath. On one side, there's nothing but a stained quilt and matching pillows, which can go straight in the bin. I sit back on my heels for a minute, not sure whether to be impressed at my ability to compartmentalise or furious that I'm multi-tasking for Dukkha's benefit, but common sense – or maybe it adds to my alibi – wins out and I pause to collect black bin bags, a duster and a couple of plastic packing boxes that are crammed into the glory hole under the stairs.

It's very cathartic, chucking things away. I'm careful only to get rid of things nobody could want – the bedding, forgotten shoes, Tupperware boxes with missing lids – with anything I'm not sure of (people have the strangest sentimental attachments) packed neatly into one of the clear containers. That includes Ravi's shelved books, that I take down one by one, shake, and pile up. There's nothing interesting in any of them, aside from the fact they are not law books, but instead HND Business Administration; titles that were innocent that first time I saw them but now take on a whole new double meaning.

It's not accidental that I've left the three desk drawers till last. If there's anything in here to find, this is where it will be. I could be mistaken and need to check through the clutter of the lounge or the detritus in the loft, but my gut tells me that Ravi has the sense to cover up his own dirty work. I must say, there's a sense of satisfaction in stripping back his old belongings, as if he's got fewer and fewer places to hide, until I get to see the real Ravi Tilak. Of course, I hesitate in opening the top drawer, if I'm wrong, then I'll feel terrible, but – hesitation again, and a crushing disappointment – I'm not wrong.

Ravi has lied to me.

I don't know if his family are in on it, or if he's lying to them too, and I'm not sure which is worse. But no, they have to be covering for Ravi, because it's only – only, ha! – taken me a couple of months to out him so there's no way he could have fooled them for years.

With grim determination, I sort through the papers in the top drawer: random birthday cards from a few years ago, a wallet full of rupees and an old passport, an alarm clock with a hand missing. It all goes in the storage box. The second drawer is empty, and my hear is thumping as I pull open the third. I feel like someone about to unearth the treasure, already knowing it's a Pandora's Box but unable to stop. My dramatic sister would be spouting on – with unadulterated relish – about the Pharoah's Curse (arguing with me for saying, scientifically, it was all total superstitious crap). Actually, the first couple of sheets of paper aren't what I was expecting, they're pages ripped from a newspaper or magazine and I'm about to toss them when I look closely – and don't know whether to laugh or cry. Each of the half a dozen sheets is a variation on 'How to woo your Hindu bride'. I'm deadly serious. There's a section dedicated to engagement gifts and I run my finger down them: flowers, chocolates, a cuddly toy, quirky joke items relating to her life or job, a gold pen...check, check, check. From the mis-spelled chocolate to Minnie Mouse to the tam o shanter to the gold pen with his name on it, Ravi sent me them all.

'Should I be touched? Or is he?' I say aloud. It's less the idea – who hasn't done a women's magazine quiz to Secure your Soulmate or Make your Match or whatever – than the taking it so seriously and following the advice. Unless...he did it all as a joke? Which turns Ravi from a romantic, clueless softy into something more calculated and unpalatable. Muttering, 'Benefit of the doubt, Anoushka,' and – ever practical – mindful of time ticking, I park the thought and reach for the paper folder lining the drawer. Inside, as if waiting for me, neatly filed, are Ravi's cycling proficiency certificate, a Bronze Life Saving Award, and his O-Level and CSE results: two Ds and three grade Cs and a grade B; his A-Levels: a C in General Studies and a D in History. (No, I'm not proud of the automatic, how the hell did he get to do A-Levels? that passes through my mind.) And there at the bottom is what I'm looking for: a Higher National Diploma in Business Studies, from Bradford College, dated June 1989, four years ago.

Barring all extenuating circumstances, Ravi is no more a lawyer than I am. He's not a solicitor, a paralegal or even a law student. He's the office boy. The runner. The gopher. I'm not being snobbish, there's nothing wrong with any of those unless you lie about it, your family lies about it...to your wife, to her family and base your married life on that lie.

I take a deep breath, put the folder on the desk and place the 'Keep' boxes on the floor just inside the door. I haul the black bags downstairs and into the bin and unlock the front and back doors. I prepare the evening food, leaving it covered on the stove, and then I go and lock myself in the bathroom with a clean set of clothes. All the time, one word is rattling around my head. Why?

Why, Ravi, why?

I climb into the shower and under the noise of the boiler and running water, let myself cry, big blobby tears of humiliation, mingling with the shower and running down the plug hole with my self-respect.

My so-called marriage is built on a bed of lies and I've been too fucking stupid to notice it.

Part 6
The Pregnancy

Chapter 34

I don't want to dwell on what happened next. It's ugly, shameful, and it shows none of us in a good light. It also set off an unravelling of immense proportions – think dominoes tumbling one after another, all fall down. But now, I've kind of crashed and putting it in black and white is my way of summarising the situation I'm in and deciding – and defending – my way forward. Because whatever I do, some people aren't going to like it.

I want to confront Ravi like a scientist: considered facts and rationale, a calm debate (though that's a fallacy; there's nobody more zealous than a scientist who is convinced by their findings) in a neutral environment. How I actually do it, is in cheated-on – it might not be another woman but that's how it feels – bride mode, throwing his qualifications at his feet with a full-on rant, a litany of his misplaced confidence and false promises, a deconstruction of every phone conversation we had in which his prevarication is now evident, and a rundown of his evasiveness and absences since our marriage…I go on and on. Albeit in a vicious whisper, so as not to have his mother gang up on me and gloat – which makes me furious with myself for being such a coward.

'Why?' I hiss. 'Just tell me why? You've lied to me, Ravi, you've lied from the very first phone call between my dad and yours.'

He doesn't try to deny it; worse, he doesn't even need to ask what I'm talking about. He just stands there, model-perfect with his jacket slung over his shoulder, staring at the meek and mild Anoushka he knows transformed into a silently screeching fishwife. I run out of steam on a 'Just tell me fucking why, you…you stupid idiot,' which about sums up the Jekyll and Hyde halves of me.

Ravi swallows once or twice, his Adam's apple bobbing up and down, and he licks his lips. When he does speak, there's no bravado, no objections, he hangs his head. 'I've treated you badly, Anoushka,' he mutters.

Is that it? Not even an apology? I look at him in disbelief, which he doesn't know because he won't meet my eye. 'Yes, you have. So tell me why.' I curl my hands into fists, letting the silence hang, determined not to be the first to break it. My willpower's at breaking point when he says,

'Because you wouldn't have married me.' He slumps down on the end of the bed. 'If you knew I wasn't a rich lawyer with a fast car and a big house, you wouldn't have married me.'

When I reply with a newly-quiet, 'Yes, Ravi, I would have,' his head jerks up and there's genuine confusion in his eyes. 'And if you're going to ask me why, then you don't know me at all,' I carry on.

'I don't think we know each other at all, Anou,' he says finally, probably the most honest and insightful thing he's said throughout our entire eight-month relationship.

'Then let's get to know each other.'

'Now? But work tomorrow, the court case…' I raise my eyebrows as he falters. 'There really is a court case, Anou, and I really am at court.'

'Carrying the boxes.' I know that's cruel but in the moment I don't care.

'I do a bit more than that.' The old Ravi flares up for a second, indignant. Then he sighs. 'What do you want to know?'

The adrenaline has pumped out of me, and the urge

is to say, 'Nothing,' and curl up with my head under the pillow but I'm not a fool; now I know, I can't un-know. It's a deceitful, sorry tale that makes me alternately pity Ravi and despise him. He did his A-Levels in Mumbai at one of the ever-popping-up English colleges, because no local sixth form would take him. He never was with an American bank, it was a financial services company where he got an office job and went on sponsored day release to do his HND. They downsized at the same time as some vague talk of a gambling issue: 'Unsubstantiated, I swear. It wasn't me and they gave me a reference' – I don't push this, some details might as well stay in the past – and he was taken on by Kendricks, Patel and Leigh. Apparently there's still some vague plan about him going back to study for a law degree. His car is clapped-out and the new one is fantasy; there was never a luxury honeymoon, just a cobbled-together loan because my heart was set on Barbados; his wage is less than mine as an ASO, and he's no savings, due to paying off some (unexplained) debt; my family's misunderstanding over the whole Hoxton Hall house thing was apparently unintentional, 'Although,' he says, 'I'm not sure that my mother didn't plan it that way,' and I believe that.

'Do they know?' I interrupt. 'Your parents – are you hiding all this from them? Or are you all hiding it from me?'

'You've lived with my Mum and Dad long enough, do you even need to ask that?' He gives a wry sort of non-laugh. 'Keeping up appearances and being superior is what she does. Why do you think my brothers and sisters all left home? She's a laughing stock, but she – we – live off my sister, Heera, who is kind and clever and rich, and very well-connected. Nobody says anything because of that.'

'Your mother is a bully,' I say, and he doesn't argue, just raises his hand to his cheek and runs his thumb over it; I doubt he realises he's doing it, but it proves she did hit him the other day and god knows how many other times. Well, I've known from the start that my mother-in-law is a calculating, gaslighting old cow – even with the benefit of the doubt – but at least Ravi isn't. He's just weak and dishonest and under her thumb – 'just'! Fantastic marriage I have when this is a bright spot in my husband's personality. It doesn't take away from the fact that there are still more plot holes in his story than a crap action film.

'Don't your parents have any money of their own? What about their business, the factories?' His face tells me everything. 'Oh. I suppose your sister is subsidising those.'

'Anou, you're so clever in lots of ways and so naïve in others.' He reaches out, presumably to take my hand, but pulls back. 'Heera isn't subsidising anything. My parents don't own anything. The business is hers, the factories here and in India are hers. She employs my mum and dad to do the least possible harm for the largest possible salary.' This time his laugh is harsh. 'It's the best kept open secret in the Indian community.'

Clearly his face didn't tell me everything. It's all coming so thick and fast, I can't be surprised at anything else. 'What exactly was I supposed to bring to the table, then?' I all but spit. 'It's not like I have old money or family connections or, the more I listen to this, even the brains I thought you all admired.'

'Respectability,' he says. 'From a family far enough away not to know about these rumours and keen to marry their eldest daughter. A pleasant and traditional-enough wife to give me above-average children…'

'Go on, Ravi, please don't spare my feelings now. I asked for the truth.' My hand itches to slap him, to match Dukkha like for like on that other unblemished cheek of his, as he – unknowingly? – annihilates me. Instead, I dig my nails into my palms. I won't be like her. 'Well?' I challenge. 'Someone self-obsessed enough in her own escape plans and career path that she wouldn't notice what was under her nose?'

'You said it.' He sounds bitter. 'But I liked you, Anou. In spite of all this,' he sweeps his hand vaguely around, 'and the fact that I was sick of being paraded on the marriage market only to be rejected when the rumours started and–'

'How many matches did you try before me?' I snap out the question, daring him to lie, but he realises what he's said and deflates in front of me.

'Four. You were the fifth. But two of them were in India,' he says, as if they don't count, 'and I think Heera stopped…' He stops digging, but it's too late. And I've had enough.

'So you were all going to just keep the pretence up – what? Forever?'

'I don't know, Anou.' He shrugs. 'It's all fucked up. I'm fucked up. My family is.'

'But how could you think I wouldn't find out?' It's a sticking point. 'I suppose you were banking on getting away with it long enough – you know, maybe till we had a couple of children, or something – to make me, the girl with the PhD, look a fool if I said anything. Hoping I'd be too embarrassed to leave you.'

'No…' he objects. 'No. I thought if I got promotion soon and got sponsored to start the law degree, then it would all work out and you wouldn't need to know this.'

The saddest thing is, I can see he absolutely believes both of these things are even a possibility.

'I love you, Anoushka,' he blurts out suddenly. 'I do love you. I didn't expect that to happen, but you are clever and funny and pretty, and you don't let my mother get you down, and I would like us to have children and be happy.'

Maybe he means it, maybe he's saying it in a means justifies the end sort of way; it's probably both. Hope flickers in his eyes, as I say, 'I love you, too, Ravi,' then fades with my, 'Or I thought I did.' That much is true because I'm not sure at all what love is or if this is it – this…this finding the monsters and staying to play, not immediately running away.

'Are you leaving me?' he asks.

The million-dollar question, and I'm not stringing out the answer just to toy with him. 'Is there anything else, anything at all that you haven't told me?' I ask.

'Isn't this enough?' He sounds incredulous. When I just look at him, he eventually says, 'No. There's nothing else. I swear.'

It's his truth, I can see that, but whether it's the truth, who knows. 'I'm not leaving you, Ravi–'

'Thank you, Anou. Thank you so much.' He grabs at me and pulls me into a hug, muttering all kinds of promises. 'We'll start again, right now. I'll get the promotion and save up and we can move into our own house and–'

'I was going to say I'm not leaving you right now.' Gently, I disentangle myself, needing to see his face. 'If we can work through this, honestly, and we still like each other, then maybe we have a future. I'm not blameless either…' I pause there, but he doesn't take me up on it, he's just nodding eagerly in a way that shows he'll agree with anything I say at this moment in time.

'I'll do anything, Anou…I know!' He looks excited like a little boy. 'I'll even come to Edinburgh with you instead of going to India. That will show Mum we're serious, you and me. She'll be furious. She's already fed up because you said you didn't mind spending the holidays without me.' He frowns. 'What is it, what have I said?'

'Backtrack a little,' I say. 'What do you mean? I thought the arrangement was that you and I were going to Edinburgh and they were going to India. That's what I agreed to.' Even as he's explaining, 'No, she told me she asked if you would rather go to Scotland...' I'm running my once-more simmering thoughts over the conversation in question, and letting them boil over as I realise we were set up – genuinely in my case; as with the house, I made assumptions, and Dukkha knew that and didn't correct me – to be at cross purposes. Bitch.

'I'm going for a bath.' I stand up abruptly. 'And you'd better eat something. It's late.'

As I lay, submerged, holding my breath under the water, coming up to take a gasp of air before going down again, like a weird form of meditation, I try to process all that's come to light. On the plus side – hollow laugh – we've talked more and more honestly than ever before, although a nagging doubt suggests that Ravi is, if not a liar, a fantasist; he believes the stories woven around him. On the negative side, I've married into the most dysfunctional family since Dallas on telly and am now colluding in an outrageous fabrication, whether or not I let on to Dukkha that I know their sordid secrets. And I will let on, because there's no way Ravi will be able to keep it from her if she starts an interrogation. I doubt there's anything about him, about us, that she hasn't extracted from him. That gives me the creeps. The other thing that's interesting (for want of a better word), is that this is all about Ravi – he called me self-obsessed, well, he didn't,

I called myself it, but that's what he meant and it still rankles, both ways, yet when I blatantly said I wasn't blameless, it didn't occur to him to take me up on it and ask what I meant. Was he being tactful? No way, he hasn't the subtlety. And, he hasn't asked me how I found out about his job.

'Remind me, why am I not leaving right now,' I mutter to myself as I finally climb out of the bath. Is it the adult thing to do, to stay and work at this, or is it childish to leave with my head held high? Too soon to decide. I'm just swapping one sodding invisible cage for another, whatever I do.

Ravi's not in our bedroom, but he's turned on my bedside light and turned down my side of the bed. I bet he's also washed his own dishes downstairs, rather than leaving them in the sink as he usually does. And if I look in the wardrobe all my clothes will be ironed. When he doesn't appear after half an hour, I figure he's probably ironing all my clothes as a token of love and intention; I snort to myself, wishing I didn't half believe it. When I hear the shower running, I turn off the lights and lie still, not wanting to talk any more. However, I listen to him being quiet as he gets into bed beside me and feel the tension of him about to say something.

'Anou? Are you awake?' he whispers just before I burst.

'Yes. Sort of.'

'Do you want to make love?' he asks.

What, make-up sex? I stifle a slightly hysterical laugh. Do I? Not really, as it's not much fun. On the other hand, it won't take much to make it painful, and concentrating on some physical pain, will be a release. Shit. I'm as screwed up as the Tilak clan; perhaps I do belong here. 'Alright,' I say.

But it's no good. Ravi tries and tries, starting out

gentle enough, then grunting with impatience and frustration, but he can't do it. He rubs at himself till he must be sore, but he doesn't ask me to touch him, and I don't offer. Neither does he offer to touch me, and I don't ask. It's hard to say who ultimately lies awake the longest; it's like that first night in the Manchester Airport Hotel all over again, but this time with far less hope.

Chapter 35

Diwali come and goes. The festival of lights, celebrating the triumph of light over darkness, good over evil and the human ability to overcome. Ironic, really, and it fails to bring much light to my soul. Even Mata Rani seems to have deserted me, although maybe not, because I'm not un-happy, or not all the time. My PhD is starting out fine, my lab job is interesting enough but not taxing, and in an absence makes the heart grow fonder kind of way, I'm looking forward to going home for the Christmas holidays. Alone.

Ravi has repeated his offer to come with me to Edinburgh, but I've not tested his resolve and taken him up on it. Had he confronted Dukkha during one of her many, many references to the long-awaited family trip, and given me a fait accompli, I'd have put a good spin on it, giving us space as a couple without a toxic Tilak (coined by Laly, not that I've breathed a word of all this latest horror) in sight. We'd still be under the gaze of the meddling Malhotras (the best I can do in the spirit of Laly) but I've come to appreciate how my extended family is comfortably within a confidence interval of oddly normal, whereas Ravi's lot are the ones to seriously skew the probability. Anyway, it doesn't matter. Ravi's going to India, but coming up to Scotland on his return, to bring me and Laly back – if she still wants to come after I've decided what to tell her. I've no idea if Dukkha realises I misunderstood her but I'm not giving her the satisfaction. I also don't know exactly what Ravi has told her about my new-found knowledge of their dirty linen but it's something because she's less full on. In fact, I might be invisible, such is her ghosting rather than gas-lighting of me.

Long may it last.

Ravi's sister, Heera, doesn't come and stay here, after all. She's holed up in a suite at the Leeds Metropolitan, ostensibly because she made a last-minute decision to bring two of her directors with her, and to interview for senior positions back at the mothership in Mumbai. I don't buy that for a second, because since when do captains of industry do anything at the last minute, especially setting up international job interviews, but Dukkha's parroting it as the party-line. I quite like what I've seen of Heera, which isn't much, and I don't know if that's because none of them have seen as much of her as they imply or if Dukkha is keeping me away from her because she no longer knows exactly what I know and therefore can't control what I might say…Oh, listen to me! It's all conspiracy theories and narrow-eyed glances. I haven't a bloody clue about their family dynamics. But like I said, Heera comes across as shrewd and – dare I say it – honest. I'm sure there was pity in her eyes when we were introduced, that was imbibed with a sliver of respect when she said goodbye. Her regret that I wouldn't be visiting Mumbai in December seemed genuine.

So the upshot is, Dukkha now has a spick and span spare room (until she fills it with the cluttery crap that's invaded the rest of the house) and, should anyone ever ask, I have a genuine reason for having found Ravi's documents – and put two and two together and made about a hundred but I hope nobody will ever see the glaring loopholes – without ever needing to mention Donald and the Kendricks, Patel and Leigh brochure.

I ponder over what to tell Donald, torn between spilling my guts or playing it down: least said soonest mended or a problem shared etc…He's the sanest person I know so do I draw on that or do I avoid contaminating him with insanity? I still haven't made up my mind by the time we're due to meet again, in a few hours' time.

'Dr Johnstone is giving me a lift into the department today,' I tell Dukkha politely as she's finishing her breakfast; I've taken to having mine earlier, allegedly with Ravi but he's often out the door with a snack box under his arm. 'If you'd like to stay and say hello.'

'I don't think so, beta,' she says. 'I'm sure you have plenty of work to do.'

'Yes, of course. You, too,' I say, watching her flush (or maybe that's wishful thinking). 'I'll give him your good wishes.'

She looks at me if to say, 'Why would he want them?' which is a fair point. All I'm doing is ensuring she has no call to mention to Ravi any trouble-making suspicions about my perceived carrying-on with another man. Well, that and making mischief.

By the time Donald's car draws up, Dukkha and Kabir are long gone to their actual jobs as accounts manager and pay roll clerk, and I briefly toy with the idea of inviting him in for tea. We'd be uninterrupted but it feels, well, too close to home and, at the same time, not my home, if that makes any sense. So instead, I'm out the door and in the car practically before he can pull on the handbrake.

'Woah, quick getaway,' he says. 'Are you going to yell, "Follow that van?" because I'm not sure this old jalopy is made for hot pursuits. And the car isn't much better.'

'I'm glad you didn't lose your sense of humour with the chickenpox,' I say happily. 'How is that, by the way? No lasting effects?'

'All cleared up and a clean bill of health, bar a few ugly scars,' he says indicating out of the Close. 'And those are in places a red-haired Scot is never going to display in public so I'm good to go.'

By tacit agreement we talk about work, science-y stuff, on the drive in, and once in the lab in the Richmond Building, both of us are absorbed in the current experiments. It's later on, once again in the café at the NMFP that the subject of Ravi, the brochure and me crops up.

'Thank you, Donald, for sending that,' I say, stirring my hot chocolate far more than necessary. 'Seriously. I would have found out in the end but the longer it went on the bigger fool I'd be.'

'You're not a fool, Anoushka. You simply trusted what someone you trusted told you.' He pulls a face. 'If you see what I mean.' There's a pause, then, 'Do you want to tell me what's going on? Or would you rather hear some more about the intricacies of chickenpox when you're a bit older than six?'

I give him the bare bones, then, unable to shut up in the face of his quiet acceptance, all the meat as well. When I eventually stop, I down my now lukewarm drink in two gulps and slump back, prepared to be hit with a wall of anxiety over sharing, but all I do feel is relief. 'Wish you'd shared your chickenpox shame now?' I say.

Donald looks as if he's planning carefully how to reply. 'If you don't mind me saying so, Anoushka,' he says at last, 'and please don't take offence, but you have married into a bunch of flaming lunatics.' He shakes his head. 'I thought my sisters had some mad-as-a- brush in-law stories but you're taking the packet of biscuits here…If you don't mind me saying,' he repeats.

We look at each other and burst out laughing. The release is immense; take me out of the equation and the absurdity of the situation hits.

'What are you going to do?' he asks.

'That's the question.' I sigh. 'I'm still not sure. I think I love Ravi, but am I mistaking that for feeling sorry for him?' I catch the outraged look on Donald's face, even if he manages to bite back the words. 'Too much? Shall we go back to chickenpox or further back to proteonomics?'

'It's not that–'

'Ah. You think I should be angry with him, don't you?'

'I jolly well hope you were angry with the lot of them and have just had time to calm down,' he says fiercely. 'But yes, Ravi has a lot to answer for. However scared of his mother he is, he's a grown man. Where are his balls? Sorry, Anoushka, but honestly.'

'I think his mother has them in the palm of her hand and is squeezing tight,' I say – and immediately feel bad for making fun of Ravi. My husband. For better or worse. I change the subject, in a slant direction. 'Was I just in love with the idea of being married rather than being in love?' I say, startling myself – at the philosophical statement and that I'm sharing it with Donald, my lab colleague, a man who a few months ago knew me only as Anouskha, BSc Group 2, dissecting partner. Then I feel ashamed all over again for downgrading him.

'If you'll forgive me again,' he says, 'and you'll have to because we're way past the stage of niceties, you never seemed particularly in love with getting married. It was more the next big thing you had to tick off after exams and graduation.'

He's right. He's a hundred per cent right. I let life happen around me without taking enough notice. Getting married was always the roundabout way to start a PhD.

'So what are you going to do?' he asks again.

'Stay for now.' I shrug. 'See if there's enough…enough something for Ravi and me to make a go of it. It's that or go home to my mum and dad, and they will not take this well. Believe me. Odds on I'd be sent back to try harder. Or shipped off to India to Auntie Sonu's village.'

'Are you sure? Are you not underestimating them?'

I shake my head. 'If I was being beaten black and blue then they might, might, take me in without a fuss. But a few lies and a frankly odious mother-in-law – that's just the subplot of a happy-ever-after Bollywood movie.' I grin to show I'm joking, mostly, and he smiles in sympathy.

'Dance it till you fake it and make it?'

'Something like that.'

'There is another possible solution, you know,' Donald says a bit later as he walks me over to the bus station.

'Murder by lethal toxin? Insulin between the toes?' Mata Rani forgive me; comedy and tragedy are closely intertwined.

'Don't be silly, the biologist would be prime suspect. No, seriously, what if you and Ravi moved away? Went back to Scotland. Hundreds of miles away from the wicked witch of West Yorkshire.' He stops walking and looks at me. 'It would give you independence without being a statement and you'd be near your family for support, which makes sense. And you could see through the PhD with a wee rearrangement of location and supervisors.'

The last bit makes me laugh. 'Getting Dukkha to agree to that is less likely than it being a wee interdepartmental, inter-university, supervisor swap.'

Donald starts walking again. 'Ah, but our secret weapon is Dr-soon-to-be-professor-Moffat – but don't tell her I told you that bit as it's not official yet. Our

Gillian still has a soft spot for you, and she definitely
wants to see you reach your potential. As for your
mother-in-law – what's her name? Dukkha – well, it's
not up to her, is it? And if her son got a promotion and
had to move offices, then how could she argue?'

'If he did. And it would probably be to Hull,' I say
gloomily.

'If he didn't, he could always tell a lie,' Donald says,
looking at me sideways.

I poke my tongue out at him. 'I've just realised why
we get on so well. You're just like my sister, Laly, but
less ditsy and not so mouthy.' I'm joking but actually,
it's true.

'Thanks, pal, I think there's a compliment in there. It
makes a change being the older brother. My sisters
would hoot if they thought I was giving advice.'

'Are you older than me?' I've no idea when he was
born or what his birthday is.

'Och, a couple of months younger, I think, but that's
immaterial, I'm still being a big brother here.'

'True.' I consider his idea. 'It's an option, a real one.
I wonder why I never thought of it.'

'You can't see the rainforest for the wood, let alone
the wood for the trees. If you're not in danger or
desperately unhappy, don't rush into a decision.'

'I'm not,' I reassure him.

'Then keep calm and do biology, as the sign says.
And if you do need to leave, well, you've got your
running away money, right?'

'Right.' I tap the pocket where my purse is.

I'm waiting at the bus stand, gazing at nothing but
feeling much brighter, when I see Ravi emerge from
the station, three colleagues fractionally ahead of him.
It's like a reconstruction, right down to the sorting of
thick documents and Ravi buckling under a legal box. I
step back slightly, hiding behind the man in front of

me – not that Ravi is likely to look this way –
instinctively feeling it would be humiliating for me to
call him and draw attention to his role. I watch him
gather himself as the others leave him, and if his suit
seems a little less sharp, his shoes a little less shiny,
and his shoulders just a bit more hunched, I'm sure it's
all in my imagination.

Chapter 36

My return to Edinburgh and my family, as a married woman, is acknowledged with a half hour burst of excitement and welcome, then it's business as usual. The absence of my new husband bothers nobody: 'Ravi Tilak is on business. The family business back in India, you remember,' my mother tells all and sundry without turning a hair. 'He's following Anoushka here as soon as he returns.' If anything, it ups my status – wife of a businessman – leaving me wondering if lies, half-truths, white-lies, all tripping off the tongue, has always been the norm and I was oblivious. Laly's an expert through and through, unashamedly when caught out, and I admit that the white kind helped me successfully navigate growing up with an over-protective, exacting and Indian-living-in-Scotland family. It's a slippery slope, Anoushka, I warn myself, all the while hearing Laly's unequivocal, 'If you can't beat 'em, join 'em,' approach.

We don't celebrate Christmas as in the belief system that lies beneath (Jesus Christ, Saviour of the world, birthday) but like everyone I know, who isn't a Christian, we celebrate the public holiday, the over-indulging, and the partying – I mean, how much more Indian can you get? Christmas Tree Indians, as Laly coined it. We even buy gifts. When I was very small, I remember the excitement of Dad coming home from work with a Christmas box. In hindsight it wasn't that inspiring, but it had things I'd never seen before and that in itself made it covetable. There was always a turkey (that Mum enjoyed turning her nose up at its providence and weight but never failed to cook alongside our quality meat; she also used it as a status tool, boasting that only senior management got a bird and the biggest size Christmas Pudding). It was the gaily-wrapped chocolate Santas, the teeth-aching sweet tablet and Tunnocks teacakes that I – and later, Laly and our brothers – drooled over. The years passed but the contents of the hamper barely changed, and a sneak peek assures me that the same goes for this year. And alongside the box, Dad would invariably have the odd bottle of wine or calendar or gift pack of hankies (mystifying us then as now; why? In whose world is something you blow your nose on a present? 'It's like giving somebody a six-pack of toilet rolls but without the puppy,' I recall a disappointed Laly saying one time, when she was still quite little and obsessed with the Andrex Labrador) and he insisted it was only good manners to return the sentiment. I wonder now if the strange Indian sweets so normal to us were fallen upon with as much glee as us and the Tunnocks, or if they were put away with puzzlement and suspicion, to gain dust, eventually opened on a drunk night six months later; the latter I'd guess.

It continued when, one by one, we went to school: random, brown-skinned children with neat uniforms and Scottish accents, who went to assembly without protest and were sheep or wisemen in the Nativity Play. In the late seventies, it wouldn't occur to anybody from the headteacher down to my classmates – including me – that I wasn't automatically part of it. I mean, what would they have done with me otherwise? Occasionally there would be a right-on, politically aware parent at a party, ahead of their time, who tried to make allowances for Indian culture, but that was just mortifying.

So Christmas is Christmas, and we feast, squabble, doze in front of Morecombe and Wise, have an opinion on the Queen's Speech (my mum adores the queen, she's less impressed with her children, Princess Anne aside) and are delighted to get away from each other when Normal Life resumes.

This year isn't any different. Aside from Mum's loaded, gloating remarks to family and friends, nobody remembers I'm a married women and haven't been living in the house since August. I slot right back in and, to be honest, even I forget about my other life for hours at a time. I have the same chores, the same responsibilities and the same excuses (studying) as ever. Some nights I lie in bed and wonder if anyone – here or in Bradford – would actually notice if I just kept quiet and never went back…

But then there's the issue of my pregnancy.

Oh, it's totally phantom, dreamed up by my mother with the same hungry hawk-eye eye as Dukkha had on our return from honeymoon. She hasn't asked me outright yet, just tutted at my looking 'sickly and wan' (I look the same as ever) and being off my food, which isn't true, it's just that months of a vegan diet has shrunk my ability to eat as much meat as I used to – I'm working on it, though, like a chipmunk stockpiling nuts in its cheek for the winter famine. I'll know I've succeeded when she shifts to oblique referrals about 'eating for two'. I could just announce I'm not pregnant, of course, but then she'll put on a pious-cum-mystified face and say that was my business and she wouldn't dream of interfering. That's verging on Dukkha tactics, and I can't be arsed with it when I'm allegedly on holiday. And the upside is that I can say – occasionally – 'I'm tired,' lie down in front of the telly and get away with it. Laly's so mad when she tries it and gets short shrift.

Nobody asks me if I'm happy, which I suppose is a blessing. Neither does it occur to them – why would it? – that any of the Tilaks are other than what they seem (house aside) so it's easiest for me to keep my mouth shut. I've unloaded on Donald, but I'm fairly sure if I did the same with my parents, they'd stick their fingers in the ears and I'd be the failure, and there's no accounting for Laly: she'll either find it hilarious or make a list of ways I can a) turn the situation to my advantage or b) beat them at their own game. Since she's coming back to Bradford with me, I don't want to give her free rope to hang us with.

Ravi phones twice from Mumbai, but it's not a good line, and once we've established he's fine, I'm fine, his family is fine, my family is fine, and that he'll see me as planned on the twenty-ninth, we run out of steam. When he says, 'I miss you,' I echo it, wondering how true it is, or is it just something you say. In the kitchen there's a collective aaah from the eavesdropping aunties, who would be shocked that I could probably count in hours the actual time Ravi and I have spent together since the honeymoon – during it, even. Better that than being in each other's pockets.

'Come, sit down and tell us about married life, Mrs Tilak.' Auntie Sonu pats the chair beside her, while I blink away the image of Dukkha still perched on my shoulder every time I'm called that.

Auntie Deepti pours me tea, and they all look expectant as I buy time sipping it. 'She's shy,' Auntie Deepti says, inducing another sigh and murmurs of, 'So sweet.' I look coy, milking it, and soon they're off down memory lane, vying for attention with their own new bride tales. Anything that diverts them from the fact that I'm still studying biology in the lab rather than baby books in Mothercare. My mind flits to Donald's remark that Ravi and I could move up here for a proper fresh start, but would it be? Lots of the time Dukkha ignores me; there's nobody round this table guilty of that – unfortunately. Being blunt, I've jumped once from the frying pan into the fire, would I just be jumping back?

'…day-dreaming about her man…' Auntie Sonu pokes me in the ribs, and I come back to find them all leering at me. 'He returns tomorrow, right, Ravi? Driving, ha?'

'By bus–'

'National Express Coach, she means.' Mum shoots me a look; alright, Mum, fancy bus. 'A refreshing change from aeroplanes and fast cars, I'm sure.'

The aunties need more than that to convince them, but I'm weary suddenly, not playing along. 'Or maybe he's just plain broke…' I pause for the sharp intake of collective air '…after all that high living in Mumbai.' I give them a brilliant smile and watch as their half-frowns melt away. Of course they want riches-to-rags gossip, but not this close to home. 'Do you mind if I go for a rest?' I push my chair back and stand up slowly. 'I'm so tired suddenly.'

I've no need to hear the comments that follow me along the hall and up the stairs, I can guess them perfectly. 'No, I'm not pregnant,' I mutter under my breath. And no, I'm not happy, but I'm not unhappy either, but I don't expect you to understand. You never did.

Years ago in P3 or P4, we did an all-school production of Jospeh and the Amazing Technicolour Dreamcoat. The return of the prodigal son was drummed in – even to those of us starring as third wheatsheaf – and that's exactly how Ravi is treated from the second he sets foot in the door.

And he thrives on it. Dad and the boys come with me to meet him at Waterloo Place, so we've no time alone, but as he leans forward to hug me, he whispers, 'Do they know?' and I shake my head; there's no need for him to elaborate. Either the fact that his secrets are apparently safe, or he's been treated as a conquering hero already in Mumbai, probably both, he plays the perfect young husband. Boyish with a slightly shy charm when handing round a selection of gifts (scarves for the females, shirts for the men), he morphs into confident and cool, as he finds his feet – not hard, because Mum and the aunties are bowing at them. Even Dad and the boys sit up a bit straighter as Ravi lounges elegantly in his new clothes from Heera's 'faithful tailor'. This is the Ravi from those pre-wedding phone calls, all status and promises, and he treats me, well, lovingly but distantly, is the nearest I can describe. When he suggests to Mum that he's happy to eat meat, wink, wink, don't tell my folks, but your food is so, so good, mama-ji, she's beside herself. Like a good Indian mama she demurs at first, because, 'Oh, Ravi, what would your dear mother say?' but it seems that every visit to Mumbai he's corrupted by Heera who doesn't subscribe to the veganism of Dukkha's complex and confusing Hindu-esque beliefs.

'Look at her,' Laly says of Mum. 'She's almost wetting her knickers.'

So the honeymoon wasn't a one-off, I think, remembering Ravi tucking into ribs and fish and creamy pina coladas. Am I the mug, then, cooking endless dairy-less vegetable dishes just to please his parents? What if it's all front, and they're scarfing down burgers and duck-fat-cooked chips in the factory canteen. I wouldn't be surprised.

I go to bed long before him; he and my dad are watching The Bridge Over the River Kwai, in lieu of a televised football match to bond over, depriving Mum of the chance of excruciating 'there go the lovebirds' comments as we climb the stairs. When he does come up, fumbling in the dark. it's like watching an actor or an undercover cop swap roles: the bravado slips and he's less shiny, more vulnerable. Ours is the small-talk of those first nights together, and I'm not sorry, it's awkward being in my old bed in my childhood room, my parents a wall away.

'That went well,' Ravi says. 'I'm glad I came up. I'm glad they like me.'

I wonder if he knows he's such a chameleon, or if he's so used to being whoever other people want him to be, he's lost himself somewhere along the way. I wonder if I'll ever really know him – any version.

Chapter 37

Laly is less than impressed with the modest proportions and messy interior of the Tilaks' house – I point out it's far less messy than it was five months ago, thanks to me; she says, 'More fool you, Cinderella' – but takes it in her stride. Lured (by Ravi, on the quiet), to the bright lights of the city is clearly trade-off enough. I don't know what's she expecting: she lives in Edinburgh, Glasgow's on her doorstep, but she quickly enlightens me.

'Mum and Dad are in Scotland, Anou. I'm technically in a different country. How mega huge is that? You're so vanilla-y white and the sun shines out of Ravi's bum, so I'm free to party like an almost-eighteen-year-old.'

Good luck with that, I think. Madam Dukkha won't have it for a second. She'll be in her element lording it over two Malhotra girls; two servants for the week. But then again, I'm reckoning without Laly.

'Why are you eyeing me up like that?' she says. 'Like you're measuring me. I'm not wearing any of your mother-in-law's tatty old clothes, however respectful it would be.'

'There are going to be fireworks,' I declare. 'No, not real ones, you idiot. I mean, you and Dukkha under one roof.'

'Bring it on.' Laly gives me a withering glance. 'I'm not being a doormat – no offence, Anou, but you need to show her who's the boss of her baby boy now.'

Mum and Dad gave Ravi a lot of cash just before we left. They said nothing to me, but I watched the way his eyes lit up; it was more than a few pounds. A bit later I find him on our bed, counting it, and stuffing the notes into his wallet. I say nothing. Dad takes me aside and hands me a much thinner envelope, asking me to pass it on to Dukkha. In the envelope to give my mother-in-law, is an extra one hundred pounds. I know that, because once we're back in Bradford and Ravi and his parents are back at work, Laly steams it open. For something nice for Anoushka. It's Mum's writing. I'm guessing there might be baby news in the not-too-distant future.

'What? Pregnant?' Laly screeches. 'You're not?'

'No, I'm not.' How could my mum do that? I feel tears well up and blink them back. I shove the money back into the envelope and rip up the note. 'I'm keeping this, and you don't breathe a word. I'll never see it otherwise'

'Way to go, big sister.' Laly looks at me admiringly. 'I thought you were too goody two shoes to steal.'

'It's not stealing. It's mine. I'm just…taking out the middleman.'

'You get more like me every day.' She sounds supremely satisfied. 'What are we spending it on?'

'We're not spending it on anything. I'm saving. For a rainy day.' Adding it to Donald's running away money, actually.

It turns out to be fun having Laly around. For some obscure reason, maybe to keep me in my place, Dukkha adores my little sister. Whatever her remark or demand or behaviour, Dukkha smiles, tolerantly – exactly as she does with Ravi, until she turns on him and makes him cry. But I'm not worried. Let her try that with Laly and we'll see who comes out on top – and treats her like a child. If anything, I'm the one who should be put out; there's Laly lazing or running noisily about the house as if she's ten, whereas I might as well be a forty-year-old dowager daughter-in-law. Ravi's not much help. He got a PlayStation in India and is glued to it like Laly's twin ten-year-old. Why doesn't my face fit?

'You're too clever,' Laly tells me. 'Madam Mole-Face wants a smart d-i-l fit for her legal-eagle darling boy so she can boast about you as a power-couple, but she doesn't like the reality that you're much, much cleverer than her. And quite pretty, in an older sister kind of way.'

'Damning with faint praise,' I murmur.

'See?' Laly wags her finger at me. 'I haven't an effin clue what you're talking about half the time, and I've lived with you all our lives. She's scared of you, Anou, and you're scared of her. One day you're gonna have to get your claws out and see who wins.'

'You're not just the prettiest Malhotra face, are you?' I ruffle her hair, making her squirm out of the way and check it anxiously in the bedroom mirror.

'No,' she agrees. 'But I ain't never gonna cure cancer like you, am I? Or,' she lowers her voice so I can pretend I don't hear it, 'live in a dump like this with a witch and a wishy-washy husband who's nearly as pretty as me and knows it.'

I wish Laly had more ambition. She could probably run the country single-handedly; her Cabinet wouldn't know what had hit them. It's amazing what a bit of company, full of down-to-earth moral support, will do for you. I find myself wishing I could move Laly down here permanently. Not that she'd come, or that Mum and Dad would let her, not to anything less than the real Hoxton Hall Estate.

'Do you want one, anyway?' Laly says now. She's on my bed henna-ing her hands and getting the dye all over my bedclothes. I'm supposed to be reading some notes through.

'Do that somewhere else, will you?' I swat at the crumpled tissues and the henna tube. 'Do I want one what?'

'Durr. A baby, of course. Isn't that what we were talking about?'

'Were we?' I consider the question though. 'Yes, of course, I do, sometime. But I can't make it happen, can I...? What's that look for?'

'Nothing.' She's put her head on one side, like a dog trying to make sense of a command. 'I just thought you'd say not until your PhD thing was finished.'

'I could do both,' I say. 'I mean there wasn't much point in getting married if I didn't want children.'

'S'pose. As long as you're doing all the fun stuff practising.' Laly gives me a Carry On film-type nudge and smirks.

'Mind your own business, beta,' I say. 'I'm shocked.' As would she be if I tell her how much fun it isn't.

Halfway through our week together, Laly learns that it's Anoop's thirtieth birthday on the Saturday, and that there's a big party planned. 'They want him married off,' she tells me. 'Like, he's turned down more girls than a maid has beds. They were shipping the best ones in from India but zilch. Now they've decided a Yorkshire girl will do, so they're using his birthday party as a massive secret audition.'

There's probably some truth in all this, but I'm more taken up with the fact that nobody's bothered to mention a party to me. I say as much to Dukkha, who looks mystified.

'Did Ravi not tell you?' She tuts. 'Silly boy. Did you think you would stay at home like Cinderella?' Her tinkling laugh is not sincere. 'I've brought you a lovely silk dress from Mumbai.'

Shite. Maybe I can 'gift' it to Laly. I catch her eye, and she puts on a sad face; she knows exactly what I'm thinking.

'Shame I have to go home on Saturday. I'll miss it.

I'd like to go to a big party and have a new dress.' She looks under her lashes at Dukkha. What is my sister playing at?

'Child, of course you must go,' Dukkha says grandly. 'Your parents can come to Anoop's birthday celebration and take you home afterwards. I will phone and tell your mother immediately.' She sweeps out of the room.

Laly sits back, grinning.

'What are you doing?' I whisper. 'Do you really want to go to this party? It'll probably be brutal.' I look at her in horror. 'You don't fancy Anoop? He's far too old for you—'

'And far too poor.' She raises her eyebrows. 'As if. You won't remember cos you were so loved-up, but at your wedding there were a few tasty cousins or neighbours or something of ancient-Anoop's family. I'm just getting the lie of India-boy land before I'm up for the big match. Scotland's too small and nobody's shipping me off to India…Ssh.'

'All settled.' Dukkha's all gloating smiles. 'They were delighted to accept. I don't think your poor parents have had a night out since your wedding, Anoushka. Never mind, we can look after them and introduce them to some very nice people. And you can leave your little science books at home and be an ordinary girl.'

Condescending cow. 'Will any of Ravi's work friends be there?' I ask, knowing it's not the way to go but not caring. 'None of them were at our wedding. I wonder why not? He's always working, I'd like to meet them.'

'It's Anoop's party,' she snaps. I get a daggers look. 'Why would Ravi's colleagues be there?'

'Silly me,' I say. 'Who wants tea?'

'What was all that about?' Laly asks when Dukkha's

gone off to unpack the dresses she brought home.

'Nothing.'

'Something!' she retorts. 'I smell secrets. Spill.'

I curse myself; Laly is not one to let things go. But for all her smart mouth, she's just a kid, and I don't want to admit the lawyer fiasco to her. There's no way of knowing if she'll blab to the world or plan a vendetta. I cross my fingers behind my back. 'Ravi needs more exams to get promotion,' I prevaricate; I know my sister. 'It's a bit of a sore point. Don't say anything, Lal.'

'Oh. Yawn.' As predicted, she loses interest. 'Let's go and see these fabulous dresses then. Though she can do one if she thinks I'm wearing some old-auntie village bazaar cast-off.'

Saturday night arrives and Laly is all packed and ready to go home. Thanks, I'm sure, to my sister, we both get dressed in some lovely Indian silk outfits. Ravi's mother can't help pampering my sister and my sister won't, on principle, leave me behind. There's nothing Laly likes more than getting one over on a 'grown-up', so Dukkha has paid for us both to get our hair done as well. I haven't the heart to tell Laly it's bound to come out of our joint account via what's left of my first PhD funding cheque.

Dukkha's cooing over Laly is to make me jealous but it's never going to work. I'm never going to be jealous of my own sister. She's even got out a selection of the ton of Indian goodies she's stashed away and is gushing on to Laly, who's stuffing her face, about Heera, and about Galu, Ravi's big brother and his family – the pedestal is getting crowded with Laly almost up there too – who Dukkha's misses so much since they moved away.

'Why don't they all live here then with you, mama-ji?' Laly asks innocently, swiping another handful of chocolates, as Dukkha works on a flustered reply. 'Or why don't you move to Mumbai?' Laly pushes on, ignoring my glare.

That stops Dukkha in her tracks. 'That is my dearest wish,' she says. 'If only we weren't all tied up here.' She's probably talking about the factory, keeping up the pretence, but I'm sure she shoots a look at me.

Ravi saves the day, appearing all scrubbed and polished in – surely – a new suit? I hold my tongue but can't help wondering if my grant paid for that too. I hate this mean individual I've turned into and compliment him loudly to mask it. I even kiss him on the cheek, which appears to surprise everyone, and he hugs me back. Dukkha's eyes widen at this tiny display of public affection, and I just know that once again, her eyes are sliding to my waistband. If it's thickening, I'll be glad to tell her it's the result of all the meat and dairy Ravi and I consumed in Scotland. Kabir gets out his camera, and with the inevitable remark about 'a rose between two thorns', takes a photo of me, Ravi and Laly. In the moment it's made up of genuinely happy smiles – which become somewhat forced as Dukkha turns it into an impromptu family photoshoot.

We arrive late, timed, I think to make an entrance, at the hall where Anoop's party is in full swing. I spot Mum and Dad straightaway, stuck in a corner with determined smiles on their faces. Their looks of relief and then pride, when they see Laly and me, make me hug them harder than I did in the holidays. Laly's already babbling on about what a week she's had, 'despite that Dukkha being as crackers as we all thought,' and Mum, mortified, is trying to shush her. Luckily the music is so loud that the woman in question, sashaying across to patronise my family, sees only broad smiles that she takes to be thanks for this invitation.

It's a nice evening. Laly is disappointed by the lack of 'Indian-man-talent' but manages to down enough secret alcoholic drinks – courtesy of a grinning Ravi – to keep her happy. And I stick close to Mum and Dad, for once appreciating them in the moment and reminding myself I must do this more often. At one point, after Dukkha has patronised them just a little bit too much, I'm ready to blurt out the Tilak secrets but I don't. Anoushka, make a scene? Never. But as they're ready to drive off – Dukkha hasn't offered a bed, or a sofa, or even the floor for the night and I don't feel I can do so on her behalf – I feel suddenly bereft and have to hold back the tears. I want to go home, I think.

Mum hugs me tight, no doubt assuming this is hormonal, and tells me to come back soon; four months is too long. And Dad says, if I need him to come and get me, just to say. They're ordinary, family things to say, but not often said in our family. Do they know I'm not that happy? Do they suspect? I'm probably just projecting. What does strike me is Dukkha's barely hidden jealousy at the obvious affection I have for my family, all the worse when Ravi bounds over, tipsy and full of bonhomie, to wish them a safe journey. She puts her arm through his and drags him away, and I see her open her handbag – Dukkha always takes a huge tote bag to dinners and functions, and I've learned it's so she can steal food from the buffet; the fridge is crammed with it the next morning – and give him a wodge of money. Everyone's turning a blind eye to the gambling going on in a back room – where Anoop is spending his time hiding from the desperate parents of ageing brides-to-be; call me cynical, it's true – and Ravi skips off to lose a good month's housekeeping. Any residual guilt over my keeping that hundred pounds Dad sent, gently slips away.

Chapter 38

Something happened in India. I've no idea what, but once Laly has gone home, Dukkha reverts to type and starts acting weird. Weird even for her, I mean. She's taking it out on Ravi, too. Night after night I lie in bed listening to her shouting about how wicked he is, a turncoat, how marriage has changed him. She doesn't even bother keeping her voice down now.

'I've spent my entire life raising you, cultivating and cherishing you–' Really? As if he's a bloody pot plant– 'But you, you do not care a damn about me. I am an untouchable. I should bow to you, my son, let me bow down to you.'

It's unhinged. She's relentless, calculatedly relentless, like Japanese water torture: drip, drip, pause, drip… Up here, I'm curled into a tense, waiting ball, so how it's affecting Ravi downstairs, I can only imagine. Why does he put up with it, why doesn't he just walk out – out of the room, out of the house, out of her life? The rest of his brothers and sisters have done it. But that's it isn't it, that's why Ravi can't, won't. She's not going to let her last remaining son – and by default her resident daughter-in-law – get away.

Tonight it's reaching a new low.

'You're rubbish,' she taunts. 'A peon in a third-rate office, no better than your uncles in Dharavi fifty years ago. You want to kiss my feet, huh? Then lick my soles, like a dog. Go on, coward.'

With creeping horror, I hear the scuffle of Ravi on his knees, snivelling and crying and doing as she says. Surely, no. He won't; he's not so weak? My eyes fill with tears because I know that he is. And much as he's the victim, I despise him just a little bit for that. You're no better, whispers a little voice in my head. It sounds enough like Dukkha's to make me jump. Hiding yourself away, all distant and superior. Reluctantly, my heart hammering, I untwist my taut muscles and get slowly out of bed; I can't let this go on. I've told myself that Ravi's self-respect is hanging on by the thread that pretends to me all is well. But this is no longer humiliation, it's abuse. It's cruelty.

My hand is on the door, when the howling starts. There's a crash as if a chair has fallen, and then Dukkha's voice, increasingly high-pitched. 'My son, my beloved son, what am I doing? Forgive me, sweet one. Come, kiss me–' my insides curdle – 'Get up, get up, and forgive me. I'm not ready to share you, that is all. You are my everything boy.'

There's sobbing then, and a muffled, 'Sorry, sorry, sorry,' over again, and I can't tell which of them it is, or both.

'Call me names, insult me. Hit me – here, I offer you my cheek,' Dukkha wails. 'Punish me.'

'You're a stupid cow. You're a bloody bitch,' Ravi's voice pipes up obediently, like a little boy who's being encouraged to goad a rabid dog. 'I'm leaving you, Mummy. I hate you.'

There's some more sobbing, but I don't know what comes next, I don't want to. Such lows of depravity make me heave – literally. I rush into the bathroom and slam the door, retching over the toilet bowl. I know what the actual meaning of incest is, of course I do, but this is as bad. Their relationship is unhealthy, sick. And where is Ravi's father? The very same place as you are, that devil voice invades my ear again. I lie down on the bathroom floor, trying to relax, knowing the show – the worst one by far – is over. Until next time.

I can't face Ravi tonight. Not that he ever really

turns on me or even cries on my shoulder, he pretends nothing has happened but in a sad and silent, 'Ask me, ask me,' way. When I do, he clams up, saying, 'Stop asking me. Leave me alone,' that shows me he's his mother's son. It gives me a shuddering glimpse into the future. My current role is to be sympathetic but non-committal – if I touch on what I think about Dukkha, he gets defensive on her behalf and will try to pick a fight with me, before going back to apologise to her, even when she's wrong. And she's always wrong. You'd expect a woman to be able to confide in her husband, to laugh or cry with him privately, but Ravi can't keep a secret from his mother, so I've learned how everything I say – about anything from whether I like the colour green to my views on proteonomics in cancer research – gets back to her. I watch what I say every day.

When she's been at her meanest, he'll try to have sex with me, and it invariably won't work properly. In the early hours of the morning, I'll wake to find him having another go and it's rough. I hate myself for allowing it but justify that it's only a few minutes, then he goes off to work appeased and I can wash it all off in a long, hot shower. Of all the things about sex I did and didn't expect, it ending in a sticky and wet puddle wasn't one of them. The biologist in me snorts her disapproval, but I find myself thinking pregnancy is a lottery; only a persistent few of those little sperm swimmers even going the right way.

I'm shocked now there's a gentle tap on the bathroom door and I scramble to my feet even though I'm certain it's locked. 'Sorry,' I say, amazed that my voice sounds totally normal. 'I'll be out in a second.'

'No hurry, dear. I've brought you a cup of tea, warm and sweet. I'll leave it on your bedside table.' It's not Ravi, looking for access to the shower, it's Dukkha.

Warm and sweet as the tea she's inexplicably offering. I swear to god my first thought is that she's killed Ravi and I'm next, that this is her lacing my tea with strychnine or digoxin.

'Um, thank you.' I turn on the taps and call over them, straining to hear her slippers pad along the hall to her own room. When I figure she's had sufficient time to be gone, I quietly unlock the door, ready to tiptoe across the landing – straight into her waiting arms.

'Anoushka, beta,' she croons through her rictus smile. 'We heard you vomiting. Poor little girl. Take my arm and we'll get you back into bed.'

'I wasn't…' Yes, I was puking, or dry-retching anyway, I can't lie because they heard me. 'I mean, I'm fine now. I think I ate a…er…something bad in the Student's Union.' Listened to something bad in the kitchen, more like.

'Is that so, dear?'

Why is she humouring me? I hug the wall so as not to touch Dukkha's outstretched hand. She follows me into the bedroom, where Ravi is perched on the bed, already in his pyjamas. He's also smiling at me, as if we're a game of updated Happy Families, Ravi Tilak, the Indian's son, and all we need now is Kabir to complete the set. Momentarily disorientated, I smile back, colluding with all the pretence, before scuttling round the bed and slipping under the covers. I lean against the headboard and reach out for the tea. I don't really think it's poisoned, but the way they're both staring at me is unsettling. As is their united front, when I think back a few minutes. I should confront them, I think. Go on, grow a backbone.

'Is everything alright?' I croak. 'I thought I heard voices.' Way to go, Anoushka, understatement of the year.

'Oh, that. All over now,' Dukkha dismisses it lightly. 'Apologise to your wife, son.'

'He doesn't need–'

'Sorry for disturbing you, Anou,' Ravi says quickly. 'Is your tea alright?'

I sip it gingerly. It tastes stewed yet weak, over-powered with cardamom, and the reheated condensed milk leaving a slimy trail on my tongue; exactly as Dukkha always botches it. Two gulps get it down, and I pass the cup to Ravi, who hands it to his mother.

'We'll have a little talk in the morning,' she coos at me. 'Ravi, into bed, now.'

A little bubble of laughter escapes my lips, which I disguise as a hiccup. If it weren't so inappropriate, this would be funny; Ravi and I like five-year-olds being put to bed.

I brace myself but Ravi doesn't make his usual move – putting his hand on my thigh – and if he doesn't do it straightaway, I know he's not going to. Emboldened, I say, 'Ravi? What happened in India?'

He turns his head to face me. 'In India? What do you mean?'

'Your mum…' is almost bursting with mental-ness and acting like someone see-sawing with manic-depression, is what I'm tempted to say, but I settle for, 'Your mum seems different since you got home, as if she's got something specific on her mind.' When he doesn't answer, I add, 'Do you know what it is?'

'It's nothing,' he says finally. 'She's always a bit funny after being in Mumbai, she has to adjust to being back here, you know? For my mum and dad – yours too – they live here but India is always home.'

He's right. His explanation is perfectly reasonable. Yet I can't help but think he's not telling me the whole truth. Then, just when I think he's fallen asleep, he goes on unexpectedly,

'She saw a clairvoyant. The women at the Club, her friends, they were all going on about him, this priest who could see the future. They went off, giggling like a hen party, to have their hands and face read.'

'And?'

I can feel his shoulders rise in a shrug. 'She wasn't laughing when she came back, and she wouldn't tell us what he'd said. Dad said it was nonsense, and he forbade her from going back. I think she ignored him.'

Nothing new there. I bite back the words. It sounds like the kind of superstitious antics Dukkha would be up for, worrying away at the psychic till she got the results she wanted. Maybe this one wouldn't give in. I feel relief, until Ravi adds sleepily,

'She took a photo of me and you with her. I forgot to ask her why.'

I stay awake thinking of plenty, mostly variations on whether her darling boy's wife is a dud, and grateful for the protection of Mata Rani and safe in the knowledge that a priest-clairvoyant seeing gaggles of middle-aged women in the back streets of Mumbai s nothing but a charlatan.

Dhukka's mood hasn't soured by morning. She asks me how I slept, and would I like some raw tea and dry toast to line my stomach? She's as solicitous as a normal mother-in-law. I can't think of anything less appetising and help myself to my usual fruit and coconut yoghurt, promising myself a bacon roll in the Richmond Building cafeteria. For once she nods approvingly as I fill my bowl. Then the penny drops. She's not being nice because she's suddenly ashamed of being a vicious bully – oh no. She's back to thinking I'm pregnant.

Sure enough, she holds out for a few minutes, but when I say nothing and am a couple of spoonfuls away from finishing, she says brightly, 'Is there anything you want to tell me?'

I look at her, spoon raised. 'I don't think so,' I say. 'Can't think of anything. Why?'

I enjoy the range of emotions that flash across her face, the mole trembles.

'Oh, come on, dear,' she says coyly. 'Morning sickness isn't always in the morning and, ' she eyes my perfectly normal-sized breakfast, 'surely to clock in you are eating for two…'

I leave her hanging for a few happy seconds, then prick her balloon. 'Do you mean, am I pregnant? No, I'm not.'

Her face falls. And along with it, the mask falls, laughingly instantaneous. 'Are you sure?' she says sharply.

'Yep.' I get up and put my bowl in the sink. 'Maybe next month.'

The last thing I hear as I leave the house – delighting in a stupid sense of one-upmanship – is her shouting disagreeably at Kabir to move his behind and get out the car – if she must be forced to work in that hell-hole of a factory, the least he can do is get her there to clock in on time.

The thing is, though, I'm not sure at all. My cycle isn't regular and some months I'm struck down with excruciating pain, others come and go without fanfare. I've never kept a diary with a little red dot tracking the days and weeks, like I know Sharmila has done since she was thirteen. Perhaps I should, even if it is a bit late in the day. I try counting back and my best guess is that my period is a couple of weeks 'overdue'. Maybe. It's not out there unusual but it's on the long side.

The bus is late today, and the traffic crawling, so it's a brisk walk down the hill, but the Richmond lifts are on my side – you can wait five minutes for one of the three to trundle its way up and down twelve floors – and I'm on time, just. It only strikes me as I put my lab coat on, stash my bag, and tie up my hair that nobody actually cares. Nobody else is signed in on the board, yet I know three of us are scheduled to work this morning. It's a revelation. And as if to underline the point, one of the admin staff pokes her head around the office door.

'I thought I heard someone,' she says, waving a piece of toast at me. 'We're in the backroom, having a sly second breakfast. We saved you a bun. Were you stuck in traffic too? Pile-up on the bypass, I believe.'

'Thanks,' I say, pleased to be one of them – not everyone gets included on the breakfast run. 'Can I have it later? I want to finish early this morning,' Go, Anou. 'I've got some shopping to do in town.'

'Course you can, lovey. Oh – wait.' She crams the last of the bread into her mouth, brushes her jumper free of crumbs, and rummages through the pile of post on her desk. 'This came for you. Not sure why it came here and not to your home address – I can update that for you today – but it'll be your next funding cheque, so I kept it safe.'

'Brilliant. I'll take it straight to the bank,' I say, the cogs in my brain whirring.

It's a long time since I haven't given one hundred per cent concentration to my work or study, but this morning, my brain is working on two parallel lines and by noon I'm going back towards the city centre with a half-formed plan. First stop is the Skipton Building Society, where I cross my fingers and send a quick request to Mata Rani, that Diana is working. She is, and she remembers me, because she waves a greeting and mimes that I should wait until she's dealt with the elderly couple in front of her.

'Hello,' she says a few minutes later, as I move to one of the recently vacated seats in front of her desk. 'How are you getting on? What can I do for you today?'

'I'm fine, thank you.' I hesitate. 'Can I open a new account? One with just my name on it? What do you need…?'

She's already nodding furiously. 'Every woman needs her own account,' she announces, then lowers her voice, 'It's what I want to tell everyone, but him over there says it's not my place and if I want to get promotion, I need to follow procedure.' She rolls her eyes. 'Anyway, I can open you a new account today. What kind do you want? Current, savings?'

'I'm not sure.' My turn to hesitate.

'Why don't you tell me why you want it, and I can advise you,' she says kindly.

'I've got my funding cheque to pay in – I'm a student, doing a PhD. I want to save some of the money but spend it if…when…I need to.'

'Easy. We'll do you a student account. You get a pass card and all kinds of perks.' She rattles on as she fills out a form, telling me about the interest rate and record shop vouchers and discounted railcards. When I'm signing my name on the application form, she adds, 'Do you ever go out in town? You could come with me and my mates, if you wanted?'

'Me? I…' I'm not sure what to say; I'm a bit tearful, if I'm honest. Two people being so simply nice today makes me realise how hateful Dukkha really is. Of all the good people in the world and I end up with her. 'I live out, the other side of Drighlington,' I say hurriedly, in case she thinks I don't want to, she already looks a bit concerned. 'So, evenings are…tricky. But,' I add, feeling shy – I'm not used to offering invitations – 'Maybe at lunchtime one day? If you get a lunch break and you're free…'

'It's a date,' she says as if it's the most natural thing in the world. 'Here, this is my phone number.' She scribbles in tiny writing on the bottom of my carbon copy. 'Keep it quiet, it's probably against the law according to the boss. And I'll always be in here anyway. Call in any time.'

'I will.' I fold up the paper and all the discount information into my purse. 'Erm, do you think I could pick up the pass card here? Instead of it being sent to my address, I mean?'

'Sure. Come in early next week.' She smiles. 'Bye, Anoushka.'

'Bye, Diana.'

'Thank you for your custom,' she calls as I make my way, also smiling, out through the glass doors.

First mission accomplished. I make my way towards Boots next, and in the wide anonymous aisle, I pick up one pregnancy testing kit after another and read the instructions. They're all pee-on-a-stick similar, in boxes of two, so I choose the cheapest and pay for that and a KitKat with £20 borrowed from Donald's running away money. Making my way back to the uni campus, I think analytically about the pros and cons of being pregnant: I do want a baby, and I know enough to know the timing will never be perfect. Ravi will want a baby if his mum tells him he wants one. Both families definitely want me to have one. I'm sure I can fit being a mother around studying and – I'm slightly hazy here – but I expect I can get maternity leave from my lab job. I'm even fairly sure there is a creche for staff somewhere. So far so good. I don't want a baby looked after by Dukkha, or even really living in Dukkha's house. But beggars can't be choosers and look how she dotes on Heera and her brood and how she took to Laly.

'The pros win,' I mutter to myself. Emotionally, I'm not so sure: I don't feel strongly either way, which probably makes me a total weirdo. Maybe a stronger response will kick in when I see if it's one or two lines on the test kit. Unwilling to wait, I ride up to the twelfth-floor loos and do the necessary, as carefully – though far less hygienically – as any experiment, counting aloud the two minutes and adding twenty more seconds, as a sort of confidence interval.

It so happens I told Dukkha the truth this morning: the test is negative. It's genuinely not good or bad news, it just is. I wrap up the spare test for next time, chuck the used one away and get on with my afternoon in the library.

Chapter 39

I've suspected since day one that Dukkha goes through my things when I'm out but I've no real proof beyond clothes folded differently to the way I do it, and my bedside drawers slightly out of kilter. It's not a big deal – I've nothing to hide and if she does it to me, she'll be doing it to Ravi, too – and unlike, say, Laly, who would be incandescent over the alleged breach of privacy (which is a smokescreen because she wouldn't be above doing it herself and she doesn't want Mum reading her outrageous and totally fictitious diary) this is one battle I've just decided not to fight. If my mother-in-law gets her thrills checking out my boring underwear and Ravi's tame-enough gambling IOUs (yes, I know about them; he calls them expenses) then all power to her.

As it happens, she outs herself.

Turns out that if I'd waited another day and a half, I wouldn't have needed to borrow from my running away money; my period has come with a vengeance. It's Saturday and Ravi goes off at the crack of dawn with some team-building outdoor day with his office – for those who are management material, apparently; I say I thought he wanted to go back and study law, he says there is a fast-track option to both, I say, 'Okay. Sounds good,' and stick the pillow over my head to muffle my screams – the agony of stomach cramps or his self-delusion, I'm not sure which. Dukkha doesn't generally surface before noon, unless she's on a mission to do the shopping early (to spoil any lie-in Ravi and I might be having) or has a series of odd jobs lined up for Kabir that need her supervision. Last week she'd heard on the grapevine (aka the factory floor)

307

that the Interfaith Community Centre in Leeds had been gifted a truckload of imported ghee that was past its UK-approved sell-by date and was free to all comers. Dukkha and Kabir were there, queuing, before the organisers even opened up. They arrived back here with pounds and pounds of the stuff, which is now shoved into carrier bags going rancid in the garage. Don't ask me why! My mother-in-law loves a bargain and would mow you down for freebies. Anyway, it means I have free rein to huddle down with a hot water bottle, drug myself up, and wallow in self-pity.

The pain dulls to that blissful almost-gone nagging ache, and I must drift off to sleep, because when she bursts through the door at the back of nine, shrieking, 'Are you a liar, girl? Would you lie to your mother-in-law, the hand that feeds you, the mind that nurtures you, the body that works to give you a home?' I'm more discombobulated than disturbed. This seriously annoys her.

'A liar even when caught in the act!'

'What? Dukkha, what do you mean?'

'You know.' She plonks herself down on the end of my bed and glowers at me. Gone is the saccharine smile from a couple of nights ago when she all but tucked me and Ravi in.

'I don't. What did I lie about?' I shuffle myself upright and rack my brains, because of course I've lied – or by emission or prevaricated – about a million little things, and some bigger ones. The new bank account and my second funding cheque are flashing in accusatory neon lights in my half-asleep brain.

She's wearing one of those tabard apron things and she gropes in the long pocket across the stomach. 'This!'

She's brandishing the now battered Clear Blue box with the remaining pregnancy test inside. 'You told me you weren't pregnant, but you did a test.'

'Yes, and it was negative–'

'So you must have thought you were pregnant. You lied, my girl. Admit it.'

I'm failing to follow her logic, and it's not because I'm still woozy from sleep and painkillers. 'I didn't lie. You asked me and only afterwards I realised I was late so...' Why am I even explaining? Especially as another thought strikes me. 'That test kit was in my bedside drawer. Did you search through my things?'

She barely falters. 'I was cleaning.' Right. But her tone, if not her words, becomes more conciliatory. 'Prove it to me, then. Do the second test.' She tosses the box onto the bed. 'I want to see.'

Sighing and irked but not surprised, I invoke my inner Laly and reach down under the covers and pluck out the hot water bottle. Then I lean over to the bottom of the bedside cabinet and pull out a box of open sanitary pads. 'I have my period. It's really bad, which is why I'm still in bed. If you look in the linen basket, you'll find some wet underwear that I rinsed through because there was blood on it.'

And guess what – she does. She really does. She gets up and takes the lid off the wicker basket that I intend taking down to the washing machine once I'm up. That's just plain...weird, but when she sticks her hand in and pulls out the damp and still slightly stained knickers, it turns into something unpleasant. Gross, in fact. I'm so taken aback I don't even say anything – to be honest, what is there to say? – just watch her drop the white cotton back down and wipe her hands on her apron. Then she flounces out and slams the door.

I lie down again, almost wondering if I've had a random hallucination, so surreal is the encounter. But I can't settle. Queasiness is creeping over me again, and it's not just the recurring pain, it's the image of my mother-in-law all but sniffing my dirty underwear. I bet she searched the bins for the used pregnancy test stick. Oh help, does she listen at our bedroom door? Does she pull back these bed covers and feel for a wet patch? I get up, strip the bed and cram the sheets – crushing the offending pants – into the laundry basket, before taking a hot and long shower, scrubbing myself. She's the grubby one, yet I feel dirty.

When I return to the bedroom, I'm disconcerted again, this time to find that the bed has been neatly remade with freshly ironed sheets, even down to the scatter cushions placed atop of the pillows. What's she up to now? Dukkha doesn't change beds (I do), and she certainly doesn't do the ironing (Ravi does). I tiptoe around the edges of the room, as I dress, eyeing up the double divan as if she's booby-trapped it. An apple-pie bed, I think crazily. I've never been sure what one of those is, but in Enid Blyton books, the Malory Towers girls used to show their displeasure via them.

'Anoushka?' A perfectly normal, friendly voice floats up from the foot of the stairs. 'How are you feeling? Would you like your breakfast in bed?'

I really can't fathom…

'Anoushka?'

'No. Thank you,' I call back. 'I'm coming down.' Which I do, reluctantly. Her mercurial nature is far more exhausting than her nastiness.

'You poor child. Sit down, sit down,' she says as I appear in the doorway. 'Anoushka. I'm so sorry. So very sorry.' She pulls out a chair. 'Sit down.'

Sit down? I'm about to fall down. There's a sting in the tail forthcoming but even after years of watching Laly's antics, I can't see it. Dukkha's ability to manipulate is world class. 'That's alright,' I say automatically – foolishly, because it's really not – but curiosity gets the better of me. 'Sorry for what?' Your words or your actions, I add mentally.

'You, beta.' She taps my shoulder, which I think is meant to signify sympathy, though it's the brisk action most people use when they want to gain your attention. 'I forgive that little outburst upstairs, don't think of it again.' What? Me? 'You don't have to save my feelings, and you shouldn't hide your own.' Double what? 'We should talk frankly, mother to daughter.'

'Me not being pregnant?' I hazard a guess. 'Dukkha, I didn't really–'

'Anoushka! Call it what it is.'

I shake my head. 'I don't understand–'

'Say the word, and it can't hurt you,' she says, like the parody of a self-help manual. 'Miscarriage. You've had an early miscarriage, dear. It happens to most of us.'

It takes me a minute to compute that, then I shake my head again. 'Oh, I see. But I really haven't. Honestly.'

'I knew you'd deny it. But for all your cleverness you can't fool me. We'll go to the doctor on Monday morning, just to ensure all is well. Then you can try again.'

She's made up her mind and she's in one of her untouchable, I know best moods now, but I have to try. 'I'm sure it's not a miscarriage, Dukkha. I think I'd know. I really never was pregnant.'

'Then you should be,' she flares up. 'It's six months. Our family are all expecting well within six months. Either way, you need to see a doctor.'

I can hardly tell her it took us a while to get started, and even now, I'm not sure we're what professionals might call maximising our chances. I haven't looked into when I'm ovulating or anything like that. The GP will laugh me out of the surgery or blame me for wasting NHS resources. 'I don't think–'

'Monday morning. I will phone at 8am.'

She plonks a plate in front of me: limp toast swimming in a watery reconstituted tofu and mung bean mix that masquerades as eggs. Even if I was on top form my stomach would flip. I put a hand to my mouth and I'm not acting. 'It's not the food. I'm sorry,' I gasp as I make a dash for the downstairs loo.

'I know it's not,' is the smug reply I hear over my retching. 'Miscarriage shouldn't be taken lightly.'

I crawl back to bed, heave over some more painkillers but manage to keep them down and draw my legs up to my chest. Let her call it what she wants.

By the time I hear Ravi come home I'm feeling almost back to normal, but I am going to milk this and hide away. I'm peckish now – as long as I don't think about Dukkha's fake eggs – and I'm sure Ravi will bring me some food up here. Saturday night is takeaway night, when Ravi's been out being sporty and all the fat and carbohydrates of a cheesy, meaty pizza is just what my body is craving. He goes way out of the way to this one mom-and-pop place in Pudsey that allegedly does a non-dairy, non-meat option that publicly appeases my in-laws, though a good few slices of the real thing always mysteriously vanish in private. Apparently, pizza is so processed that it's not real food and it's tolerated for Ravi and me as a treat. The dietary (and religious) rules in this house, as my dad would say, are more complex than grandmaster chess and change like the tides.

Unusually, Ravi doesn't come up to change before I hear the front door slam again, but Dukkha will have told him the miscarriage story and that I'm resting – I'll set him right later on – and he's embarrassed by all the nitty-gritty of women's reproductive systems so any excuse to stay well away. It's only after a good hour has passed, and then two, that I notice how silent the house is, and realise they've all gone out, and have been far too long to be collecting pizza. Oh, well. I'm not sorry to be missing some function that Dukkha has 'forgotten' to tell me about. There's no food ready downstairs, as I've neither been grocery shopping or done any cooking of course, so I grab some crackers and an apple and help myself to a big dish of the coconut and pistachio kulfi that's stashed in the garage freezer, constantly replenished, and nobody ever talks about. Upstairs, with my John Grisham novel, I'm probably as happy as I've been any Saturday night since I got married. Even as I have the thought, the contentment dissipates a little because it's actually a really sad state of affairs. In lieu of any other solution, I shovel the ice-cream down and absorb myself in the legal affairs of The Client.

It's late when Ravi and his parents come home and I'm not hungry, but when I hear his tread, and the cautious opening of the bedroom door, I sit up and do my best to look appreciative of whatever it is he's bringing me – luckily not too appreciative, as it turns out to be nothing.

'Mum said you were sick, women's things,' he says awkwardly, 'so I didn't disturb you. Are you feeling better?'

'Much,' I reply. 'It wasn't a miscarriage, Ravi, if that's what she told you. Just, the usual…'

'Yes, yes,' he says hastily. 'I know. But you should go to the doctor anyway. She won't let up.' He shuffles his feet. 'And she's kind of right that all the others had honeymoon babies. Maybe a check-up is a good idea.' I bite back the retort that it would be impossible for us to have a honeymoon baby because he knows it and I'm about to refuse to waste the doctor's time, when he adds, 'She says if you won't go, she'll phone your mum for your own good—'

'She…' The witch. She's got me. If Dukkha even breathes the word miscarriage to Mum and Dad, it'll be an emergency of nuclear proportions and never lived down. 'Fine,' I agree, tight-lipped at being blackmailed. 'Right. So. Did you have a good day?'

Ravi looks mightily relieved at my abrupt change of subject. 'It was a great session,' he says enthusiastically. 'Paintballing. We thrashed the Hull team. I'll be black and blue with battle scars tomorrow.' His grin suggests there's no higher accolade. 'Tonight's pizza never tasted so good.'

'Pizza?'

'Yeah, we went to the restaurant. Anoop and his folks met us. Great fun…Sorry you missed it, Anou.'

I keep my tone neutral. 'Did you bring me some?'

'Pizza? Nah. Did you want some?' Ravi frowns. 'You were sick. Mum said not to bother, we'd be doing you a favour. She cooked you lunch and you threw it all up, didn't you? Shall I make you some toast?'

'No, I'm fine,' I tell him, and let him witter on about how hilarious it was when x got spattered in the eye with paintball dye and y and z banged heads and saw stars. I swear he's one step away from joining the Army, shooting each other is such a hoot. Meanwhile, all I'm musing on is the fact that it's not the big things that eat away at a relationship, that wreck a marriage, it's the little ones. Like a single slice of lukewarm pizza.

Chapter 40

I let Dukkha have her way and make me an appointment with her GP practice. I do need to register, and it's either here or with the University Medical Centre – who are probably far more versed in preventing conception than encouraging it. I bite my tongue on hearing her insist on an emergency appointment due to my spontaneous early miscarriage, but it works in my favour, as they offer a ten o'clock slot on Wednesday morning and Kabir reminds Dukkha she can't easily skive off work because she's got a Health and Safety Assessment booked. She's pissed off, which makes me amenable to going (alone) so she gives in, and they drop me off, tolerably early as I've yet to register, on their way to the factory.

I feel lucky that the doctor is middle-aged, comfortably mumsy and waves away my concerns at being a time-waster. She accepts that my period is my period, and that less than six months of not-really-trying for a baby is far too soon for fertility tests; her eyes twinkle as I politely explain the peccadilloes of my mother-in-law. Instead, she suggests she'll do a general MOT. 'We'd call you in anyway, once you're registered as a new patient, so I might as well do it now,' she says cheerfully and sets about my blood pressure, heart rate, eyes and ears, quickly giving me a clean bill of health.

'When was your last cervical smear test?' she asks finally, raising her eyebrows when I say I've never had one. 'Hmm. Well, have you any objection to having one now? It'll be something to tell your mother-in-law.' She winks.

So I go behind the screen, take off my bottom half

clothes – wishing I'd worn a skirt not jeans – and get up on the examination couch, pulling the blue paper towel stuff over my modesty. The GP brandishes a speculum at me, saying, 'Sorry. I won't tell you to try and relax, but well, try and relax…' and goes on to explain matter-of-factly what she's about to do. I let my knees fall apart as she requests and screw up my eyes, waiting from the sharp cold metal to stretch my insides. Nothing happens. I look down the bed to see the doctor's head still bent between my thighs, then she straightens up and frowns.

'Change of plan,' she says, catching my eye. 'Nothing's wrong, Anoushka, don't worry, but I'm not doing the smear test today. Get dressed and we'll talk about it.'

Kind as the GP is, I hurry out of the surgery ten minutes later, utterly mortified. I can hardly bear to think about what she's just explained to me, and I've no idea how I'm going to tell Ravi. When she stopped, I thought there might be some residual bleeding or, for a horrible second, polyps or even a tumour. As it is I'm lucky – lucky! – that the doctor can't do the test because my tissue linings are intact; I'm still a virgin. I don't know who was more shocked, the GP or me. I could see her struggling to ask me, the PhD biology student, the right questions to work out how I could possibly have thought I was having penetrative sex. I muttered about the half-erect and short-lived thrusting and jabbing, the soreness and the fluid, and she said that at least explained the extensive bruising and chafed skin down there. I even had to reassure her that no, I'm not being abused, not a victim of forced marriage or domestic violence. Then, when I asked could she not just do the test and break the hymen herself, she said that was inhumane. She said we, me and Ravi, need help – counselling – to understand the physical act and explore our emotional barriers.

The more I play it over and over in my head, the more shameful it gets. I am a fool, an idiot, thick as two short planks.

I walk home, miles and miles, all the while rehearsing what I'll say to Ravi. It wouldn't be so bad, not quite so bad, if it was just between him and me, but his mother will dig and snipe and bully him till she gets at the truth. Then, god knows how she'll react. There's no way I cannot tell him…But that gets me thinking, and eventually I work out how exactly to not tell him. Sort of.

Back at the empty house I pick up the phone and dial Ravi's office. He won't like being disturbed at work, but I can't talk to him here.

'I went straight into work,' I lie. 'So I thought I could meet you in town for lunch. There's a couple of things the doctor said about getting pregnant,' I lower my voice even though I'm home alone, 'you know, how to increase the odds.' Maybe appealing to his gambling side is intentional, I don't know. There's a pause, then:

'Yes, sure,' Ravi says pleasantly. 'I'll see you at 1 o'clock at…er…'

'The Wimpy on Broadway,' I reply quickly. He's in a busy office, he won't turn me down but best not to chance it. 'Got to dash. See you then.'

I've plenty of time to get there first and order him a Wimpy Grill – let Dukkha smell that on his breath and dare to complain after the pizza fiasco. I'm at the window, sipping a Coke, when I see him hurrying in my direction. There's no doubt about it that my husband is a very good-looking man, beautifully dressed. It's just a shame–

'I've ordered,' I say, cutting off my thoughts as he

sits down opposite. 'The food should be here any minute.'

'Why did you phone? Why are we here?' he asks immediately. 'I'm glad to see you, of course.' This is added hurriedly, probably prompted by the appearance of the waitress and two plates of food.

I tell him quietly about the soft side of the GP visit: I'm fine; not pregnant; no miscarriage; have a smear test – which I very loosely explain. Even then, he looks round uneasily. 'Do we have to do this here?' he whispers. 'Why not at home, later.'

'Your mum.' I'm deliberately blunt. 'She'll either worm it out of me first, listen in to us, or make you tell her everything.' To his credit he doesn't argue, just stabs his fork sulkily at a few chips. 'Brace yourself,' I go on breezily, 'because I've more to say. You eat, I'll talk.' Poor Ravi. The topic isn't funny, and it's not great that I've chosen to be less than fully honest – mostly because I don't want him so traumatised he becomes impotent – but his reaction is a picture. All I say is, 'We're not doing it right. You have to go in further–'

'Anou, please!'

'And more often.'

'Stop, Anousha. No more.'

He's scandalised. Well, good. I went through the mortification of the appointment and I'm here saving his feelings, so I call the shots. But I'm done anyway. I sit up straighter and take a big bite of the burger I've no appetite for. When I open my mouth again, he's shushing me before any words come out. I hold up my hands. 'I'm done, Ravi. All I need is your promise that we can do it–'

'Ssh.'

'Go in further and more often,' I temper it. 'Promise?'

'Yes, yes, alright,' he agrees.

'Oh, and one more thing – you tell your mum whatever you want about this, but she's not going to hear anything from me. It's our business.'

He nods, which I take with a pinch of salt, but my cards are on the table, at least. I pick up the menu just as the smiling waitress comes to remove our plates. 'Time for a Knickerbocker Glory?' I ask him.

Unsurprisingly, Ravi has to hurry back to work.

Very surprisingly, it works. Either he's desperate never, ever to have that kind of 'conversation' again, or he's secretly relieved to have a bit of simple guidance (however vague), or he just responds well to women wearing the mantel of his mother and giving him orders – which is my least favourite but most likely option – however, Ravi rises (pun sort of intended) to the occasion. Over the next few weeks, we have sex a bit more often and with intermittently more success. I can pinpoint the night he, well, properly penetrates me for the first time because there's a sharp sting, tightness, and more than a smear of blood, (I can hear Laly saying, 'Eww, too much information, Anou,'). I teach myself to relax and it gets easier if not thrilling. If I had to look at the experiential results, it would be that seven out of ten times, he's in the right place for the few important seconds. Theoretically, it's enough to get me pregnant now. Practically, nothing happens. I keep telling myself nature knows best. My mind wants a baby, it always did, but deep down, in the wee small hours, there's a part of me that wishes that it was in a very different situation, and I wonder if my body is rebelling.

Whatever the reason, there's a semblance of normality over the house as the new year turns into spring. Dukkha and Kabir take a few days holiday and go to visit Galu and his family. Ravi is firm for once and says, no, we (she really only wants him) can't go because of work; other people with children should get the Easter break. Dukkha pouts but presumably isn't that bothered; she'll be well versed in playing off one son against another and if my faults are highlighted in the daughter-in-law stakes, then I'll take that for a few days' blissful peace here. Instead, the first weekend I go up to Edinburgh while Ravi has a mammoth card game, and then for my birthday, we go to Scarborough and stay in a B&B overnight. A couple of times I catch myself comparing the trip to how it would be with Donald, and it comes to me it's the formality of life with Ravi that makes it, frankly, less fun. I don't want to be married to Donald, he's still the big brother I'd love, and we can eat fish and chips from the paper and make silly in-jokes because we've plenty in common, work and study-wise anyway. With Ravi, it's all about appearances and style – and I understand more and more – the only thing we have in common is being Indian. And probably having got married to please – and escape (or try to, in his case) – our parents; totally messed-up and complicated. It's quite a strain spending two whole days and a night together. It's the longest time we've spent together full stop – even on our honeymoon Ravi's diving course took up hours and hours – and while it's not awkward or unpleasant, we're like acquaintances stuck together on a long train journey, we run out of things to talk about every ten minutes.

Dukkha and Kabir have arrived back in our absence, and I brace myself for the third degree, but she's full on busy with Galu and his family. Unlike the majesty of Heera and the (outward) golden boy status of Ravi, Galu comes across as a middle-of-the-road son in Dukkha's eyes. One minute she's extolling the virtues of his pleasantly ordinary lifestyle – his talented children's sports activities and musical abilities is a big one – the next she's dissing it as constant running around after them and paying extortionate fees, instead of spending the time and money on Dukkha. Okay, I've inferred the last bit there, but I bet it's true.

In true Dukkha style she's also returned with bags of leftover food and pre-prepared meals, which are lodged precariously in the fridge and piled on the kitchen table for 'someone' to put away. I do it without being told, ignoring her sitting there talking at me and implicitly comparing me poorly to Galu's traditional wife (and mother of his three children) who insisted that they bring back all these specially-made treats. I'm simply grateful to the woman; it means I can reheat rather than cook from scratch.

I expect that Ravi will rush out as soon as he's showered and changed, but for once he doesn't and it's strange setting a table for four people and arranging a family dinner. We generally eat in sittings whenever we're at home and so inclined, pulling out whatever I've left ready or snacking on toast and jam if I haven't. It's exactly like being in the car together, except with food and sitting opposite each other; Ravi and Kabir share an odd thought, I sit quietly, and Dukkha keeps up a rumbling monologue. I've realised I automatically deconstruct her words and reply to them in my head, my own passive-aggressive incredulity, a variation on I can't believe she just said that and she's a fine one to talk. Should I be challenging her? Or am I picking my battles wisely? I don't know, but I don't much like the person I am around her.

So, expecting a fight, I retrieve a carton of kulfi – what the hell, two cartons of different flavours – from the depths of the chest freezer and plonk it defiantly in front of them. I expect lowered eyes from my husband and father-in-law (if they could they'd put their fingers in their ears and hum lah-lah-lah to distance themselves) and an attitude from Dukkha. Instead, in that infuriating way she has, of pulling the rug from under me, she's all smiles. They all are, and they're looking expectantly at me, which makes me very suspicious.

'Mum got you a gift,' Ravi pipes up first.

I look down at my setting and sure enough, the plate's been pushed aside, and a thick white envelope is propped up against my glass, my name in curlicue ink on the front.

'Open it, go on,' Ravi encourages me.

Kabir nods along. 'Happy birthday, my dear,' he says. 'Many happy returns.'

Dukkha sits there like the queen of the cats who have brought her all the cream.

I sit down heavily and run my finger under the loosely stuck flap. If I were to guess, I'd say it's an invitation or a gift voucher. Now, who wouldn't love a luxury spa day or a ride in a hot air balloon, or…whatever, but all I can imagine is the four of us partaking together – massage tables all in a row followed by a Turkish bath, oh my god. But no, it will be something that serves Dukkha, so best case scenario is a cordon bleu course at a fancy hotel. Worst case scenario is that the hotel is in Mumbai.

'Thank you,' I say, putting off the evil moment. 'Do you know what it is?' I can't help asking Ravi.

He shakes his head. 'Total surprise. Just open it, Anou.' He says it good-naturedly but then shares an indulgent what is she like? smile with his mother, which makes me feel like a five-year-old. Especially when he adds, 'Do you want mango or coconut kulfi? I'll serve you.'

I'm glad they're partially distracted by the sweet, because when I see what the gift is, all laid out in fancy print on heavy card, I wish it was only as horrible as a group massage or cooking in India. I know I let out a gasp, but no doubt they all think it's with pleasure. For my birthday, Dukkha has given me an appointment with a fertility consultant, a specialist doctor.

'He's private, of course,' Dukkha adds now. 'You can see him immediately, at his rooms in Leeds.' She announces his location in inverted commas, nothing as common as a clinic for Dr Karim Arnab.

Not even a woman, certainly not a down-to-earth Yorkshire woman like my kind GP, who I might just tolerate seeing again. Oh no, a man. An Indian man, no doubt sourced from Dukkha's extended social circle, all of whom will be aware of, 'My poor daughter-in-law's miscarriage and failure to get pregnant.'

All of this flashes through my mind like an Intercity train, along with wondering – for the millionth time – if Dukkha is cluelessly tactless or incisively calculating. Her face is impassive as she waits for me to thank her; Kabir clearly has no idea what the 'gift' is, nor does he care as he eats his ice cream; Ravi's look confirms he didn't know what was in the envelope and his reaction will depend on whether he's expected to attend the consultation.

'What an original gift,' I say. 'Full of thought and consideration.' Yeah, of a totally weird kind, and I'm buggered if I'll thank her. 'I can honestly say I wasn't expecting this. I don't quite know what to say.' That's true, at least.

She inclines her head, regally. 'I'll chaperone you. And the sooner the better. After all, dear, you're not getting any younger, are you?' She cackles away between slurps of kulfi, clearly delighted with herself.

Chapter 41

Resigned to the ordeal, I figure it's best to get the fertility consultation over sooner rather than later. Ravi distances himself, it being 'women's problems', even though I'm fairly sure there is no problem. My hint that he might need to get involved, if I'm given a clean bill of health – falls on determinedly deaf ears. Well, I'll deal with it when it happens, right now, I'm in a nightmare that might just be bearable as long as Dukkha isn't allowed in to see the doctor with me. When I make the appointment, I'm snootily assured of confidentiality by a woman who is clearly Indian, and short of bluntly asking whether I can ban my mother-in-law and thus becoming a joke, a pity case, or the subject of the local Indian community gossip, I accept the superior one's word. She's not the friendliest; I doubt she'll be sympathetic. Surely if I agree to attend, Dukkha will content herself with the waiting room. Even my mother would reluctantly agree to that.

I'm too taken aback to broach it as we climb the stairs to the doctor's 'rooms'. I'd envisioned a Leeds version of Harley Street, all Chesterfields and filter coffee machines in a waiting area carefully designed to resemble a posh sitting room. Instead, the taxi deposits us outside a row of three-storey terraced houses in a nondescript backstreet. Of the six grubby bells, the middle one is labelled Dr Arnab and a tinny voice tells us to go up. The carpet is worn and grubby, there's a faint smell of cooking oil and the doors we pass all have nameplates without any indication of the businesses within. I swear if Hollywood were casting for an illegal abortionist circa 1965, then this would win hands down. I steal a look at Dukkha's face, knowing that if she were anyone else, we'd bolt. However, she doesn't appear to think anything of the place, just marches on in through the door marked Karim Arnab M.D., me trailing like a puppy being dragged to the vet. Dukkha greets the woman behind the desk with a familiarity that makes my heart sink, my only saving grace being that whoever she is, she doesn't seem that enamoured by my mother-in-law's fawning Hindi words. Mind you, she doesn't pay me any attention at all. She just tells us to knock on the door and go straight in, the doctor is waiting. That alone throws me, because whoever gets shown straight into an empty surgery for an on-time appointment?

Dr Arnab has thick glasses, a clean white coat, and a smile that isn't a smile bearing crooked yellow teeth. There's no sign of cigarettes but the cramped room stinks of smoke with an undercurrent of disinfectant wipes. One side is portioned off with a kind of shower curtain and beyond it I can see an examination couch. At this moment in time, I'm actually grateful for Dukkha's presence – and she is speechless – which indicates the sleazy predicament I think I'm in.

There are no pleasantries. The doctor gestures at us to sit down and opens proceedings with, 'I understand you wish to become pregnant and are failing. Let's find some answers.' Then he launches into a quickfire round of intimate questions, which are so clinical and detached it's not that hard to answer them at all. Dukkha has a face like (I imagine) a Peeping Tom at a spyhole and when I say outright what the GP told me, I hear a sharp intake of breath. Well, tough. If she can't take hearing the explicit details of her darling little boy's sex life, she shouldn't have forced this meeting. There's a reason why talking about sex is taboo in Indian families, mama-ji. My dignity is out the window and legging it over the chimneyed roofs of the Leeds suburbs, my remaining self-respect in hot pursuit, so I might as well spill all the beans. Dr Arnab's response, whatever I say, is only to scribble on a jotter in front of him. Then there's silence.

'Go behind the curtain and take off your clothes.' He has a high-pitched, squeaky voice, but it still makes me and Dukkha jump. He peers at her and says, 'You stay here while I examine her.' She shrinks back and a little bit of me thrills with the fact that she's bitten off more than she can chew, whereas I'm doing alright; this medic has the bedside manner a pathologist would be ashamed of and is going to look at my naked body the same way I examine microbes under a microscope.

I do as I'm told, finding a folded paper gown to wear, and perch on the bed reading the single framed medical certificate crooked on the wall. The glass has a crack across it and it might be fifty years old, certifying someone called Karim Arnab Chatterjee as a graduate of the Manohar Prasad Medical Institute, Bangalore. I've no idea if that is the person about to manhandle me, but my standards are now so low, I'm impressed he's thoroughly washing his hands before beginning.

First, he checks my breasts in a way that suggests authority, next he indicates I should lie down and raise my knees while he slaps on a pair of blue surgical gloves. There's no speculum or ultrasound in sight, so I ask politely, 'What are you going to do?' to which he replies, 'Check the position of your womb.' That's the limit of our interaction, until I'm told to get dressed.

I'm done while he's still scrubbing his nails, peering at them intently, the water heater screeching and steaming; I'm almost inclined to apologise he had to approach my unclean body.

Once back behind his desk, he says abruptly, addressing a spot between us. 'You're fine. She's fine. Stop being impatient. Practise intercourse frequently and correctly. If there is no pregnancy in six more months, go to your NHS doctor. Take your husband. He will require tests too.'

There's a quickly stifled half-snort from Dukkha, but Dr Arnab's already dismissing us with a wave of his hand.

'Thank you, doctor,' I say over my shoulder. Dukkha says nothing, not even to the woman in the outer room. She just stomps down the stairs. I can't help but feel a sense of satisfaction. Serves her right. I hope she paid that dodgy set up a fortune. In the taxi on the way home, I wait for Dukkha to turn on me, and although it takes her a good few miles to decide her tactics, she doesn't disappoint. Two minutes from the Close, she turns to me and hisses,

'You, madam, have no right to put my son down. Did you hear yourself, saying those things to that man?' She sucks air up through her teeth, making a whistling sound. That man, I think, the great fertility doctor has been demoted to that man, yet I'm still the one in the wrong 'A wife, asking for sexual relations from her husband, demanding it two or three times a week! Disgusting. Men make the first moves, not girls. Even if those ridiculous accusations were true, how could my son perform his duty well under such pressure.' She looks me up and down in the way I'd expected Dr Arnab might and didn't. 'Think on that my girl,' she spits out.

Dukkha pauses in her whispered vitriol to pay the taxi driver, march up the driveway, and fumble with the front door key. Despite myself – or maybe because she's so unfair, so vicious – I'm struggling to blink away the tears I know would make her day. Her parting shot, as she stalks up the stairs to her bedroom, is, 'Because if you can't get pregnant normally, like a nice well-brought up Indian girl, then your role here will change.'

'Divorce?' I find my voice. 'You'd have Ravi divorce me? That wouldn't look good–'

She backtracks to look over the banister at me, a horrible smile on her evil face. 'Oh no, dear. You entered into a contract, you don't escape it. But you can be put in your rightful place by a second wife, a fertile and amenable wife.'

Has she gone mad? At least incredulity dries my tears. 'A second wife? 'Ravi wouldn't do that.' Would he? 'That's not even legal anyway.'

She laughs in a way that makes me feel like a rabbit caught in a snare: trapped, desperate – just what she wants. 'It's legal enough in India,' she says. 'If the families will it, who's to stop it? As for Ravi, of course he would. Ravi does as I tell him. Haven't you learned anything yet?'

Part 7
The Cage Door Opens

Chapter 42

The light and shade of Dukkha's behaviour is slowly driving me insane. It might sound overly dramatic, but I do mean that literally. On the darkest days, when I take two paracetamol for a headache, I even wonder what it would be like to cram a handful of pills into my mouth, swallow then, and just go to blissful sleep. Shit. Just saying that makes me feel….guilty? Panicked? Out of control…? Luckily, knowledge is a powerful thing and the biologist in me knows the risks of overdosing on paracetamol are horrible. Neither am I about to raid the university laboratories for random white powders. Jumping off a cliff isn't an option in this part of Yorkshire, and neither is doing that to my parents, so I'll have to fucking jog on. If that sounds facetious, too bad. Nobody else is ever, ever going to know that I've harboured such thoughts, especially not Dukkha. Her pseudo-grieving over my mental health is enough to drag me up from the doldrums.

That said, seriously, if it wasn't for weekdays at the university, studying or working, irregular meetings with Donald, and long and increasingly silly chats with Laly on the phone, I think I would have snapped by now. I've no idea what that 'snapping' would look like – fight, flight, depression, mania – but she's chipping away at me, bit by bit, covering the wounds with balm and plasters, then ripping them off – sometimes fast, sometimes slow – to start chipping away again. It's like there's a sculpture of the real Anoushka out there somewhere, that Dukkha is moulding into something cowed and deformed. Call me fanciful and stupid, I don't care; she's already called me every name under the sun.

And then, just when the sculpture is about to crack beyond repair, she places it on a pedestal and goes at it with a half-arsed repair job; too little too late.

So, the cycle continues.

I know it's her and not me. I know it's not just me, it's what she does with Ravi. Maybe it's why all her children live away from home and why her husband is a cardboard cut-out of a man, re-animated for public occasions. But divide and conquer, behind closed doors, street angel (sort of) – house devil…all of those things make her cruelty slippery, inadmissible.

She hasn't hit me physically yet, and actually I don't think she will. She does that to Ravi because she decided long ago he's not clever enough for her mind games. Me, though, with my notions of being better than I should be, I'm ripe for mental manipulation. The sad thing is that I'm not as intelligent as she gives me credit for, because she's winning.

Perhaps I'm grasping at straws, but I do think Ravi and I might stand a chance if we were left alone. We'd have to work hard at getting to know each other properly, and hard work is second nature to me; to Ravi though? He has ideas and intentions but his ambition is missing, either bashed out of him by his mother or it just never developed. He works during the day, gambles at night, and lives like an electronic Peter Pan in the fantasy world of his PlayStation.

I've tried to talk to him about the whole sex-fertility-pregnancy thing – despite last month's awful session with Dr Arnab (who I subsequently looked up in the medical library and I'm fairly sure was struck off the GMC or never registered at all) and Dukkha's nasty aftermath – but it reminds me of my mum's futile attempts to get my brother Akash to wear his glasses and do his exercises when he was diagnosed with a lazy eye. But Akash was seven years old. Ravi promises to make love and then gets a headache, backache, or feels a cold coming on. One time recently – I kid you not – he had a paper cut on his thumb and cried off on pain of that. If he'd just say, 'No. I don't want to do it tonight,' I'd have some respect but to him those things aren't excuses, they're real. Then there's been once or twice when he has got hard at inopportune moments and called me excitedly to come to bed quickly. That's quite funny – not that I'd let on. I don't know whether he'll ever agree to see a doctor. Fair enough, my experience isn't encouraging and Ravi is non-committal when I bring it up. 'Kismet,' he'll say, and shrug. Destiny. If we're meant to have a baby, we will. Then I want to shake him and say, 'Fuck kismet. It's science,' but what's the point? The root of it is, that his mother has told him I'm to blame and he blindly believes.

So, I'm changing tack. I've decided that since Dukkha is the villain of the piece, I'm going to milk that for all it's worth. Our lives will only ever be half-lives whilst she's in close proximity, so she has to go. Or we do. As I can't take a knife to her or bash her over the head with a rock, because even with just cause I'm still opposed to murder, then it's over to us, me and Ravi, to get out. I'm playing with fire because it's a 'me or her' ultimatum, which could go either way, and might seem like bully tactics learned from my mother-in-law herself. but it's worth the dual risk.

There's no real way around the classic, 'We need to talk,' and all its connotations, so that when I say it, Ravi's eyes are filled with alarm. I catch him when his parents are out, ironically at the factory's Personnel Manager's wedding, and he's ironing his and Kabir's five work shirts each for the next week. This, card games and PlayStation aside, is Ravi's happy place. If I were a psychologist, I could probably find significance in his control of making smooth order out of creased cotton.

'You're leaving me this time, aren't you,' he says flatly.

'That's up to you,' I reply, which sounds like a cop-out but is true. 'I don't want to leave you but honestly, Ravi, we can't go on like this.' I've got a whole speech prepared but before I can launch into it, he speaks.

'What do you want me to do?'

I flounder, off course. 'It's not about–'

'Don't give me a crock of shit, Anou.' He lays one sleeve the length of the ironing board and picks up the sizzling iron. 'Just tell me what you want me to do.'

'I want us to move out.' There. Said it. I hold my breath.

He runs the iron back and forth over the blue pinstripes. 'Move out where?'

'Well, I thought either nearer the city centre so we're close to your office and the university or…or if you want to go further, Scotland. Not to my parents, not even Edinburgh, which is too expensive, but somewhere you could get a new job and I could commute to the uni there.'

I wait it out through him ironing the front, the back, the tricky shoulder places of the shirt, then him buttoning it and hanging it over the back of a chair, ready to transport upstairs. It's not a tense silence.

'I need to think about it,' he says finally. 'Let me think.'

He reaches for another shirt and I realise he means now, he wants to think about it now. It's more than I expected so I don't tempt fate but leave him to it. Crossing my fingers that he thinks it through before his mother gets back, reads his face and makes his decision for him.

In reality, it takes him two weeks to decide. I have

to zip my mouth and draw on every gram of dwindling patience not to prod him. Since there's the distinct possibility he's hoping for the ignore it and it'll go away scenario I do remind him, backing off when I get the irritated, 'Yes, yes, I know, Anoushka. Don't hassle me. I'm thinking.' The saving grace, the reason I believe him, is that he doesn't tell his mum about the ultimatum – she'd have been down on me like ten tonnes of granite blocks if he had.

She does know something's up, though; those beady little greedy eyes are following us both. It's because Ravi is arriving from work even later than normal, grabbing some food and coming straight to our room – the only way he can keep any secret from her is not to see her. Interestingly, she isn't seeking him out with pointless little subterfuges like opening a stubborn jar of pickles or to come and say hello to Heera's children on the phone. I'm guessing she thinks we're shagging the evenings away, determined to produce a baby ASAP, me doing my wifely duty – at Ravi's behest and having taken fright over Dukkha's mad threat about second wives in India. If she knew I was babying her son along in whispers about whether he chooses me or her to live with for the rest of his life – and let's not pretend it's anything less than that – then my mother-in-law would burn the house down with me in it, or have me committed to an institution for 'Hysteria', just like they did in Victorian times...I only wish I were exaggerating.

'I'll move out with you,' Ravi says abruptly, coming in and removing his tie, then his shoes, whilst speaking. 'We'll have to move away though because I can't stick to it if I'm near here. She'll have a way of stopping us from renting a place or turn up on our doorstep and talk me round.'

I don't say anything immediately, trying to take that

in. My initial feeling is disbelief, closely followed by shock, as I realise, first, I've been assuming Ravi will choose his mother and try and talk me into staying, and second, that he has the insight to see that she will – certainly – be a siren luring him onto the rocks.

'Well, say something. You don't seem very pleased.' He throws himself on the bed and stares up at the ceiling, arms crossed under his head.

And in that second, I don't know if I am. 'Neither do you,' I say quietly, deflecting that thought. 'Are you sure?'

'Yes…No…I don't know. It's too hard,' he admits and I respect him for not lying to me, even if the underlying counterpoint is clearly, 'It's also not fair and it's your fault,' But I'm not going down that route, I'm taking this at face value. Calling his bluff, if you like.

'So, it's Scotland, then?'

He nods miserably.

'Good.' I start talking about deciding where to start looking for a flat, depending on him finding a job: the chicken and egg of it, when he drops it into the one-sided conversation that there's an office job for the taking in a solicitor's office in Stirling. 'What? Well, that's great. Tell me about it,' I interrupt myself to say.

'What's to tell? It came up in the team meeting. We're opening an office in Stirling so it's an internal vacancy. It's a sideways move and I'll have to have an interview but of course I'll get the job. Who could be better qualified? I can do it all backwards. Might even put in for office manager while I'm at it.'

That bit of the confident Ravi I first met shines through the gloom and stops me asking again, for a different reason, 'Are you sure?' Fingers crossed the stars are aligned, Mata Rani's on my side, and my marriage is meant to be more than a washout. We need this, if there's any chance of us surviving together. Even if we can just scrape together the money for a student-type flat, I'll get a GTA job in addition to lab work; I'll cut back on the PhD until we're on our feet; I'll put my cards on the table in front of Dr Moffat and call Donald in as back-up; I'll go cap in hand to my parents...I make those, and more, bargains with whatever god is open to a deal before having to add that 'Are you sure?'

'I don't want to go but I can't stay,' he says. 'But I wish it was over. I wish we could just take our stuff and go now.' We both know, I wish we didn't have to face my mother, is what he's really saying.

I lie awake half the night, worrying, planning, up and down. Sometimes I can see how it will work out, luck on our side – and hell are we due some luck – but other times it feels like we're two small children playing at running away.

Chapter 43

'So, we're agreed. We will sit your parents down and tell them in a proper fashion what we both want to do and why. Ravi?' I want to snap my fingers in his face to prove that he can hear me. He's frowning at a barely-there crease in his trousers. 'Ravi, we have to be together on this.' I don't need to remind him his mother will destroy our allegiance in seconds if it's in any way tentative. 'This conversation is going to be the test of our marriage, I'm not exaggerating.'

'I know. Don't go on, Anou. I'm with you a hundred per cent.' He shudders. 'I just wish it were over. She's going to go apeshit.'

No, she's not. She's far too clever for that, but the fallout will be far worse than a bit of shouting. 'Come on.' I put out my hand to pull him up and he takes it, his palm soft and damp.

Downstairs, the kitchen table is lavish with sweets and snacks, Dukkha has even made chai in a pan on the stove. My heart sinks because she's so got the wrong end of the stick. Alright, then, as Ravi says, she's going to go apeshit.

'A family conference,' she says gaily. 'What could this be about? Sit down, sit down. Kabir?' She bustles to the back door and calls him in. 'The children are waiting for you.'

Ravi and I sit down side by side. Under the table, I put my hand firmly on his thigh, because he looks like a spooked horse that might bolt any minute.

'You said you have an announcement.' Dukkha looks expectantly over the top of her mug. 'Eat, eat,' she urges.

I drop a galubjamon on my plate, where it swims in

its juice like a lonely testicle, and Ravi reaches blindly for a handful of sweet rice. He is petrified. 'We said we'd come to a decision.' I correct Dukkha against my better judgement but the sooner she knows this is not a pregnancy announcement the better.

'Yes, yes,' she snaps, her smile faltering only momentarily. 'Well?'

Ravi just stares into space, no eye contact even with me. I sigh. I explain to them it's time that Ravi and I become a proper couple. We need our own independence, to make our own decisions and our own mistakes. That we need to be treated like adults not children. That we need our own space. 'In our own house,' I add firmly.

Silence.

'In our own house in Scotland.' There's a quavery shrill note in my voice now. 'We're moving to Stirling. Not India.' I have to release Ravi's thigh to wipe my hand, it leaves a sweaty print that he'll hate. 'We'll still be there for you, of course–'

'What about the baby?' Dukkha interrupts harshly. 'Ravi, son, why do you let your wife speak? Are we to be denied our own grandchild?'

'Dukkha, there is no baby,' I say quietly when I see that Ravi's lips move wordlessly. 'No baby, I am not pregnant.'

There is a pause, a whole ten seconds – I start counting to calm my nerves – then Dukkha gets up abruptly and leaves the room.

At first I think she's gone to the toilet, because it's either the downstairs cloakroom door or the front door that we hear opening. When she doesn't come back, Kabir, who sits drumming his fingers on the table – not a single word to say to his son, or to me – gets up and follows her. I stare at Ravi, and when I can't put up with him ignoring me any longer, I, too, go and see what's happening. We've got to finish this now.

The next thing I see, the front door is wide open my father-in-law is running down the path – in his slippers; Dukkha won't like that, I think automatically – calling out. I rush outside, to see him in pursuit of Dukkha, who's halfway down the close, clutching herself and bawling. Kabir shouts at her in Hindi, asking her where she's going in such a state and her reply is that she doesn't know, her life is over. Oh, please. He grabs her by the upper arm and tries to drag her back but she's having none of it. They wrestle like that for a couple of minutes and then Dukkha seems to give up. She crumples, and as if in slow motion, falls to the pavement and is still. Drama queen, I think, she should get a standing ovation – and doing this in public. Kabir bends over her, speaking rapidly, trying to make her see reason, I suppose, when suddenly his body goes rigid and he slaps her face. My smile dies as he looks back at me, panicked, and shouts out.

'Anoushka, help! Phone an ambulance. She's had a heart attack. She's not breathing. Help.'

I back into the hall and with shaking hands, dial 999, and pull my wits together to explain what's happened. The dispatcher tells me to hold the line, the ambulance is on its way and does anyone know CPR, she can talk us through it. I tell her I do and then call out to Ravi to come and hold the phone. Suddenly he's galvanised into action and emerges from the kitchen like a bat out of hell.

'What? What's happening?' His eyes are wild, like someone coming out of a catatonic state, and he shakes me.

'Oh, Ravi,' I sob at him, 'thank goodness. Your mum…she's…she's having a heart attack. Quick, take the phone so I can–' I hold it out but it falls with a crash to the table, Ravi is flying past me, pushing me roughly aside so that I bang my head on the glass panel in the front door. He pauses, mid-flight, and I think it's to catch me, to apologise, but no. His hand shoots out and he slaps my face.

'Don't you dare go near her. This is your fault,' he shouts. 'If my mother dies, I'll never forgive you. I'll kill you. I hate you, Anoushka. I hate you.'

She's carted off in an Emergency Ambulance, a crowd of sympathetic neighbours crowded around, their faces illuminated in the flashing lights. Ravi goes with her, holding her hand, and Kabir trudges back to the house to collect his car keys and follow them. I'm lurking in the doorway, reeling less from the collapse than from Ravi's attack on me.

'She'll be alright,' he says wearily. 'They say she'll be alright.'

'Kabir,' I manage. 'I'm sorry. I didn't...' But what didn't I? I just look at him.

'Not now, Anoushka.' He shakes his head.

'Shall I come? To the hospital.'

'Best not, eh?'

I stand there, slumped in the doorframe until he's gone, and all the neighbours have gone, too. Despite their surreptitious glances, none comes over. I don't want them to, but I do beat myself up, they're probably blaming me, too. God knows what Ravi or even Dukkha said out there. More likely they just don't know me; they probably think I'm a bride shipped in from India without a word of English. It's not like I've ever made an effort to say hello.

I go upstairs and climb into bed, fully clothed, and hide my face in the pillow until there's not a chink of light visible. The very worst thing of all is not that my mother-in-law had a heart attack and it's my fault, nor is it that Ravi hit me, or that he hates me. No. The very

worst thing is that the strongest feeling I had, watching
her out there, paramedics in attendance, was that I
wished, wished, she was dying. It's passed, of course, I
don't want that, really, I don't, but I can't unthink it.
But what kind of person does it make me?

It wasn't a heart attack. Nothing to do with her heart;
she's as strong as an ox. They took her in to Bradford
Royal Infirmary as a precaution because her pulse rate
was sky-high and she was hyperventilating and
hysterical. In other words, Dukkha had a panic attack. I
wouldn't usually be so dismissive, but surely this was
self-induced? I've gone over and over the scenario and
I was firm, yes, but gentle and reasonable – in tone and
in mine and Ravi's simple, ordinary expectation of a
life of our own. Yes, I feel guilty still, but I'm hopping
mad that I do.

'Ravi took no responsibility and then fucking
blamed me; Kabir sat there adding to the cowardly
silence, standing up for nobody – not even his wife –
and she brought it on herself.' I rant to Laly down the
telephone the next morning, after Ravi has deigned to
phone me with an update. Stiffly, he also apologises
for hitting me and for what he said, 'In the heat of the
moment'. Equally stiffly, I say, 'That's alright,' even
though it really isn't. I meant to talk to Mum, to play it
down, just in case the story got back to her any other
way (not least by Dukkha herself) but she and Dad are
out, and Laly is such a receptive audience I can't help
myself. 'All she needed was a glass of water, and a
paper bag to blow into. Instead, she tied up an
Emergency Ambulance and A&E staff when a real
patient needed them.'

'Wicked witch of West Yorkshire having a lickle
tantrum.' Laly puts on a baby voice. 'I'd have thumped
her before she could chuck herself down. You'd better

be ready to tell the bitch to grow up and get a life instead of sucking the joy out of yours.'

I know I shouldn't encourage my little sister to disrespect and violence, but with or without me, she's already the type of person who'd be great at inciting a riot against, well, anything, or drumming a concert crowd into frenzied support of an atrocious support act.

'I'll be thinking it, anyway,' I say gloomily.

'Wuss. Hey, so does this mean you and Ravi are moving to Scotland still?'

'Laly, shush! I told you not to tell anyone. Please.' I'd meant to keep the plan to myself and Ravi until it was all settled, but I caved in and whispered it, on pain of death, to my sister. But it's a good question. Does it? Wherever we live he can hit me, springs to mind, whatever stunts his mother pulls to keep us in line.

I get myself together and go into the university as usual. I've work to do in the lab, and hysterical mother-in-law and cowardly husband feel like dog-ate-my-homework excuses to cry off. Dukkha is bound to have got a sick-note for however long and it won't be me she wants as nursemaid, Ravi will have to take time off. Whether she's in avenger or martyr mode I can't cope any more. I'm no longer afraid of what I might be tempted to do myself, but what I might do to her.

Of course Ravi changes his mind about moving out; I'm just waiting for him to tell me. He does take compassionate leave from work after his mother's near-death experience and after three full days at home, waiting on her like a bearer in the British Raj, he's brainwashed. He won't ever leave his parents, he says, because he loves them and he promised he would care for them all their lives. He should never have had his head turned by me, he adds – which I know are

Dukkha's words, not his – only a weak man would abandon his parents.

'Abandon?' I'm incredulous. They're fit, in their sixties, work, and have plenty of money. How precisely are we abandoning them. It would be different if they were old and sick. An image of Dukkha, bones crumbling with osteoporosis, leaking urine and babbling with dementia floats before my eyes, and call me hard-hearted but no, there is not enough self-sacrifice in the world to send me down that path.

'It would be moral abandonment,' he says piously, and I wonder if he has any thoughts of his own left. 'I can't do it, Anou, I should never have agreed.'

'So what are you saying?'

He pauses, like an actor unsure of his lines and straining to hear the out-of-sight prompt; Dukkha looming invisible at his shoulder. 'My family is important to me,' he says finally, 'and you are part of that family. So is my mother. Equal parts…Oh, my father too, of course.' That's an afterthought, if ever I heard one. 'My duty is obedience to my parents – let me finish, Anou – and the care and protection of my wife and any future children. I need to be in a place where I will be able to fulfil both of those roles.'

Crap. Mealy-mouth parroting. I sigh. 'What does your mother want, Ravi?'

He won't look me in the eye.

'Well?'

'She wants us all to go to live in India,' he mutters.

'What? Whose idea is that?' Why am I even asking. 'Are you insane?' I'm no longer sure about my husband's mental health but in Laly's words, his mother is bat-shit crazy.

'There's no need to be rude, Anou,' Ravi says. Then he must see the look on my face because he hurries on.

'For a few months, at least? Heera's home is large and comfortable. The sun will shine. You will have company. You can transfer your studies to the university nearby. Heera will help you do that, Mum will talk to her…'

'Oh, will she?' I let that really sink in. 'So this has always been the plan, has it? Does your sister need a nanny for her children? Or a new cook?'

'Of course not. She has enough servants.'

Is he deliberately missing the point? I realise that despite everything that's gone on, today is the first day that I actively dislike Ravi. He's not clever and in control, he's a little boy in a pretty man's body. I want to bang his and Dukkha's heads together. There are many things I could say, explanations to give him, facts to share but his ears are deaf.

He mistakes my silence for compliance. 'Just try it – yes?' he begs. 'For me. For our marriage. For your family's sake.'

That's a low blow – family honour at stake. And no mention of me in the list, what's good for me. We're at an impasse. 'I'm not going to India, Ravi,' I say quietly.

He does look at me now and laughs, a bark of mirthless laughter and it chills me. 'Oh, yes, you are,' he says in a way that's half miserable and half triumphant. 'We both are. My mother will make sure of it.'

Chapter 44

I can bury my head in the sand with the best of them. Some might say I've been doing that since my family's first approach to the Tilak family as a match. Actually, this is more a case of being stubborn: if Dukkha thinks she can take me to Mumbai, then she'd better broach it with me face to face, not using her son as a mouthpiece. Does she really think I'll pack my trunk and meekly board the plane and living together on another continent will make it a happy ever after? I'm on tenterhooks but it's a tacit stand-off, the two of us circling each other but co-existing, not interacting. Then:

'You're very jealous of my daughter, aren't you, Anoushka,' comes out of the blue. Dukkha's lying on the sofa, recuperating from her heart episode, as she's describing it to everyone she phones with the news. Evidently, she's been waiting for me to pass the lounge door and call this out; her timing is perfect.

I'm stunned.

'I expect you hate her, don't you.' She carries on eating a bowl of fruit salad as if she's musing on my feeling towards spiders. 'Don't try driving my darling son away from her. It won't work and you'll make enemies. You're worth less than the value of my daughter's shoes.'

I'm tempted to roll on by but she's relentless; if we don't do this now, it'll be worse later, so I ignore her insult and manage to find my voice. 'I'm not doing anything like that. Ravi should do whatever he can to help his brothers and sisters. I would for mine.'

'Not true, though, is it, dear.' She flashes a sideways glance at me. 'I know Ravi has talked to you about our

345

move to India. He wants to live in Mumbai, you know, near Heera and her beautiful family. He was so happy, so relaxed there in December. You're the one stopping him.' Before I can respond she goes on, 'Whenever I bring up her name, your face changes. Don't you like me talking about my own daughter? If you don't, I won't mention her name in front of you ever again.'

'What?' Even for her that sounds unhinged.

Dukkha shakes her head, as if in sorrow. 'My hands are tied. I've tried converting you into an honest and pure girl but some things are impossible. Do you know, dear, I don't think I'm going to bother with you anymore.' The sing-song voice that's freaking me out, suddenly turns menacing. 'But remember this, Anoushka, once the bride moves into her husband's family, she has to forget everything subsequent to marriage. We are now everything to you. One way or another, we will be going to live in India. I am telling you that now, and as far as my son is concerned, I am judge and jury.'

My, 'How can you say this to me...' is lost in the ether as she pointedly turns over to face the sofa cushions and pulls a blanket up to her ears.

Right, so this is the way she's playing the India question. What a load of rubbish. I run upstairs and find my Ventolin inhaler. I'm not being awkward; it's more than not wanting to leave my family and my work and my studies. Last time we did a family visit to India, I was Laly's age. That trip, which lasted two weeks, was a living nightmare. Temperatures were in the high thirties and pollution levels through the roof. My parents spent a lot of time in old Delhi, with Auntie Sonu's extended family, and from their house you could smell the open sewers. I spent the whole time gasping for breath, which was laughed off as being the poor little Scottish girl being dramatic, but as

soon as we got back home, Mum frog-marched me to
the doctor. I'd not needed an asthma inhaler since I
was four, and we left Mumbai for the UK, but after that
summer I did. I've still got them, for when the pollen
count here is very high.

There's no way I'm going through that again,
however much I'm promised air-conditioning and state
of the art filtration systems – which is what I'm sure
Heera has. It's still India. It's still the city. I can't be
holed up twenty-four hours a day like a medical house
arrest. I stand over her but my explanation falls on deaf
ears; showing Dukkha the medication elicits nothing
more than a disdainful shrug and a barbed remark
about people being too good for their roots.

'Do what you want,' she says. 'It's up to you what
you do with your life. But whatever actions you take,
they affect all of us not just you. Most wives and
daughters-in-law would consider our feelings and
what we want. They would stop being so selfish.'

'Well, isn't that a hoot. When have I ever truly
prioritised what I want? What I keep bloody doing is
looking after every whim you lot have.' I mutter this
under my breath, which she can't possibly hear but her
face darkens.

'And this muttering you do, talking to yourself,
another bad habit. Oh, Anoushka, when will you
cleanse your mind and body?' She adds piously, 'Our
house is a temple and only honesty and clean living
exists here.'

I glance around at the clutter and think about the
stash of sweets and junk she keeps locked in her
bedroom, wondering how she can say that with a
straight face.

'We'll be going in September,' she calls after me as I
go into the kitchen. 'Plenty of time for you to hand in
your notice or whatever at that little job of yours. In

Mumbai, Heera's contacts can find you a nice teaching job. Far better than playing with germs in a nasty laboratory. Just until the babies come. And there will be babies in India, you can be sure of it.'

She's delusional – and trying to draw me into another altercation with such a loaded remark. I don't rise, just hold my breath, braced for more, but when I don't engage, she clearly decides to let me stew until I do give in.

I recount the gist of this to Donald when we meet up during the week. Even a few weeks ago I would have felt as if I were telling tales out of school, betraying Ravi's trust, but that's just being whittled away. And Donald doesn't seem to mind being my confessor. He says it's called being a friend. I say how easy life would be if everyone was like him.

'She can't make you go, Anoushka…Can she?' Donald's brow furrows. 'I mean, at the risk of sounding like an ignorant racist, there's no ancient Hindu rule that makes you her property and bound to obey her? What?' He looks mortified because I'm grinning.

'No, Donald, there isn't. She's not going to lock me in a trunk and ship me out there, or disguise me in a hijab and make me 'disappear' – because all brown people look the same, don't they?'

His face turns scarlet. 'Jesus, Anoushka, I mean…I mean, I didn't mean–'

'I know you didn't. I'm just teasing.' I let him off the hook. 'It makes me feel almost normal, you know having a conversation with someone ordinary.'

'Thanks for that.' His turn to smile. 'I'd rather be ordinary than racist.'

'You're neither.' I stir my hot chocolate, wishing I could read the dregs like tea leaves. 'But to answer your question properly, she can't physically force me, she can just make my life hell. All she needs to do is get on to my mum and dad and whine about marriage vows and family honour and respect. It'll be an ultimatum: I'm either a dutiful daughter-in-law who unquestioningly goes to Mumbai with them, or I'm sent back to Edinburgh in disgrace, a failed wife. The gossip-mongering will go wild and my parents will be unbearable, probably forever.'

'You haven't told them yet? They might surprise you?'

'I haven't told them any of it,' I admit. 'Not about Ravi's job, or the big business that's really Heera's. Or that I'm not very happy…They'd just brush the lies under the carpet and tell me marriage isn't all about happiness and to try harder. They'll definitely want me to go to India.'

'Hmm. Just as well you can spend today doing something easier, like finding a cure for breast cancer,' Donald says. 'Speaking of which…' He shows me his watch, and we both scramble ourselves together and rush up ten flights of stairs to make it to the lecture with twenty seconds to spare.

'This must be a crisis.' Donald pants exaggeratedly, holding open the classroom door. 'Nothing has ever before made this dream-team almost late for a lecture.'

There's no space in my brain to dwell on it all for the next few hours. We move from a presentation to a spot-test, to the lab for a demonstration. Donald and I are split into different groups, so even the tea-breaks are fully professional. Dr Moffat is down from Edinburgh, one of the co-presenters on her own research, and it's nice that she makes a beeline for me. She's so careful not to ask me how I am or how married life's going, all the usual stuff, that I suspect Donald has given her the lie of the land. She's soon carted off by one of the admins, and her only personal words to me are, 'I wish we could entice you back to Scotland, Anoushka. If life works out that way, I've still got a cubicle in my lab with your name on it.'

I nod and smile and agree to arrange a date for a proper supervision session before the end of the semester, wondering if I'm reading too much into her perfectly innocent words. What I can count on, is that Dr Moffat is an ally if ever I need one. It's a bit of a sad thought, though, that I'm mustering people I can count on if – when – my marriage shit hits the fan.

In what's become our routine, Donald walks with me back to the Interchange, though there's no leisurely cake at the NFPT today. The bus stop is just ahead and I turn to tell him there's no need to wait with me; he came down on the train today so is watching the time too, but he puts out a hand and stops me.

'Wait, Anoushka. I've been thinking about the,' he hesitates and pulls a face, 'the pickle you're in. I've got an idea. It's a bit off the wall, but any port in a storm is worth sailing into as my granny used to say.'

'Wow. Go on then, tell me?' I say. 'I'll listen to anything.'

He hesitates again. 'I wrote it down. For you to read on the bus.' He reaches into his pocket and pulls out a sheet of A4, folded in half. 'Don't worry, it's not as life-changing as the last thing I sent you. Neither,' his eyes widen, 'Oh God, neither is it a declaration. I'm not being a knight in shining armour. Crap. I'm putting all my feet in it today.' He thrusts the paper at me. 'Just read it, okay. See what you think.'

'I will. Thanks, Donald.' There is no solution other than going to India or divorce, but I'm really touched he cares enough to try and help.

'Phone me,' he calls as he heads off to the trains.

I choose a seat near the back of the bus and open the

note, which is, exactly as I'd expect, to the point:

Anoushka,

I've been offered a semester's research at McGill University in Toronto. It's an exchange thing, Dr M's doing. Starts in August. It's not me they want specially, just a PhD biologist. Why don't you go instead? Get away from everything for a bit. No strings (except you're buying the hot chocs forever) and Dr M is up for it.

D.

Well. How about that, then? The perfect solution. Or no solution at all. What it does is get me thinking: Canada is a long way away, whether you go there...or whether you just tell people you've gone there.

Chapter 45

The pros and cons of absconding to a totally unknown Toronto fill the bus ride home, my walk up to the Close, and whilst I fumble for my front door key. I can hear the phone ringing just behind the glass but I don't bother hurrying, as presumably Dukkha has sent Ravi out for provisions and has the extension at her elbow by the sofa. It's still going when I get through the door and there's the phone on the hall table, no sign of my mother-in-law, lazy cow, so I snatch up the receiver with a brusque, 'Yes?'

'Mrs Tilak?' the voice says.

'Just a minute.' I pick up the handset, making sure the extra-long cord is trailing behind me, not tripping me up, and march into the lounge. 'Dukkha, it's for you– Oh.' She's not there. I run up the stairs, a cursory knock on her bedroom door – not there either. Must have made a miraculous recovery and gone out. I remove my hand from the receiver, and start to apologise, but the dour voice – a man now, not the female who spoke originally – overrides me.

'Mrs Tilak, my time is money,' he says in Hindi.

I'm about to put him right, when he goes on, 'This is Dr Arnab,' and I realise it's fifty-fifty he's looking for me, not Dukkha; he's one of the few who would routinely call me Mrs Tilak. It's unsettling.

'Hello, yes?' I say cautiously, frowning over why he'd be phoning either of us. Most likely, Dukkha hasn't paid his bill and I'll be instructed to withdraw it from our joint account.

'It is possible for me to administer the prescribed hormone injections,' he says abruptly. 'You will need to procure them directly as they are not licensed in the

UK. You would do well also to keep a record of written consent from the girl–'

'Wha–'

'Let me finish, Mrs Tilak.' He sighs. 'As I was saying, your daughter-in-law needs to accept there are potential side effects for her and for a foetus, should she become pregnant – which is not, as I've already told you, by any means a certainty. However, if she's as desperate as you say she is, the risk might be worth taking. Is that clear?' There's a pause, before he says, irritably, 'Mrs Tilak? Are you still there?'

I cough. 'Yes, I'm here.' I try to make my voice deeper. It sounds nothing like Dukkha's but I can't imagine the doctor really cares which of us he's talking to.

'I strongly suggest you purchase the hormone injections and the corresponding drugs in India. I can give you details of a reliable source. If you must, you can bring them to me to administer. That will incur a significant fee per episode for my time and the risk involved to me as a medic working outside of the system. If there should be complications and your daughter-in-law needs medical attention, the NHS will ask uncomfortable questions.' He fires this out in a very detached manner, ending with, 'Your plan of residing in Mumbai is by far the best option. Ideally, you and the girl – and her husband, naturally – will remain there for the duration of the treatment, plan on not less than six months, where provision and follow-up will be less troublesome.'

'I understand,' I croak. 'Er, thank you.'

'My bill is in the post. Cash, please. Good day, Mrs Tilak.' And he rings off.

I sink down onto the stool beside the telephone table. I don't know how long I sit there with the phone in my hand, but it's long enough for the automated voice to order me to replace my handset. I do as I'm told, then go to the kitchen for a glass of water. I genuinely feel faint, my head spinning, as I run over Dr Arnab's words again. And again: hormone injections; drugs; pregnancy; risks; written consent from the girl. I've no trouble understanding it, I just can't take it in. It's too horrific, sickening. Dukkha might as well be experimenting on me, as if I'm nothing more than a lab rat. Her motivations to move to India – as well as the big house and the rich family connections – are here in a nutshell. It all makes perfect sense...except, I realise as I gulp down the cold water, for one thing. My mother-in-law is willing to risk my life to have Ravi's child – that, very sadly, I can see. But why, when she already has a whole host of grandchildren is it so important?

Does it matter? I look out of the window into the garden and think, My mother-in-law hates me. My life is expendable.

It's a defining moment.

There are many times I've felt like running away, back home to Edinburgh. But my upbringing has been based firmly on very high Hindu morals that will not allow me to do that. Once an Indian girl is married, she's married, there's no get out card or extenuating circumstances. Many times I've heard the words, 'Only her coffin would leave her husband's house.' When I married Ravi, I accepted that. I agreed with it. Over the last year, like it or not, I've accepted it and agreed with it.

But now? How do I feel now?

I've tried, Mata Rani, I've tried. I want to shout the words out loud, but even louder, I want to ask, 'How much more do I have to do?' And as if Mata Rani herself has spoken, the answer, quietly and with certainty, is in me. Any girl, Indian or otherwise, whose husband's family has made her life a living nightmare, should not stand for it. She – I – should leave them immediately. Their lives are not worth the sacrifice of your own – my own – life. Hinduism or any culture does not tell you – me – to accept suffering at the hands of people who are supposed to love you – me. No human being has the right to treat another human being as somehow less.

I have to leave, that's the bottom line.

'I have to leave.' I say it aloud to hear how it sounds, how it makes me feel, and it sounds right. Feels right. It is right. Impossible, but right. It's more than not going to India. It's more than living elsewhere with Ravi. It's about survival.

I don't know when and I don't know how but I'm leaving this house, this marriage, this family I should never have agreed to become part of and will never be mine.

Chapter 46

I can't stomach seeing any of them tonight but I've nowhere else to go, and all I want to do is crawl into bed and into oblivion. It's a vain hope that a night's sleep will bring clarity but it's all I have right now. As a last resort, I shower, then root around under the bathroom washbasin where there's a mishmash of medicines and find a sticky but barely out-of-date bottle of Night Nurse and a card of antihistamine tablets. Then I lock my bedroom door, and leave Ravi a note taped to it:

Having a really, really heavy period. I've drugged myself up, put in ear plugs, and gone to bed. Would you mind sleeping in your old room tonight? The bleeding is bad. Anou.

There's enough in that to have him run a four-minute mile, let alone beat a hasty retreat to a room across the landing. Using something as yucky as menstruation as my alibi seems quite pleasing in the circumstances and Ravi will have no clue as to whether the dates remotely tally. His mother might, but let him tell her whatever he likes. If she asks. I debate the drugs but can't remember if the antihistamine is the drowsy or non-drowsy one, so go for taking a generous dose of the codeine-filled Night Nurse. I could swallow an antihistamine as well, I dither, but I want to knock myself out for a few hours, not potentially cause some awful interaction. It would probably be fine but I've got a first class biology Masters, my pride won't let me. So, I set an alarm, block my ears, and set my mind to considering Donald's offer of Canada.

Surprisingly enough, I do sleep right through till about 5am, and I do feel brighter: no codeine hangover and not quite so shell-shocked by Dr Arnab's message. It feels like the crisis I've been unconsciously waiting for has come, and now the worst has happened, I will be able to act. Long may that last.

Making a miraculous recovery, I get dressed and sort my backpack in silence, leave the bedroom door open with a note on the bed: Much better. Early start and didn't want to wake you, creep down the stairs and go straight out the front door. It's impossible to shut quietly but if anyone does wake up, I'll be down the road and out of the estate before they gather it's me and they're not likely to throw on clothes and follow me. The first bus is at five to six, I checked, and it's a nice morning. It's a very peaceful time; maybe I should leave the house at dawn every day and come home at dusk, limiting all my future communication to notes. I'm grinning at the thought, when it occurs to me that's more or less how Ravi copes – and marriage hasn't made much difference.

The bus driver, one I recognise, though he's never said a word to me before, waves me on with, 'Beating the masses today. Best time to travel,' and it's a tiny ray of happiness, a slimmer version of Diana-in-the-building-society's friendliness and the uni office staff including me in food runs. Sure enough, the bus eats up the miles and I'll need to get a security guard to open up the lab at this hour. Walking past the Alhambra, and down Great Horton Road, I notice there's a tiny café already open so without giving myself to analyse the decision, I push the door open, squeeze past the half a dozen Formica-topped tables and stare up at the blackboard. It's criss-crossed with every possible variation of an English Breakfast.

'What'll it be, love?' A huge women, her smile the biggest thing about her, slides out from a side door behind the counter. 'I can do you anything you fancy if

357

we've got the ingredients. Or is it just a cuppa?'

'Can I just have tea and toast?' I ask.

'Course you can. Brown or white? Or there's a croissant just out the oven.'

'Erm…' She's smiling encouragingly, and looks so kind, I blurt out, 'I've never been in a café on my own before.' I'm racking my brains, but it's true; I've never eaten alone outside home – or college, but mostly that's a vending machine.

The woman leans her bulk across the counter and winks at me. 'I'd say that calls for an everything omelette, two croissants and a big mug of tea. Indulge me, pet. I spend my day buttering bacon baps and drowning sausage sarnies in brown sauce. Let me spoil you.'

I could cry. Instead I blink furiously and manage an enthusiastic nod. 'Yes, please. Thank you.'

She nods her head towards the tables and mismatched chairs. 'Take the weight off. Not that you've much to take off.' Guffawing at her own joke, she disappears into the back, and I sit down and take out my book. Even if I were relaxed enough to read it, the print would blur as I've too much to think about. I'm not going to take up Donald's offer. It would be a sticking plaster on a cut that needs stitches; a temporary reprieve until I had to come back and pick up where I left off. With the smell of onions and garlic frying behind me, and the burble of Terry Wogan on Radio 2 in the background, I ditch the novel, tear a page from my notebook and write a reply to Donald.

I appreciate this more than I can say and I'm so tempted but I'm going to say, no, thank you. I'm not being polite (I don't expect you to believe that!) but I woke up this morning and realised I've never done anything entirely on my own before. I need to prove to myself I can and prove to everyone else that I'm serious. I'm starting out right now by sitting in Gloria's Canteen. If I can have breakfast alone, I can do anything alone, right? But keep an eye out while you're in Canada in case I fail and come running.

A.

Decision made. And I know it's the right one. Even if it leaves me with no bloody idea whatsoever what I'm going to do instead.

The breakfast when it comes is lovely. And so enormous I wonder if a whole carton of eggs has gone into the making of it. Partly ravenous after missing dinner last night and partly wanting to show my appreciation, I eat all of it and a whole croissant. I take my empties back up to the counter and the lady heaves her bosom off the counter and puts her newspaper to one side.

'Now that's what I like to see, a clean plate.' She grins broadly. 'I didn't think you had it in you, a slip of a thing like you. More tea? Cake? Tiffin traybake or Victoria Sponge.' She raises her eyebrows.

'I couldn't.' I groan. 'That was so good I won't need to eat for a week. But,' I look at the home-baking beside her, 'could I take some of the cakes away? The others in the office would love them.'

As she slices generous wedges, and places them in paper bags, I ask her, 'Are you Gloria? As in Gloria's Canteen.'

She gives a big rumbling laugh and I really hope she's always this good-natured; nobody could possibly be down after meeting her. 'Me? No, love. I'm Bernice. It's named after the great Gloria Gaynor – I Will Survive?' She sings a few bars in a remarkably tuneful alto. 'Rented the place after my divorce. Worked twelve hours a day with my kids in their prams in the corner. Now they're grown and flown and I own the place.' Bernice gazes proudly around her empire. Then her eyes return to me. 'Am I right in thinking the Good Lord sent you to me today?'

'I...'

As I flounder in the face of such unexpected faith, she goes on comfortably. 'I'm a great believer in him moving in mysterious ways. You looked lost when you came in, pet. You look better now. Or maybe you were just hungry!'

'Both.' I smile back. 'I'm Anoushka. Thank you for everything, Bernice,' I say as I hand over what seems to be far too few coins for a huge breakfast and a mountain of cake.

'Don't be a stranger now,' she calls over the ping of the door.

I do cry a couple of tears as I walk down the road. Who'd have thought Mata Rani and Gloria Gaynor would combine forces to send me a sign via Bernice that I will survive this. Corny but comforting, scientist or not.

The cakes are so well-received I doubt they'll last till tea-break. I sign in to the lab, get my coat and look up the protocols for the day, all the time reminding myself that I can have a lovely, perfectly normal life just like this without Ravi and his family and their crackpot ideas in it. Deep breaths, Anou. Before I give in to my heart racing with anxiety, I concentrate on setting out my station, testing the equipment and logging the samples. It's a great stress reliever. Once I'm immersed in the work I can forget everything else, that's my superpower. I'm writing up my notes when the internal phone rings, and as I'm nearest, I answer it.

'Anoushka?' Brenda from the office says. 'Are you going to be long? You've got a visitor.'

'Me? Are you sure?' I'm not expecting Donald or Dr

Moffat and nobody else would look for me here.

'Yes. She's called on the off-chance, she says. Your sister-in-law. Heera. She says she can wait.'

'Heera...' I rub my forehead. I go to say again, 'Are you sure?' then stop myself, changing it to, 'Five minutes. Will you make her some coffee, Brenda?'

'Already on it.'

All kinds of scenarios run through my mind as I pack away and wash my hands but none of them make sense. Heera, here. Why? How? It can't be good. Any optimism I have trickles away like sand through my fingers.

She's in the tiny beige staff room, hovering like a bright and exotic butterfly, all gold jewellery and sunshine yellow salwar kameez. Sunglasses are perched like a hairband on her head. Unlike me, Heera isn't made to blend in. Even in a city full of Indians and Pakistanis and Bangladeshis, she will always stand out; Laly will adore her – if they ever get to meet.

'Heera,' I say uncertainly from the doorway. We saw each other in November, when she chose not to stay with us in Hoxton Close but it would be an exaggeration to say we'd spent much time together. That doesn't faze her. She crosses the room in two strides and envelopes me in a cloud of Chanel No.19.

'Anoushka. Sorry to gatecrash but I've only got a couple of hours and I wanted to see you. Is there somewhere we can talk?'

'Take my cubby hole,' Brenda jumps in. 'I'm off to get some lunch and there'll be nobody much around till two.'

'I won't beat about the bush,' Heera says, perched on the edge of a very messy desk while I lean against the wall. 'And I'd rather you didn't tell my mother I was here. She doesn't know I'm over for a flying visit, or that I've made it my business to see you.'

'She hasn't sent you here?' Things are getting weirder by the second.

'Hell, no.' She gives a mock shudder. 'Did you think I was here to give you a good telling off – you did! I'm on your side. I can't imagine the shit you have to put up with from her, Anoushka, now that there's only you and Ravi left in the house. No. I'm here to talk about this sudden move to India. She says you don't want to come.'

'It's very kind of you,' I say hastily because if I don't say my piece I'll lose my nerve. 'And I know you have a lovely home and space for us, which makes me ungrateful–'

'Anoushka, you misunderstand me.' She holds up a hand. 'You'd be a bloody fool to give in and I need to tell you that in person. Don't come to India. My mother has got some mumbo jumbo from a fake priest she met last December…I don't know how much to say, I don't want to upset you.'

I manage a half smile. 'About the fertility drugs I'm going to be given and the second wife waiting in the wings if they don't work?'

'The what drugs? Don't tell me, it can't do any good. I knew you were too smart for them.' Heera shakes her head. 'She's my mother but she's a manipulative control freak who's a law unto herself. I am where I am in spite of her. We all got away, except Ravi. She's not letting him go and she's sucking you in.'

'I've tried. But the heart attack–'

'That isn't a heart attack, it will be wheeled out every time she doesn't like something you do. Bottom line, don't come to India. If on the other hand,' she looks at me closely, 'you decide you can't leave my brother then of course you are welcome in my home – and so, though, is my mother.' She sighs. 'I'm loyal to my family, Anoushka, but not at the expense of another woman whose life is in their – our – hands.'

'Thank you,' I say, still trying to process that she's here, what she's saying. 'I appreciate–'

'Don't appreciate me. I'm committing the taboo act of telling you to consider leaving your husband, my little brother. You need to decide what's the lesser of the evils.' Heera stands up and smooths her outfit; this interview is over. 'I throw money at things. I have it to throw. If you need money, Anoushka, get off your high horse and ask. Alright?' From her small cross-body bag she gives me her card. 'Here.'

'Heera?' I put a hand out to stop her sweeping out of the office. 'How did you know what I do, and where I'd be today?'

She laughs. 'It wasn't difficult. Your life is an open book. Now remember, I was never here, as they say. Got to go, I've a plane to catch.'

How different would life be, if Heera and her family were still at home, I think, as she leaves me, my head whirling. Even India mightn't be so bad…'Yes, it would,' I tell myself firmly. 'Dukkha is still her mother.' Not to mention second wives and illegal hormone injections.

Chapter 47

When I get back in the early evening, I'm more confused than I've ever been. And I'm so terrified I'll let slip I've had today's visit that I might as well be wearing a badge saying, 'Heera was here'. I also have no idea if I should confront Dukkha about Dr Arnab's phone call; she'll work it out soon enough when his bill appears in the post. Shite. My spirits sink when I see the car on the drive; they must all be home. Double shite. My chances of sneaking in un-noticed are slim but what I don't expect is Ravi calling me into the living room. He and his parents are in there, looking like judge and jury.

Coldly, I go. I'm not going to get wound up, I'm not going to argue but I'm not going to India. Whatever her ruse, whatever her threat.

'Yes?' I say, standing in the doorway.

Dukkha is on the sofa, a tape recorder and a pile of tapes on the coffee table in front of her. She wants me to listen to music? Surely we're not expected to sit round and bond over some Indian music or some religious speeches about the call of the homeland. Scotland is my homeland and I'm a second generation Indian, I haven't an ounce of nostalgia in my body for India.

She looks me up and down with a glint in her eye and a knowing smile. 'Have you anything you'd like to tell us, Anoushka?' she asks.

It's like being called to the headmistress's office, being given the opportunity to own up to some misdemeanour and so lessen a punishment. But what – specifically – have I done this time? She's either found out about my taking the telephone call from Dr Arnab or about Heera visiting me. I look at Ravi and Kabir and their eyes are on their feet. As usual.

'I'm not pregnant and I'm not going to India,' I recite, like a news reel on repeat. Play dumb, I tell myself, until you know what she knows.

'You're certainly not,' Dukkha says pleasantly – and my head jerks up to meet her gaze. What? 'And you're no longer my daughter-in-law and you're no longer my son's wife,' she goes on, so nicely that I have trouble computing the words. With anyone else there would be a punchline and 'you got me' laughter.

I just stand there, like a gaping fish, opening and closing its mouth. then suddenly, something in me wakes up. I'm too weary for another session of game-playing or her histrionics and me being blamed for unheard of wrongdoings. I turn to leave the room, but in a flash, she's beside me, yanks my arm and pushes me down onto the armchair.

'Sit, Ravi,' she snaps. 'Here.' She points to the sofa and makes Ravi squeeze in between her and Kabir. The three of them are in a row looking across at me. I might as well be interviewing for the job as housemaid.

'Ravi...?' I start but he just shrugs, and even if he wants to say something, Dukkha jumps in.

'Shut up,' she directs at me. 'And listen. You wicked, wicked girl.' With a self-righteous finger, she presses Play on the tape recorder and after some static and a couple of squawks, I hear a voice, tinny and distant, saying:

'...just the same as usual. I was in trouble today for putting the Coke bottle on the wrong shelf of the fridge...I wasn't even the one who had left it out...That's what I said...There's no pleasing the old bag...'

Frowning with concentration – it sounds familiar; a Scottish accent, female – I realise with a jolt that it's me.

My voice. But how…? And then it clicks: it's a tape recording from one of my telephone conversations with Laly. Dukkha has been recording my telephone calls.

'You can't do that–'

'Shut up!' She shouts at me this time. 'Shut up and listen.'

Again, I look to Ravi or Kabir for support. Again, neither catches my eye, let alone stands up for me.

'Don't you dare look at them for help,' Dukkha shrieks. 'These are your words, girl.' She smashes a hand down on the machine, pulls out one tape and jams in another. 'Nobody can help you now, unless it's to wash out your filthy gutter mouth with carbolic soap.'

I'm numb and slack-jawed; I can't seem to move, let alone run – and where will I run to anyway? My voice goes on and on; gaps for Laly – it's mostly Laly Dukkha plays – to reply. She must have hours of recordings, going right back to my first phone call home, the one she encouraged me to make last August. That's innocuous enough. Most of the ones to my mum are, with long periods of silence as she's doing the bulk of the talking and the recording is all one-sided. There are two or three with Donald, nothing more than arrangements for a lift or a reminder to bring a particular book, but:

'Dirty. Dirty, dirty, dirty.' Dukkha attacks me. 'Talking to another man, meeting him. You brought him here, to this house, your marital home. Disgusting.'

'There was nothing wrong–' I find my voice, a croak, but she's having none of it.

'Shush. Sshh,' she hisses.

Stupidly I do. My own voice mocks me, growing louder and louder as Dukkha turns up the volume, until my words almost consume us. 'The freezer is full of ghee,' bellows out. 'I mean, who's greedy enough to go and bring all that back just because it's free…Yes, I know. It's like a sickness, the house is stashed with goodies that are supposed to be secret – and they're not vegan at all…' Then the room reverberates with manic, clown-like laughter. 'You really shouldn't call her that, even if she is a haggy mole face. '

Dukkha snaps the tape off at that point and the room is silent. My face is burning with shame; I'm rude, I'm childish, and most of all I'm embarrassed at being caught out. How on earth can I apologise and recover from this? Ravi looks stunned, Kabir confused, Dukkha downright triumphant.

That's what gets through to me. With a start, my brain cogs fire up, and I remember that while I might have said a whole stack of silly things, moaned on about trivia, called my mother-in-law rude names, she is the one who has invaded my privacy, broken any sense of trust, 'And recorded my phone calls! How could you?' I say that last bit out loud, very loud. 'Why would you do that? You're the one really in the wrong.' I've said nothing half as bad as some of the horrible things she's thrown at me over the last few months.

Now she's gloating, delighted how I'm provoked. She sits back, playing tape after tape, smiling at how clever she's been to catch me out:

'…All she needed was a glass of water, and a paper bag to blow into. Instead, she tied up an Emergency Ambulance and A&E staff when a real patient needed them…'

And that's the finale.

'I'd ask you again, if you have anything to say for yourself, but I think you've said enough, don't you?' Dukkha cackles at her little joke.

In all honesty, I can expect nothing else of Dukkha, and Ravi appears more shell-shocked than me – if that's at his mother's actions or my indiscretions or both, I've yet to discover – but it's strangely Kabir who is the biggest let-down. This grown man, who made such promises to my father to care for me, to treat me as a daughter, who publicly turned down a larger dowry, all of that and more, yet he's sitting here in neutral silence. He hasn't even the gumption to back up his wife.

'I'm going to be the one making a telephone call now.' Dukkha leans in confidentially. 'Do you want to know who to? I'm going to phone your parents and tell them what a rude, ungrateful liar of a daughter-in-law you are. And how you've corrupted not only my son but your own little sister.' She spits – literally, spits on the floor. I'm revolted, watching the shiny little globule wobble and sink into the carpet fibres. 'Shame on you. Shame on your family. Ravi!' She turns to him and I'm shocked at the way he jumps, as if she's physically jabbed him with an arrow. 'You're her husband. Take some action. Send her back to her parents for six months. Let her disgrace be known.'

'Wait a second.' I sit up straight. 'Ravi, you are my husband. What have you got to say about all this?'

'He has nothing to say,' Dukkha snaps. 'He is nothing without me. And you madam, are less than nothing, full stop. How low we sank with you…'

Something explodes in my brain and for a second I think I'm going to collapse. I never understood that saying about the red mist before now. In the ensuing slanging match, I'm not sure if I'm proud or ashamed to report that I give as good as I get. A small voice in my head is telling me to stop it because I can't win and I can lose quite badly, but it's too late. Months of pent-up frustration burst out of me and I tell Dukkha exactly what I think of her, how those conversations were just the tip of the iceberg and I have plenty more where they came from. She's incandescent – not at what I say, she can't hear it because she's roaring over me – but because I'm daring to stand up to her. I inform her that the whole Tilak family is of very low mentality to stoop to such a low deed; she says they can do what they like and if need be, they will do it again. She threatens again to call my parents; I threaten to call the police. She says she can do as she likes in her own home; I say that phone tapping is illegal (though I've no idea if it is) – as are illegal fertility drugs and hormone treatments. Whoops. I wait for the shit to hit the fan and decorate the room but she's so riled up, I doubt she's taking in the substance of my insults. Maybe there's a momentary hesitation before she roars how I've betrayed their trust and I remind her, po-faced, of Kabir and Ravi's promises to treat me as their own. Dukkha starts swearing magnificently, saying I belong to a very low-class family; I reply that the Tilaks fitted that class perfectly well long before I came along.

She attacks my degree for being made of dirt; I point out that at least I have one and didn't palm off my office-boy son on false pretences of being a hotshot lawyer, when I had a menial job in a factory…I regret stooping to that even as I say it, but am glad I've no chance to retract it when she insults my mum as an uneducated, sucking-up woman and my father a naive and blundering idiot. I'm this far away from betraying Heera with, 'At least I'd tell my Mum every time I was in the country,' but there are some boundaries that are uncrossable.

In the aftermath, I'm not sure which of us slaps the other's face first but we both do it, fast and stinging. And I'm not sure about her, but it brings me to my senses. I bite back the instinctive need to apologise, standing there, breathing heavily and holding my burning cheek. I realise that Ravi and Kabir are still just sitting there, frozen, and in that second I despise both of them more than I do Dukkha. It must be the one thing we see eye to eye on because she looks at them, too, and curls her lip. 'Like father, like son,' she snarls.

The words are out before I can decide if it's a good move or not. 'You made them that way,' I say quietly.

She tells me to get out of her house immediately and never come back. She shrieks it. And it just makes me want to laugh, it's more melodramatic than her collapse in the close. None of us moves, and something in the air changes. Dukkha opens her mouth again and this time, the same words emerge, cold and menacing.

'Get out of my house. Get out now and never come back.' There's pure hatred in her eyes. 'Get. Out.'

Still we don't move, Kabir seemingly as rooted to the spot as Ravi and me. It occurs to me in the seconds that feel like hours, that this is the crunch. This is the point which will make or break my marriage; I'm waiting for Ravi to act. I'm waiting for him to grab my hand, run out of that front door, and go. And if he can't do that, at least to tell his mother, 'No.'

It doesn't happen. Instead, the idiot – my husband – rushes forward and punches the wall. Once. Twice. Right hand. Left hand. He hits out at the unyielding wall like a boxer in the ring, and when he stops, he throws his head back, eyes turned to the ceiling and howls like a werewolf. It's as if twenty-five years of pent-up misery and frustration are pouring out of him. Finally, the cry dies to a whimper, but my in-laws and I still stand there in petrified silence. As if in a stupor he fumbles with his hands, pulls off his wedding ring and flings it at me; the bracelet my dad paid a fortune for, follows. I think Ravi is about to fall to his knees and instinctively reach out to catch him – when he rushes forward towards the front door, stumbles – and puts his hand right through the glass.

He's bleeding badly and suddenly Dukkha's all over him like a rash; her own recovery a miracle given that she's allegedly weaker than a Victorian heroine on total bed-rest. I run to the kitchen and raid the freezer for ice – thinking it might freeze the bleeding; I don't know – and the drawer for tea towels. I chuck all of these at Dukkha's feet, expecting to be verbally abused, but she's crooning over her whimpering son. Once we've stemmed the blood from his palm, we haul him up, an arm each – for the first time (and probably the last, pops into my mind) working as a team – out to the car that Kabir is already revving up.

None of us says anything on the way to the hospital. Ravi's head is lolling against the back seat, his eyes closed. Anyone who thinks a brown-skinned man can't go pale should take a look at his face, I think oddly, but he's fully conscious. His knee is jiggling up and down and he keeps licking his lips. From the front seat – of course Dukkha's in the back with her boy – I turn to take surreptitious looks at the makeshift bandage and it's not changing colour. It probably looked worse than it is, and Ravi's reaction now, is shock. I'd lay my life on the fact he's not in any danger, anyway, and I take a deep breath. Adrenaline stops pumping, leaving me empty, not uncaring but not caring much either.

'I think it's okay, Ravi,' I say to the car in general. 'I think you need stitches and probably a tetanus jag but that's all–'

'All! That's all,' Dukkha spits. 'Stupid girl, this is your fault. Just like my heart attack was your fault. What do you know about what my son needs. He'll probably need surgery! And,' her face twists, 'Speak

English if you won't speak Hindi. What's a jag? Call yourself a scientist.'

'Mum, please,' Ravi whispers.

I don't know if he's sticking up for me or himself, but it works. She shuts up immediately, stroking his arm, his face, and muttering it will be alright.

We're four hours in Casualty. Ravi is triaged and told to wait – he's not an emergency. Good news, I'd have thought, but Dukkha is raging. When he's called through, I remain in the waiting room with Kabir, who gets us colourless tea from a vending machine. A few minutes later, Dukkha comes to tell us, with a face that suggests amputation and blood transfusion are on the cards, that Ravi needs stitches and a tetanus jab. I don't say a word.

I'm tempted to leave them to it and get the bus home but that would mean asking for a set of house keys – I didn't pick mine up in the chaos – which would surely rekindle a fight based on my indifference and selfishness. Instead, I go for 'some fresh air' away from the grim and overcrowded A&E department. There's a row of phone boxes in the foyer and on impulse I phone my mum; I don't know what to say when she answers so I blurt out a garbled, heavily sanitised version of what's happened. Being economical with the horrible truth is automatic; even as I doctor the facts, I wonder why I can't say how it is to my Mum, of all people.

'Ravi's in hospital?' Mum screeches. 'What did you do to him?'

Which answers my unspoken question: she assumes I'm to blame. I'm stung. 'Ravi did it to himself,' I say. 'An accident. It was Dukkha and me who were arguing. As usual. He didn't even try to take my side.'

Unbelievably, she laughs. 'Oh, is that all? You had me worried for a minute, Anoushka.' I can feel her rolling her eyes at whoever's passing her as she sits in our hall, shaking her head at my 'nonsense'. 'It's just a fight–'

'It's another fight, and it's getting worse. She's horrible to me, Mum.'

'Come on now. You knew what you were getting into with Dukkha Tilak,' Mum says briskly. 'I don't deny she's a piece of work but you're a clever girl, just keep your head down and toe the line.'

'But Ravi…'

'Ravi, what?'

Ravi what, indeed. Where on earth do I start? 'He's too scared of his mother to do anything,' I start, but she interrupts.

'He's very respectful of his parents,' she corrects me, blithely unaware of how wrong she is. 'I expect he's learned to pick his battles and today he got a little overheated. Maybe you should apologise.'

It hits me like a punch to the stomach that all these months I've said too little, too late. Who's going to believe me now about even a diluted version of what's gone on. I've continually glossed over the crap and been all Pollyanna – except to Laly, and even to her I've made life seem more of an inconvenience, if not a joke. As if she can read my mind, Mum changes tack.

'And what have you been saying to Laly, my girl? Filling her imagination with crazy stories. I've been meaning to have a word with you about that. If you call your mother-in-law even a quarter of the silly names, Laly repeats, or complain about humdrum petty differences, then I'm not surprised the woman feels the need to rebuke you. I would do the same myself and well you know it.'

'It's not the same. You're not unkind, not…not vicious. It's not fair.' I hear the whine in my voice and stop it before she loses patience. In one last ditch attempt, I add, spontaneously, 'Can I come home, Mum? Just for a bit?'

There's a pause, and I'm hopeful.

'It's just a fight,' Mum repeats – and my hopes are dashed. 'You're a married woman, Anou, you won't always see eye to eye with your husband or your mother-in-law. If you leave for every little thing, you'll always be packing your bags.'

'But Mum–'

'No, Anoushka. I promise you you'll regret this conversation tomorrow when you and Ravi make up.' She's resolute; there's no point arguing. 'I'm doing you a favour. Just try harder.'

Which is how it always ends: going to school; making friends; studying; being Indian in Scotland; being Scottish in India…'Try harder, Anoushka.' It'll be the epitaph on my gravestone.

'You're on your own, girl,' I tell myself as I circle the perimeter of the carpark. 'Dig deep.'

Chapter 46

'You'll need to bring our food into the lounge,' Dukkha says to me when we arrive home. 'Ravi is weak from loss of blood and my heart is palpitating with the strain. We need to rest.'

Are we just supposed to carry on as if nothing has happened?

A normal person wouldn't have thought there was any way of coming back from that row, but Ravi's accident overshadows it completely. Dukkha doesn't even mention the tape recordings again. She sweeps the machine and the tapes into a drawer to make room for all the things Ravi needs – tea, water, tissues, painkillers, magazines, the phone extension – after she's tenderly led him in by his good hand and settled him on the sofa. He falls into playing the part of the invalid spectacularly. Her threat to call my parents was apparently as empty as mine to call the police. Of course, I remind myself, that Dukkha thrives on fighting, it's her lifeblood, like food or air for the rest of us. The only newness in our altercation was my finding the gumption to argue back. Proud, not proud. She'll glow with the thrill of having goaded me, broken me.

It is a strange thing, that now we've aired our feelings I feel reckless, careless – adrenaline pumping and I should harness it – but there's nowhere to go with the acute feelings unless I pack up and leave immediately, and the one thing I am now fully clear on, is that I am going – but not without a proper plan. The first step is to play my cards very close to my chest.

Like the good girl I'm not, I plate up, microwave, and serve two generous meals to my husband and mother-in-law. Laly would tell me to spit in it but I'm not that bad ass; I do it mentally. I see and ignore the pleading, puppy-dog eyes in Ravi's perfect face, as he mutters, 'Thank you, Anou.' I'm past the point of analysing what he's trying to semaphore. Dukkha takes her food with the grace of a goddess who's had to discipline a wayward disciple and is now giving her a magnanimous second chance – yet the light of battle still shines from her eyes and she's spoiling for any provocation to go in for the kill. She'll turn the knife well and truly. I'm not trading my power that easily.

'Mama-ji, I forgot that Dr Arnab phoned you yesterday,' I say pleasantly, enjoying her momentary freeze. Oh, I've got your number, lady. 'Something about the medication you enquired about is best found in Mumbai. He's to send you contact details and his own fee. I hope that makes sense,' I add, innocence personified. 'I was rushing in the door and might not have taken it in properly.'

She draws breath in through her nose. 'Ayurvedic supplements. For you.' Clever lie. 'I'll see to it. When we get to Mumbai…' She leaves that hanging; Ravi gulps as if World War Three might break out but I simply turn and call upstairs to Kabir that his dinner's on the kitchen table. I sit opposite him and toy with my food; it's been a manic twenty-four hours, as if a year or two of life has been squeezed into a day, and my stomach is churning in competition with my mind. I channel an unlikely inner trinity of Laly, Bernice and Heera as I force some noodles down. I'm going to leave for good a year to the day since my graduation. Four and a bit weeks away. There's something symbolic in choosing that date – a year on I'll have finally reached the first day of the rest of my life when I am answerable only to me. It also means there's no first wedding anniversary to sob over and regret. Well, it makes sense to me, and it gives me a deadline. I shiver in anticipation – neither nerves nor excitement, just a physical response to making it real. Kabir, eating in companionable enough silence, notices. A couple of times I think he might be about to speak but he holds back, as do I. It's very surreal sitting opposite your father-in-law at a weekday dinner and calmly planning to walk away from your marriage – the one he helped arrange.

When the phone rings, I gladly set down my fork but Kabir is on his feet before me. 'I'll get it,' he says. 'Today has been hard on you,' which has nothing to do with answering the phone but is the best he can do to show a modicum of solidarity. He's in the same boat as Heera, of course, and probably Galu and the others: divided loyalties; life being bearable, mostly, when Dukkha gets what she wants.

'Hello?' I hear him say as I get up to clear our dishes. 'Kabir Tilak speaking.' There's a pause and then his tone changes to one of surprise. 'Oh – hello, there. Of course.' Another pause. 'Yes, she is. Er, just one moment, please.' The receiver goes down and he crosses to close the lounge door. Dukkha mumbles something and he replies, 'Work. No need to disturb your programme.' I move to do likewise with the kitchen door, but he shakes his head in my direction and cups his ear, as if I should listen. Alright, then.

'Dev, my friend, please talk freely,' Kabir says, and I nearly drop the Tupperware containers I'm lining up in the fridge. Dad? Why is my dad phoning to speak to Ravi's dad?

My initial thought, that something is wrong with Mum or Laly or one of the boys is obvious in the worried face I thrust into the hall. Kabir puts his hand over the receiver and mouths, 'Everyone is fine, don't worry.' I nod, but only half-placated. Nobody might be dead or dying but my dad doesn't make social phone calls. He says a quick hello and hands over the phone to Mum like it's a scalding potato. Kabir is holding the handset equally awkwardly, yet I'm sure neither man has a problem communicating by phone at work.

Dad is speaking but Kabir's face is neutral; I can't guess what's being said. Finally, my father-in-law says, 'Ravi's accident was his own fault but it's true to say that Anoushka and my wife had a falling out that may have, er…escalated matters. Heated words were said, accusations made.' Another pause. 'She spoke without thought on the telephone, girlish uncomplimentary nonsense to her sister.'

Ah, the nitty-gritty. I stiffen.

'My wife took offence and she, er…' He coughs. 'I'm afraid she acted out of turn and taped the conversations. Which she now regrets.'

Like hell she does.

'And for which I apologise profusely.'

Not to me you didn't.

'Please, Dev, there is no need for you to apologise on her behalf.'

For fuck's sake. How could my dad?

'Anoushka is not to blame. If anything, we have failed her. There is no reason for her to leave.'

He sounds sincere, but words are cheap, and it changes nothing. Kabir is giving my dad the current edited highlights with none of the months of backstory–

Wait a second, rewind. I'm so indignant, I almost miss the worst of it:

'…the move to Mumbai remains a strong possibility, yes. I'm sure Anoushka just needs time and encouragement…'

They know? My parents have known all along that India is on the cards? How? When were they talking?

I'm literally winded; it's the biggest blow of all. I have to sit down, thoughts like a tornado. Is my forehead really painted with 'loser', 'victim' and 'last to know'? What else does my family know about the crap I've been putting up with – and have let me go it alone?

I'm in this on my own, I think with sudden clarity. I knew it before, but now it's with certainty.

'I'll pass the phone to your daughter, Dev,' Kabir is saying. 'She can reassure you, I hope.'

'Dad, what's going on?' I say briskly, taking the phone and feeling amazed I sound normal.

'Your mother said you sounded unhappy when you spoke to her earlier,' he says, no preamble. 'You know how your mum gets ideas, but she took it upon herself to ask Laly if she thought everything was alright with you and…'

'You know what Laly's like,' I say flatly. Sorry, Laly.

'Well, yes, but she was very specific. But if you're sure?' When I say nothing, he goes on, 'It appears you've behaved very childishly, Anou. However, I accept that taping your conversations is equally as misguided, so let's say no more.' He clears his throat then says some more. 'The precious bond between two families is too easily broken and broken for good. Someone always has to step up.' Dad infers that, this time, the person should be me. It's a matter of izzat, respect – the most important thing an Indian family can demonstrate.

'If I was really unhappy, would you and Mum let me come home?' I ask suddenly. 'How bad would it have to be, before I could leave. Hypothetically.' I have to know but it throws him off course.

'We have a responsibility to all our children and we take it seriously,' he says finally. 'If you, our eldest, were in a situation of danger or true misery, if all else failed, then it would be our duty to accept you back.'

It's the impersonality of that response that leaves me cold. He – my dad – takes the question at face value and answers it like a manifesto. All I wanted him to do was say yes, to ask, 'Are you unhappy, Anou?' But he doesn't. Why would he? He doesn't know the half of it.

Feeling a hundred years older, I let the Tilaks carry on with their plans to relocate to Mumbai, on a 'six months trial basis'. I presume they see my lack of further argument as acquiescence, that I've come to my senses. I don't know if Dukkha orders the hormone injections or if she's waiting till 'we' get there, but there's no repercussions from my impromptu conversation with Dr Arnab. In the meantime, I quietly get on with my own arrangements. I ask for, and am granted, a short leave of absence from my PhD, and I've resigned my lab assistant's job for the summer. Following a meeting with my supervisors – in which I delicately indicate all might not be well in my arranged marriage – it's also rapidly agreed there is no reason why I can't return to Edinburgh if it's in my best personal and professional interests and if Dr Moffat will have me. (She will). Donald knows the gist of what's going on, is sworn to secrecy, and eventually stops asking me if I'm sure I don't want to go to McGill university in his place.

'We'll meet by the fourth-floor vending machine next February, in Edinburgh' I tell him, laughing – he's one of the few people with whom I'm still laughing. 'It'll be like old times.'

'If we plan it right, we can eke out our PhDs and be eternal students,' Donald agrees. 'We'll be urban myths. Undergrads will come and stare in awe.'

On one of our last sessions at the NFP, he tries to press more running away money on me but I assure him I don't need it, and yes, I will ask him if I get stuck. With Heera's contact details in my purse, never have I been so potentially well off, but it's the extraordinary, unconventional moral support rather than the financial that I really, really value. Money, anyway, isn't an immediate problem. A couple of visits to Diana in the building society and I've both cash withdrawn and evidence of enough saved to last a good few weeks. She also offers me a bed in her flat share if ever I need it. A bit too close to home, I tell her, but I do take her address and phone number to keep in touch; she and her boyfriend ('If he lasts the distance,') are up for the Edinburgh Fringe, and she'll look me up. It's all these normal little encounters that keep me sane.

Ravi and I get along as we always have. I've no idea if he truly believes that I've done an about turn and am heading to Mumbai to play Happy Families in Heera's mansion. He seems to. He's all taken up with little boy excitement: giving in his notice at work and making grand plans for everything he's going to do in India – leasing a fleet of Ambassador cars to start a taxi firm and tapping Heera to invest in a chain of casinos set up by a friend of his cousin Anoop's vie for the top of the list. When he suggests we should take a break from sex until we get over there and I'm taking Dhukka's mythical Ayurvedic fertility supplements, I don't disagree – and privately sigh in relief. I can't dislike Ravi. Fantasist, compulsive liar, gambler, he's not bad. He's a pawn of his mother as much as she's tried making me.

I've spent evenings pouring over my notebook, composing letters to him and to my parents. I'm explaining but not apologising and it's excruciating. Ravi's is by far the hardest because I'm leaving him and I know he doesn't want me to; it's easier if I don't. But Dukkha will convince him that a quick divorce and a second marriage is the solution. To Mum and Dad,

I'm simply telling them what I'm doing. As for Dukkha, I thought about a few home truths but I've nothing polite to say to her and she'll wash her hands of me the instant I'm gone anyway.

'By the way,' Donald says, with an unexpected hug goodbye. 'What are you going to be doing until we meet again?'

'Disappearing,' I say.

Chapter 47

When the end of my marriage comes, it's without fanfare. There should be a grand finale, surely? A soundtrack and closing credits, an ending that's also a beginning, as I walk off into the sunset. Nope. There's one actor, an unaware supporting cast, and no question of audience.

The lead-up to my leaving has hurtled through the month of planning, un-planning, re-planning; of fear, loathing and regret. I can't bring myself to look forward to a new start when I'm failing at marriage, and it's too soon to accept fully the dual truth that one unsuccessful year out of twenty-three is a good return and the real failure would be staying. But the day itself – today – is ordinary. I think back to that temple visit years ago when I was a child, and the proclamation that I'll be unhappy for years to come – well, it ends now.

Once Ravi and his parents have gone to work, I take down my suitcase from the loft – from on top of the chest that still contains all the unclaimed, unused burrie Dukkha showed me after our honeymoon – and pack it from a list already fine-tuned. In my handbag, I have my money, my passport, bank card, prepaid telephone card, all the documents relating to my PhD and a diary full of contact numbers. It seems remarkably little, but I check and check again and it's everything I need.

I've got a taxi booked for noon, and at ten to, I'm waiting by the door, anxious to be gone before I lose my nerve. My house keys are on the kitchen table; on the pillow upstairs is my letter to Ravi. The one to my parents is in the post, and should arrive, Royal Mail willing, tomorrow morning. That way, even if Ravi phones them tonight – or rather, Dukkha phones them, irate and bemoaning my lack of gratitude – they won't have time to worry. I'm not a monster and neither are my Mum and Dad; they will worry about me, and ultimately – I'm ninety per cent sure – they'll forgive me. Mum will just need time to reformulate what I've done and make it palatable for all the friends, neighbours and acquaintances who will be shocked – delightfully, gossipy – by my inexplicable defection from the perfect marriage. I will, though, be answering to my actions for the rest of my life.

The taxi is taking me to Leeds because there's a greater choice of direct destinations than from either of the Bradford stations. That matters because I've set myself a challenge.

I don't know where I'm going.

Nobody else knows where I'll be.

I'll be totally alone.

All for the first time ever – except for that single spontaneous breakfast at Gloria's Canteen.

I'm not brave enough to take a flight somewhere abroad and even if I was, it would feel like a holiday. I want to end up somewhere I can find a library and study, explore the area like a new resident, seek out a temporary summer job – okay, that might be a stretch but there's bound to be an Indian restaurant or newsagent somewhere – and live on my own. My aim is to be away for eight whole weeks, but that depends how cheaply I discover somewhere safe to stay – I'm not a masochist. And I'm not going to London, that's too big, too obvious and would swallow me up. Otherwise, choosing on the spot narrows the options and the dithering.

Leeds station is humming, tinny announcements directing shoals of people to platform after platform. I follow the signs for the Ticket Office, just another traveller. When it's my turn to trundle forward, pulling my case, the man behind the counter smiles.

'Where can we get you to today?' he asks.

'I know this sounds mad,' I say, 'But where's the next InterCity train going?'

He looks at a screen I can't see and I watch his eyes flicker back and forth. 'That would be London Kings Cross in twenty-eight minutes,' he announces. I'm about to say anywhere but London, when he frowns. 'But it's terminating at Peterborough–'

'That's it. Peterborough,' I get in quickly. 'A single ticket to Peterborough, please.'

'Right you are.' He presses a few buttons, and while he's waiting for the ticket to print, says, 'Next train on Platform 4. Arrival time is 15.04.'

I pass a twenty-pound note over the counter, and on impulse say, 'Do you know is there a hotel near the station? I need something nearby for tonight.'

'I do, indeed. The Great Northern.' He leans to one side and with my change and ticket, gives me a tourist information brochure. 'Number's in there. Best phone ahead to be sure – pay phones over there on the left. Have a good trip.'

And that's how, with ten minutes still to go, I have a ticket, a room booked at The Great Northern Hotel, and I'm sitting on the train to the city of Peterborough – not far away at all in miles but a place I know nothing about. One that will open up another world. I'm exhausted, pleased with myself, full of trepidation. When the guard blows his whistle and the train chugs out of the station, picking up speed – mirroring my life – I think, nobody knows where I am, and steel myself for panic. It doesn't come, instead I feel a release.

I've lived in an invisible cage my whole life, not just this last year, and today is the day the cage door opens.

And if that sounds overblown and sensationalist, well, tough. It really is that big a deal.

Anoushka Malhotra is flying free.

THE END

Acknowledgements

I would like to thank everyone who has supported me and helped make this book a reality — you know who you are. I am especially grateful to my editor, Anne Hamilton, for the incredible work she put into this project, and to Claire for her valuable contributions.

A heartfelt thank you to my sister, Manju, and my brother Ajay who have stood by me through the years with unwavering support and guidance. To my partner, Gordon — my rock — thank you for your constant strength and encouragement. I am also deeply thankful to my dear friend, Neet.

Printed in Dunstable, United Kingdom

75815005R00228